What I Loved

What I Loved

Siri Hustvedt

W F HOWES LTD

This large print edition published in 2004 by
W F Howes Ltd
Units 6/7, Victoria Mills, Fowke Street
Rothley, Leicester LE7 7PJ

1 3 5 7 9 10 8 6 4 2

First published in 2003 by Hodder & Stoughton

Copyright © Siri Hustvedt

The right of Siri Hustvedt to be identified as
the author of this work has been asserted by her
in accordance with the Copyright, Designs and
Patents Act, 1988.

A CIP catalogue record for this book is available
from the British Library

ISBN 1 84505 639 6

Typeset by Palimpsest Book Production Limited,
Polmont, Stirlingshire.
Printed and bound in Great Britain
by Antony Rowe Ltd, Chippenham, Wilts

For Paul Auster

ONE

Yesterday, I found Violet's letters to Bill. They were hidden between the pages of one of his books and came tumbling out and fell to the floor. I had known about the letters for years, but neither Bill nor Violet had ever told me what was in them. What they did tell me was that minutes after reading the fifth and last letter, Bill changed his mind about his marriage to Lucille, walked out the door of the building on Greene Street, and headed straight for Violet's apartment in the East Village. When I held the letters in my hands, I felt they had the uncanny weight of things enchanted by stories that are told and retold and then told again. My eyes are bad now, and it took me a long time to read them, but in the end I managed to make out every word. When I put the letters down, I knew that I would start writing this book today.

'While I was lying on the floor in the studio,' she wrote in the fourth letter, 'I watched you while you painted me. I looked at your arms and your shoulders and especially at your hands while you worked on the canvas. I wanted you to

3

turn around and walk over to me and rub my skin the way you rubbed the painting. I wanted you to press hard on me with your thumb the way you pressed on the picture, and I thought that if you didn't, I would go crazy, but I didn't go crazy, and you never touched me then, not once. You didn't even shake my hand.'

I first saw the painting Violet was writing about twenty-five years ago in a gallery on Prince Street in SoHo. I didn't know either Bill or Violet at the time. Most of the canvases in the group show were thin minimalist works that didn't interest me. Bill's painting hung alone on a wall. It was a large picture, about six feet high and eight feet long, that showed a young woman lying on the floor in an empty room. She was propped up on one elbow, and she seemed to be looking at something beyond the edge of the painting. Brilliant light streamed into the room from that side of the canvas and illuminated her face and chest. Her right hand was resting on her pubic bone, and when I moved closer, I saw that she was holding a little taxi in that hand – a miniature version of the ubiquitous yellow cab that moves up and down the streets of New York.

It took me about a minute to understand that there were actually three people in the painting. Far to my right, on the dark side of the canvas, I noticed that a woman was leaving the picture. Only her foot and ankle could be seen inside the frame, but the loafer she was wearing had been rendered

4

with excruciating care, and once I had seen it, I kept looking back at it. The invisible woman became as important as the one who dominated the canvas. The third person was only a shadow. For a moment I mistook the shadow for my own, but then I understood that the artist had included it in the work. The beautiful woman, who was wearing only a man's T-shirt, was being looked at by someone outside the painting, a spectator who seemed to be standing just where I was standing when I noticed the darkness that fell over her belly and her thighs.

To the right of the canvas I read the small typed card: *Self-Portrait* by William Wechsler. At first I thought the artist was joking, but then I changed my mind. Did that title next to a man's name suggest a feminine part of himself or a trio of selves? Maybe the oblique narrative of two women and a viewer referred directly to the artist, or maybe the title didn't refer to the content of the picture at all, but to its form. The hand that had painted the picture hid itself in some parts of the painting and made itself known in others. It disappeared in the photographic illusion of the woman's face, in the light that came from the invisible window, and in the hyperrealism of the loafer. The woman's long hair, however, was a tangle of heavy paint with forceful dabs of red, green, and blue. Around the shoe and the ankle above it, I noticed thick stripes of black, gray, and white that may have been applied with a knife, and in those dense

5

strokes of pigment I could see the marks left by a man's thumb. It looked as if his gesture had been sudden, even violent.

That painting is here in the room with me. When I turn my head I can see it, although it too has been altered by my failing eyesight. I bought it from the dealer for $2,500 about a week after I saw it. Erica was standing only a few feet away from where I am sitting now when she first looked at the canvas. She examined it calmly and said, 'It's like looking at another person's dream, isn't it?'

When I turned to the picture after Erica spoke, I saw that its mixed styles and shifting focus did remind me of the distortions in dreams. The woman's lips were parted, and her two front teeth protruded slightly. The artist had made them shiny white and a little too long, almost like an animal's. It was then that I noticed a bruise just below her knee. I had seen it before, but at that moment its purple cast, which was yellow-green at one edge, pulled my eyes toward it, as if this little wound were really the subject of the painting. I walked over, put my finger on the canvas, and traced the outline of the bruise. The gesture aroused me. I turned to look at Erica. It was a warm September day, and her arms were bare. I bent over her and kissed the freckles on her shoulders, then lifted the hair off her neck and kissed the soft skin underneath it. Kneeling in front of her, I pushed up the material of her skirt, ran my fingers along her thighs, and then I used my tongue. Her

6

knees bent slightly toward me. She pulled down her underpants, tossed them onto the sofa with a grin, and pushed me gently backward onto the floor. Erica straddled me and her hair fell forward onto my face as she kissed me. Then she sat back, pulled off her T-shirt, and removed her bra. I loved that view of my wife. I touched her breasts and let my finger circle a perfectly round mole on the left one, before she leaned over me again. She kissed my forehead and cheeks and chin and then began fumbling with the zipper of my pants.

In those days, Erica and I lived in a state of almost constant sexual excitement. Just about anything could spark off a session of wild grappling on the bed, the floor, and, once, on the dining room table. Since high school, girlfriends had come and gone in my life. I had had brief affairs and longer ones, but always there had been gaps between them – painful stretches of no women and no sex. Erica said that suffering had made me a better lover – that I didn't take a woman's body for granted. On that afternoon, however, we made love because of the painting. I have often wondered since why the image of a sore on a woman's body should have been erotic to me. Later, Erica said that she thought my response had something to do with a desire to leave a mark on another person's body. 'Skin is soft,' she said. 'We're easily cut and bruised. It's not like she looks beaten or anything. It's an ordinary little black-and-blue mark, but the way it's painted makes it stick out. It's like he loved doing it, like he wanted to make a little wound that would last forever.'

Erica was thirty-four years old then. I was eleven years older than that, and we had been married for a year. We'd literally bumped into each other in Butler Library at Columbia. It was late on a Saturday morning in October, and the stacks were mostly empty. I had heard her steps, had felt her presence behind the dim rows of books illuminated by a timed light that gave off a low humming sound. I found the book I was looking for and walked toward the elevator. Except for the lamp, I heard nothing. I turned the corner and tripped over Erica, who had seated herself on the floor at the end of the stack. I managed to keep my footing, but my glasses sailed off my face. She picked them up, and as I bent over to take them from her, she began to stand up and her head knocked against my chin. When she looked at me, she was smiling: 'A few more like that, and we might have something going – a regular slapstick routine.'

I had fallen over a pretty woman. She had a wide mouth and thick dark hair cropped to her chin. The narrow skirt she was wearing had moved up her legs in our collision, and I glanced at her thighs as she tugged at her hem. After adjusting her skirt, she looked up at me and smiled again. During the second smile, her bottom lip quivered for an instant, and I took that small sign of nervousness or embarrassment to mean that she was susceptible to an invitation. Without it, I'm quite sure I would have apologized again and walked away. But that momentary tremor in her lip, gone in a moment, exposed a softness in her character and offered me a glimpse of what I guessed was her carefully guarded sensuality. I asked her to have coffee with me. Coffee turned into lunch, and lunch into dinner, and the following morning I was lying next to Erica Stein in the bed of my old apartment on Riverside Drive. She was still sleeping. The light came through the window and illuminated her face and hair. Very carefully I put my hand on her head. I left it there for several minutes while I looked at her and hoped she would stay.

By then we had talked for hours. It turned out that Erica and I came from the same world. Her parents were German Jews who left Berlin as teenagers in 1933. Her father became a prominent psychoanalyst and her mother a voice teacher at Juilliard. The Steins were both dead. They died within months of each other the year before I met Erica, which was the same year my mother died: 1973. I was born in Berlin and lived there for five years. My memories of that city are fragmentary, and some may be false, images and stories I shaped from what my mother told me about my early life. Erica was born on the Upper West Side, where I ended up after spending three years in a Hampstead flat in London. It was Erica who prompted me to leave the West Side and my comfortable Columbia apartment. Before we married, she told me she wanted to 'emigrate.' When I asked her what she meant, she said that it was time for her to sell her parents' apartment on West Eighty-second Street and take the long subway ride downtown. 'I smell death up here,' she said, 'and antiseptic and hospitals and stale Sacher torte. I have to move.' Erica and I left the familiar ground of our childhoods and staked out new turf among the artists and bohemians farther south. We used the money we had inherited from our parents and moved to a loft on Greene Street between Canal and Grand.

The new neighborhood with its empty streets, low buildings, and young tenants freed me from bonds I had never thought of as constraints. My father died in 1947, when he was only forty-three years old, but my mother lived on. I was their only child, and after my father was gone, my mother and I shared his ghost. My mother grew old and arthritic, but my father remained young and brilliant and promising – a doctor who might have done anything. That anything became everything for my mother. For twenty-six years she lived in the same apartment on Eighty-fourth Street between Broadway and Riverside with my father's missing future. Every once in a while, when I was first teaching, a student would refer to me as 'Dr Hertzberg' rather than 'Professor,' and I would inevitably think of my father. Living in SoHo didn't erase my past or induce forgetfulness, but when I turned a corner or crossed a street, there were no reminders of my displaced childhood and youth. Erica and I were both the children of exiles from a world that has disappeared. Our parents were assimilated middle-class Jews for whom Judaism was a religion their great-grandparents had practiced. Before 1933 they had thought of themselves as 'Jewish Germans,' a phrase that no longer exists in any language.

When we met, Erica was an assistant professor in English at Rutgers, and I had already been teaching at Columbia in the art history department for twelve years. My degree came from Harvard, hers from Columbia, which explained why she was wandering in the stacks that Saturday morning with an alumni pass. I had fallen in love before, but in almost every case I had arrived at a moment of fatigue and boredom. Erica never bored me. She sometimes irritated and exasperated me, but she never bored me. Erica's comment about Bill's self-portrait was typical of her – simple, direct, and penetrating. I never condescended to Erica.

I had walked past 89 Bowery many times without ever stopping to look at it. The run-down, four-story brick building between Hester and Canal had never been more than the humble quarters of a wholesale business, but those days of modest respectability were long over by the time I arrived to visit William Wechsler. The windows of what had once been a storefront were boarded up, and the heavy metal door at street level was gouged and dented, as if somebody had attacked it with a hammer. A man with a beard and a drink in a paper bag was lounging on the single front step. He grunted in my direction when I asked him to move and then half-rolled, half-slid off the step.

My first impressions of people are often clouded by what I come to know about them later, but in Bill's case, at least one aspect of those first seconds remained throughout our friendship. Bill had glamour – that mysterious quality of attraction that seduces strangers. When he met me at the door, he looked almost as disheveled as the man on the front step. He had a two-day beard. His thick black hair bushed out from the top and sides of his head, and his clothes were covered with dirt as well as paint. And yet when he looked at me, I found myself pulled toward him. His complexion was very dark for a white man, and his clear green eyes had an Asiatic tilt to them. He had a square jaw and chin, broad shoulders, and powerful arms. At six-two, he seemed to tower over me even though I couldn't have been more than a few inches shorter. I later decided that his almost magical appeal had something to do with his eyes. When he looked at me, he did so directly and without embarrassment, but at the same time I sensed his inwardness, his distraction. Although his curiosity about me seemed genuine, I also felt that he didn't want a thing from me. Bill gave off an air of autonomy so complete, it was irresistible.

'I took it for the light,' he said to me when we

walked through the door of the loft space on the fourth floor. Three long windows at the far end of the single room were shining with the afternoon sun. The building had sagged, which meant the back of the place was considerably lower than the front. The floor had warped as well, and as I looked toward the windows, I noticed bulges in the boards like shallow waves on a lake. The high end of the loft was spare, furnished only with a stool, a table constructed from two sawhorses and an old door, and stereo equipment, surrounded by hundreds of records and tapes in plastic milk crates. Rows of canvases had been stacked against the wall. The room smelled strongly of paint, turpentine, and must.

All the necessities for daily life had been crowded into the low end. A table knocked up against an old claw-foot bathtub. A double bed had been placed near a table, not far from a sink, and the stove protruded from an opening in an enormous bookcase crammed with books. There were also books piled in stacks on the floor beside it, and dozens more on an armchair that looked as if it hadn't been sat on in years. The chaos of the loft's living quarters revealed not only Bill's poverty but his obliviousness to the objects of domestic life. Time would make him richer, but his indifference to things never changed. He remained curiously unattached to the places where he lived and blind to the details of their arrangements.

Even on that first day, I felt Bill's asceticism, his

13

almost brutal desire for purity and his resistance to compromise. The feeling came both from what he said and from his physical presence. He was calm, soft-spoken, a little restrained in his movements, and yet an intensity of purpose emanated from him and seemed to fill up the room. Unlike other large personalities, Bill wasn't loud or arrogant or uncommonly charming. Nevertheless, when I stood next to him and looked at the paintings, I felt like a dwarf who had just been introduced to a giant. The feeling made my comments sharper and more thoughtful. I was fighting for space.

He showed me six paintings that afternoon. Three were finished. The three others had just been started – sketchy lines and large fields of color. My canvas belonged to the same series, which were all of the dark-haired young woman, but from one work to another, the woman's size fluctuated. In the first painting, she was obese, a mountain of pale flesh in tight nylon shorts and a T-shirt – an image of gluttony and abandon so huge that her body appeared to have been squeezed into the frame. She was clutching a baby's rattle in her fat fist. A man's elongated shadow fell across her right breast and huge belly and then dwindled to a mere line at her hips. In the second, the woman was much thinner. She was lying on a mattress in her underwear looking down at her own body with an expression that seemed to be at once autoerotic and self-critical. She was gripping a large fountain pen in her hand, about twice the size of a normal

14

pen. In the third picture, the woman had gained a few pounds, but she wasn't as plump as the person in the canvas I had bought. She was wearing a ragged flannel nightgown and sitting on the edge of the bed, her thighs casually parted. A pair of red knee socks lay at her feet. When I looked at her legs, I noticed that just below her knees were faint red lines left by the elastic of the socks.

'It reminds me of Jan Steen's painting of the woman at her morning toilet, taking off her sock,' I said. 'The small painting in the Rijksmuseum.'

Bill smiled at me for the first time. 'I saw that painting in Amsterdam when I was twenty-three, and it got me thinking about skin. I'm not interested in nudes. They're too arty, but I'm really interested in skin.'

For a while we talked about skin in paintings. I mentioned the beautiful red stigmata on the hand of Zurbarán's Saint Francis. Bill talked about the skin color of Grünewald's dead Christ and the rosy skin of Boucher's nudes, whom he referred to as 'soft porn ladies.' We discussed the changing conventions of crucifixions and pietàs and depositions. I said Pontormo's Mannerism had always interested me, and Bill brought up R. Crumb. 'I love his rawness,' he said. 'The ugly courage of his work.' I asked him about George Grosz, and Bill nodded.

'A relative,' he said. 'The two are definitely artistic relatives. Did you ever see Crumb's series *Tales from the Land of Genitalia*? Penises running around in boots.'

15

'Like Gogol's nose,' I said.

Bill showed me medical drawings then, a field I knew little about. He pulled out dozens of books from his shelves with illustrations from different periods – diagrams of medieval humors, eighteenth-century anatomical pictures, a nineteenth-century picture of a man's head with phrenological bumps, and one from around the same time of female genitalia. The latter was a curious drawing of the view between a woman's splayed thighs. We stood beside each other and stared down at the detailed rendering of vulva, clitoris, labia, and the small blackened hole of a vaginal entrance. The lines were harsh and exacting.

'It looks like a diagram for machinery,' I said.

'Yes,' he said. 'I never thought of that.' He looked down at the picture. 'It's a mean picture. Everything is in the right place, but it's a nasty cartoon. Of course the artist thought it was science.'

'I don't think anything is ever just science,' I said.

He nodded. 'That's the problem with seeing things. Nothing is clear. Feelings, ideas shape what's in front of you. Cézanne wanted the naked world, but the world is never naked. In my work, I want to create doubt.' He stopped and smiled at me. 'Because that's what we're sure of.'

'Is that why you've made your woman fat and thin and in between?' I said.

'To be honest, it was more of an urge than an idea.'

'And the mixture of styles?' I said.

Bill walked to the window and lit a cigarette. He inhaled and let the ash drop on the floor. He looked up at me. His large eyes were so penetrating. I wanted to turn away from them, but I didn't. 'I'm thirty-one years old, and you're the first person who ever bought one of my paintings, unless you count my mother. I've been working for ten years. Dealers have rejected the work hundreds of times.'

'De Kooning didn't have his first show until he was forty,' I said.

'You misunderstand me,' he said, speaking slowly. 'I don't ask that anyone be interested. Why should they be interested? I'm wondering why *you* are interested.'

I told him. We sat down on the floor with the paintings in front of us, and I said that I liked ambiguity, that I liked not knowing where to look on his canvases, that a lot of modern figurative painting bored me, but his pictures didn't. We talked about de Kooning, especially one small work that Bill had found inspiring, *Self-portrait with Imaginary Brother*. We talked about Hopper's strangeness, and about Duchamp. Bill called him 'the knife that cut art to pieces.' I thought he meant this in a derogatory way, but then he added, 'He was a great con artist. I love him.'

When I pointed out the razor stubble he had

included on the thin woman's legs, he said that when he was with another person, his eyes were often drawn to a single detail – a chipped tooth, a Band-Aid on a finger, a vein, a cut, a rash, a mole, and that for a moment the isolated feature took over his vision, and he wanted to reproduce those seconds in his work. 'Seeing is flux,' he said. I mentioned the hidden narratives in his work, and he said that for him stories were like blood running through a body – paths of a life. It was a revealing metaphor, and I never forgot it. As an artist, Bill was hunting the unseen in the seen. The paradox was that he had chosen to present this invisible movement in figurative painting, which is nothing if not a frozen apparition – a surface.

Bill told me that he had grown up in the New Jersey suburbs, where his father had started a cardboard-box business and eventually made a success of it. His mother volunteered for Jewish charities, was a den mother for the Cub Scouts, and had later gotten a real estate license. Neither of his parents had gone to college, and there were few books in the house. I imagined the green lawns and quiet houses of South Orange – bicycles in driveways, the street signs, the two-car garages. 'I was good at drawing,' he said, 'but for a long time baseball was much more important to me than art.'

I told him that I had suffered through sports at the Fieldston School. I was thin and nearsighted and had stood in the outfield and hoped that

18

nobody would hit the ball in my direction. 'Any sport that required a utensil was impossible for me,' I said. 'I could run and I could swim, but put something in my hand and I dropped it.'

In high school, Bill began his pilgrimages to the Met, to MoMA, to the Frick, to galleries, and, as he put it, 'to the streets.' 'I liked the streets as much as museums, and I spent hours in the city wandering around, inhaling the garbage.' When he was a junior, his parents divorced. That same year he quit the cross-country team, the basketball team, the baseball team. 'I stopped working out,' he said. 'I got thin.' Bill went to college at Yale, took studio art, art history, and literature courses. That was where he met Lucille Alcott, whose father was a professor at the law school. 'We were married three years ago,' he said. I found myself looking for traces left by a woman in the loft, but I saw nothing. 'Is she at work?' I said to him.

'She's a poet. She rents a little room a couple of blocks from here. That's where she writes. She's also a freelance copy editor. She copy-edits. I paint and plaster for contractors. We get by.'

A sympathetic doctor saved Bill from Vietnam. Throughout his childhood and youth he had suffered from severe allergies. When they were bad his face swelled up and he sneezed so hard he got a neckache. Before he reported to the draft board in Newark, the physician added the phrase 'with a tendency toward asthma' to the word 'allergies.' A couple of years later, a tendency might not have earned Bill 1-Y status, but this was 1966 and the full force of Vietnam resistance was still in the future. After college, he spent a year working as a bartender in New Jersey. He lived with his mother, saved all his earnings, and traveled in Europe for two years. He moved from Rome to Amsterdam to Paris. To keep himself going, he took odd jobs. He worked as a desk clerk for an English magazine in Amsterdam, a tour guide of the catacombs in Rome, and a reader of English novels for an old man in Paris. 'When I read to him, I had to lie on the sofa. He was very particular about my position. I had to take off my shoes. It was important to him that he had a clear view of my socks. The money was good, and I put up with it for a week. Then I quit. I took my three hundred francs and left. It was all the money I had in the world. I walked into the street. It was about eleven at night, and there was this wasted old man standing on the sidewalk with his hand out. I gave the money to him.'

'Why?' I said.

Bill turned to me. 'I don't know. I felt like it. It was stupid, but I never regretted it. It made me feel free. I didn't eat for two days.'

'An act of bravado,' I said.

He turned to me and said, 'Of independence.'

'Where was Lucille?'

'She was living in New Haven with her parents. She wasn't very well then. We wrote to each other.'

I didn't ask about Lucille's illness. When he

mentioned it, he looked away from me, and I saw his eyes narrow in an expression of pain.

I changed the subject. 'Why did you call the painting I bought a self-portrait?'

'They're all self-portraits,' he said. 'While I was working with Violet, I realized that I was mapping out a territory in myself I hadn't seen before, or maybe a territory between her and me. The title popped into my head, and I used it. Self-portrait seemed right.'

'Who is she?' I said.

'Violet Blom. She's a graduate student at NYU. She gave me that drawing I showed you – the one that looks like machinery.'

'What's she studying?'

'History. She's writing about hysteria in France at the turn of the century.' Bill lit another cigarette and glanced at the ceiling. 'She's a very smart girl – unusual.' He blew the smoke up, and I watched its faint circles combine with specks of dust in the window light.

'I don't think most men would portray themselves as a woman. You borrowed her to show yourself. What does she think?'

He laughed for an instant and then said, 'She likes it. She says it's subversive, especially because I like women, not men.'

'And the shadows?' I asked him.

'They're mine, too.'

'Too bad,' I said. 'I thought they were mine.'

Bill looked at me. 'They can be yours, too.' He

gripped my lower arm with his hand and shook it. This sudden gesture of camaraderie, even affection, made me unusually happy. I have thought about it often, because that small exchange about shadows altered the course of my life. It marks the moment when a meandering conversation between two men took an irrevocable turn toward friendship.

'She floated through the dance,' Bill said to me a week later over coffee. 'She didn't seem to know how pretty she was. I chased her for years. It was on again and off again. Something kept bringing me back.' Bill made no mention of Lucille's illness in the following weeks, but the way he talked about her led me to think she was frail, a woman who needed protection from something he had chosen not to talk about.

The first time I saw Lucille Alcott, she was standing in the doorway of the Bowery loft, and I thought she looked like a woman in a Flemish painting. She had pale skin, light brown hair, which she had tied back, and large, almost lashless blue eyes. Erica and I had been invited to have dinner on the Bowery. It was raining that November night, and while we ate we heard the rain on the roof above us. Somebody had swept the floor of dust and ashes and cigarette butts for our visit, and somebody had put a large white cloth over Bill's worktable and set eight candles on top of it. Lucille took credit for cooking the meal, a tasteless

22

brown concoction of unrecognizable vegetables. When Erica politely inquired after the name of the dish, Lucille looked down at her plate and said in perfect French, 'Flageolets aux légumes.' She paused, raised her eyes, and smiled. 'But the flageolets seem to be traveling incognito.' After stopping for a second, she continued, 'I would like to cook more attentively. It called for parsley.' She peered down at her plate. 'I left out the parsley. Bill would prefer meat. He ate a lot of meat before, but he knows that I don't cook meat, because I have convinced myself that it is not good for us. I don't understand what it is about recipes. I am very particular when I write. I am always worrying about verbs.'

'Her verbs are terrific,' Bill said and poured Erica more wine.

Lucille looked at her husband and smiled a little stiffly. I didn't understand the uneasiness of the smile, because Bill's comment had been made without irony. He had told me several times how much he admired her poems and had promised to give me copies of them.

Behind Lucille, I could see the obese portrait of Violet Blom and wondered if Bill's craving for meat had been translated into that huge female body, but later my theory was proven wrong. When we had lunch together, I often saw Bill chewing happily on corned-beef sandwiches, hamburgers, and BLTs.

'I make rules for myself,' Lucille said about her poems. 'Not the usual rules of metrics, but an anatomy I choose, and then I dissect it. Numbers are helpful. They're clear, irrefutable. Some of the lines are numbered.' Everything Lucille said was characterized by a similarly rigid bluntness. She seemed to make no concessions to decorous conversation or small talk. At the same time, underneath nearly every remark she made, I felt a strain of humor. She talked as if she were observing her own sentences, looking at them from afar, judging their sounds and shapes even as they came from her mouth. Every word she spoke rang with honesty, and yet this earnestness was matched by a simultaneous irony. Lucille amused herself by occupying two positions at once. She was both the subject and object of her own statements.

I don't think Erica heard Lucille's comment about rules. She was talking about novels with Bill. I can't imagine that Bill had heard it either, but during the discussion between them, rules came up again. Erica leaned toward Bill and smiled. 'So you agree, the novel is a bag that can hold anything.'

'*Tristram Shandy*, chapter four, on Horace's *ab ovo*,' Bill said, pointing his index finger at the ceiling. He began to quote, as if he were hearing an inaudible voice somewhere to his right. '"Horace, I know, does not recommend this fashion altogether: but that gentleman is speaking only of an epic poem or a tragedy – (I forgot which); – besides, if it was not so, I should beg Mr Horace's pardon; – for in writing what I have set about, I shall confine myself neither to his rules, nor to any man's rules that ever lived.' Bill's voice rose on the final clause, and Erica threw back her head and laughed. They meandered from Henry James to Samuel Beckett to Louis-Ferdinand Céline as Erica discovered for herself that Bill was a voracious reader of novels. It launched a friendship between them that had little to do with me. By the time our dessert arrived – a weary-looking fruit salad – Erica was inviting him to Rutgers to speak to her students. Bill hesitated at first, and then agreed.

Erica was too polite to ignore Lucille, who was sitting beside her, and some time after she asked Bill to visit one of her classes, she focused all her attention on Lucille. My wife nodded at Lucille when she listened, and when she talked her face was a map of shifting emotions and thoughts. In contrast, Lucille's composed face betrayed almost no feeling. As the evening went on, her peculiar remarks gained a kind of philosophical rhythm, the clipped tone of a tortured logic, which reminded me a little of reading Wittgenstein's *Tractatus*. When Erica told Lucille she knew of her father by reputation, Lucille said, 'Yes, his reputation as a law professor is very good.' After a moment, she added, 'I would have liked to study law, but I couldn't. I used to try to read my father's law books in his library. I was eleven. I knew that one sentence led to another, but by the time I got to the second sentence, I had forgotten the first, and then during the third, I forgot the second.'

'You were only eleven,' Erica said.

'No,' she said. 'It was not my age. I still forget.'

'Forgetting,' I said, 'is probably as much a part of life as remembering. We're all amnesiacs.'

'But if we've forgotten,' Lucille said, turning to me, 'we don't always remember that we forgot, so that to remember that we forgot is not exactly forgetting, is it?'

I smiled at her and said, 'I'm looking forward to reading your work. Bill's talked about it with a lot of admiration.'

Bill lifted his glass. 'To our work,' he said loudly. 'To letters and to paint.' He had let himself go and I could see he was a little drunk. His voice cracked on the word 'paint.' I found his high spirits endearing, but when I turned to Lucille with my glass lifted for the toast, she smiled that tense, forced smile a second time. It was hard to tell whether her husband had brought on that expression or whether it was merely the result of her own inhibition.

Before we left, Lucille handed me two small magazines in which her work had appeared. When I shook her hand, she took mine limply. I squeezed her palm in return, and she didn't seem to mind. Bill hugged me good-bye, and he hugged and kissed Erica. His eyes were shiny with wine, and he smelled of cigarettes. In the doorway, he put his arm around Lucille's shoulder and pulled her close to him. Next to her husband, she looked very small and very self-conscious.

It was still raining when we stepped outside onto the Bowery.

After I put up our umbrella, Erica turned to me and said, 'Did you notice that she was wearing the loafers?'

'What are you talking about?' I said.

'Lucille was wearing the shoes, or rather the shoe, in our painting. She's the woman walking away.'

I looked at Erica, absorbing her statement. 'I guess I didn't look at her feet.'

'I'm surprised. You looked pretty closely at the rest of her.' Erica grinned, and I saw that she was teasing me. 'Don't you find that evocative about the shoe, Leo? And then there's the other woman. Every time I looked up, I saw her – that skinny girl looking down at her underpants, a little greedy and excited. She looked so alive, I felt like they should have set a place for her at the table.'

I pulled Erica toward me with my free hand, and holding the umbrella over us, I kissed her. After the kiss, she put her arm around my waist and we walked toward Canal Street. 'Well,' she said, 'I wonder what her work is like.'

All three of the poems Lucille had published were similar – works of obsessive, analytic scrutiny that hovered somewhere between the funny and the sad. I remember only four lines from those poems, because they were unusually poignant, and I repeated them to myself. 'A woman sits by the window. She thinks / And while she thinks, she despairs / She despairs because she is who she is / And not somebody else.'

The doctors tell me that it won't come to blindness. I have a condition called macular degeneration – clouds in my eyes. I have been near-sighted since I was eight years old. Blur is nothing new to me, but with glasses I used to see everything perfectly. I still have my peripheral vision, but directly in front of me there is always a ragged gray spot, and it's growing thicker. My pictures of the past are still vivid. It's the present that's been affected, and those people who were in my past and whom I still see have turned into beings blotted by clouds. This truth startled me in the beginning, but I have discovered from fellow patients and from my doctors that what I have experienced is perfectly normal. Lazlo Finkelman, for example, who comes several times a week to read to me, has lost some definition, and neither my memory of him from before my eyes dimmed nor my peripheral vision is enough to sustain a clear picture. I can *say* what Lazlo looks like, because I remember the words I used to describe him to myself – narrow pale face, tall bush of blond hair that stands straight up at attention, black glasses with large frames over small gray eyes. But when I look straight at him now, his face won't come into focus, and the words I once used are left hanging. The person they are meant to delineate is a clouded version of an earlier picture I can no longer bring fully to mind, because my eyes are too tired to be always peeking at him from the side. More and more, I rely on Lazlo's voice. But in his even, quiet tone as he reads to me, I have found new sides to his cryptic personality – resonances of feeling that I never saw on his face.

Even though my eyes have been crucial to my work, poor vision is preferable to senility. I can't see well enough anymore to wander through galleries or return to museums to look at works I know by heart. Nevertheless, I keep a catalogue in my mind of remembered paintings, and I can leaf through it and usually find the work I need. In class, I have given up using a pointer for slides, and refer to details instead of pointing at them. My remedy for insomnia these days is to search for the mental image of a painting and work to see it again as clearly as possible. Lately, I've been calling up Piero della Francesca. Over forty years ago, I wrote my dissertation on his *De prospectiva pingendi*, and by concentrating on the rigorous geometries of his paintings I once analyzed so closely, I fend off other pictures that rise up to torment me and keep me awake. I shut out noises from the street and the intruder I imagine is lurking on the fire escape outside my room. The technique has been working. Last night, the Urbino panels began to melt into my own semisleep dreams, and soon after, I lost consciousness.

For some time, I have had to struggle to ward off dread when I lie alone and try to sleep. My mind is large, but my body feels smaller than it once did, as though I am steadily shrinking. My fantasy of reduction is probably connected to growing older and more vulnerable. The circle of a lifetime has begun to close, and I've been thinking more often about my early childhood – what I can remember from Mommsenstrasse 11 in Berlin. It isn't that I recall every part of the apartment where we lived, but I can still take the mental walk up two flights of stairs and past the window with etched glass to our door. Once inside, I know that my father's office is to the left and the parlor rooms lie ahead of me. Although I have retained only a few details of the apartment's furniture and objects, I have a general memory of its spaces – of its large rooms, high ceilings, and changing light. My room was located down a small corridor off the apartment's biggest room. That was where my father played the cello on the third Thursday of every month with three other musical doctors, and I remember that my mother would open the door to my room so that I could hear them play while I was lying in bed. I can still walk through the door of my room and climb up onto the window casement. I climb, because in memory I am as tall as I was then. Below I can see the courtyard at night, detect the lines of the paving bricks and the blackness of the bushes. When I take this walk, the apartment is always empty. I move through it like a phantom, and I have begun to wonder what actually happens in our brains when we return to half-remembered places. What is memory's perspective? Does the man revise the boy's view or is the imprint relatively static, a vestige of what was once intimately known?

Cicero's speaker walked through spacious, well-lit rooms he remembered and dropped words onto tables and chairs where they could be easily retrieved. No doubt I have assigned a vocabulary to the architecture of my first five years – one mediated through the mind of a man who knows the horror that would arrive after the little boy was gone from the apartment. During the last year we were in Berlin, my mother left a light burning in the hallway to calm me before I slept. I had nightmares, and I would wake to a strangling fear and the sound of my own screaming. *Nervös* was the word my father used – *Das Kind ist nervös*. My parents didn't speak to me about the Nazis, only about our preparations to leave home, and it's hard to know to what degree my childish fears were related to the fear that every Jew in Germany must have felt at the time. The way my mother told it was that she was taken by surprise. A party whose views had seemed absurd and contemptible suddenly and inexplicably took hold of the country. Both she and my father were patriotic, and while they were still in Berlin, they regarded National Socialism as something distinctly un-German.

On August 13, 1935, my parents and I left for Paris, and from there we traveled to London. My mother packed sandwiches for the train – brown bread with sausage. I remember the sandwich on my lap, because beside it on a wrinkled square of wax paper was a *Mohrenkopf* – a ball of pastry filled with custard and covered with chocolate. I have no memory of eating it, but I distinctly recall my delight at the thought that it would soon be mine. The *Mohrenkopf* is vivid. I see it in the light of the train window. I see my bare knees and the hem of my navy blue shorts. That is all that remains of our exodus. Around the *Mohrenkopf* is emptiness, a void that can be filled with other people's stories, historical accounts, numbers, and facts. Not until I turned six do I have anything like a continuous memory, and by then I was living in Hampstead. Only weeks after I was sitting on that train, the Nuremberg Laws were passed. Jews were no longer citizens of the Reich, and the opportunities to leave had diminished. My grandmother, my uncle and aunt, and their twin daughters, Anna and Ruth, never left. We were living in New York when my father found out that his family had been pushed onto a train for Auschwitz in June of 1944. They were all murdered. I keep their photographs in my drawer – my grandmother in an elegant hat with a feather standing beside my grandfather, who would be killed in 1917 at Flanders. I have the formal wedding portrait of my Uncle David and Aunt Marta, and a picture of the twins in short wool coats with ribbons in their hair. Beneath each girl in the white border of the photo, Marta wrote their names, to avoid confusion. Anna on the left, Ruth on the right. The black-and-white figures of the photographs have had to stand in place of my memory, and yet I have always felt that their unmarked graves became a part of me. What was unwritten then is inscribed into what I call myself. The longer I live the more convinced I am that when I say 'I,' I am really saying 'we.'

In Bill's last finished portrait of Violet Blom, she was naked and starved. Her entire body was darkened by the enormous shadow of an unseen spectator who loomed over her. When I stood close to the canvas, I noticed that parts of her body were covered with a fine hair. Bill called it 'lanugo' and said that the starving body often grows hair for protection. He said that he had spent hours studying medical and documentary photographs to get it right. Her skeletal body was painful to look at, and her huge eyes gleamed as if she had a fever. Bill had painted her emaciated body in color, first rendering her with painstaking realism and then going over her body with bold, expressionistic strokes, using blue and green and dabs of red on her thighs and neck. The black-and-white background resembled an aging photograph, like the ones I keep in my drawer. On the floor behind Violet were several pairs of shoes – men's, women's, and children's, painted in gray tones. When I asked Bill if this portrait referred to the death camps, he said yes, and we talked about Adorno for over an hour. The philosopher had said there could be no art after the camps.

*   *   *

I knew Bernie Weeks through a colleague at Columbia, Jack Newman. The Weeks Gallery on West Broadway had done well, because Bernie had a talent for sniffing out new artists, and he had connections. He was one of those people in New York who was purported to 'know everybody.' 'Knowing everybody' is a phrase that denotes not having many relations with people but having relations with a few people generally thought to be significant and powerful. When I introduced Bernie to Bill, Bernie was probably about forty-five, but his age was subsumed by his youthful presence. He wore immaculate, up-to-the-minute suits with brightly colored sneakers. The casual shoes gave him a faint air of eccentricity always welcome in the art world, but they also added to what I thought of as Bernie's bounce. He never stopped moving. He ran up stairs, hopped into elevators, rocked back and forth on his heels when he examined a piece of art, and jiggled his knees through most conversations. By drawing attention to his feet, he alerted the world to his indefatigable go-getting and nonstop pursuit of newness. He had a breathless patter to go with the bounce, and his speech, although sometimes fractured, was never stupid. I pushed Bernie to look at Bill's work and had Jack call Bernie as well. Jack had already been to Bill's studio and had become a convert to what he called 'the growing and shrinking Violets.'

I wasn't on the Bowery when Bernie came to look at the work, but it ended as I had hoped. The paintings were shown the following fall. 'They're weird,' Bernie said to me. 'Good weird. I think the fat/thin angle is going to fly. Everybody's on a diet, for Christ's sake, and the self-portrait bit. It's good. It's little risky to show new figurative work right now, but he's got something. And, I like the quotations. Vermeer, de Kooning, and Guston after his revolution.'

By the time the show opened, Violet Blom had flown off to Paris. I met her just once before she left – on the stairway in 89 Bowery. I was coming. She was going. I recognized her, introduced myself, and she paused on the steps. Violet was more beautiful than Bill's paintings of her. She had large green eyes with dark lashes that dominated her round face. Curling brown hair fell over her shoulders, and although her body was hidden under a long coat, I came to the conclusion that she was not thin but didn't qualify as chubby either. She shook my hand warmly, said she had heard all about me, and added, 'I love the fat one with the taxi.' She then said she was sorry she had to run and raced down the stairs. As I continued my climb, I heard her call my name. When I turned around, I saw that she was already standing in front of the door to the street. 'You don't mind if I call you Leo, do you?' I shook my head.

She ran back up the stairs, stopped a couple of steps below me, and said, 'Bill really likes you.' She hesitated. 'I'm going away, you see. I'd like to be able to think that you're there for him.'

I nodded. She took a couple more steps, reached up for my shoulder, and squeezed it as if to confirm that she really meant what she was saying. Then she stood very still and looked straight at me for several seconds. 'You have a nice face,' she said. 'Especially your nose. You have a beautiful nose.' Before I had time to respond to this compliment, she had turned around and was running down the steps. I watched the door slam behind her.

That night when I brushed my teeth and for many nights after, I examined my nose in the mirror. I turned my head to one side and then to the other and tried to catch a glimpse of my profile. I had never spent much time on my nose, had rather disparaged it than admired it, and I can't say that I found it particularly attractive, but that feature in the middle of my face was nevertheless changed forever, transformed by the words of a beautiful young woman, whose image I saw every day hanging on my wall.

Bill asked me to write an essay for the show. I had never written about a living artist and Bill had never been written about before. The little work I called 'Multiple Selves' has now been reprinted and translated into several languages, but at the time I regarded its twelve pages as an act of admiration and friendship. There was no catalogue. The essay was stapled together and handed out at the opening. I wrote it over a period of three months, between correcting papers and committee meetings and student conferences, jotting down thoughts as they came to me after class and on the subway. Bernie knew that Bill needed critical support if he was going 'to get away with' his work at a moment when minimalism reigned in most galleries. The argument I made was that Bill's art referred to the history of Western painting but turned its assumptions inside out, and that he did it in a way that was essentially different from earlier modernists. By including a viewer's shadow in each canvas, Bill called attention to the space between the viewer and the painting where the real action of all painting takes place – a picture becomes itself in the moment of being seen. But the space the viewer occupies also belongs to the painter. The viewer stands in the painter's position and looks at a self-portrait, but what he or she sees is not an image of the man who has signed the painting in the right-hand corner but somebody else: a woman. Looking at women in painting is an established erotic convention that essentially turns every viewer into a man dreaming of sexual conquest. Any number of great painters have painted pictures of women that subvert the fantasy – Giorgione, Rubens, Vermeer, Manet – but as far as I know not a single male painter has ever announced to the viewer that the woman was himself. It was Erica who elaborated the point one evening. 'The truth is,' she said, 'we all have a man and a woman inside us. We're made from a father and a mother, after all. When I'm looking at a beautiful, sexy woman in a picture, I'm always both her and the person who's looking at her. The eroticism comes from the fact that I can imagine I'm him looking at me. You have to be both people or nothing will happen.'

Erica was sitting up in bed reading the indecipherable work of Jacques Lacan when she made this statement. She was wearing a sleeveless cotton nightgown cut low at the neck, and she had tied her hair back, so that I could see her soft earlobes. 'Thank you, Professor Stein,' I said to her, and put my hand on her belly. 'Is there really someone in there?' Erica put her book down and kissed me on the forehead. She was almost three months pregnant, and it was still our secret. The exhaustion and nausea of the first two months had lifted, but Erica had changed. There were days when she shone with happiness and other days when she seemed always to be on the brink of tears. Erica had never been steady, but her moods were even more volatile now. One morning at breakfast she sobbed noisily over an article about foster care in New York City that featured a four-year-old boy named Joey who had been booted out of one home after another. One night she woke up weeping after she dreamed that she left her newborn on a ship and it sailed away as she stood on the dock. Another afternoon, I found her sitting on the sofa with tears streaming down her cheeks. When I asked her what was the matter, she sniffed and said, 'Life is sad, Leo. I've been sitting here thinking about how sad it all is.'

These changes in my wife, physical and emotional, also affected my essay on Bill. Violet's body, which grew and shrank in the canvases, did more than hint at fertility and its transformations. One of the fantasies between the viewer/painter and the female object had to be impregnation. After all, conception is plurality – the two in the one – the male and the female. After he read the piece, Bill grinned. He shook his head and felt his unshaven face before he said a word to me. In spite of my confidence, I felt a rush of anxiety. 'It's good,' he said. 'It's very good. Of course half of it never crossed my mind.' Bill was silent for about a minute. He hesitated, seemed about to speak, and then paused again. Finally, he said, 'We haven't told anybody yet, but Lucille is two months pregnant. We've been trying for over a year. The whole time I was working with Violet, we were hoping that we would have a child.' After I told Bill about Erica, he said, 'I've always wanted kids, Leo, lots of kids. For years I've had this daydream about traveling around the world and populating the earth. I like to imagine myself as the father of hundreds, thousands of children.' I laughed when he said it, but I never forgot that fantasy of extravagant potency and multiplication. Bill dreamed of covering the earth with himself.

About halfway through his own opening, Bill

disappeared. He told me later that he went to Fanelli's for a Scotch. He had looked pretty miserable from the start as he stood under the NO SMOKING sign, inhaling deeply on a cigarette and tapping the ashes into the pocket of a jacket that was too small for him. Bernie always attracted a good crowd. The guests milled about the big white space with glasses of wine and talked loudly. My essay sat on the desk in a pile. I had given papers at conferences and seminars, had published in journals and magazines, but my work had never been distributed as a leaflet. The novelty pleased me, and I surveyed the takers. A pretty redhead picked it up and read the first few sentences. I felt particularly gratified when she moved her lips as she read. It seemed to suggest an added interest in my words. The piece had also been taped to the wall, and a few people glanced at it. One young man wearing leather pants appeared to read it in its entirety. Jack Newman showed up and slouched around the gallery, one eyebrow raised in an expression of bemused irony. Erica introduced Jack to Lucille, and he cornered her for a good half hour. Every time I looked up, I saw him leaning over her, an inch closer than he should have been. Jack had been married and divorced twice. His lack of success with wives hadn't stopped him from pursuing less permanent encounters, and his wit more than compensated for his lack of physical charm. Jack was comfortable with his jowly face, big belly, and stubby legs, and he made women comfortable with them, too. I had seen him go after the most unlikely people time and time again and succeed. He seduced them with the well-turned compliment. I watched his mouth move as he stood beside Lucille, and I wondered what baroque quips he was using on her that evening. When Jack sidled up to me later to say good-bye, he rubbed his jaw, looked me straight in the eyes, and said, 'So what about Wechsler's wife? Do you think she melts in the sack or stays frozen?'

'I have no idea,' I said. 'But I hope you don't have any leanings in that direction. She's not one of your student nymphettes, and she's pregnant, for God's sake.'

Jack lifted his palms toward me and gave me a look of mock horror. 'Heaven forbid,' he said. 'The thought never entered my mind.'

Before Bill escaped to Fanelli's, he introduced me to his parents. Regina Wechsler, who had become Regina Cohen after her second marriage, was a tall, attractive woman with a large bust, thick black hair, considerable amounts of gold jewelry, and a sweet, lilting voice. When she spoke, she cocked her head sideways and glanced up at me from under her long eyelashes. She undulated her shoulders as she declared the evening 'wonderful' and referred to the toilet, before she went off to use it, as 'the powder room.' And yet Regina wasn't all artifice. She sized up the soberly dressed crowd in a few seconds, pointed to her red suit, and said, 'I feel like a fire engine.' She let out a deep, sudden

41

laugh, and her humor cut straight through her posing. Her husband, Al, was a pink-faced man with a square jaw and a deep voice, who seemed genuinely interested in Bill and his work. 'They take you by surprise, don't they?' he said about the paintings, and I had to agree.

Before Regina left, I saw her hand Bill a letter. I was standing right beside her, and I suppose she thought I deserved an explanation. 'It's from his brother Dan, who couldn't be here tonight.' An instant later, she turned to Bill and said, 'Your father just walked in. I'm going to say hello to him before we leave.'

I watched Regina approach a tall man who had just come out of the elevator. The resemblance between father and son was striking. Sy Wechsler had a narrower face than Bill, but his dark eyes and skin, his broad shoulders and strong limbs were so much like his son's that the two could have been mistaken for each other if viewed from behind, a fact I would remember later when Bill began a portrait series of his father. While Regina spoke to him, Sy nodded and answered, but his expression was vague. I guessed that the encounter was awkward for him and that he was bearing up by adopting a polite but distant attitude toward his ex-wife, but the expression on his face never changed. When he approached Bill, he stuck out his hand and Bill shook it. He thanked his father for coming and introduced me. When we shook hands, I looked into the man's eyes and he returned the look, but there was little recognition in his face. He nodded at me, said, 'Congratulations and good luck,' and then turned to his pregnant daughter-in-law and said exactly the same thing. He did not comment on his forthcoming grandchild, who by then was a small bump under Lucille's dress. He glanced at the paintings as if they were the work of some stranger, and left the gallery. I don't know whether the suddenness of his father's arrival and departure rattled Bill enough to make him leave or whether it was just the pressure of finding himself under scrutiny by an art world he feared might reject him.

As it turned out, the critics both rejected and accepted him. That first show set the tone for the rest of Bill's career. He would always have passionate defenders and violent detractors, but as painful or pleasant as it might have been for Bill to be hated by some people and worshiped by others, he would become far more important to reviewers and journalists than they ever would be to him. By the time of his first show, Bill was already too old and too stubborn to be swayed by critics. He was the most private person I have ever known, and only a few people were ever allowed to enter the secret room of his imagination. It is ironic and sad that perhaps the most important inhabitant of that room was and would always be Bill's father. Alive, Sy Wechsler was the incarnation of his son's unfulfilled longing. He was one of those people who were never fully present at the events of their own lives. A part of him was not there, and it was this absent quality in his father that Bill never stopped pursuing – even after the man was dead.

Bill showed up for the small dinner at Bernie's loft after the opening, but he was mostly silent, and we all went home early. The next day, a Saturday, I went to see him on the Bowery. Lucille was visiting her parents in New Haven, and Bill told me the story of his father. Sy's parents were immigrants who had left Russia as small children and ended up on the Lower East Side. Bill told me that his grandfather had abandoned his wife and three children when Sy, the oldest, was ten. The story in the family was that Moishe ran off to Canada with another woman, where he became a wealthy man and fathered three other children. At his grandmother's funeral, Bill had met a woman named Esther Feuerstein, and it was through Esther that he learned what no one in the family had ever mentioned. The day after her husband left, Rachael Wechsler had walked into the tiny kitchen in their tenement on Rivington Street and stuck her head in the oven. It was Sy who had pounded on Esther's door and Sy who helped Esther pull a screaming Rachael away from the gas. Despite her encounter with early death, Bill's grandmother lived to be eighty-nine years old. His description of the old lady was unsentimental. 'She was nuts,' he said. 'She used to howl at me in Yiddish, and when I didn't understand her, she'd whack me with her purse.'

'My father always favored Dan,' Bill said. He didn't make this statement with any bitterness. I already knew that Dan had been an unstable, high-strung child and that sometime in his early twenties he had had a schizophrenic breakdown. Since then, Bill's younger brother had been in and out of hospitals and halfway houses and mental health clinics. Bill said that his father was touched by weakness, that he had a natural attraction to people who needed a helping hand. One of Bill's cousins had Down's syndrome, and Sy Wechsler had never forgotten Larry's birthday, although he sometimes forgot his older son's. 'I want you to read the note Dan sent me,' Bill said. 'It will give you a good idea of what goes on in his head. He's mad, but he's not stupid. I sometimes think he's got the life of at least five people in him.' Bill handed me a wrinkled, smudged piece of paper, written by hand.

CHARGE BRO THE RS W.!
REACH THE ACHE!
HEAR THE BEAT.
TO THE ROSE, THE COAT,
THE CAR, THE RATS, THE BOAT.
TO BEER. TO WAR.
TO HERE. TO THERE.
TO HER.
WE WERE, ARE
HER.
LOVE, DAN (I) EL. (NO) DENIAL.

After I read the note, I said, 'It's a kind of anagram.'

'It took me a while to figure it out, but if you look at it closely, all the words in the poem are made up of the letters in the first line – except the last ones, when he signs off.'

'Who is the "her"? Did he know about your paintings?'

'My mother might have told him. He writes plays, too. Some of them rhyme. Dan's sickness isn't anybody's fault. I think my mother always felt that something was wrong, even when he was a baby, but at the same time, it didn't help that my parents were, well, not really together. By the time he was born, my mother was pretty disappointed. I don't think she had had any idea who she was marrying. By the time she found out, it was too late.'

I suppose we are all the products of our parents' joy and suffering. Their emotions are written into us, as much as the inscriptions made by their genes. That afternoon, sitting in a chair not far from the bathtub, while Bill sat on the floor, I told him about my father's death, a story I had only told to Erica. I was seventeen when my father died. He had three strokes. The first one paralyzed his left side, which distorted his face and made speaking difficult. He slurred his speech. He complained of a cloud in his brain that snatched words from his consciousness, and he spent hours typing out sentences with his good hand, often pausing for minutes to retrieve a missing phrase. I hated the sight of my debilitated father. I still dream that I wake up and find that a leg or arm is paralyzed or has simply dropped off my body. My father was a proud, formal man whose relation to me was principally one of answering my questions, sometimes more thoroughly than I wished. A question of only a few seconds could easily yield a half-hour lecture. My father didn't talk down to me. He had great confidence in my understanding, but the truth was that his discourses on the nervous system or the heart or liberalism or Machiavelli often bored me. And yet, I never wanted him to stop talking. I liked to have his eyes on me, liked to sit near him, and I would wait for the signs of affection that always concluded his talks – a pat on my arm, on my knee, or the tender quiver in his voice when he rounded off his speech by saying my name.

In New York, my father read the *Aufbau*, a weekly paper for German Jews in America. During the war it published lists of missing people, and my father read every name before he read anything else in the paper. I dreaded the arrival of the *Aufbau*, dreaded my father's absorption, his hunched shoulders, the blank look on his face as he read down the lists. The hunt for his family took place in silence. He never said, I am checking to see if their names are here. He said nothing. My mother and I choked on his silence, but we never never interrupted it by speaking.

The third stroke killed him. My mother found

him dead beside her in the morning. I had never seen or heard my mother cry, but that morning she let out a terrible wail that brought me running to my parents' bedroom. She told me in a strange, tough voice that Otto was dead, shooed me out of the room, and closed the door behind her. I stood outside the door and listened to her low guttural noises, to her muffled cries and hoarse gasps. It was never clear to me how long I stood there, but after some time she opened the door. Her face was calm then and her posture unusually erect. She told me to come in, and we sat beside my father's body for several minutes before she stood up and walked into the other room to use the telephone. My father wasn't terrible to look at, but the change from life to death scared me. The blinds on the windows were still drawn, and along their bottoms I noticed two brilliant lines of sun. I studied them as I sat there in the room alone with my father.

When Erica and Lucille were both about five months pregnant, I took a snapshot of the two of them in our loft. Erica is grinning at the camera, and she has her arm securely around Lucille's shoulders, who looks small and shy but contented at the same time. Her left hand is laid protectively on her belly and her chin is lowered as she looks up. One side of her mouth has twisted itself into an obliging smile. Pregnancy suited Lucille. It softened her, and the picture is a reminder to me of a gentleness

48

in her personality that was more often hidden than not.

In her fourth month, Erica started humming, and she hummed until our son was born. She hummed at breakfast. She hummed on her way out the door in the morning. She hummed at her desk while she worked on her 'Three Dialogues' paper – the one on Martin Buber, M. M. Bakhtin, and Jacques Lacan, which she delivered at a conference at NYU two and a half months before she gave birth. The humming drove me crazy, but I strove to be tolerant. When I asked her to stop, she would always look up at me with startled eyes and say, 'Was I humming?'

During their pregnancies, Erica and Lucille became friends. They compared internal kicks and belly size. They went shopping for minuscule outfits and laughed like two conspirators about their squashed bladders, protruding navels, and large bra sizes. Erica laughed louder. Although Lucille never lost her reticence, she seemed to relax more with Erica than with other people. And yet, after the babies were born, there was a shift in Lucille toward Erica – a barely perceptible hint of coolness. I did not see it or feel it until Erica pointed it out, and even then I doubted the truth of it for a long time. Lucille was not socially graceful. Her manners had a blunt, uncivil edge and, on top of that, she was probably exhausted from the rigors of caring for an infant. My arguments usually convinced Erica until she felt it again: the tiny sting of possible rejection – always ambiguous, always subject to many interpretations.

When I saw Lucille, we talked about poetry. She continued to give me the little magazines that published her, and I took time with the poems and made comments on them. My comments were usually questions – about form, about choices she had made or not made, and she talked eagerly to me about her use of commas and periods and her preference for simple diction. Her ability to focus on these details was extraordinary, and I enjoyed our conversations. Erica didn't like Lucille's poems. She once confided in me that reading them was 'like eating dust.' Lucille may have divined Erica's distaste for her work and instinctively withdrawn from that disapproval, or she might not have liked the fact that Erica eagerly embraced Bill's literary opinions and sometimes called him for a reference or just to ask him a question. I don't know, but as time wore on, I understood that the two women were no longer close, and that the more Lucille withdrew from Erica, the more she seemed interested in me.

About two weeks after I took the photograph of Erica and Lucille, Sy Wechsler dropped dead of a heart attack. It happened early one evening after work while he was taking in the mail. Wechsler lived alone, and it was his brother Morris who found him the next morning, lying near the kitchen table with bills, a couple of business letters, and several catalogues on the floor beside him. No one had expected Wechsler to die. He did not smoke or drink, and he ran three miles a day. Bill and his Uncle Morris made the funeral arrangements, and Sy's youngest brother flew in from California with his wife and two children. After the funeral, Bill and Morris cleaned out the big house in South Orange, and when that task was over, Bill started drawing. He drew hundreds of pictures of his father, both from memory and from photographs. Bill had produced very little since his first show, not because he didn't want to work but because he needed to earn money. Two of the Violet paintings had sold to collectors, but the money they brought in had disappeared quickly. Once Bill knew he and Lucille were going to have a child, he had taken every plastering job he was offered, and after grinding days on a contracting site, he was often too tired to do anything but sleep. Sy Wechsler left $300,000 to each of his sons, and with his share of the money, Bill transformed his life.

The loft above us at 27 Greene Street was up for sale. Bill and Lucille bought it, and by early August of 1977 they had moved in. The rent on the Bowery was low, and Bill kept it as his studio. The money, Bill told me, 'will buy us time to do our own work.' But that summer, Bill had few hours to spare for painting. All day, every day, he sawed, hammered, drilled, and breathed in dust. He erected Sheetrock walls in the raw space to make rooms. He laid tile in the bathroom once the plumber had installed the fixtures. He built closets and put in lights and hung

51

the kitchen cabinets, and at night he would return to the Bowery and his sleeping wife and draw his father. It was grief as energy. Bill understood that his father's death had given him a new beginning and that the gargantuan physical labors of that summer were finally spiritual. He worked in the name of his father for his unborn son.

In early August, only days before Matthew was born, Bernie Weeks and I walked to the Bowery in the late afternoon to take a look at Bill's early plans for a new series of paintings – which were developing out of the drawings of his father. While Bernie was flipping through the drawings of Sy Wechsler – sitting, standing, running, sleeping – he paused at one and said, 'You know, I had a nice conversation with your father once.'

'At the opening,' Bill said flatly.

'No, it was a couple of weeks after. He came back to look at the paintings. I recognized him, and we chatted for two or three minutes.'

In a startled voice, Bill said, 'You met him in the gallery?'

'I thought you knew,' Bernie said casually. 'He was there for at least an hour. He took his time, going very slowly. He would look at one for quite a while and then move on to the next one.'

'He went back,' Bill said. 'He went back and looked at them.'

The story of his father's return visit to the Weeks Gallery never left Bill. It became the single concrete sign he had of his father's affection for him.

Before that, Sy's long days at the box business, his appearances at the occasional Little League game, school play, or first art opening had had to suffice as markers of his father's paternal duty and goodwill. Bernie's story added a layer to Bill's internal portrait of his father. It also had the irrational effect of confirming his loyalty to the Weeks Gallery. Bill confused the messenger and the message, but it hardly mattered. As Bernie rocked back and forth on his heels in front of several mounted drawings of Sy Wechsler and ran his fingers through the keys and papers and debris that Bill said would be mounted onto the canvases, I sensed his excitement. Bernie was in for the long haul.

Birth is violent, bloody, and painful, and all the rhetoric to the contrary will not convince me that I am wrong. I have heard the stories of women squatting in the fields, snapping umbilical cords with their teeth, strapping their newborns onto their backs, and picking up the scythe, but I wasn't married to those women. I was married to Erica. We went to Lamaze classes together and listened attentively to Jean Romer's breathing advice. A stocky woman in bermuda shorts and thick-soled sneakers, Jean referred to birth as 'the great adventure' and to the members of her class as 'moms' and 'coaches.' Erica and I watched films of athletic, smiling women doing deep knee bends during their labors and breathing their babies out of them. We practiced panting and blowing as we silently corrected Jean's grammar every time she told us 'to lay down on the floor.' At forty-seven, I was the second-to-oldest father-to-be in the class. The oldest was a bullish man in his sixties named Harry who had been married before, had grown-up children, and was now working on his second child from his second wife, who looked like a teenager but was probably well into her twenties.

Matthew was born on August 12, 1977, at St Vincent's Hospital. I stood beside Erica and watched her agonized face, squirming body, and clenched fists. Every once in a while I reached for her hand, but she batted me away and shook her head. Erica did not scream, but down the hallway in another labor room, a woman shrieked and wailed at the top of her lungs, pausing only to swear both in Spanish and in English. She too must have had a 'coach' with her, because after a few seconds of surprising silence, we heard her yell, 'Fuck you, Johnny! Fuck you and your fucking breathing! You fucking breathe! I'm dying!'

Near the end, Erica's eyes took on a bright, ecstatic gleam. She clenched her teeth and growled like a animal when she was told to push. I stood beside the doctor in my surgical gown and watched the wet, bloody, black head of my son emerge from between Erica's legs, followed immediately by his shoulders and the rest of his body. I saw his bloated little penis, saw blood and fluid gush from Erica's closing vagina, heard Dr Figueira say, 'It's a boy,' and felt dizzy. A nurse pushed me into a chair, and then I had my son in my arms. I looked down at his wrinkled red face and soft lopsided head and said, 'Matthew Stein Hertzberg,' and he looked me in the eyes and grimaced.

It had come to me late. I was a graying, wrinkling father of an infant son, but I took to parenthood with the enthusiasm of the long deprived. Matt was an odd little creature with thin red limbs, a purplish umbilical stump, and downy black hair on only part of his head. Erica and I spent a lot of time studying his peculiarities – his greedy slurping noises when he fed, his mustard-colored bowel movements, his waving arms and legs, and his absorbed staring, which suggested brilliance or idiocy, depending on how you looked at it. For about a week, she called him 'our naked stranger,' but then he became Matthew or Matt or Matty boy. In those first few months after he was born, Erica showed a competence and ease I hadn't seen in her before. She had always been nervous and excitable, and when she was really heated her voice would take on a shrill, anxious timbre, a register that affected me physically – as if someone were running a fork over my skin. But Erica had few outbursts during Matt's early days. She was almost serene. It was rather like being married all over again to someone slightly different. She never slept enough, and the skin beneath her eyes was dark with lack of sleep, but her features were milder than I had ever seen them. When she nursed Matt, she would sometimes look at me with a tenderness that was nearly painful in its intensity. Often, I was still reading in bed while Erica and Matt slept together beside me, his head on her breast as she held him. Even while she slept, she was aware of him and would wake to his smallest squeak. Sometimes, I would put down my book and look at the two of them in the light of my reading lamp. I now think I was lucky that I wasn't young. I knew what I might not have known earlier – that my happiness had come. I even told myself to fix the image of my wife and son in my mind while I watched them sleep, and it is still there, a clear picture left by my conscious wish. I can see Erica's profile on the pillow, her dark hair falling over her cheek, and Matt's little head, about the size of a grapefruit, turned in toward his mother's body.

We tracked Matt's development with the precision and attentiveness of Enlightenment scientists, noting each phase of his growth as if nobody had ever smiled, laughed, or rolled over before him. Erica once called me loudly to his crib, and when I arrived beside her, she pointed at our son and said, 'Leo, look! I think he knows it's his foot. Look at the way he's sucking on his toes. He knows they belong to him!' Whether Matt had actually discovered the perimeter of his own body by then or not remained a moot point, but he increasingly became someone with a personality we could identify. He was not a loud person, but I suppose that if every time you utter a barely audible noise, one of your parents comes running, you do not become loud. For a baby he seemed weirdly compassionate. One evening when Matt was about nine months old, Erica was getting him ready for bed. She was carrying him around with her and opened the refrigerator to retrieve his bottle. By accident two glass containers of mustard and jam came with it and smashed on the floor. Erica had gone back to work by then, and her exhaustion got the better of her. She looked at the broken glass and burst into tears. She stopped crying when she felt Matt's small hand gently patting her arm in sympathy. Our son also liked to feed us – half-chewed bits of banana or pureed spinach or mashed carrots. He would come at me with his sticky fist and push the unsavory contents into my mouth. We read this as a sign of his generosity. From the time he could sit, Matt showed great powers of concentration, and when I saw other children his age, I found I hadn't exaggerated this trait. He had a long attention span, but he did not speak. He gurgled and babbled and pointed, but the words were very slow in coming.

When Erica returned to work, we hired a nanny for Matt. Grace Thelwell was both tall and fat, a woman in her fifties who had grown up in Jamaica. She had four adult children and six grandchildren and the posture of a queen. She walked noiselessly around our house, spoke in a low musical voice, and exuded a Buddha-like calm in the face of all agitation. Her refrain consisted of two words:

'Never mind.' When Matt cried, she would hold him and sing the words, 'Never mind.' When Erica rushed in after a day at Rutgers and ran into the kitchen, looking wild-eyed and harried, Grace would place a hand on her shoulder and say, 'Never mind' before she helped Erica put the groceries away. When Grace came to us, her practical philosophy arrived with her, and it soothed all three of us – like a warm Caribbean breeze blowing through the rooms of the loft. She would always be Matt's fairy godmother, and the longer she was with us the more I felt that she was not an ordinary person but someone of feeling and intelligence, whose ability to distinguish between the important and the trivial often put me and Erica to shame. When Erica and I went out in the evenings and Grace stayed home with Matt, we would return to find her sitting in his room while he slept. The lights were always out. Grace did not read or knit or busy herself with anything. She sat in silence on a chair looking over him, content with the fullness of her own thoughts.

Mark Wechsler was born on August twenty-seventh. We were now two families, one on top of the other. Although the physical closeness made visiting easy, I saw Bill only a little more often than before. We loaned each other books, shared articles we had read, but our domestic lives were mostly contained within the walls of our separate apartments. All first babies shock their parents to one degree or another. Their demands are so urgent, their emotions run at such a high pitch that families close in on themselves to answer their calls. Bill would sometimes bring Mark with him to visit me when he returned home after a day at the studio. 'Lucille's taking a nap,' he would say. 'She's exhausted,' or, 'I'm giving her a break. She needs silence.' I accepted these comments without question, although I did hear the occasional note of worry in Bill's voice; but then he had always worried about Lucille. He was easy with his son, a small, blue-eyed version of himself who struck me as placid, well-fed, and slightly dopey. My obsessive interest in Matthew did not carry over to Mark, but the fact that Bill's affection for his own son was at least as passionate as mine for Matt solidified my sense that our lives were parallel – that in the hectic, grubby ordeal of caring for a baby, he and Lucille, like Erica and me, had discovered new strains of joy between them.

Only Lucille's weariness wasn't like Erica's. It had an existential cast – as though she suffered from more than being up at night. She didn't come to see me often, perhaps once every two months, and she always called days ahead of time to arrange the meeting. At the appointed time, I would open the door to find Lucille standing in the hallway with a sheaf of poems in her hand. She always looked pale and drawn and stiff. Her hair hung around her face uncombed, usually dirty. Mostly she wore jeans and old-fashioned blouses in dull colors, and yet her disheveled appearance didn't

59

disguise her prettiness, and I admired her lack of vanity. I was always glad to see her, but Lucille's visits augmented Erica's feeling that Lucille had forgotten her. Lucille always greeted Erica politely. She would endure Erica's questions about Mark, answer them in curt, precise sentences, and then she would turn to me. Her economical but resonant poems were written in a voice of complete detachment. Inevitably they contained autobiographical references. In one poem a man and a woman lie beside each other in bed, unable to sleep, but neither one says a word to the other. They don't speak, out of deference to the other, but in the end, the woman feels the man's consideration as a presumption that he knows what she is thinking. Her annoyance with him keeps her awake long after he has gone to sleep. Lucille called the poem 'Aware and Awake.' A baby turned up in some works, a comic character referred to as 'It.' 'It' wailed and clung and kicked and spat up, rather like a windup toy whose mechanism had gone haywire and couldn't be controlled. Lucille never acknowledged in any way that the poems were personal. She treated them as objects that might be remanipulated with my help. Her coolness fascinated me. Every once in a while she would smile to herself as she read a line, and I couldn't penetrate the source of her humor. While I sat next to her, I had the sense that she was always somewhere ahead of me, and that I was running after her. I would look down at the blond hairs on

60

her slender arm and ask myself what it was about her I couldn't grasp.

One evening before she left to go upstairs, I watched as she began to gather up her papers. I had learned to turn away, because I knew that if I looked at her, she would feel uncomfortable and might drop her pencil or eraser. When I shook her hand good-bye, she thanked me and opened the door. It was when she began to walk through it that I had an uncanny sensation of resemblance, followed by a sudden certainty that I was right. In that moment, Lucille reminded me of Sy Wechsler. The link between them was neither physical nor spiritual. Their personalities had little in common except what they both lacked – a quality of ordinary connectedness to other human beings. Lucille didn't elude only Bill, she eluded everyone who knew her. The old adage 'He married his mother' had to be revised. Bill had married his father. Hadn't he said, 'I chased her for years'? As I listened to the sound of her feet on the stairs, I wondered if he wasn't chasing her still.

In the spring before Matt turned two, I overheard a fight between Bill and Lucille. It was a Saturday afternoon and I was sitting in my chair by the window. I had a book in my hand, but I had stopped reading it because I was thinking about Matt. Erica had taken him out to buy new sneakers, and just before the two of them had left, he had spoken his first words. Matt had pointed at his mother, at himself, and at the shoes he was wearing. I had said I hoped his new shoes would be beautiful, and then Matthew had eked out two garbled sounds – 'ooo neets,' which Erica and I had joyfully translated as 'new sneaks.' The child was learning how to talk. I had opened the window to let in the warm breeze. The windows above must have been opened, too, because Bill's booming voice interrupted my reverie about Matt's verbal breakthrough.

'How could you say that?' Bill screamed.

'You weren't supposed to hear it. She shouldn't have told you!' Lucille's voice rose with each word. Her anger surprised me. She was always so controlled.

Bill growled back. 'I don't believe that. She tells everybody everything. You told her because you knew she would tell me, and then you could refuse to take responsibility for your own words. Do you deny you said it? No! So – did you mean it?'

There was silence.

'What the hell am I doing here?' Bill yelled. 'Tell me that!' I heard a loud crash. Bill must have hit or kicked something.

'You broke it!' I heard rage in Lucille's voice, trembling, hysterical rage, and it cut through me. Mark started crying. 'Shut up!' she shrieked. 'Shut up! Shut up!'

I went to close the window. The last thing I heard was Bill saying, 'Mark, Mark. Come here.'

The following day, Bill called me from his studio and told me he had moved out of Greene Street and was living on the Bowery again. His voice sounded dull with misery. 'Do you want me to come over?' I asked. He didn't answer me for a few seconds. Then he said, 'Yeah, I think I do.'

Bill didn't mention the mysterious woman who had played a pivotal role in the argument I had overheard the day before, and I couldn't ask him about her without telling him that I had eavesdropped. I let him talk, even though most of what he said explained little. He told me that although Lucille had said over and over again how much she looked forward to being a mother before Mark was born, after the birth she had seemed disappointed. 'She's been really low and irritable. Everything about me seems to annoy her – I swallow too loudly when I eat. I brush my teeth too vigorously. I pace when I'm thinking and it drives her nuts. My socks smell. I touch her too much. I work too hard. I'm gone too long. She likes me to take care of Mark, but she doesn't like the way I do it. I shouldn't sing Lou Reed songs to him. They're inappropriate. The games I play are too rowdy. I throw him off his schedule.'

Lucille's complaints were banal – the familiar stuff of joyless intimacy. I've always thought that love thrives on a certain kind of distance, that it requires an awed separateness to continue. Without that necessary remove, the physical minutiae of the other person grows ugly in its magnification.

From where I sat opposite Bill, he looked to me like the Byronic ideal of male beauty. A black curl had fallen onto his forehead as he inhaled a cigarette and squinted in thought. Behind him were the seven unfinished paintings of his father he had decided to show. For two years he had been working on portraits of Sy Wechsler. There must have been fifty canvases of the man in various positions, but Bill had chosen to exhibit only seven – all of them of his father viewed from the back. He called the series 'Missing Men.' The afternoon light sank in the windows, the big room grew darker, and we didn't speak for minutes on end. For the first time, I pitied Bill, and a pain settled in my chest at the thought of his suffering. Around five o'clock I told him that I had promised Erica I would be home in ten minutes.

'You know, Leo,' he said, 'for years I've been thinking that Lucille was somebody else. I deceived myself. That's not her fault. It's mine. And now I have a son.'

Instead of responding directly to this, I said, 'It might not be much, but I'm here for you if you need me.' As I said it, I remembered Violet running up the stairs toward me and what she had said to me about my being 'there' for Bill. For a few moments, I wondered if she had known something I didn't about Bill and Lucille, and then I forgot about her and her comment for almost a year.

★   ★   ★

64

Lucille stayed on in the Greene Street loft, and Bill lived on the Bowery. Mark shuttled back and forth between his parents – half the week with Lucille, the other half with Bill. They talked on the phone every day, and neither Bill nor Lucille ever mentioned divorce. Trucks and fire engines and baby wipes appeared in the Bowery loft, and sometime in July, Bill made his son a beautiful bed that looked like a boat. He constructed a stand that allowed it to rock back and forth like an oversized cradle, and he painted it a deep marine blue. Bill read to his son and fed him and encouraged him to at least try the plastic potty in the little room with the toilet. He worried about his appetite and fretted about him falling down the stairs, and he picked up most of his toys, even though he had no gift for housekeeping. The loft was filthier than it had ever been because Bill never bothered to clean it. The sink turned colors I had never seen before on porcelain – a palette that ranged from pale gray to orange to a deep, mucky brown. I didn't mention the dirt. The truth was that father and son seemed comfortable enough in the big crooked room. They didn't mind living among the towers of soiled laundry that rose up from a dusty, ash-covered floor.

Bill didn't say much more to me about his failing marriage. He never complained about Lucille, and when he wasn't taking care of Mark, he worked long hours and slept little. But the truth was that when Erica and Matt and I visited Bill and Mark that summer, I often felt relieved when we left them

65

and walked outside into the hot street. The studio had an oppressive, nearly smothering atmosphere, as if Bill's sadness had leaked into the chairs, the books, the toys, and the empty wine bottles that piled up under the sink. In the paintings of his father, Bill's sorrow took on a palpable beauty that was executed with a rigorous, unflinching hand, but in life his pain was merely depressing.

When the portraits of Bill's father were shown in September, Lucille did not come to the opening. I'd asked her if I would see her there, and she'd said that she was editing a manuscript and would have to work into the night. Her answer sounded like an evasion, and I must have looked dubious, but she'd insisted. 'I have a deadline,' she'd said. 'There is nothing I can do about it.'

Every painting in the show sold, but not to Americans. A Frenchman named Jacques Dupin bought three paintings; the others went to a German collector and a Dutchman in the pharmaceutical business. After that show, Bill was picked up by a gallery in Cologne, one in Paris, and another in Tokyo. American reviewers were befuddled – acclaim by one critic was neutralized by the savage attack of another. There was no consensus about Bill among those who wrote about art for a living, and yet I noticed large numbers of young people in the gallery, not just at the opening but every time I went to look at the paintings. Bernie told me that he had never had so many artists and poets and novelists in their twenties at any exhibition as at that one. 'The kids are all talking about him,' he said. 'That's got to be good. The old fogies are going to die off, and they'll take over.'

It took me several visits to the gallery to understand that the man whose back looked very much the same from one painting to another was aging. I noticed that wrinkles formed at the back of his neck and that his skin changed. Moles multiplied. In the last painting there was a small cyst beneath Sy's ear. By some miracle of art or nature, however, his hair remained black in every one. Bill's rendering of his father, always clad in a dark suit, reminded me of seventeenth-century Dutch paintings, but without their illusion of depth. The smooth, clear image of the man's back was lit from the left side of the canvas, and every fold in the suit's material, every speck of dust on a padded shoulder, every crease in the black leather of a shoe had been painstakingly depicted. But what fascinated spectators was the material Bill had applied over this initial image, which partly obscured it – the letters, photographs, postcards, business memos, receipts, motel keys, movie ticket stubs, aspirins, condoms – until each work became a thick palimpsest of legible and illegible writing, as well as a medley of the various small objects that fill junk drawers in almost any household. There was nothing innovative about gluing foreign materials to a painting, but the effect was very different from Rauschenberg's dense layerings, for example, because the debris in Bill's canvases had been left behind by one man, and as I moved from one painting to another, I enjoyed reading the scraps. I especially liked a letter written in crayon: 'Dear Uncl Sy, Thank you for the relly neet racing car. It's relly neet. Love, Larry.' I studied the invitation that read, 'Please come and celebrate Regina and Sy's Fifteenth Wedding Anniversary. Yes, it's really been that long!' There was a hospital bill for Daniel Wechsler, a playbill from *Hello, Dolly!*, and a torn, wrinkled piece of paper with the name Anita Himmelblatz written on it, followed by a telephone number. Despite these momentary insights into a life, the canvases and their materials had an abstract quality to them, an ultimate blankness that conveyed the strangeness of mortality itself, a sense that even if every scrap of a life were saved, thrown into a giant mound and then carefully sifted to extract all possible meaning, it would not add up to a life.

Over each canvas, Bill had placed a thick piece of Plexiglas, which removed the viewer from the two layers underneath. The Plexiglas turned the works into memorials. Without it, the objects and papers would have been accessible, but sealed behind that transparent wall, the image of the man and the detritus of his life could not be reached.

I returned to the show on West Broadway seven or eight times. The last time I went, only days before it closed, I met Henry Hasseborg. I had seen him before lurking around other galleries and knew him by sight. Jack, who had spoken to him on a couple of occasions, had once called him 'man as toad.' Hasseborg was a novelist and art critic, known for his arch prose and scathing opinions. He was a tiny bald person, always dressed fashionably in black. He had small eyes, a flattened nose, and an enormous mouth. A rash that may have been eczema crawled up one side of his face and onto his head. He approached me and introduced himself. He said that he was familiar with my work and hoped that I was working on another book. He had read my 'Piero' and loved it, as well as my book of essays. 'Tremendous' was the word he used. Then he casually glanced over at a canvas and said, 'You like it?'

I told him I did and began to say why when he interrupted me: 'You don't think they're anachronistic?'

I began another sentence. 'No, I think he puts historical references to another use—'

Hasseborg cut me off again. He was almost a foot shorter than I was. As he looked up at my face, he took a step closer to me, and his proximity made me suddenly uncomfortable. 'They say he's landed galleries in Europe. Which ones?'

'I don't know,' I said. 'You should talk to Bernie if you're interested.'

'Interest might be too strong a word,' he said, and smiled. 'Wechsler's a little too cerebral for me.'

'Really,' I said. 'I feel a lot of emotion in the work.' I paused, surprised that he had let me finish, and went on. 'I seem to remember an article you wrote on Warhol. If anyone's work embodies ideas, it's Warhol. Surely that's cerebral.'

Hasseborg leaned even closer to me, his chin lifted. 'Andy's an icon,' he said, as if this answered my question. 'He had his finger on the cultural pulse, man. He knew what was coming, and it came. Your friend Wechsler's running down some side street . . .' He didn't finish the sentence. He looked at his watch and said, 'Shit, I'm late. See you around, Leo.'

As I watched him walk slowly toward the elevator, I asked myself what had just happened. The tone of his conversation had shifted from ingratiating flattery to insulting familiarity. I also realized that when he'd introduced himself, he hadn't mentioned my friendship with Bill, but as he'd continued to talk, he had insinuated our connection by asking about the European galleries and then directly referred to Bill as 'your friend Wechsler.' Finally, he had rounded off our aborted talk with the flippant use of my first name, as if we were old friends. I was not a naïf. For Hasseborg, manipulating other people was a sophisticated game that could reap him benefits: an inside scoop, a bit of art world gossip, a quote from someone who'd never intended his remark to be public. He was an unscrupulous man, but he was also an intelligent man, and in New York that combination could take you far. Henry Hasseborg had wanted something from me, but for the life of me I couldn't imagine what it was.

By then Erica and I had been together for over five years, and I often thought of our marriage as one long conversation. We talked a lot, and I liked listening to her, especially in the evenings, when she spoke about Matt or her work. Her voice was lovely when she was tired. It lost its shrillness, and her words were sometimes interrupted by yawns or little sighs of relief that the long day was over. One night, we were lying in bed together still talking hours after Matt had gone to sleep. Erica had her head on my chest and I was telling her about my essay on Mannerism, mostly Pontormo, which began with a long definition of 'distortion' – and the context needed to understand what such a word meant. She moved her hand over my belly, and then I felt her fingers stray into my pubic hair. 'You know, Leo,' she said, 'The smarter you are, the sexier you are.' I never forgot Erica's equation. For her, the charms of my body were related to the swiftness of my mind, and in light of this, I thought it wise to keep that higher organ tight, lean, and well-exercised.

Matt had grown into a thin, thoughtful boy who spoke in monosyllables and wandered around the house with his stuffed lion, 'La,' singing to himself in a high, tuneless voice. He wasn't articulate, but he understood everything we said to him. Either Erica or I read to him at night, and while Matt

71

listened, he lay very still in his new big bed, his hazel eyes open and concentrated, as if he could see the story unfold on the ceiling above him. Sometimes he would wake up at night, but he rarely called out to us. We would hear him in the next room, chattering to his animals and cars and blocks in a fluent but private language. Like most two-year-olds, Matt often ran himself to exhaustion, sobbed violently, ordered us around, and was frustrated when we refused to obey his imperial commands, but inside the toddler I felt a strange, tumultuous, and solitary core – an immense inner sanctum where a good part of his life took place.

Violet reappeared in June of 1981. I was near the Bowery, because I had bought some sausage at an Italian deli on Grand Street, and in the spirit of my summer freedom from student papers, students themselves, and the endless bickering of my colleagues in committee meetings, I decided to drop in on Bill. I was walking down Hester Street when I saw him standing with Violet outside the Chinese movie theater on the corner. I recognized Violet instantly, even though I saw her only from behind and she had cut her hair short. She was holding Bill tightly around the waist and her head was pressed against his chest. I watched him lift her face toward him with both hands and kiss her. Violet stood on tiptoe to reach him and lost her balance for a moment before Bill caught her, laughed, and kissed her forehead. Neither one of them saw me standing stock-still on the sidewalk across the street. Violet kissed Bill again, hugged him again, and then ran off down the street, away from me. I noticed that she ran well, like a boy, but she tired quickly, slowed, and began to skip down the block, turning once to blow Bill a kiss. He watched her until she turned the corner. I crossed the street, and when I approached Bill, he waved at me.

After I had reached him he said, 'You saw us.'

'Yes, I was up the street at the deli and . . .'

'It's all right. Don't worry about it.'

'She's back.'

'She's been back for a while.' Bill put his arm around my shoulder. 'Come on,' he said. 'Let's go upstairs.'

While Bill talked to me about Violet, his eyes had the steady concentrated gleam I remembered from the first year I met him. 'It started before,' he said, 'when I was painting her. Nothing happened between us. I mean, we didn't have an affair, but the feeling was there. God, I was careful. I remember thinking that if I so much as brushed against her, I was finished. Well, then she left, and I couldn't stop thinking about her. I thought I'd get over it, that it was a sexual attraction that would pass if I ever saw her again. When she called me a month ago, a part of me hoped I'd take one look at her and say to myself, "You spent years obsessing about this broad? Were you nuts?' But she walked through the door and . . .' Bill rubbed his chin and shook his head. 'I fell apart the second I saw her. Her body . . .' He didn't finish the sentence. 'She's so responsive, Leo. I've never experienced anything like it. Not even close.'

When I asked him if he had told Lucille about Violet, he shook his head. 'I've put it off, not because she wants me back. She doesn't, but because Mark . . .' He hesitated. 'It's much more complicated when you have a child. The poor kid's pretty confused already.'

We talked about our sons for a while. Mark was articulate but easily distracted. Matt said little but could amuse himself alone for a long time. Bill asked about Pontormo, and I talked about elongation in *The Deposition* for a few minutes before I said I had to leave.

'Before you go, I want to show you something. It's a book Violet lent me.'

The book had been written by a Frenchman, Georges Didi-Huberman, but what interested Bill were its photographs. They had all been taken at the Salpêtrière Hospital in Paris, where the famous neurologist JeanMartin Charcot had conducted experiments on women suffering from hysteria. Bill explained that a number of the patients had been hypnotized for the photographs. Some were twisted into positions that reminded me of contortionists in the circus. Others looked at the camera with blank eyes as they held out their arms, which had been pierced through with pins the size of knitting needles. Still others were kneeling and appeared to be praying or beseeching God for help.

The photograph on the book's cover is the one I remember best, however. A pretty dark-haired girl was lying in bed with the sheets over her. She had twisted her body to one side and was sticking out her tongue. The tongue seemed unusually thick and long, a fact that made the gesture more obscene than it might have been. I also thought I saw a glint of mischief in her eyes. The photograph was carefully lit to bring out the voluptuous roundness of the girl's shoulders and torso under the sheets. I stared at the picture for some time, not quite sure what I was seeing.

'Her name was Augustine,' Bill said. 'Violet's particularly interested in her. She was photographed obsessively in the ward and became a kind of pinup girl for hysteria. She was also color-blind. Apparently, many of the hysterics saw colors only when they were hypnotized. It's almost too perfect – the poster girl for an illness in the early days of photography sees the world in black and white.'

Violet was only twenty-seven then, still writing furiously on her dissertation about long-dead women whose illness included violent seizures, paralyzed limbs, stigmata, obsessive scratching, lewd postures, and hallucinations. She called the hysterics 'my lovely lunatics,' and referred to them casually by name, as if she had met them not long ago in the ward and regarded them as friends or at least as interesting aquaintances. Unlike most intellectuals, Violet didn't distinguish between the cerebral and the physical. Her thoughts seemed to run through her whole being, as if thinking were a sensual experience. Her movements suggested warmth and languor, an unhurried pleasure in her own body. She was forever making herself more comfortable. She wriggled into chairs, adjusted her neck and arms and shoulders. She crossed her legs or let one dangle over the edge of a sofa. She had a tendency to sigh, take deep breaths, and bite her bottom lip when she was thinking. Sometimes she would gently stroke her arm while she talked or finger her lips while she listened. Often she would reach out and touch my hand very lightly when she spoke to me. With Erica she was openly affectionate. She would stroke Erica's hair or let her arm lie comfortably around her shoulders.

Beside Lucille, my wife had looked loose and open. Next to Violet, Erica's nerves and the relative tightness of her body seemed to redefine her as reserved and cautious. The two women liked each other immediately, however, and the friendship between them would last. Violet seduced Erica with her stories of feminine subversion – tales of women who made daring escapes from hospitals and husbands, fathers and employers. They chopped off their hair and disguised themselves as men. They climbed over walls, jumped out windows, and leapt from roof to roof. They boarded ships and sailed out to sea. But Erica especially loved the animal stories. Her eyes widened and she smiled as she listened to Violet tell about an outbreak of meowing among girls who attended a convent school in France. At exactly the same hour every afternoon, the girls went down on their hands and knees and meowed loudly for several hours until the whole neighborhood pulsed with the noise. Another incident involved canine behavior. Violet reported that in 1855 every single woman in the French town of Josselin succumbed to a fit of uncontrollable barking.

Violet captivated Erica with her own stories, too, most of them kept secret from me and only hinted at, but I gathered that Violet had been in and out of many beds in her young life, and that not every bed had had a man in it. For Erica, who had slept with exactly three men in the course of her thirty-nine years, Violet's erotic adventures were more than intriguing anecdotes. They were tales of enviable daring and freedom. For Violet, Erica embodied feminine reason, an idea that most of history has relegated to an oxymoron. Erica had a patience of mind that Violet lacked, a dogged willingness to tease a thought to fruition, and there were days when Violet would come to our door with a question for Erica, usually about German philosophy – Hegel, Husserl, or Heidegger. Violet became Erica's student then. She would lie on our sofa, her eyes fixed on her teacher's face, and while she listened she squinted, frowned, and pulled at strands of her hair, as though these gestures could help her puzzle out the tortuous mysteries of being.

I doubt that either Erica or I would have taken to Violet so quickly had she not been with Bill. It wasn't only that we knew him and were well-disposed to the woman he had fallen for so hard, it was that we liked Bill and Violet together. They were beautiful, those two, and my mind is still crammed with memories of their bodies from the early days of their love affair: Violet with her hand in Bill's hair or on his thigh or Bill leaning over her, his mouth grazing her ear. Every time I saw them, I had the impression that they had just made love or were about to make love, that their eyes never left each other. Infatuated people often look ridiculous to others; their nonstop cooing, touching, and kissing can be intolerable to friends who have left that stage behind them. But Bill and Violet didn't embarrass me. Despite their obvious passion for each other, they played at restraint, holding back when Erica or I were in the room, and I think the tension they created together was what I liked best. I always felt that there was an invisible wire between them, stretched nearly to its breaking point.

Violet had grown up on a farm near Dundas, Minnesota, a town with a population of 623. I knew almost nothing about her corner of the Mid-west, with its alfalfa fields, Holstein cows, and stolid characters with names like Harold Lundberg,

Gladys Hrbek, and Lovey Munkemeyer, but I imagined it nevertheless, stealing images from movies and books of a flat landscape under a large sky. She had graduated from high school in the neighboring town of Northfield and attended St Olaf College in that same town before she fled east to graduate school at NYU. Her great-grandparents on both sides had emigrated from Norway and made their way across the country to start their farms and fight the earth and weather. Violet's rural childhood still clung to her. It appeared not only in her long midwestern vowels and in her references to milking machines and feedbags, but in the earnestness and weight of her spirit. Violet had charm, but it was not cultivated charm. When I spoke to her, I had the feeling that her thoughts had been nourished in wide-open spaces where talk was sparse and silence ruled.

One afternoon in July I found myself alone with Violet. Erica had taken Matt and Mark back to Greene Street, along with the first chapter of Violet's dissertation, which she had promised to read. Bill had gone off to Pearl Paint for supplies. The light shone on Violet's brown hair as she sat cross-legged on the floor in front of a window and told me the story of Augustine, which turned into a story about herself.

In Paris, Violet had rummaged through documents, files, and case studies called *observations* from the Salpêtrière hospital. From these accounts, she had cobbled together a few sketchy personal histories. 'Both her parents were servants,' Violet told me. 'Not long after she was born, they sent her away to live with relatives. She stayed with them for six years but then was sent away again to a convent school. She was an angry girl – unruly and difficult. The nuns thought she was possessed by the devil, and they threw holy water in her face to calm her. When she was thirteen, the nuns expelled her, and she went back to her mother, who was working in a house in Paris as a chambermaid. The case study doesn't mention what happened to her father. He must have disappeared. It does say that Augustine was hired "on the pretext" that she teach the children of the house to sing and sew. For her efforts she was allowed to sleep in a little closet. It turned out that her mother was having an affair with the master of the house. In the records, they just call him "Monsieur C." Not long after Augustine moved in, Monsieur C. began making sexual advances toward her, but she refused him. Finally he threatened her with a razor and then raped her. She started having convulsive fits and bouts of paralysis. She hallucinated rats and dogs and big eyes staring at her. It got so bad that her mother took her to the Salpêtrière, where she was diagnosed as a hysteric. She was fifteen.'

'A lot of people would go crazy after that kind of treatment,' I said.

'She didn't have a chance. You'd be surprised how many of the girls and women I've been reading about came from similar backgrounds. Most of them were dirt-poor. A lot of them were shuttled back and forth between one parent or relative and another. They were always being uprooted as children. Several of them had been molested, too, by a relative or employer or somebody.' Violet stopped talking for several seconds. 'There are still psychoanalysts who talk about "hysterical personality," but most pyschiatrists don't even consider hysteria a mental illness anymore. The one thing that's left on the books is "hysterical conversion" or "conversion disorder." That's when you wake up one day and can't move your arms or legs and there's no physical reason for it.'

'You're saying that hysteria was a medical creation,' I said.

'No,' Violet said. 'That's too simple. The medical establishment was certainly part of it, but the fact that so many women had hysterical attacks, not just women who were hospitalized for them, goes beyond doctors. Swooning, thrashing, and foaming at the mouth were a lot more common in the nineteenth century. It hardly happens anymore. Don't you find that strange? I mean, the only explanation is that hysteria really was a broad cultural phenomenon – a permissible way out.'

'Out of what?'

'Out of Monsieur C.'s house, for one thing.'

'You think that Augustine was pretending?'

'No. I think she was really suffering. If she had been admitted to a hospital today, they would have said she was schizophrenic or bipolar, but let's face it, those names are pretty vague, too. I think her illness took the form it did because it was in the air, floating around like a virus – the way anorexia nervosa floats around today.'

While I thought about her comment, Violet continued. 'When we were kids, my little sister, Alice, and I used to spend a lot of time in the barn. The summer after I turned nine and Alice turned six, we were playing with our dolls up in the hayloft. We were sitting across from each other making our dolls talk when suddenly Alice got this strange look on her face and pointed at the little window. "Look Violet," she said, "there's an angel." I didn't see anything except the little square of sunshine, but I was spooked, and then for a second I thought that there might be a figure there – a pale, weightless thing. Alice fell over and started kicking and choking. I grabbed her and tried to shake her. At first, I thought she was fooling, and then I saw her eyes roll up into her head and I knew she wasn't. I started screaming for my mother, and then I was gagging on my own spit. I was kicking and rolling around in the hay. My mother came running out of the house and climbed up the ladder to us. I was all crazy, Leo. I was yelling so loud I got hoarse. It took my mother a couple of minutes to figure out which one of us was in trouble. When she did, she had to push me out of the way, really hard, because I was holding on to Alice's knees and I wouldn't let go. My mother carried Alice out of there and down the ladder and drove her to the hospital.' Violet took a big, shuddering breath and continued. 'I stayed home with my father. I was sick with shame. I had panicked. I did everything wrong. I wasn't brave at all, but worse than that, a part of me knew that I had been acting flipped out, and that it was only partly real.' Violet's eyes filled with tears. 'I went into my room and started counting. I counted way up to four thousand and something, and then my father came into my room and told me Alice was going to be all right. He had talked to my mother at the hospital, and I cried all over him for a long time.' Violet turned her head away from me. 'Alice had had a grand mal seizure. She's an epileptic.'

'You shouldn't blame yourself for being scared,' I said.

Violet looked at me, her eyes suddenly shrewd. 'You know how Charcot began to understand hysteria? The hysterics just happened to be housed right next door to the epileptics at the hospital. After a little while, the hysterics started having seizures. They became what they were near.'

In August Erica and I rented a house on Martha's Vineyard for two weeks. We celebrated Matt's fourth birthday in the small white house about a quarter mile from the beach. After he woke up that morning, Matt was unusually quiet. He seated himself at the breakfast table across from me and Erica and looked soberly at the presents that were piled in front of him. Behind his head through the kitchen window I could see the green expanse of the small lawn and the shine of dew on the grass. I waited for him to begin tearing off the wrapping paper, but he didn't move. He looked as if he were about to say something. Matt often paused before a speech, collecting himself for the sentence ahead. His verbal abilities had improved dramatically in the past year, but they still lagged behind most of his friends'.

'Don't you want to open your presents?' Erica said to him.

He nodded at the pile, looked over at us, and said in a clear loud voice, 'How does the number get inside my body?'

'The number?' I said.

'Four.' Matt's hazel eyes widened with the question.

Erica reached across the table and put her hand on his arm. 'I'm sorry, Matty,' she said, 'but we don't understand what you mean.'

'Turn four,' he said. I could hear the insistence in his voice.

'Oh, I see,' I said slowly. 'The number doesn't go inside you, Matt. People say you're turning four, but nothing happens in your body.' It took us a while to explain numbers to Matt, to make it clear that they didn't magically lodge themselves inside us on our birthdays, that they were abstract symbols, a way of counting years or cups or peanuts or anything else for that matter. I thought about Matthew's four again that night when I heard Erica's voice coming from the bedroom. She was reading 'Ali Baba and the Forty Thieves,' and every time she read 'Open sesame,' Matt sang out the magic words with her. It wasn't strange that he had stumbled over the phrase 'to turn four.' His body had miraculous properties, after all. It had an invisible inside and a smooth surface with openings and passageways. Food went into it. Urine and feces came out of it. When he cried, a salty liquid streamed from his eyes. How could he possibly know that 'turning four' didn't signify yet another physical transformation, a kind of corporeal 'open sesame' that allowed a brand-new number four to take its place beside his heart or in his stomach or maybe find a home in his head?

That summer I had begun taking notes for the book I was planning to write about changing views in Western painting, an analysis of the conventions of seeing. It was a large, ambitious project and a dangerous one. Signs have often been confused with other signs, as well as with the things that lie beyond them in the world. But iconic signs function differently from words and numbers, and the problem of resemblance has to be addressed without falling into the trap of naturalism. As I worked on the book, Matt's four was often with me, a little reminder to avoid a very seductive form of philosophical error.

In Violet's first letter to Bill, dated October 15, she wrote, 'Dear Bill, You left me an hour ago. I didn't expect you to vanish from my life so

85

abruptly, to disappear without any warning at all. After I walked you to the subway and you kissed me good-bye, I came home, sat down on the bed, and looked at the pillow squashed by your head and the sheets wrinkled from your body. I lay down on the bed where you were lying just minutes before and realized that I wasn't angry and I didn't want to cry. I just felt amazed. When you said that you had to go back to your old life for Mark's sake, you said it so simply and sadly that I couldn't argue with you or ask you to change your mind. You were resolved. I could see that, and I doubt whether tears or words would have made any difference.

'Six months isn't such a long time. That's how long it's been since I came to see you in May, but the fact is it's been much longer than that. We've spent years living inside each other. I've loved you since the first second I saw you, standing at the top of the stairs in that ugly gray T-shirt with black paint on it. You stank of sweat that day, and you looked me over like I was some object you were about to buy in a store. For some reason that cold, strict look in your eyes made me crazy with love for you, but I didn't show you a thing. I was too proud.'

'I think about your thighs,' she wrote in the second letter, 'and the warm, moist smell of your skin in the morning, and the tiny eyelash in each corner of your eye that I always notice when you first roll over to look at me. I don't know why you are better and more beautiful than anybody else. I don't know why your body is something I can't stop thinking about, why those little flaws and ridges on your back are lovely to me or why the pale soft bottoms of your New Jersey feet that always wore shoes are more poignant than any other feet, but they are. I thought I would have more time to chart your body, to map its poles, its contours and terrain, its inner regions, both temperate and torrid – a whole topography of skin and muscle and bone. I didn't tell you, but I imagined a lifetime as your cartographer, years of exploration and discovery that would keep changing the look of my map. It would always need to be redrawn and reconfigured to keep up with you. I'm sure I've missed things, Bill, or forgotten them, because half the time I've been wandering around your body blind drunk with happiness. There are still places I haven't seen.'

In the fifth and last letter, Violet wrote, 'I want you to come back to me, but even if you don't, I'm in you now. It started with the paintings of me that you said were of you. We've written and drawn ourselves into each other. Hard. You know how hard. When I sleep alone, I can hear you breathing with me, and the funniest part of it is that I'm fine alone, happy alone, able to live alone. I'm not dying for you, Bill. I just want you, and if you stay with Lucille and Mark forever, I will never come and take back what I gave you the night when we heard the man singing about the moon behind the trash cans. Love, Violet.'

Bill's separation from Violet lasted five days. On the fifteenth, he moved in upstairs and resumed his marriage. On the nineteenth, he left Lucille for good. Both Bill and Violet called on the first day to tell me and Erica what had happened, and neither one of them betrayed any emotion when delivering the message. I saw Violet only once during that time. On the morning of the sixteenth, I met her in the hallway at the bottom of the stairs. Erica had been trying in vain to reach Violet since she'd called with the news. 'She sounded calm,' Erica had said, 'but she must be devastated.' But Violet didn't look 'devastated.' She didn't even look sad. She was wearing a small navy blue dress that hugged her body. Her lips were shining with red lipstick and her hair had been artfully touseled. Her high-heeled shoes looked new, and she gave me a brilliant smile when she saw me. In her hand, she was holding a letter. When I asked her how she was, she responded to the sympathy in my voice with a cool, crisp tone that warned me I had better remove all traces of pity from mine. 'I'm fine, Leo. I'm delivering a letter to Bill,' she said. 'It's faster than the post office.'

'Speed is important?' I said to her.

Violet fixed her eyes on mine and said, 'Speed and strategy. That's what matters now.' With a single, emphatic gesture, she dropped the letter on top of the mailbox. Then she swiveled on her high heels and walked toward the door. I felt sure that Violet knew she was living one of her finest moments. Her straight posture, her slightly elevated chin, the sound of her heels as they clicked on the tile floor would have been wasted without an audience. Before she left, she turned around and winked at me.

Bill had never told me that he was reconsidering his marriage, but I knew that after he told Lucille about Violet, Lucille began to call him more often. I also knew that they had met several times to discuss Mark. I don't know what Lucille said to him, but her words must have reached both Bill's guilt and his sense of duty. I felt sure that if he had abandoned Violet, he had done it because he truly believed it was the only path he could take. Erica thought Bill had lost his mind, but then Erica had taken sides. Not only did she love Violet, she had turned against Lucille. I tried to articulate to Erica what I had long sensed in Bill – a rigid current in his personality that sometimes pushed him toward absolute positions. Bill had once told me that by the age of seven he had adopted a strict but private code of moral behavior. I think he recognized that it was somewhat arrogant to hold himself to higher standards than he did other people, but for as long as I knew him, he never let go of the idea that he lived with special restrictions. I guessed that it came from a belief in his own gifts. As a child Bill could run faster, hit harder, and play ball better than any other boy his age. He was handsome, good in school, drew like a wizard, and, unlike many other talented children, was acutely aware of his own superiority. But for Bill, heroism came with a price. He would never blame others for wobbling indecision, ethical weakness, or muddy thinking, but he wouldn't allow it himself. Faced with Lucille's willingness to try the marriage again and Mark's need for a full-time father, he obeyed his inner laws, even when they told him to act against his feelings for Violet.

Bill and Violet liked the story of their brief crack-up and reunion. They both told it in the same way, very simply, as if it were a fairy tale, without ever mentioning what was in the letters: One morning, Bill woke up and told Violet he was leaving her. She walked him to the subway and they kissed each other good-bye. Then, for five days in a row, Violet delivered a letter to 27 Greene Street, and every day Bill carried the letter upstairs and read it. On the nineteenth, after he had read the fifth letter, he told Lucille that the situation between them was hopeless, left our building, walked to Violet's apartment on East Seventh Street and declared his undying love for her, after which she burst into tears and sobbed for twenty minutes.

I've come to see the five days they were apart as a battle between two strong wills, and now that I've read the letters, it's clear to me why Violet won. She never questioned Bill's right to do whatever he felt he had to do. She argued persuasively that he should choose her over his wife without appearing to argue this at all and by mentioning Lucille's name only once. Violet knew that Lucille had time, a son, and legitimacy on her side, all reinforced by Bill's unflinching sense of responsibility, but she never tangled with Bill's moral code. She wore him down with the only truth she had to offer him, that she loved him fervently, and she knew that passion was exactly what Lucille lacked. Later, when Violet spoke about the letters, she made it clear that she had written them carefully. 'They had to be sincere,' she said, 'but they couldn't be maudlin. They had to be well written, without a shred of self-pity, and they had to be sexy without being pornographic. I don't want to gloat, but they did the trick.'

Lucille had asked Bill to come back. He told me this openly, but I think that as soon as he returned to her, the desire she had felt for him began to wane. He said that after only a couple of hours, she had criticized both his dishwashing and a story he was reading to Mark – *Busy Day, Busy People*. Lucille's coolness and unavailability had been her most alluring features for Bill, particularly because she seemed oblivious to the power they had over him. But nagging is a strategy of the powerless, and there is nothing mysterious about it. I suspect that Violet's cause, set forth with blazing awareness of purpose in the letters, was helped along by the dreary sound of Lucille's domestic complaints. I never heard Lucille talk about those days, so I can't be sure of what she felt, but I suspect that whether she knew it or not, a part of her pushed Bill away, a possibility that made Violet's victory a little less remarkable than she may have supposed.

Violet moved into 89 Bowery with Bill, and as soon as she arrived, she started cleaning. With a zeal that must have come from a long line of Scandinavian Protestants, she scrubbed and bleached and sprayed and polished until the loft took on a foreign, naked, almost squinting appearance. Lucille remained our upstairs neighbor, and the four-year-old Mark, whose divided life had been given a five-day reprieve, resumed his back-and-forth existence. Bill never spoke to me of his relief and joy. He didn't have to. I noticed that he started slapping my back again and affectionately grabbing my arm, and the odd thing was that not until he began touching me again did I realize that he had stopped doing it.

The days came and went with an almost liturgical dependability, incantations of the ordinary and intimate. Matt sang to himself in the mornings in his high, tuneless voice while he dressed himself very, very slowly. Four days a week Erica sailed out the door with her briefcase and an English muffin in her hand. I walked Matt to school and then took the IRT uptown. On the subway I composed paragraphs in my head for my chapter that focused on Pliny's *Natural History*, while I half-saw the faces and bodies of other riders. I felt their bodies pressed against mine, smelled their tobacco, sweat, and cloying perfumes, their medicinal creams and herbal remedies. I took the Columbia boys and a few Barnard girls through a survey course on Western art and hoped some of those images would stick with them forever – the gold-and-blue abstraction of a Cimabue or the estranging beauty of Giovanni Bellini's *Madonna in a Meadow* or the terror of Holbein's dead Christ. I listened to Jack moan about the docile students. 'I never thought I'd find myself actually longing for those characters from SDS.' After work Erica and I found Matt and Grace at home. He was often in her lap by then, a place he had named 'the soft house.' We fed him and bathed him and listened to his stories about Gunna, a wild redheaded boy from a country called 'Lutit' that was somewhere in the 'north.' He fought us, too, especially when he metamorphosed into Superman or Batman and we had the gall to challenge his omnipotence with directives about teeth brushing and bedtime. Erica helped edit Violet's dissertation. Ideas flew between them and they excited each other, and sometimes at night I would rub Erica's back to ease the tension that made her head ache after long talks on the telephone with Violet about cultural contagions and the problem of the subject.

When he didn't have Mark with him, Bill worked far into the night on the hysteria constructions. Violet was often asleep by the time he finished. She told me that he rarely sat down to eat, and when he did, he would sit with the plate on his lap in front of the piece and say nothing. Neither Bill nor I had much time for coffees or lunches that year, but I also knew that Violet had altered the outlines of our friendship. It wasn't that Bill actively neglected me. We spoke on the phone. He wanted me to write about the hysteria works, and whenever I saw him he brought me something to read – a *Raw Comics* or a book of medical photographs or an obscure novel. The truth was Violet had opened a passage in Bill that had taken him further into his own solitude. I could only guess at what had passed between them, but I sometimes felt that their intimacy had a courage and fierceness that I had never known, and the awareness of this lack in myself made me vaguely restless. The feeling lodged itself in my mouth as a dry taste, and I suffered from a longing that nothing could satisfy. It wasn't hunger or thirst or even sex that I wanted. It was a dim but irritating need for something nameless and unknown that I had felt from time to time since I was child. There were a few nights that year when I lay awake beside my sleeping wife with that emptiness in my mouth, and I would move into the living room and sit on the chair by the window to wait until morning.

For a long time I thought of Dan Wechsler as another missing man in a family of missing men. Moishe, the grandfather, had disappeared. Sy, the father, had stayed, but had sprinted away emotionally. Dan, the youngest of these three generations of men, had been hidden away in New Jersey, the phantom resident of either a halfway house or a hospital, depending on his state of mind. That year, Bill and Violet hosted a small Thanksgiving dinner on the Bowery, to which Dan was invited. For days Dan called Bill. One day he cancelled. The next day he reinstated himself. The day after, he called again to say he wasn't coming. But at the last moment, Dan found the courage take the bus to the Port Authority bus terminal, where Bill picked him up. We were seven, altogether: Bill, Violet, Erica, Dan, Matthew, Mark, and I. Regina had gone to Al's family for the day, and the Bloms had felt it was too far and too expensive to travel to New York for the holiday. Dan's craziness wasn't hidden. His fingernails were heavily rimmed with dirt, and his neck was thickly covered with ash-colored flakes of drying skin. His shirt had been buttoned wrong, giving his whole upper body a lopsided appearance. At dinner I found myself seated beside him. While I was still unfolding my napkin and putting it on my lap, Dan had already picked up his dessert spoon and was pushing turkey and stuffing into his mouth at an astonishing speed. His ravenous eating lasted for about thirty seconds. Then he lit a cigarette, sucked on it deeply, turned abruptly to me, and said in a loud excited voice: 'Leo, do you like food?'

'I do,' I said. 'I like most foods.'

'That's good,' he said, but he sounded disappointed. With his free hand he began to scratch his forearm hard. His nails left red stripes on his skin. Then he fell silent. His large eyes, which looked very much like his brother's except that their irises were darker, suddenly withdrew from me.

'Do *you* like food?' I said to him.

'Not much.'

'You were eating crackers when I called you yesterday, Dan,' Bill said, interrupting us.

Dan smiled. 'That's right. I was!' He said this happily and then stood up from the table and began to pace. With his shoulders hunched and his head lowered toward the floor, he made a curious gesture with his left hand as he walked. He turned his thumb and index finger into an O, then closed his hand into a fist, and after a second of clenching repeated the O sign again.

Bill ignored his brother and continued his conversation with Erica and Violet. Matt and Mark sat for a few minutes longer and then jumped up from the table and began to run, announcing loudly that they were 'superheroes.' Dan paced. The warped floorboards creaked as he trod back and forth, back and forth. While he paced he muttered to himself and interrupted his own monologue with short bursts of laughter. Violet glanced at him repeatedly and then looked at Bill, but Bill shook his head at her, telling her not to interfere.

When we had finished dessert, I noticed that Dan had retreated to the far end of the room and was sitting on the stool near Bill's worktable. I stood up and walked toward him. As I came closer, I heard him say, 'Your brother won't let you go back to that stinking joint.

Mother's old now. She just pretends to like you anyway.'

I said his name.

The sound of my voice must have startled him, because I saw his whole body jerk to attention. 'I'm sorry,' he said. 'I hope it's okay to be here. I had to think. I've been thinking pretty hard.'

I sat down beside him. I could smell him. Dan reeked of sweat, and there were big wet patches under the arms of his shirt. 'What are you thinking about?'

'Mystery,' he said. He pulled at several hairs on his forearm and began to twist them into a small knot. 'I told Bill about it. It's funny, because it has two sides – male and female.'

'Does it?' I said. 'In what way?'

'It's like this – it can be Mr Ree or Miss Tery. You see what I mean?'

'Yes, I do.'

'They're the hero and heroine of the play I'm writing.' He gave the hairs on his arm a severe wrench, lit another cigarette, and stared at the ceiling. Dan's eyes were circled with blackness, but his gaunt profile resembled Bill's, and for a moment I imagined the two of them as small boys standing in a driveway. Dan lapsed into his own thoughts and the O sign reappeared, his fingers going through the motions urgently and rapidly. He stood up and paced again. Violet interrupted us.

'Would you like to join us at the table for a cognac?' she said.

'Thank you, Violet,' Dan said politely. 'But I'd rather smoke and pace.'

After several minutes Dan did come to the table. He seated himself next to Bill, leaned close to his brother, and vigorously began to pat his shoulder. 'My big bro,' he said. 'Big Bill, old B.B., the Big Boom Bill . . .'

Bill stopped Dan's patter by putting his arm around him. 'I'm glad you decided to come. It's good to have you here.'

Dan grinned hugely and took a sip from the snifter that was standing in front of him.

An hour later, the dishes had been washed and put away. The two boys were playing with blocks near the windows while Violet, Erica, Bill, and I stood over the mattress where Dan had fallen into a dead sleep. He was curled up into a tight ball, hugging his knees as he wheezed softly with his mouth open. A broken cigarette and his lighter lay on the blanket beside him. 'I probably shouldn't have let him have that brandy,' Bill said. 'It might have interacted with the lithium.'

Dan didn't come often to the Bowery, but I know that Bill spoke to him on the telephone regularly, sometimes every day. Poor Dan was all cracks. His life was a daily struggle to ward off a breakdown that would land him in the hospital again. Wracked by bursts of paranoia, he would call to ask Bill if he still liked him or, worse, if Bill was out to kill him. And yet despite his illness, Dan had traits that linked him to his brother. They both coursed with emotions that weren't easy to contain. In Bill that potent feeling found an exit in work. 'I work to live,' he once told me, and after meeting Dan I understood far better what he had meant by those words. Making art was necessary for Bill to maintain a minimal equilibrium, to keep himself going. Dan's plays and poems were mostly unfinished, the tattered products of a mind that ran in circles and could never leap out of itself. The older brother's brain and nerves and private history had given him the strength to withstand the strains of ordinary life. The younger brother's had not.

I heard Lucille walking above us every day. She had a particular step, light with a little drag to it. When I met her on the stairs, she would always smile self-consciously before we began to talk. She never mentioned Bill or Violet, and although I always asked her about her work, she never asked me to read her poems again. At my urging, Erica invited Lucille and Mark for an early dinner that spring. She put on a dress for the occasion, an odd beige sack that was very unflattering. Although her body was hidden under it, the badly chosen dress touched me. I read it as yet another sign of her unworldiness, and rather than repelling me, I found its ugliness poignant. As she sat across the table from me that evening, I wondered at the strict composure of her pale oval face. Her restraint gave her an aura that was almost inanimate, as if by some supernatural fluke she were a painting of herself made centuries before she was born.

That night Mark and Matt dug out their Halloween costumes and roared about the room. Mark wore a thin nylon skeleton suit, black with white bones printed on it, and Matt was a skinny midget Superman in blue pajamas with a red felt S sewed onto the chest and a cape in the same material. Matt began calling Mark 'Skeley-man' and 'Boney-head.' After a couple of minutes, the nicknames turned into a loud chant: 'Bones bones dead down.' The two little boys tromped in a circle near the windows of our loft. Like two mad grave diggers, they repeated the chant over and over again: 'Bones! Bones! Dead! Down!' Erica watched them, and I turned my head several times to make sure they were not working themselves up into a frenzy that would end in tears, but Lucille didn't seem to notice her son or hear the song Matt had made up for their game.

She told us that she was considering taking a job she had been offered teaching creative writing at Rice University in Houston. 'I have never been to Texas,' she said. 'I hope that if I take the job, I will meet a cowboy or two. I have never met one.' Lucille often avoided contractions in her speech, a small tic I hadn't noticed until that dinner. She went on. 'Cowboys have interested me since I was a child, not real ones, of course, but the ones I invented for myself. The real thing might disappoint me terribly.'

100

Lucille took that job and left for Texas with Mark in early August. By then she and Bill had been divorced for two months. Five days after the divorce was final, Bill and Violet were married. The wedding was held in the Bowery loft on June 16th, the same day Joyce's Jewish Ulysses had wandered around Dublin. A few minutes before the exchange of vows, I noted that Violet's last name, Blom, was only an *o* away from Bloom, and that meaningless link led me to reflect on Bill's name, Wechsler, which carries the German root for change, changing, and making change. Blooming and changing, I thought.

Bill and Violet had wanted to be married in Paris away from family and friends. That is what they had told Regina and Violet's parents they were doing, but the romantic fancy was stymied by a tangle of French laws, and they married quickly before they left for France. The only people who actually witnessed the event were Matt and Dan and Erica and I. Mark and Lucille were on Cape Cod with her family. Regina and Al were on a cruise somewhere, and the Bloms planned a reception for the couple in Minnesota later that year.

The six of us sweltered as the temperature rose to near a hundred degrees. The ceiling fan pushed the sultry air round and round, squeaking as it turned through the short ceremony conducted by a small bald man from the Ethical Culture Society. After saying a few words and reading 'The Good-Morrow' by John Donne, he pronounced Bill and

Violet husband and wife. Only minutes later, the wind rose and blew in through the windows and it rained. It rained in sheets and it thundered while we danced to tapes of the Supremes and drank champagne. We all danced. Dan danced with Violet and Erica and with Matt and with me. He pounded the floor with his feet and let out a low rumbling laugh every now and again, before he was lured away by the desire to pace and smoke in a corner alone. Erica had dressed Matt in a blazer with a bow tie and gray pants, but he danced barefoot in nothing but his white shirt and underpants. He wiggled his hands over his head and swayed back and forth to the music. The bride and groom danced, too. Violet shimmied and kicked and threw her head back, and Bill moved with her. On a sudden impulse, he picked her up, carried her through the loft's door, out onto the landing, and then returned with her.

'What's Uncle Bill doing to Violet?' Matt asked me.

'He's carrying her over the threshold.' I crouched down beside him to explain the symbolism of doors. Matt stared at me with wide eyes and wanted to know if I had done it to Mommy. I hadn't, and when I looked in his face, I felt my masculinity pale a little beside vigorous Uncle Bill's.

Bill hadn't wanted Lucille to leave New York with Mark, but the more he'd insisted that she stay, the more stubborn Lucille had become, and he'd lost that first battle over his son. Bill kept the loft that had been bought with his inheritance. His truck, his savings account, the furniture he and Lucille had bought together, and three portraits of Mark disappeared in the agreement. By the time Bill and Violet returned from France, Lucille and Mark had flown off to Texas, and the loft above us had been stripped bare except for Bill's books. Violet cleaned it hard and then they moved in. But in late September, only weeks after her move to Texas, Lucille called Bill and told him that she was unable to take care of Mark and teach her classes. She put Mark on a plane and sent him home to his father. Mark landed back on Greene Street with Bill and Violet, in the same place where he had lived with his mother for a couple of years. It must have looked very different to him. Lucille was an indifferent housekeeper. Although not as slovenly as Bill, she had lived with piles of books on her floor, toys underfoot, and a large family of dust mice. Violet inhabited the new apartment with typical zeal. The largely empty rooms sparkled from her severe purgings. The day I first saw it in its new incarnation, a clear glass vase had been placed on a simple new table that Bill had built and Violet had painted a deep shade of turquoise. The vase was filled with twenty brilliant red tulips.

By the time the hysteria pieces were up for exhibition in late October of 1983, the SoHo Erica and I had moved to in 1975 was gone. Its mostly vacant

103

streets and quiet dumpiness had been replaced by a new sheen. One galley after another opened – their doors stripped and freshly painted. Clothing stores popped up suddenly to display seven or eight dresses, skirts, or sweaters in huge pale rooms, as if those garments were also works of art. Bernie renovated his large, white second-floor gallery on West Broadway into a smoother, larger, whiter second-floor gallery, and as his art sales mounted, Bernie ran faster and bounced higher. Whenever I bumped into him on a corner or in a café, he rocked and jiggled and rattled on about this new artist or that one, grinning broadly about sold-out shows and rising prices. Bernie wasn't queasy about money. He embraced it with an exuberance and immodesty I couldn't help but admire. Booms and busts have come and gone in New York with rhythmical succession, but I have never felt so close to large sums of money as I did then. Those dollars pulled hordes of unfamiliar people into the neighborhood. Buses made stops on West Broadway and unloaded tourists, most of them female and most of them middle-aged. These women padded around the neighborhood in groups, visiting one gallery after another. They were usually dressed in running suits, a fashion that had the distasteful effect of making them look like aging infants. Young Europeans arrived and bought up lofts. After decorating their new digs according to the minimal fashion of the time, they headed for the streets and restaurants and galleries, where they loitered for hours, as shiftless as they were well-dressed.

Art is mysterious, but selling art may be even more mysterious. The object itself is bought and sold, handed from one person to another, and yet countless factors are at work within the transaction. In order to grow in value, a work of art requires a particular psychological climate. At that moment, SoHo provided exactly the right amount of mental heat for art to thrive and for prices to soar. Expensive work from every period must be impregnated by the intangible – an idea of worth. This idea has the paradoxical effect of detaching the name of the artist from the thing, and the name becomes the commodity that is bought and sold. The object merely trails after the name as its solid proof. Of course, the artist himself or herself has little to do with any of it. But in those years, whenever I went for groceries or stood in line at the post office, I heard the names. Schnabel, Salle, Fischl, Sherman were magic words then, like the ones in the fairy tales I read to Matt every night. They opened sealed doors and filled empty pouches with gold. The name Wechsler wasn't fated for full-blown enchantment then, but after Bernie's show, it was whispered here and there, and I sensed that slowly Bill too might lose his name to the strange weather that hung over SoHo for a number of years before it stopped, suddenly, on another October day in 1987.

In August, Erica and I were invited to look at

three of the finished hysteria pieces on the Bowery. Dozens of smaller works on the same theme, paintings, drawings, and little constructions, were still under way. When we entered the room, I saw three huge shallow boxes – each ten feet high, seven feet wide, and a foot deep – standing in the middle of the room. Canvas had been stretched across their frames, and the material glowed, lit by electric lights sealed inside the boxes. At first, all I noticed were their surfaces: hallways, stairs, windows, and doors painted in muted colors – browns, ochers, deep greens, and blues. Steps led to a ceiling with no access to another floor. Windows opened onto brick walls. Doors lay on their sides or were tilted at impossible angles. A fire escape seemed to crawl through a hole from a painted outside to a painted inside, bringing a long cluster of ivy with it.

A covering that reminded me of Saran Wrap was pulled tightly over the fronts of the three painted boxes. Texts and images had been impressed into the plastic, leaving an imprint but no color. The effect of these words and pictures was more subliminal than anything else, because they were hard to make out. Near the bottom of the right-hand corner of the third box was a three-dimensional man, about six inches tall, dressed in a top hat and a long coat. He was pushing on a door that appeared to be ajar. Looking closer, I saw that the door was real. It opened on a hinge, and through the crack I could see a street that looked like ours – Greene Street between Canal and Grand.

Erica found a door in the first box and opened it. Drawing close to her, I peeked into a small room, harshly lit by a miniature ceiling lamp that shone on an old black-and-white photograph that had been pasted to the far wall. It showed a woman's head and torso from behind. The word SATAN had been written in large letters on the skin between her shoulder blades. In front of the photo was the image of another woman kneeling on the ground. She had been painted on heavy canvas and then cut out. For her exposed back and arms, Bill had used pearly, idealized flesh tones reminiscent of Titian. The nightgown she had pulled down over her shoulders was the palest of blues. The third figure in the room was a man, a small wax sculpture. He stood over the cutout woman with a pointer, like the ones used in geography classes, and seemed to be tracing something onto her skin – a crude landscape of a tree, a house, and a cloud.

Erica withdrew her head and said to Violet, 'Dermagraphism.'

'Yes, they wrote on them,' Bill said to me. 'The doctors traced their bodies with a blunt instrument and the words or pictures would appear on their skin. Then they took photographs of the writing.'

Bill opened another door, and I looked into a second room in the same box. Its back wall was covered with the painted image of a woman looking out a window. Her long dark hair had been pulled to one side to bare her shoulders. The style of the painting was straight from seventeenth-century

Holland, but Bill had complicated the image by lightly drawing over it in black. The drawing was of the same woman, but the style of the rendering was different, and the sketch on top of the painting made me feel that the woman was standing with her own ghost. Written twice on her arm, once with red paint and once with black crayon, was: T. BARTHÉLÉMY. The letters appeared to be bleeding.

'Didi-Huberman mentions Barthélémy,' Violet said. 'He was a doctor somewhere in France who wrote his name on a woman, and then commanded her to bleed from the letters at four o'clock the same afternoon. She bled, and according to the report, the name remained visible for three months.' I continued to look into the small illuminated room. On the floor in front of the painting of Augustine were tiny articles of clothing – a petticoat, a miniature corset, stockings and tiny boots.

Violet pulled open a third door. This all-white room was lit from above by a small electric chandelier. A tiny painting in an ornate gold frame had been propped against the back wall. The canvas showed a fully dressed man and a naked woman in what appeared to be a hallway. You couldn't see the woman's face, but her body reminded me of Violet's. She was lying on the floor as the young man straddled her back. Gripping a large pen in his left hand, he appeared to be writing vigorously on one of her buttocks.

The middle box had two doors. Behind the first was a small doll who made me think of Goldilocks – long blond curls, checkered dress, and white pinafore. The little figure was having a tantrum. Her eyes were screwed shut and her mouth was stretched wide in a silent scream as she clamped her arms around a pole that divided the little room in half. In her fit she had contorted her body to one side so that her dress had twisted up around her waist, and when I scrutinized her little face more closely, I saw that a long bloody scratch ran down one of her cheeks. On the walls that surrounded her, Bill had painted ten shadowy male figures in black and white. Each man was holding a book and had turned his gray eyes toward the howling girl.

The second door in the middle box contained a black-and-white painting that resembled a photograph from the Salpêtrière. Bill had used one of the photographs of a woman in a crucifixion pose to render his version of Geneviève, a young woman whose medical ordeals had mimicked the trials of saints – paralysis, seizures, and stigmata. Four Barbie dolls were lying face-up on the floor in front of the photo-painting. Blindfolds had been tied around their eyes and their mouths were taped. As I studied the dolls, I noticed that words had been printed on the mouth tapes of the three first dolls: HYSTERIA, ANOREXIA NERVOSA, and EXQUISITE MUTILATION. The fourth tape was blank.

The third box, with its lone figure at the bottom pushing open a door, contained two other well-hidden doors. I found the first one, its knob disguised among a dozen others that had been painted in a trompe l'oeil style. I looked into a brightly lit room that was much smaller than the others. On its floor lay a miniature wooden coffin. That was all. Erica opened the last door to reveal another nearly empty room. It had nothing in it except a dirty, ragged piece of paper with the word *key* written on it in a tiny cursive hand.

Erica bent down to examine the little sculpture of the man in the top hat walking out the door to Greene Street. 'Is he a real person, too?' she said.

'She,' Violet said. 'Look closely.'

I crouched down beside Erica. I could see the figure's breasts underneath the jacket. The suit looked large. It bagged at her ankles.

'It's Augustine,' Violet said. 'That's the end of her story – the very last entry in her *observation: '9 septembre – X . . . se sauve de la Salpêtrière déguisée en bomme.'*

'X?' I said.

'Yes, the doctors shielded their patients' identities by using letters and codes. But it was definitely Augustine. I've traced it. On September ninth, 1880, she escaped from the Salpêtrière dressed as a man.'

It was early evening by then. Erica and I had both come straight to the Bowery from work. Hunger and weariness had begun to weigh on me. I thought of Matt at home with Grace, and I wondered how to write about these boxes as

I watched Bill put his arm around Violet, who was still talking to Erica. 'They turned living women into things,' she said. 'Charcot called the hypnotized women "artificial hysterics." That was his term. Dermagraphism makes the idea more potent. Doctors like Barthélémy signed women's bodies just as if they were works of art.'

'It smacks of fraud,' I said. 'Bleeding names. A mere touch of the skin and drawings appear.'

'They didn't fake that, Leo. It's true that the whole scene was pretty theatrical. Charcot had his study done completely in black. He was fascinated with historical accounts of demonism, witchcraft, and faith healing. I suppose he thought he could explain it all through science, but the dermagraphism was real. Even I can do it.'

Violet sat down on the floor. 'It takes a little while,' she said. 'Be patient.' She closed her eyes and began to breathe in and out. Her shoulders sank. Her lips parted. Bill glanced down at her, shook his head, and smiled. Violet opened her eyes and looked straight ahead. She held out her forearm and traced the inside of it lightly with the index finger of her free hand. The name Violet Blom appeared on her skin as a pale inscription, which at first was the color of a pink rose and then deepened slightly. She closed her eyes, breathed again, and an instant later, she opened her eyes. 'Magic,' she said. 'Real magic.'

Violet rubbed the looping letters with her fingers

as she held her arm out for us to examine. While I continued to look at the words on the flushed skin of her inner arm, the distance between me and the doctors in the Salpêtrière closed. Medicine had granted permission to a fantasy that men have never abandoned, a muddled version of what Pygmalion wanted – something between a real woman and a beautiful thing. Violet was smiling. She lowered her arm to her side, and I thought of Ovid's Pygmalion kissing, embracing, and dressing the girl he had carved out of ivory. When his wish comes true, he touches her new warm skin and his fingers leave an imprint. The name inscribed on Violet's arm was still visible as she sat cross-legged on the floor with her arms in her lap. The hypnotized women had obeyed every command: Bend over, kneel, lift your arm, crawl. They had dropped their blouses over their shoulders and turned their naked backs to the physician's magic wand. Only a touch was needed and the words in his mind became words in flesh. Omnipotent dreams. We all have them, but usually they live only in stories and waking fantasies, where they have license to roam. I thought of one of the little paintings I had just seen, now hidden behind a closed door – the young man presses the nub of his fountain pen into the soft buttock of the reclining woman. It had seemed comic when I'd looked at it, but remembering it caused a warm sensation in me that ended with Bill's voice. 'Well, Leo,' he said. 'Any thoughts?'

112

I answered him, but I said nothing about Violet's arm or Pygmalion or the erotic pen.

By abandoning the flatness of painting, Bill had leapt into new territory. At the same time, he continued to play with the idea of painting by opposing two-dimensional images with three-dimensional spaces and dolls. He continued to work in contrasting styles, to refer to the history of painting and to cultural images in general – including advertisements. I discovered that the plastic 'skin' on the boxes had been densely printed with old and new ads for everything from corsets to coffee. Among the ads were poems, by Dickinson, Hölderlin, Hopkins, Artaud, and Celan – the lonely poets. There were also quotations from Shakespeare and Dickens, mostly ones that had entered the language, like: 'All the world's a stage' and 'The law is a ass.' Over one of the doors, I found Dan's poem 'Charge Brothers W,' and near the poem I deciphered the title of another work I recognized: '*Mystery: A Play Cut in Half* by Daniel Wechsler.'

For several weeks, I abandoned my book to write a short essay – seven pages. Again my piece was xeroxed and put out on a table in the Weeks Gallery, this time accompanied by postcard-sized reproductions of the boxes and a few of the smaller works. Bill was pleased with the short essay. I had done all that I could reasonably do under the circumstances, but the truth was that I needed years, not a month, to think through those pieces.

At the time I didn't understand what I do now. The boxes were like three tangible dreams Bill had dreamed when his life split between Lucille and Violet. Whether Bill knew it or not, the little figure of a woman dressed like a man was another self-portrait. Augustine was the fictional child he and Violet had made together. Her escape into that familiar street was also Bill's escape, and I have never stopped thinking about what Augustine left behind her in the rooms of that same box – a tiny coffin and the word *key*. Bill could easily have put a real key into that white room, but he had chosen not to.

Erica and I both wondered if we hadn't been wrong to take Matt to the gallery to see the hysteria boxes. After his first visit, he begged for more excursions to 'Bernie's house.' A bowl of tin-foil-wrapped chocolates that lay on the front desk was partly responsible for luring Matt back to the gallery, but he also liked the way Bernie talked to him. Bernie didn't modulate his voice into the condescending tones grown-ups usually adopt for children. 'Hey, Matt,' he would say, 'I've got something in the back room you might like. It's cool sculpture of a baseball mitt with some hairy stuff growing out of it.' After one of these invitations, Matt would straighten himself up and walk in a slow and dignified manner behind Bernie. He was only six years old and already he had pretensions. But more than anyone or anything in the Weeks Gallery, Matt loved the monstrous little girl in the second hysteria piece. A hundred times, I lifted him up so that he could open the door and peek in at the screaming child.

'What is it you like so much about that little doll, Matt?' I finally asked him one afternoon after I set him down on the floor.

'I like to see her underpants,' he said matter-of-factly.

'Your kid?' a voice said.

When I looked up, I saw Henry Hasseborg. He was wearing a black sweater, black pants, and had tossed a red scarf around his neck and over one sloping shoulder in the manner of a French student. This overt touch of vanity made me pity him for a moment. He squinted down at Matt, then up at me. 'Just making the rounds,' he said in a voice that was unnecessarily loud. 'I missed the opening, but I certainly heard about it. Made a dull roar among the cognoscenti. Good piece of writing by the way,' he continued casually. 'Of course, you're just the man for it with all your training in the old masters.' He drawled out the last two words and made quotation gesture with his fingers.

'Thank you, Henry,' I said. 'I'm sorry I can't stay and talk, but Matthew and I were just leaving.'

We left Hasseborg with his red nose inside one of Bill's doors.

'That was a funny man,' Matt said to me on the street as he took my hand.

'Yes,' I said. 'He's funny, but you know he can't help the way he looks.'

'But he talks funny, too, Dad.' Matt stopped walking and I waited. I could see that he was thinking hard. My son thought with his face in those days. His eyes narrowed. He screwed up his nose and tightened his mouth. After several seconds, he said, 'He talks like me when I'm pretending.' Matt deepened his voice, 'Like this – *I'm Spiderman.*'

I stared down at Matthew. 'Well, you're right, Matt,' I said. 'He is pretending.'

'But who is he pretending to be?' Matt asked.

'Himself,' I said.

Matt laughed at this and said, 'That's silly,' and then he burst into song. 'Ha, Ha,' he sang, 'Rumpelstiltskin in my name! Rumpel, Rumpel, Rumpel, Rumpel, Rumpelstiltskin is my name!'

From the time he turned three, Matt had been drawing every day. His egglike people with arms that sprouted from giant heads soon gained bodies and then backgrounds. At five, he was sketching people in profile walking down the street. Although Matt's pedestrians had oversized noses and appeared to be moving stiffly, they came in all sizes and shapes. They were fat and thin and black and tan and brown and pink, and he dressed them up in suits and dresses and the motorcycle garb he must have noticed on Christopher Street. Bins overflowed with litter and soda cans on his street corners. Flies hovered over the debris, and he etched cracks into the sidewalks. His bulbous

116

dogs peed and shat as their owners stood ready with sheets of newspaper. Miss Langenweiler, Matt's kindergarten teacher, reported that she had never seen such detail in a child's drawings in all her years of teaching. Matthew balked at letters and numbers, however. When I showed him a *b* or a *t* in the newspaper, he ran away from me. Erica bought elaborately illustrated ABC books with large colored letters. 'Ball,' she would say and point to the picture of a beach ball. 'B-A-L-L.' But Matthew wanted nothing of balls and *B*'s. 'Read the Seven Ravens, Mommy,' he would say, and Erica would put down the tedious new alphabet book and pick up our tattered copy of *Grimm's Fairy Tales.*

I sometimes thought that Matt saw too much, that his eyes and brain were so flooded with the world's astounding particularity that the same gift that had made him sensitive to the habits of flies, to cracks in cement, and the way belts buckled made it difficult for him to learn to read. It took my son a long time to understand that in English words moved from left to right on a page and that the gaps between the clusters of letters signified a break between words.

Mark and Matthew played together every afternoon after school while Grace handed out carrot sticks and bits of apple, read them stories, and negotiated the occasional dispute. That daily routine was broken in February. Bill explained to me that Mark had been 'very upset' after his mother's

Christmas visit and that he and Lucille had decided together that Mark would be better off with her in Texas. I didn't press Bill for details. The few times he spoke to me about his son, his soft voice would tighten and his eyes would settle somewhere beyond me – on a wall or a book or a window. Bill made three visits to Houston that spring. During those long weekends, he and Mark holed up in a motel, watched cartoons, took walks, played with Star Wars men, and read 'Hansel and Gretel.' 'That's all he wants to hear – over and over and over again,' Bill said. 'I know it by heart.' Bill had to leave Mark with his mother, but he took the story with him and began to work on a series of constructions that would become his own version of the tale. By the time *Hansel and Gretel* was finished, Lucille and Mark were living in New York again. She had been offered another year of teaching at Rice but had turned it down.

Not long after Mark left for Texas, Gunna died. The death of this imaginary boy, who had been around for two years, was followed by the arrival of a new person Matt called 'the Ghosty Boy.' When Erica asked Matt how Gunna died, he told her, 'He got too old and couldn't live anymore.'

One evening after his story, Erica and I were sitting on the end of Matt's bed. 'I have the Ghosty Boy feeling,' he said.

'Who's the Ghosty Boy?' Erica asked, leaning over him. She put her lips to his forehead.

'He's a boy in my dreams.'

'Do you dream about him a lot?' I asked.

Matt nodded. 'He doesn't have a face and he can't talk, but he can fly. Not like Peter Pan, just a little bit off the ground and then he sinks down. Sometimes he's here, but other times he's away.'

'Where does he go?' Erica asked.

'I don't know. I've never been there.'

'Does he have a name,' I said, 'other than Ghosty Boy?'

'Yes, but he can't talk, Dad, so he can't say!'

'Oh yes, I forgot.'

'He doesn't frighten you, does he, Matt?' Erica said.

'No, Mom,' he said. 'He's kind of in me, you see. Half in me, and half out of me, and I know he's not really real.'

We accepted this cryptic explanation and kissed Matt good night. The Ghosty Boy came and went for years. After a while he became a memory for Matt, a personage he would refer to in the past tense. Erica and I came to understand that the boy was a damaged creature, someone to be pitied. Matthew would shake his head when he talked about the boy's feeble attempts at flight, which lifted him only inches off the ground. His tone was oddly superior. He talked as if he, Matthew Hertzberg, unlike his figment, were soaring regularly over New York City with a large and highly efficient pair of wings.

The Ghosty Boy was still active when Violet defended her dissertation in May. She and Erica

119

spent hours discussing what Violet should wear for the event. When I interrupted them to say that defense committees never look at a doctoral candidate's clothes, Erica cut me off. 'You're not a woman. What do you know?' Violet decided on a conservative skirt, a blouse, and low heels, but underneath she wore a whalebone corset that she had rented from a costume company in the Village. Before she left for her defense, she appeared in our doorway to model herself. 'The corset's for good luck,' Violet said as she spun around for me and Erica. 'It makes me feel closer to my hysterics, but it also squishes me in the right places.' She looked down at her belly. 'I've gotten kind of fat from sitting on my butt all these months.'

'You're not fat, Violet,' Erica said. 'You're voluptuous.'

'I'm pudgy and you know it.' Violet kissed Erica and then she kissed me. Five hours later, she returned in triumph. 'It must be good for something,' she said about the Ph.D. 'I know there aren't any jobs around here. Last week a friend told me there were only three positions in French history in the entire country. I'm destined for unemployment. Maybe I'll turn into one of those overeducated, hyperarticulate cab-drivers who whiz around the boroughs singing Puccini arias or quoting Voltaire to their passengers in the backseat, who keep praying they'll just shut up and drive.'

Violet didn't become a cabdriver, and she didn't

become a professor. A year later, the University of Minnesota Press published *Hysteria and Suggestion: Compliance, Rebellion, and Illness at the Salpêtrière*. The teaching jobs Violet might have secured were in far-flung places like Nebraska or Georgia, and she didn't want to leave New York. A contemporary art museum in Spain had bought Bill's three large hysteria works, and many of the smaller pieces had sold to collectors. His money worries had lifted, at least for a while. But well before her first book was published, Violet had begun research for a second book about another cultural epidemic. She had decided to write about eating disorders. Although Violet exaggerated her plumpness, it was true that her full curves had come to resemble the rounder movie queens of my youth. She knew her body was unfashionable, particularly in Manhattan, where thinness was a requirement for the truly chic. Violet's work inevitably turned on her private passions, and food was one of them. She cooked well and she ate with gusto – often dribbling in the process. Nearly every time Erica and I shared a meal with Bill and Violet, it ended with Bill, napkin in hand, delicately wiping Violet's face to clean up errant bits of food or spots of juice.

Violet's book would take years to write, and it would be more than a cool, academic study. Violet was on a mission to uncover the afflictions she called 'inverted hysterias.' 'Nowadays girls *make* boundaries,' she said. 'The hysterics wanted to explode them. Anorexics build them up.' She pored over historical materials. She studied the saints who starved themselves of earthly nourishment in order to taste the heavenly food of Christ's body in their visions – his blood, the pus from his wounds, even his lost foreskin. She dug up medical reports of girls who were said to eat nothing for months at a time, women who sustained themselves on the scent of flowers or from watching others eat. She explored the lives of the hunger artists who performed in cities all over Europe and America in the nineteenth century and well into the twentieth. She told me about a man named Sacco in London who fasted publicly in a glass box while hundreds of visitors filed past his wasted body. She also visited clinics and hospitals. She interviewed women and girls suffering from anorexia nervosa, bulimia, and obesity. She spoke to doctors, therapists, pyschoanalysts, and the editors of womens' magazines. In her small study upstairs, Violet accumulated hours and hours of tapes for her book, and every time we saw her, she had given it a new facetious title: *Blimps and Bones, Monster Mouths*, and my favorite, *Broad Broads and Tiny Teens*.

Bill invited me to his studio three or four times while the *Hansel and Gretel* works were under way. During my third visit, I suddenly realized that the fairy tale Bill had chosen was also about food. The whole story turned on the problems of eating, of not eating, and of being eaten. Bill told *Hansel and Gretel* in nine separate works. During the narrative, the figures and images grew steadily larger, reaching human scale only in the last piece. Bill's Hansel and Gretel were starved children, famine victims whose frail limbs and immense eyes brought to mind the hundreds of photographs that document twentieth-century misery, and he dressed the children in ragged sweatshirts, blue jeans, and sneakers.

The first piece was a box, about two feet square, that resembled a dollhouse – one wall lifted off for viewing. The cutout figures of Hansel and Gretel could be seen at the top of a stairway. Below them were two more cutouts of a man and a woman sitting on a sofa as a television flickered in front of them – its pulsating light provided by a small bulb hidden behind the painting. I couldn't see the man's face. His features were muted by shadows, but the woman's face, which she had turned toward her husband, resembled a tight, hard mask. The four characters had been drawn in black ink (etched in a style that reminded me a little of the Dick Tracy cartoon strip) and then set into the interior of the house, which had been painted in color.

The three pieces that followed were paintings. Each canvas was framed in the heavy gilt style of museums, and each was a little larger than the one that came before it. The colors and style of the paintings reminded me at first of Friedrich, but then I realized that they bore a closer resemblance to Rider's romantic American landscapes. The first painting showed the children from a great distance, after they had awoken in the forest to find their parents gone. The tiny figures were clinging to each other under a high, eerie moon, its cool light shining on Hansel's pebbles. Bill followed that picture with another landscape of the forest floor. A long trail of bread crumbs glowed like pale tubers under a blue-black sky. The sleeping children were barely visible in this painting – mere shadows that lay beside each other on the ground. In the third canvas, Bill had painted the birds diving for bits of bread as a thin gold sun rose through the trees. Hansel and Gretel were nowhere to be seen.

To depict the candy house, Bill abandoned framed canvases for a larger one that had been cut into the shape of a house. The children were separate cutouts attached to the roof. He had painted the house and children with broad, wild strokes, using colors far more brilliant than any that had preceded them. The two starved and abandoned children sprawled on the candy house and gorged themselves. Hansel's palm was pressed tightly against his mouth as he stuffed himself with chocolates. Gretel's eyes squinted with pleasure as she bit into a Tootsie Pop. Every sweet on the house was recognizable. Some were painted. Others were boxes and bags from real candies Bill had glued to the surface of the house – Chuckles and Hershey bars, Sweetarts, Jujyfruits, Kit Kats, and Almond Joys.

The witch didn't appear until the sixth work, also a painting. Inside another house-shaped canvas, painted in colors more subdued than the one before it, an old woman stood over the sleeping boy and girl, who had the blissful, bloated look of sated gluttons. Near the three figures was a table covered with dirty dishes. Bill had painted bread crumbs and bits of hamburger, as well as the red streaks left on their plates from ketchup. The interior of that room was as banal and dreary as any in America, but it was painted with an energy that reminded me of Manet. Again Bill had included a television, and on the screen he had painted an ad for peanut butter. the witch was wearing a dirty brassiere and a pair of flesh-colored panty hose, through which you could see her flattened pubic hair and soft swollen belly. Her shriveled breasts under the bra and the two thin rolls of skin around her waist were unpleasant to look at, but her face was truly monstrous. Distorted by rage, her eyes bulged behind the lenses of her thick glasses. Her gaping mouth looked enormous as she bared her teeth to reveal rows of gleaming silver fillings. In Bill's witch, the fairy tale's literal horror came true. The woman was a cannibal.

In the seventh piece, Bill changed the format again. Inside a real iron cage, he had placed a canvas cutout of Hansel. The flat painted boy was down on his hands and knees, and when I looked through the bars, I saw that he was much fatter than in his earlier incarnations. His old clothes

125

no longer fit him, and his belly hung out over his unsnapped jeans. At the bottom of the cage lay a real wishbone from a chicken – clean and dry and white. The eighth piece showed Gretel standing in front of a stove. The girl was a thick paper cutout that resembled her earlier cartoon self but much chubbier. Bill had painted both sides of her, back and front, because she was meant to be viewed from both sides. The stove she faced was real, and its oven door hung wide open. But inside the oven there was no burned corpse. The back of the stove had been removed, and all that could be seen was the blank wall behind it.

The last work showed two well-fed children stepping out of a doorway that had been cut out of a large rectangular canvas – ten feet long and seven feet high. No longer a candy house, the structure was a classic ranch, borrowed from the landscape of a thousand American suburbs, and it was painted to resemble a fading color photograph. Bill had included a thin white frame around the canvas, like those found on older snapshots. In their flat hands, the children were clutching a real rope. A few feet in front of them was a life-sized, three-dimensional sculpture of a man. He was kneeling on the floor as he gripped the other end of the rope and appeared to be pulling the children toward him and out of the story. Near his feet lay a real axe. The father figure had been painted solid blue. Over the blue, covering his body in white letters, was the complete story of 'Hansel and Gretel.' 'Hard by a great forest dwelt a poor woodcutter with his wife and two children. The boy was called Hansel and the girl Gretel.'

Words of rescue, I said to myself when I saw the writing on the man's body. Exactly what I meant by this I didn't know, but I thought it nevertheless. The night after I saw the finished *Hansel and Gretel*, I dreamed that I lifted my arm and discovered words written into my skin. I couldn't understand how the words had gotten there, and I couldn't read them, but I could identify the nouns, because they were all capitalized. I tried to rub off the letters, but they wouldn't go away. When I woke from the dream, I guessed that it had been inspired by Bill's father figure, but then I remembered the image of the woman with a bleeding inscription and the pale marks Violet's name had made on her skin. 'Hansel and Gretel' was a story about feast and famine and childhood fears, but Bill's work, with its skeletal children, had unearthed another association in my dreaming mind – the uppercase nouns of my first language had mutated into the numbers that were burned into the arms of people after they arrived at the Nazi death camps. My Uncle David had been the only member of my family who had lived long enough to be branded with a number. For a long time, I lay awake in bed and listened to Erica's breathing. After about an hour, I quietly left the room, went to my desk, and dug out the wedding photo of David and Marta, which I kept in my desk drawer. At four o'clock in the morning, Greene Street was remarkably quiet. I listened to a few trucks rumble down Canal and examined the picture. I studied Marta's elegant ankle-length dress and my uncle's suit. David had been better looking than my father, but I could see the resemblance between the two, especially around the jaw and brow. I have a single memory of my uncle. I am walking with my father to meet him. We are in a park and the sun that shines through the trees makes patterns of light and shade on the grass. I am looking intently at the grass, and then suddenly Uncle David is there and he has taken me by the waist and lifted me high above his head. I remember the pleasure of sailing up and then down, and that I admired his strength and confidence. My father wanted him to leave Germany with us. I don't remember that they argued that day, but I know there were many fights between them and that David adamantly refused to leave the country he loved.

When the *Hansel and Gretel* works were shown, they caused a ruckus. The man behind the uproar was Henry Hasseborg, who had written an article for *DASH: The Downtown Arts Scene Herald* with the headline GLAMOUR BOY'S MISOGYNIST VISION. Hasseborg first accused Bill of adopting 'the dressed-down macho look of the Abstract Expressionists to pander to wealthy European collectors.' He then blasted the work as 'facile illustration' and went on to call it 'the most blatant artistic expression of the hatred of women in recent memory.' In three tightly packed columns of print, Hasseborg fumed and boiled and spat venom. The article included a large photograph of Bill wearing sunglasses and looking very much like a movie star. Bill was stunned. Violet cried. Erica referred to the article as an example of 'narcissistic hatred,' and Jack chuckled, 'Imagine that little skunk masquerading as a feminist. Talk about pandering!'

My own feeling was that Hasseborg had been waiting to strike. By the time the article appeared, Bill had received enough attention to be deeply resented by a few people. Envy and cruelty inevitably accompany fame, however small that fame may be. It doesn't matter where it rises – in the schoolyard, in boardrooms, in the hallways of universities, or on a gallery's white walls. Out in the big world, the name William Wechsler meant very little, but in the incestuous circle of collectors and muscums in New York, Bill's reputation was getting warmer, and even a dim glow had the power to burn the likes of Henry Hasseborg.

Over the years, Bill would regularly inspire hatred in people who didn't know him, and every time it happened, he felt wounded and surprised. His handsome face cursed him, but far more damaging was the fact that strangers, usually in the form of journalists, dimly perceived his code of honor, that maddening certainty that accepted no compromise. To some, usually Europeans, this made him a romantic figure – a fascinating and mysterious genius. To others, usually Americans, Bill's stringent convictions were like a slap in the face, a frank acknowledgment that he was not 'a regular guy.' The truth was that much of what Bill produced he didn't show. His exhibitions were the result of severe purgings, during which he edited the work down to what he regarded as essential. The rest he hid. Some of the works he thought of as failures, others as redundant, and still others were pieces he considered unique and isolated, which meant they couldn't be displayed as part of a group. Although Bernie did sell some of the unshown work from his back room, a lot of it Bill simply kept to himself. He didn't need the money, he told me, and he liked having his paintings and boxes and little sculptures around him 'like old friends.' In light of this, Hasseborg's accusation that Bill styled himself to please collectors was laughable, but it was born of an urgent wish. For Henry Hasseborg, the admission that there were artists who were not driven by a preening vanity to advance their careers would have amounted to an annihilation of himself. The stakes were high, and the tone of the article reflected the man's desperation.

After the article was published, I asked Bernie to tell me more about Hasseborg. It turned out that before he became a writer, he had been a painter. According to Bernie, Hasseborg had produced muddy, semiabstract canvases nobody wanted, and after years of struggle had finally abandoned the calling and launched himself as an art critic and novelist. In the early seventies he published a book about a drug dealer on the Lower East Side who meditates on the condition of the world between transactions. The book had gotten some good reviews, but in the ten years since its publication, Hasseborg had not managed to finish another. He had written many reviews, however, and Bill wasn't Hasseborg's first victim. In the seventies, Bernie had shown an artist named Alicia Cupp. Her delicate sculptures of fragmented bodies and bits of lace had sold very well in the Weeks Gallery. In the fall of '79, Hasseborg ravaged her work in a review for *Art in America*. 'Alicia was always pretty fragile,' Bernie told me, 'but that article pushed her right over the edge. She was in Bellevue for a while and then she packed up and went to live in Maine. Last I heard, she was walled up in some little cabin with thirty cats. I called her once and asked her if she wanted to sell some work through me. I said she didn't have to come to New York. You know what she told me? "I don't do that anymore, Bernie. I stopped."'

The unintended twist to the story was that Hasseborg's spleen inspired three other articles on *Hansel and Gretel* – one equally hostile to it and two others that praised it. One of the positive articles appeared in *Artforum*, a magazine more important than *DASH*, and the contentious debate brought more and more people to the gallery. They came to see the witch. It was Bill's witch who had ostensibly driven Hasseborg into a fury. Her panty hose had so offended him that he had devoted an entire paragraph to the stockings and pubic hair beneath. The woman who reviewed the work for *Artforum* continued the panty-hose discursus with three paragraphs defending Bill's use of the garment. After that, several artists Bill had never met telephoned with their sympathies and praise for his work. Hasseborg hadn't meant to do it, but he had coaxed Bill's witch out into the open, and she, in turn, had cast a spell over the art world through the magic of controversy.

The witch returned in a conversation on a Saturday afternoon in April. When Violet knocked, I was sitting at my desk, looking down at a large reproduction of a Giorgione – his painted door of Judith standing with her foot on the severed head of Holofernes. After Violet dropped a borrowed book on my desk, she put one hand on my shoulder and leaned over me to get a better look at the picture. With her naked foot on the head of the man she has just decapitated, Judith seems be smiling, ever so slightly. The head is almost smiling, too, as if the woman and the bodiless head are sharing a secret.

'Holofernes looks like he enjoyed being killed,' Violet said. 'The picture doesn't feel a bit violent, does it?'

'No,' I said. 'I think it's erotic. It suggests the quiet after sex, the silence of satisfaction.'

Violet moved her hand down my arm. The intimate gesture was natural for her, but I felt suddenly conscious of her fingers through my shirt. 'You're right, Leo. Of course you're right.'

She moved to the side of the desk and leaned over it. 'Judith fasted, didn't she?' She ran her finger down Judith's long body. 'It's like the two of them are mingled, isn't it, mixed up in each other? I suppose that's what sex is.' Violet turned her head to one side. 'Erica's not home?'

'She's doing errands with Matt.'

Violet pulled up a chair and sat down opposite me. She took the book and turned the picture toward her. 'Yes, he seems to have gotten it here. It's very mysterious, the mixing thing.'

'Is this a new idea?'

'Not really,' she said. 'It started because I was looking for a way to talk about the threat anorexics feel from the outside. Those girls have overmixed, if you see what I mean. They find it hard to separate the needs and desires of other people from their own. After a while, they rebel by shutting down. They want to close up all their openings so nothing and nobody can get in. But mixing is the way of the world. The world passes through us – food, books, pictures, other people.' Violet put her elbows on the desk and frowned. 'When you're young, I think it's harder to know what you want, how much of others you're willing to take in. When I was living in Paris, I tried on ideas about myself like dresses. I was always reinventing who I was. Chasing after the stories about those girls in the ward made me itchy and restless. I used to roam around the streets in the late afternoon, stopping for a coffee here and there. One day, I met a young man named Jules in a café. He told me that he had just gotten out of prison – that very day. He had been serving eight months on an extortion charge. I thought that was very interesting, and I asked him about prison, what it was like. He told me that it was terrible, but that he had done a lot of reading in his cell. He was a very handsome guy with big brown eyes and those soft lips, you know, the slightly bruised kind that look like they're always kissing. Anyway, I fell for him. He had this idea that I, Violet Blom, was a wild young American thing, a late-twentieth-century femme fatale who had been unleashed on Paris. It was all very silly, but I liked it. The whole time I was with him, I watched myself like I was some character in a movie.'

Violet lifted her hand off my desk and gestured to her right. 'Look, there she is in a café with him. The scene is well lit, but a little fuzzy to make her look better. Cheesy music is playing in the background. She gives him that look – ironic, distant, unknowable.' Violet clapped her hands. 'Cut!' She looked across the room and pointed. 'There she is again. Dyeing her hair in the sink. She's turning around. Violet's gone. It's V. Platinum V walks out into the night to meet Jules.'

'You dyed your hair blond,' I said.

134

'Yes, and you know what Jules said to me when he saw my new hair?'

'No.'

'He said, "You look like a girl who needs piano lessons."'

I laughed.

'Well, you may laugh, Leo, but that's how it started. Jules recommended a teacher.'

'You mean you actually went just because he said you needed piano lessons?'

'It was my mood. It was a dare and a command at the same time – very sexy. And why not take piano lessons? I went to this apartment in the Marais. The man's name was Renasse. He had lots of plants, big trees and little spiky cacti and ferns – a real jungle. As soon as I walked in there, I had the feeling that something was going on, but I couldn't tell what it was. Monsieur Renasse was stiff and well-mannered. We started from the beginning. I was probably one of the only children in America who never played the piano. I played the drums. Anyway, I went to Monsieur Renasse every Tuesday for a month. I learned little pieces. He was always *très correct*, boringly so, and yet, when I sat beside him, I felt my body so intensely that it was like it wasn't mine. My breasts seemed too big. My butt on the bench took up too much room. My new white hair felt like it was blazing. As I played, I squeezed my thighs together. During the third lesson, he was a little fiercer and scolded me a couple of times. But it was during the fourth lesson

135

that he got really frustrated. He stopped suddenly and yelled, "*Vous êtes une femme incorrigible*." And then he took my index finger like this.' Violet leaned over the desk, grabbed my hand, then my finger, and squeezed it hard. She stood up, still holding on to my finger, and bent over me. With her mouth to my ear, she said, 'And then he whispered like this.' In a low, hoarse voice, Violet said, 'Jules.'

Violet dropped my finger and returned to her chair. 'I ran out of the apartment. I almost knocked down a lemon tree.' She paused. 'You know, Leo, lots of men have tried to seduce me. I was used to that, but this was different. He scared me, because the whole thing was about mixing.'

'I'm not sure I understand you,' I said.

'When he squeezed my finger, it was like Jules was doing it, don't you see? Jules and Monsieur Renasse were all mixed up together. I was afraid of it, because I liked it. It excited me.'

'But maybe Monsieur Renasse was attracted to you, and you to him, and he just used Jules.'

'No, Leo,' she said. 'I wasn't attracted to Monsieur Renasse at all. I knew it was Jules. Jules had set it up, and I was attracted to the idea of acting out one of Jules's fantasies.'

'But weren't you already Jules's lover?'

'Of course, but that's just it. It wasn't enough. He wanted a third person in it.'

I didn't answer her. I understood the story better than she imagined, and whatever had happened in that plant-filled apartment, I felt as though the story now included me, that the chain of erotic electricity continued unbroken.

'I've decided that *mixing* is a key term. It's better than *suggestion*, which is one-sided. It explains what people rarely talk about, because we define ourselves as isolated, closed bodies who bump up against each other but stay shut. Descartes was wrong. It isn't: I think, therefore I am. It's: I am because you are. That's Hegel – well, the short version.'

'A little too short,' I said.

Violet flapped her hand dismissively. 'What matters is that we're always mixing with other people. Sometimes it's normal and good, and sometimes it's dangerous. The piano lesson is just an obvious example of what feels dangerous to me. Bill mixes in his paintings. Writers do it in books. We do it all the time. Think of the witch.'

'Bill's witch, you mean?'

'Yes, "Hansel and Gretel" is Mark's story. It's like his very own fairy tale, the one that speaks to him personally. Bill painted it because of Mark. Sometimes Mark says to me, "You're my real mommy" and then, two minutes later, he gets angry and says, "You're not my real mommy. I hate you." All I can say is that every time I'm with him, she's there. She walks through every game I play with him. She whispers behind me every time I talk to him. When we draw, she's there. When we build blocks, she's there. When

137

I scold him, she's there. Whenever I look up, she's there.'

'You mean that you're always moving between good mother and witch in his eyes?'

'Wait and I'll explain,' she said. 'For over a year now, Mark and I have been playing a game after his bath. He lets me see him naked now. He never used to. The game is called Master Fremont. It goes like this. Mark is Master Fremont and I'm his servant. I wrap him up in his robe and carry him out of the bathroom to his bed. I put him down on the bed and then I start hugging and kissing my little master. He pretends to be very angry and he fires me. I promise to be good and never hug him again, but I can't control myself, and I throw myself at him and kiss him and hug him all over again. He fires me again. I beg to be given another chance. I get down on my knees. I pretend to cry. He relents, and the game starts all over again. He could play it forever.'

'You're too obscure, Violet.'

'It's Lucille, don't you see? It's Lucille.'

'The game,' I said slowly.

'Yes, it's a mixing game. He gets to reject me, send me away and then take me back over and over again. He has the power. In the game, I play Mark. He plays . . .'

'His mother,' I said.

'Yes,' Violet said. 'Lucille's never going to leave us.'

★　　★　　★

138

A month after that conversation, I found myself alone with Lucille. We hadn't been in touch during her year in Houston, and after she'd returned to the city in the fall, my encounters with her had been limited to chance hellos or short talks in the hallway when she came by to pick up Mark. Violet's stories about 'mixing' in the Giorgione painting, in the piano lesson, and in the Master Fremont game have a curious relevance to what happened between me and Lucille. I've come to think that even though she and I were the only people in the room that night, we weren't really alone.

It began on a Saturday evening. Erica and I attended a large party on Wooster Street given for the supporters of a downtown theater group. When I first saw her, Lucille was in deep conversation with a very young man, probably in his early twenties. She had put her hair up, which showed off her slender neck, and she was wearing a gray dress, far prettier then anything I had ever seen her in before. I noticed that as she talked to the man, she occasionally grabbed his forearm in an emphatic and surprisingly forceful way. I tried to catch her eye, but she didn't see me. It was one of those crowded events, during which most conversation is scattershot at best and the lights are too low to see anyone properly. After a while we lost sight of her.

We had been at the party for about a half an hour when Erica said to me, 'See that kid over there?'

I turned around. Across the room I saw a tall

thin boy with thick black glasses and a shock of blond hair that stood straight up from the top of his head, a hairdo that looked very much like the straw end of a broom. The boy was hovering near the food table. I saw his hand dart out toward a plate of food. He snatched several bread sticks and stuffed them quickly into the pockets of his long raincoat – an inappropriate garment for a warm spring night with no rain. Within minutes, he had squirreled away rolls, grapes, two whole cheeses, and at least half a pound of ham in various pockets of the coat. Apparently satisfied with his hoard and looking very lumpy, the boy began to make his way toward the door.

'I'm going to talk to him,' Erica said.

'No, don't, you'll embarrass him,' I said.

'I'm not going to tell him to put it back. I just want to find out who he is.'

Not long after that, Erica introduced me to Lazlo Finkelman. When I shook his hand, he gave a strangled nod. I noticed that the coat was buttoned directly under his chin, and he seemed to have stored more food in the vicinity of his collar. Lazlo didn't stay to chat. We watched him lumber toward the door and disappear.

'The boy's starving, Leo. He's only twenty years old. He lives in Brooklyn – in Greenpoint. He's some kind of an artist. He feeds himself by raiding happy-hour tables and crashing parties like this one. I invited him to dinner next week. I want to help him.'

'He should last a month on the haul he made tonight,' I said.

'I got his number,' Erica said. 'I'm going to call and make sure he comes.'

On our way out the door, we saw Lucille again. She was standing alone and had slumped against the wall. Erica walked over to her.

'Lucille? Are you okay?' she said.

Lucille lifted her face and looked at Erica, then at me. 'Leo,' she said. Her eyes glittered and her face had a softness I'd never seen before. The joints of her normally stiff body had loosened like a marionette's, and as we stood in front of her, her knees buckled and she began to slide down the wall. Erica grabbed her.

'Where's Scott?' she said.

'I don't know Scott,' Erica said gently. Then, turning to me, she said, 'He must have ditched her. We can't leave her here. She's had way too much to drink.'

Erica walked back to Greene Street and relieved Grace from her baby-sitting duties. I escorted Lucille home in a cab to East Third Street between Avenues A and B. By the time she was fumbling for her keys on the steps to her building, Lucille had sobered up a little. Although her flabby gestures lagged behind her will, I could see a veil of self-consciousness returning as she struggled to fit the key into the lock. The small railroad apartment on the second floor of the building was silent except for a faucet dripping somewhere in a hidden room.

There were several pieces of clothing draped over the sofa, a large pile of papers on a desk, and toys scattered on the floor. Lucille dropped down on the sofa and looked up at me. Her hair had come undone and fell in long strands over her flushed face.

'Mark's with Bill tonight?' I asked.

'Yes.' She tentatively pushed her hand through her hair, as if she was uncertain about what to do with it. 'I appreciate this,' she said.

'Are you okay?' I said. 'Can I get you any-thing?'

In an abrupt motion, she grabbed my wrist. 'Stay for a while,' she said. 'Please stay.'

I wasn't eager to stay. It was after midnight and the noise of the party had tired me, but I sat down beside her. 'We haven't really talked since you came back from Texas,' I said. 'Did you meet any cowboys?'

Lucille smiled at me. Alcohol suited her, I decided, because its effects continued to relax her features, and the smile she gave me was far less inhibited than usual. 'No,' she said. 'The closest I came was Jesse. Once in a while he wore a cowboy hat.'

'And who was Jesse?'

'He was my student, but he was also my boyfriend. It started when I edited his poems. He did *not* like my suggestions, and his anger interested me.'

'So you fell in love with this Jesse?' I said.

Lucille looked me steadily in the eyes, 'My interest in him was very strong. I followed him for two days once. I wanted to find out what he did when I was not with him. I followed him without his knowing it.'

'Did you think he was with another woman?' I said.

'No.'

'What did he do when he wasn't with you?'

'He rode his motorcycle. He read. He talked to his landlady, who had blond hair and wore a lot of makeup. He ate. He watched more television than was good for him. One night, I slept in his garage. I liked doing it, because he never knew. I arrived at his house, watched him through his window for a while, and then I slept in the garage and left before he got up in the morning.'

'That must have been uncomfortable.'

'There was a tarp,' she said.

'It sounds like love to me,' I said. 'A little obsessive maybe, but still love.'

Lucille's eyes narrowed as she continued to look at me. Her face was pale and her eyes had dark circles under them. She shook her head. 'No,' she said. 'I did *not* love him, but I wanted to be near him. Once, in the beginning, he told me to go away, but he did not mean what he said, because he was angry. I went away. He came after me and we were together again. Then, months later, he said it again. That time he was calm, and I knew he meant what he said, but I stayed until he pushed me out the door.'

I looked at Lucille in silence. Why was she telling me this? Had she enmired herself in a semantic riddle – what does love mean? – or was she confessing a lack of feeling? Why did she describe deeply personal, even humiliating stories as if they were puzzling exercises in a beginning logic textbook? When I looked into Lucille's clear blue eyes, I found their cold steadiness both fascinating and irritating, and all of a sudden, I felt like slapping her. Or kissing her. Either one would have satisfied the urge that came over me, an intense desire to smash the brittle surface of her impassive face. I leaned toward her, and Lucille responded instantly. She clutched my shoulders, pulled me toward her, and kissed me on the lips. When I returned the kiss, she pushed her tongue far into my mouth. Her aggression surprised me, because it seemed out of character, but I was no longer examining her motives or mine. As I began to unbutton her dress from the back, she moved her mouth to my neck, and I felt her tongue and then her teeth as she nipped my skin. The bite ran through my body like a small shock, and I understood its hint of violence. Lucille didn't want gentleness, and she may have felt all along that my desire for her was very close to anger anyway. I grabbed Lucille by the shoulders, threw her back onto the sofa, listened to her gasp, and then I looked down at her face. Lucille was smiling. It

144

was a dim, barely detectable smile, but I saw it and the look of triumph in her eyes, goading me on. I pushed her dress up around her waist, tugging at her pantyhose and underpants. She helped me pull them down and then kicked the beige mess onto the floor. I didn't undress. I unzipped my pants, seized her thighs, and pushed them apart. When I entered her, Lucille made a small grunting sound. After that, she didn't make much noise, but she was fierce as she dug her fingers into my back and thrust her hips against mine. While I sweated and grunted over her, the air on my skin felt warm and moist and I could smell her perfume or soap, a musky scent that mingled with the dry odor of dust in the apartment. I don't think it lasted very long. She made a throttled cry. I came seconds later, and then we were sitting beside each other on the sofa again.

She stood up and I watched her leave the room. As soon as she was gone, regret settled in my chest like an iron bar. When she returned and handed me a maroon towel to wipe myself, my body felt heavier than I could remember, like a tank that had run out of gas.

In Lucille's bathroom, I washed my penis with soap. As I dried myself with another maroon towel, I could feel a rift forming between myself and the present moment, as if I had already left the apartment. Only minutes before, my need for Lucille had been furious and real. I had acted on that need, and had taken pleasure from it, but already

145

the sex was becoming remote, like an apparition of itself. When I pulled up my pants, I remembered Jack quoting the artist Norman Bluhm: 'All men are prisoners of their peckers.' The words rose in my mind as I stood there eyeing Lucille's night creams and an ice-blue streak of toothpaste that had hardened onto her sink.

After staying in the bathroom too long, I returned to Lucille, who was sitting in her partly unbuttoned dress on the sofa. Seeing her made me want to apologize, but I knew that it would have been tactless – the admission of a mistake. I sat down beside her, took her hand and began several sentences in my mind: I love Erica. I don't know what came over me . . . Lucille, this was not . . . I think we should talk about . . . I canceled every hackneyed phrase and instead said nothing.

Lucille turned to me. 'Leo.' She spoke slowly, enunciating every word. 'I will not tell anybody.' Her eyes measured mine, and after she spoke those words, her mouth tightened. At first I felt relieved, although I hadn't come so far in my thoughts as to suspect that she might tell other people about the tryst. A second later, I wondered why she had mentioned this before anything else – that she wouldn't tell. Why had 'anybody' popped up as a character in this drama between us? I had been wondering how I might extricate myself from the entanglement without hurting her feelings. All at once I sensed that she had raced ahead of me, that she didn't want more of me at all. She had wanted this time, and this time only.

I said it then: 'I love Erica very much. She is more dear to me than anything in the world. I was rash . . .' I stopped. Lucille was smiling at me again, more broadly than before, and it wasn't a smile of satisfaction or sympathy. She looked embarrassed. Her face had turned red. 'I'm sorry,' I stuttered, the apology running out from me in spite of myself. I stood up. 'Can I get you something?' I asked. 'A glass of water? I could make coffee.' I was filling the air with speech, rattling on to block out her blush.

'No, Leo,' she said. She reached for my hand and examined it, turning the palm toward her. 'You have long fingers,' she said, 'and a rectangular palm. In a book I saw once, it said that hands like yours belong to psychics.'

'In my case,' I said, 'I'm afraid the book was wrong.'

She nodded. 'Good night, Leo.'

'Good night.' I leaned forward and kissed her cheek. As I did it, I made a great effort to check my awkwardness. And then, although I wanted to run from the apartment, I lingered, overcome by a feeling that the business between us was unfinished. I looked down at the floor and noticed a toy at my feet. I recognized the black-and-red object, because Matt had several of them. The toy, called a Transformer, could be changed from a vehicle into a robotic creature with more or less human form. The thing was in a half-and-half state – part thing, part man. On a sudden impulse, I picked it up. For some reason, I couldn't leave it untouched. I flipped one side of it downward to finish the change. It became all robot – two arms, two legs, a head, and a torso. I could feel Lucille watching me. 'An ugly toy,' she said.

I nodded and lay the Transformer on the table. We said good night again and I left.

When I crawled into bed beside Erica, she woke up for a few seconds. 'Was Lucille okay?' she said. I told her yes. Then I said she had wanted to talk, and I had stayed with her for a while. Erica rolled over and went back to sleep. Her shoulder and arm lay over the covers and I stared at the thin strap of her nightgown in the obscure light of the room. Erica would never suspect my betrayal, and her trust sickened me. Had she been a woman who doubted my loyalty, I would have felt less guilt. In the morning, I repeated the lie to Erica without flinching. I lied so well that the night before appeared to harden into what should have happened, rather than what had happened. 'I will not tell anybody.' Lucille's promise was our bond, one that would help erase the reality of my having had sex with her. As I sat with Erica and Matt at the table that Sunday morning, a basket filled with bagels in front of me, I listened to Matt talking about Ling. Ling had left the grocery next door for another job. 'I'll probably never ever see Ling again,' he said, and while he continued to talk I remembered Lucille's teeth on my neck and saw her pale brown pubic hair against her white skin. Lucille had not wanted an affair; I felt quite sure of that. But she had wanted something from me. I say *something*, because whatever it was, it had merely taken the form of sex. The more I thought about it, the more troubling it became, because I began to suspect that the *something* was connected to Bill.

I didn't see Lucille for months after that. Either I missed her comings and goings in our building or she rarely came for Mark anymore, because she had made new arrangements with Bill. But only a few weeks after I had sex with her, I asked Bill about Lucille's illness, the one he had mentioned to me years before.

His direct answer turned my years of reticence into folly. 'She tried to commit suicide,' he said. 'I found her in her dorm room with her wrists cut, bleeding all over the floor.' Bill paused and closed his eyes for a moment. 'She was sitting on the floor holding her arms out in front of her, watching herself bleed very calmly. I grabbed her, wrapped her wrists in towels, and started yelling for help. Afterward the doctors said the cuts weren't very deep, that she probably hadn't meant to kill herself. Years later, she told me that she had liked watching the blood.' Bill paused. 'She said a strange thing about it. She said, 'It had authenticity.' She was in a hospital for a while, and then she lived with

149

her parents. They wouldn't let me see her. They thought I was a bad influence. You see, when she did it, she knew I wasn't far away. She knew I would come looking for her. I think her parents thought that with me around, she might do it again.' Bill grimaced for an instant and shook his head. 'I still feel bad about it,' he said.

'But it wasn't your fault.'

'I know. I feel bad because I liked that craziness in her. I found it dramatic. She was very beautiful then. People used to say she looked like Grace Kelly. It's awful, but a beautiful, bleeding girl is more compelling than a plain bleeding girl. I was twenty years old and a total idiot.'

And I'm fifty-five, I thought to myself, and I'm still a total idiot. Bill stood up and began pacing. As I watched him move back and forth across the floor, I knew that if I wasn't careful, the secret between me and Lucille could fester like a sore. I also knew that I had to keep it. Nothing would come of confession, except my own relief. 'Lucille will always be with us,' Violet had said. Perhaps that was exactly what Lucille wanted.

After a month of delays, Lazlo Finkelman finally came for dinner. A good part of Erica's pleasure in his company that evening came from watching him eat. He ingested heaps of mashed potatoes, six pieces of chicken, and smaller but significant amounts of carrots and broccoli. After he had consumed three pieces of apple tart, he appeared to be ready for conversation. But talking to Lazlo was like climbing a steep hill. He was almost perversely laconic, answering our questions in monosyllables or sentences that evolved so slowly I was bored before he managed to end them. Nevertheless, by the time Lazlo went home, we had gathered that he had grown up in Indianapolis and that he was an orphan. His father had died when he was nine, and then seven years later his mother had died. At sixteen he had been taken in by his aunt and uncle, who, in his words, were 'okay.' When he was eighteen, however, he had left them for New York City 'to do my art.'

Lazlo had worked many jobs. He had been a busboy, a clerk in a hardware store, and a bicycle messenger. During one desperate period, he had collected bottles on the street for their refunds. At the time, he was a cashier at a store in Brooklyn with the dubious name of La Bagel Delight. When I asked Lazlo about his art, he immediately produced slides from his bag. The boy's work reminded me of the Tinkertoys my mother had bought for me not long after we arrived in New York. As I studied the oddly shaped sculptures, it dawned on me that these sticks resembled genitalia, both male and female.

'Does all your work have a sexual theme?' Erica said to him. She was smiling as she said it, but Lazlo seemed immune to her humor. He studied Erica from behind his glasses and nodded soberly.

151

His blond broom nodded with him. 'It's what I do,' he said.

Erica was the one who approached Bill on Lazlo's behalf. For some time, Bill had been talking about hiring an assistant, and Erica was convinced that Lazlo would 'be perfect.' I was more skeptical about the boy's qualifications, but Bill couldn't resist Erica, and Lazlo became a fixture in our lives. He started working for Bill on the Bowery every afternoon. Erica fed him about once a month, and Matt loved him. Lazlo did nothing to court Matthew. He didn't play with Matt or speak much more to him than he did to us. But the young man's apparent coolness didn't deter Matt in the least. He climbed onto Laz's lap and touched his fascinating hair and rattled on to him about his growing passion for baseball, and every once in a while, Matt would clasp his hands on either side of Lazlo's face and kiss him. During these onslaughts of Matt's passion, Lazlo would sit impassively in his chair, speaking as little as possible, his expression uniformly morose. And yet, one evening as I watched Matt throw his arms around the skinny Finkelman legs as they were about to stride through the door for dinner, I had the sudden thought that Lazlo's lack of resistance to Matt was in itself a form of affection. It was simply the best he could do at the time.

That January, my colleague Jack Newman began his liason with Sara Wang, a graduate student whom he had taught in one of his courses. She was a pretty young woman with brown eyes and black hair that fell to the middle of her back. There had been others before her – Jane and Delia and the six-foot-one-inch Tina, whose sexual appetite had apparently been as large as she was. Jack was lonely. His book, *Urinals and Campbell's Soup*, which he had been working on for five years, wasn't enough to fill the evening hours spent in his large apartment on Riverside Drive. The affairs didn't last very long. Jack's love objects weren't necessarily pretty, but they were always bright. He once told me rather sadly that he had never managed to get a stupid girl into bed. But even the smart girls soon tired of Jack. I suppose they understood that he wasn't serious, that he loved the game more than he loved them. Perhaps they woke up in the morning and looked over at the balding character in bed next to them and wondered what had happened to last night's magic. I don't know, but Jack lost them all. Late one afternoon, I walked down the hall to Jack's office. I had stayed on to correct papers and had come across a remarkable little essay on Fra Angelico by a young man named Fred Ciccio that I wanted to show Jack. When I put my eye to the small window of his office, I saw him and Sara in a clinch. His right hand had disappeared inside Sara's blouse, and although her hands were hidden somewhere beneath the desk, the look on Jack's face suggested that they weren't idle. As soon as I understood what I was seeing,

153

I turned around, leaned my head against the window to block the view, and fell victim to a sudden, explosive coughing fit before I knocked. Sara, rebuttoned but red in the face, fled as soon as I walked through the door.

I didn't wait to speak to Jack. I sat down in the chair across from him and gave him my standard lecture. I warned him that his lack of discretion could ruin everything for him in the department. The climate was bad for seducing students. He would have to break it off or hide her.

Jack sighed, looked at me grimly, and said, 'I'm in love with her, Leo.'

'You were in love with all of them, Jack,' I said.

He shook his head. 'No, Sara's different. Did I ever use that word before?'

I couldn't remember whether Jack had said he loved Tina or Delia or Jane. I thought of Lucille then and the curious distinction she had made between 'strong interest' and the state of being 'in love.'

'I'm not sure that love is an excuse for everything,' I told him.

On the IRT I pondered my own words. They had sprung from my lips without hesitation – a pithy comeback to Jack's confession – but what had I meant by them? Had I said it because I didn't believe in Jack's love for Sara or because I did? Not once in all the years of my marriage had I asked myself whether I loved Erica. For about a year after we met, I had been thoroughly unhinged by her.

My heart had pounded. My nerves had tensed with longing until I could almost hear them buzz. My appetite had vanished, and I had withdrawal symptoms when I wasn't with her. That mania had gradually ended, but as I walked up the steps out of the subway and into the cold gray air, I realized that I couldn't wait to see her. At home I found Erica and Grace and Matthew in the kitchen. I grabbed Erica, tipped her backward over my arm, and kissed her forcefully on the mouth. Grace laughed. Matt gaped, and Erica said, 'Do it again. I liked it.' I did it again. 'Now do it to me, Daddy!' Matt cried. I bent down, threw Matt over my arm, and gave him a kiss on his small pursed mouth. These demonstrations amused Grace so much that she pulled out a kitchen chair, fell into it, and laughed for a good minute.

It was a small incident, and yet I have often gone back to that moment in my mind. Years later, I began to imagine the episode from a distance, as though the man walking through the door had been caught on film. I watch him take off his coat and place his keys and wallet near the telephone in the entryway. I see him set his briefcase on the floor and then stride into the kitchen. The middle-aged man with a receding hairline, who is mostly but not entirely gray, grabs a tall, still-young woman with dark brown hair and a little mole above her lip and kisses her. I kissed Erica that day on a whim, and yet my sudden desire could be traced back to Jack's office, where he said that he loved

Sara, and, even further, to Lucille's sofa, where she had tied herself into linguistic knots over the same word. No one but I could track that kiss. Its trail was invisible, a muddled path of human interaction that climaxed in my impulsive gesture of reaffirmation. I'm fond of that little scene. Whether my memory is completely accurate or not, it has a sharpness that nothing I look at now can possibly have. When I concentrate, I see Erica's eyes close and her thick lashes brush the delicate skin beneath her eyes. I see her hair fall away from her forehead and feel the weight of her body on my arm. I can remember what she was wearing – a long-sleeved striped T-shirt. Its round neck was cut out to reveal her collarbones and the even pallor of her winter skin.

That August was the first of four Augusts the two families spent together in Vermont. Matt and Mark turned eight, nine, ten, and finally eleven in the big old farmhouse we rented every year – a rambling, run-down place with seven bedrooms. At various junctures during its 150 years, additions had made the house larger and then larger again to accommodate growing families, but by the time we saw it, nobody was living there during the other months of the year. An old woman had willed it to her eight godchildren, now older people themselves, and the house languished as a mostly forgotten asset. It lay on top of a hill, which the locals called a mountain, not far from

Newfane – a town pretty enough to be obsessively photographed as an archetypal village of cozy New England. The summer days have run together in my mind, and I can't always separate one vacation year from another, but the four months we spent there are now touched by a quality I can only call imaginary. It isn't that I doubt the truth of them. My memory is clear. I remember every room as though I had been in it yesterday. I can see the view from the little window where I used to sit and work on my book. I can hear the boys playing downstairs and Erica humming to herself not far from them. I can smell corn boiling. No, it's that the ordinary comfort and pleasure of that house has been reconfigured in my mind by 'the past.' Because what was has disappeared; that *was* has become idyllic. Had it been only one summer, the green mountain could never have held the magic it has for me now. Repetition enchanted it: the drive north in our car and Bill's truck, loaded down with books, art supplies, and toys, the settling into our musty rooms, the cleaning rituals led by Violet, the cooking and the eating and the reading and the bedtime songs, the four adults sitting beside the woodstove and talking into the night. There were warm days, a few sultry ones, and stretches of rain that chilled the house and rattled the windows. There were nights when we lay on blankets and studied the constellations that shone out as plain and clear as the points on an astronomical map. From our beds at night we heard black bears calling to each other in voices that sounded like owls. Deer came to gaze at the house from the wood's edge, and once a great blue heron landed a foot from the house and peered in at Matt, who was standing near the window. He didn't know what it was, and when he came to me to explain what he had seen, his face was still pale from the sudden apparition of a bird too large to be real.

Bill and Violet and Erica and I worked while the boys attended a day camp in Weston until two in the afternoon, when one of the four parents would take the twenty-minute drive to fetch them. Erica, Violet, and I worked in the house. Bill set up a studio in an outbuilding on the property, a sagging structure he called Bowery Two. Those childless hours when each of us pursued his or her work remind me now of collective dreaming. I heard the soft sound of Erica's electric typewriter as she wrote the book that was eventually published under the title *Henry James and the Ambiguities of Dialogue*. From Violet's room I listened to the hushed drone of girls speaking on tape. Once, that first summer, I walked past her door on my way to get a glass of water, and I heard a childish voice say: 'I like to see my bones. I like to see them and feel them. When there's too much fat between me and my bones, I feel farther away from myself. Do you understand?' From Bill's workplace I heard hammering, the occasional bangs and crashes, and the low and distant sound of music – Charlie

Mingus, Tom Waits, Lou Reed, the Talking Heads, arias from Mozart and Verdi, Schubert's songs. Bill was making fairy-tale boxes. Each one contained a story, and because I usually knew the story he was working on, images of impossibly long hair, overgrown castles, and pricked fingers would sometimes float into my consciousness as I bent over a reproduction of a Duccio madonna. I love the flatness and mystery of medieval and early Renaissance art, and I labored over interpreting its didactic codes in terms of the sweep of history. The triptychs and panels of the Passion, of the Virgin's life, of the lives of the saints in all their bloody Christian strangeness sometimes overlapped with Bill's magical narratives or with Violet's starving girls, young women for whom denial and self-inflicted pain were virtues. And because Erica read to me from her book almost every afternoon, I found that the attenuated sentences of Henry James (with their numerous qualifying clauses, which inevitably cast doubt on the abstract noun or nominal phrase that had come before them) sometimes infected my prose, and I had to revise my paragraphs to rid them of a writer's influence that had drifted onto my page through Erica's voice.

After camp, the boys played outside. They dug holes and filled them up again. They built forts from dead logs and old blankets and caught newts and beetles and several enormous June bugs. They grew. The two small children of the first summer had little in common with the long-legged boys of the last summer. Matt played and laughed and ran like all children, but I continued to feel an undertow in his personality that separated him from his peers, a passionate core that was taking him in his own direction. Because he and Mark had always known each other, because their relation was almost fraternal, a mutual tolerance of their differences lay at the bottom of the friendship. Mark was more easygoing than Matt. After the age of about seven, he'd become an unusually agreeable child. Whatever hardships he had endured, they seemed to have left no trace on his character. Matt, on the other hand, lived intensely. He rarely cried over cuts or bruises, but when he felt slighted or mistreated, the tears rushed out of him. His conscience was severe, even cruel, and Erica worried that we had accidentally created a child with a monstrous superego. Even before a reprimand was out of my mouth, Matt was apologizing. 'I'm so sorry, Daddy. I'm so, so sorry!' He meted out his own punishment, and Erica and I generally ended up comforting rather than scolding him.

Matt had learned to read slowly but steadily with the help of a tutor, and at night we continued to read to him. The books grew ever longer and more complicated, and they, along with several movies, strongly affected his imagination. He was orphaned and imprisoned. He led mutinies and endured shipwrecks. He explored new galaxies. For a time he and Mark had a Round Table in the

160

woods. But Matt's overriding fantasy was baseball. He carried his glove everywhere. He practiced his stance and his swing. He stood in front of the mirror in his uniform and caught imaginary balls in his glove. He collected cards, read from *The Baseball Encyclopedia* nightly, and invented games in his mind that often ended in a suicide squeeze. For Matt's sake, I sometimes wished he were a better player. When he was nine, he started wearing glasses, and his hitting improved, but the progress he made as a Little League player was more the product of his ferocious, indefatigable will than any native talent. When I watched him run the bases – the new glasses strapped to his head, his knees and arms pumping wildly – I could see that his running style had less grace than some of the other boys' and that in spite of his determination, he wasn't all that fast. But then, he wasn't alone. At least in the first years, Little League is a comedy of errors, of children who dream on the bases and forget the rules, who miss balls headed straight for their outstretched gloves or who stumble and fall once the ball is caught. Matt made every mistake except that of flagging alertness. As Bill said, 'He has the concentration of a champion.' What he lacked was a champion's body.

The intricacies of the game tightened the bonds between Bill and Matt. Like a gnostic priest initiating a young disciple into the sect, Bill fed Matt obscure RBIs and ERAs. He instructed him in methods of decoding the waving, flapping, nose touching, and ear tugging of coaching signs, and he pitched and threw to Matt in the yard until the light faded and the ball all but vanished in the darkness. His own son's interest in the game was lackadaisical. Sometimes Mark joined the two fanatics; other times he wandered off to collect insects in jars or just lie on the grass and stare at the sky. I never detected any jealousy in Mark toward Matt. He seemed perfectly contented with the growing friendship between his father and his best friend.

In a single body, Bill combined Matt's two great passions: baseball and art, and I watched as his affection for Bill gradually turned to hero worship. The last two Augusts we were in Vermont, Matt began to wait for Bill to finish working. He would sit patiently on the wooden steps outside the squat studio building, usually with a drawing on his lap. When he heard footsteps followed by the squeak of the screen door, Matt would jump up and wave the sheet of paper. I often saw this scene enacted from the kitchen, where I was engaged in my assigned task – chopping vegetables. Bill would exit the little building and pause outside the door. On warm days he would wipe his forehead and cheeks with one of the paint rags he carried in his pockets as Matt ran up the remaining stairs toward him. Bill would take the drawing, smile, nod, and often he would reach out and ruffle Matt's hair. One of those pictures was a gift to Bill – a drawing Matt had done in colored pencils of Jackie Robinson at the plate.

He'd worked for days on it. When Bill returned to New York in September, he hung it up in his studio, where it remained for years.

Although Matt was always sketching baseball diamonds and players, he never stopped drawing and painting New York City. Over time, these pictures became more and more complex. He painted the city in sunshine and under quiet gray skies. He painted it in high winds and in rain and in whirling snowstorms. He drew views of the city from above, from the side, and from below, and he peopled its streets with sturdy businessmen and chic artists and skinny models and bums and the chattering lunatics we saw every day on the way to school. He drew the Brooklyn Bridge and the Statue of Liberty and the Chrysler Building and the Twin Towers. When he brought me these urban scenes, I would always take my time with them, because I knew that only scrutiny would reveal their details – a couple entwined in the park, a child sobbing on a street corner beside its helpless mother, lost tourists, pickpockets, and three-card monte cheats.

The summer Matt turned nine, he began to include a character in almost all of his urban drawings: an older man with a beard. He was usually seen through the window of his tiny apartment, and like a Hopper recluse he was always alone. A gray cat sometimes prowled on the windowsill or curled up on the floor at his feet, but he never had any human company. In one drawing I noticed that the man sat hunched in a chair with his head in his hands.

'This poor fellow keeps coming back,' I said.

'That's Dave,' Matt said. 'I named him Dave.'

'Why Dave?' I said.

'I don't know, but that's his name. He's a lonely guy, and I keep thinking that he should meet somebody, but when I get around to drawing him, he's always by himself.'

'He looks unhappy,' I said.

'I feel sorry for him. His only friend is Durango.' He pointed at the cat. 'And you know cats, Dad, they don't really care.'

'Well,' I said. 'Maybe he'll find a friend . . .'

'You'd think I could just do it, because I made him up, but Uncle Bill says that it doesn't work that way, that you have to feel what's right, and sometimes what's right in art is sad.'

I looked into my son's earnest face and then down at Dave. Matt had included veins in the old man's hands. A coffee cup and a plate lay near his feet. It was still a child's drawing. Matt's perspective was shaky, his anatomy a little askew, but the lines that etched the body of that solitary man affected me strongly, and I began to look for Dave whenever Matt handed me one of his cityscapes.

In the late afternoons we took walks down the mountain on the dirt road. We drove to Dutton's farm stand and picked out tomatoes and peppers and beans for dinner. On sunny days, we swam in the pond that was only yards from the house. Bill rarely accompanied us anywhere. He worked longer hours than the rest of us. He never cooked – he washed dishes. But on a couple of blazing afternoons every summer, he would leave Bowery Two and join us for a dip. We would see him walking across the field and watch him strip down to his boxer shorts by the pond. Bill was ageless then. I couldn't see that he looked a day older than when I had met him. He entered the pond slowly and made shocked noises as he waded farther and farther out. Often he held a cigarette between his thumb and index finger, elevating the smoking butt over the water's surface. Only once in the five summers we were in Vermont did I see him duck, wet his head, and actually swim. On that occasion, however, I noticed that his strokes were both strong and fast.

The summer after I turned fifty-six, I suddenly noticed that my body had changed. It happened the day Bill swam, and I listened to Matt and Mark cheer him on as he moved across the pond. I had been swimming myself and was sitting by the water in my black bathing trunks. When I looked down at myself, I discovered that my toes were gnarled and bony. A long varicose vein had popped out in my left leg, and the wispy hairs on my chest had turned white. My shoulders and upper body seemed oddly diminished, and my pale skin was now marred by red and brown discolorations. But more surprising to me were the soft white folds of fat that had lodged themselves around my middle. I had always been lean, and although I had noticed a suspicious tightness around my waist when I zipped my pants in the morning, I hadn't been particularly alarmed. The truth was that I hadn't kept up with myself. I had walked around with a self-image that was completely out-of-date. After all, when did I actually see myself? When I shaved, I looked only at my face. Occasionally I caught a reflection of myself in a window or glass door in the city. When I showered, I scrubbed myself but didn't study my flaws. I had become an anachronism to myself. When I asked Erica why she hadn't mentioned these unattractive changes in me, she pinched the flesh around my waist and said, 'Don't worry, darling. I like you old and fat.' For a time, I entertained hopes for a metamorphosis. I bought dumbbells during an outing in Manchester and made attempts to eat more of the broccoli on my plate and less of the roast beef, but my resolve soon vanished. My vanity simply wasn't strong enough to endure deprivation.

The last week of every August, Lazlo arrived to help Bill pack up his work. I can still see him hauling materials from Bowery Two across the field to Bill's truck, wearing tight red pants, black patent-leather boots and a deadpan expression. It wasn't Lazlo's face but his hairdo that gave him character. The blond brush that rose from his head suggested strains of humor hidden deep within the

Finkelman persona. Like a silent comedian's prop, it spoke for him – lending him the look of a hapless and naive fictional hero, a contemporary Candide, whose response to the world was one of profound and never-ending surprise. In truth, Lazlo was a mild and diffident person. He would examine a frog carefully when Matt presented him with one, would make brief pronouncements on any subject when asked, and would dry dishes very slowly and methodically when called upon. It was this evenness of temper that made Erica pronounce him 'sweet.'

Erica launched every August with a migraine, which often lasted two or three days. The white or pink stars that floated in the periphery of her left eye were followed by pain so fierce she writhed and vomited. The headache stole all the color from her face and turned the skin under her eyes nearly black. She slept and she woke. She ate almost nothing and didn't want anyone near her. Every noise hurt her, and throughout it all she would blame herself and continually mumble to me that she was sorry.

When Erica fell sick for the third summer in a row, Violet intervened. The day the headache hit, the weather was damp and humid. Erica sequestered herself in our bedroom, and early that afternoon I went to check on her. I opened the door and found the shutters closed. Violet was sitting on Erica's back, kneading her shoulders. Without speaking, I pulled the door shut. When I returned an hour later, I heard Violet's voice from inside the room – a barely audible but steady sound. I opened the door. Erica was lying on the bed with her head on Violet's chest. At the sound of the door opening, she lifted her face and smiled at me. 'I'm better, Leo,' she said. 'I'm better.' I don't know whether Violet had miraculous healing powers or whether the migraine had simply run its course, but whichever it was, Erica turned to Violet after that. When the pain arrived in the first week of our stay, Violet performed her ritual of whispering and massage. I never asked what Violet said to Erica. The affinity between them had thickened into a relationship I interpreted as darkly feminine – a girlish intimacy between women that included caresses, giggling, and secrets.

There were other intimacies in that house as well – most of them entirely banal. I saw Violet in her pajamas and she saw me in mine. I discovered that bobby pins helped along the tousle in her hair. I noticed that although Bill always washed with turpentine and soap before dinner, he bathed infrequently, and that he was sullen before his cup of coffee in the morning. Erica and I heard Violet moan to Bill about housework he didn't do and listened to Bill complain about Violet's impossible domestic standards. Bill and Violet heard Erica accuse me of forgetting groceries and of wearing pants I 'should have thrown away years ago.' I picked up Mark's socks that had turned stiff with dirt and his frayed underpants along with

Matt's. One evening, I saw spots of blood on the toilet seat and knew that it wasn't Erica who was menstruating. I took a sheet of toilet paper, wet it, and wiped away the stains. At the time, I didn't know that those spots were important, but that same night, Erica and I heard Violet sobbing from the bedroom down the hall, and through the crying, we heard Bill's low voice.

'She's crying about the baby,' Erica said.

'What baby?'

'The baby she can't have.'

Erica had been keeping a secret. For over two years, Violet had been trying to get pregnant. The doctors hadn't found anything wrong with either her or Bill, but Violet had started fertility treatments, and so far they had failed. 'She got her period today,' Erica said.

Just as Violet's crying stopped, I remembered Bill saying that he had always wanted children – 'thousands of children.'

There was no television in the house, and its absence returned us to the entertainments of another era. Every evening after dinner, one of the adults read stories aloud, usually a fairy tale. When it was my turn to read, I would page through one of the many volumes of collected folk-tales Bill had brought with him and choose a story, carefully avoiding the ones that began with a king and queen who longed for a child. Bill was the best reader among us. He read quietly but with nuance,

169

changing the tempo of his sentences according to their meaning. He paused for effect. Sometimes he winked at the boys or pulled Mark, who was usually leaning on him, a little closer. Bill never tired of the stories. All day he reinvented those tales in the studio, and at night he was ready to read more of them. Whatever Bill's project happened to be, it became the obsessive thread of his existence, one he would follow indefatigably to its end. His enthusiasm was infectious and also a little wearing. He quoted scholarly articles to me, handed over xeroxed drawings, discoursed on the significance of threes – three sons, three daughters, three wishes. He played folk songs that were distantly related to his investigations and put penciled X's by works he thought I must read. I rarely resisted him. When Bill came to me with a new thought, he never raised his voice or showed excitement with his body. It was all in his eyes. They burned with whatever insight he may have had, and when he turned them on me, I felt I had no choice but to listen.

In five years, Bill produced over two hundred boxes. He illustrated a book of poetry written by a friend, continued to make paintings and drawings, many of them portraits of Violet and Mark, and he was usually building some contraption or vehicle for the boys. These brightly colored playthings rolled or flew or spun like windmills. Mark and Matt were particularly fond of a crazed-looking boy puppet who performed a single trick: when you pulled a lever in his back, his tongue popped out of his mouth and his trousers fell to his ankles. Making toys was a vacation for Bill from the grueling work of the fairy-tale boxes. They were all the same size – about three feet by four feet. He used flat and three-dimensional figures, combined real objects with painted ones, and used contemporary images to tell the old stories. The boxes were divided into sections that resembled small rooms. 'They're two-D and three-D comics without the balloons,' he told me. But this description was misleading. The miniature proportions of the boxes drew on the ordinary fascination people have with peeping into dollhouses and the pleasures of discovering them, but the content of Bill's small worlds subverted expectation and often created a feeling of the uncanny. Although their form and some of the magical content recalled Joseph Cornell, Bill's works were larger, tougher, and far less lyrical. The tension inside each work reminded me of a visual argument. In the early pieces, Bill counted on the spectator's familiarity with a story to retell it. His dark-skinned and dark-haired Sleeping Beauty doll lay in a coma on a bed in a hospital room. IV tubing and the wires of a heart monitor entangled themselves with elaborate floral arrangements sent by well-wishers – gigantic gladioli, carnations, roses, birds-of-paradise, and ferns that choked the room. Ivy from a pink basket wove itself into her hair and curled into the receiver of the Princess telephone that lay on a table beside her bed. In a later scene, a cutout of a naked man with an erect penis hung in the air over her bed as she slept. The man held a large pair of open scissors in his hand. In the final image the girl was seen sitting up in bed with her eyes open. The man had disappeared, but the flowers, tubes, and wires had all been cut and were lying in a knee-deep mess on the floor.

Later, Bill adapted more obscure stories for the boxes, including one we had read together in Andrew Lang's *The Violet Fairy Book*: 'The Girl Who Pretended to Be a Boy.' A princess disguises herself as a young man in order to save her father's kingdom. After numerous adventures, including rescuing a captured princess, the heroine finds that her trials have transformed her into a hero. The final image of nine squares showed the story's protagonist standing in front of a mirror dressed in a suit and tie. At her crotch was the unmistakable bump of manhood.

The summer of 1987, Bill finished a piece called *The Changeling*. It's still my favorite work of that series. It was Jack's favorite work, too, though for him the piece was about contemporary art – a play on identities, replicas, and pastiche. But I was closer to Bill than he was, and I couldn't help but believe that the artwork with its seven rooms was a parable of sorts taken from his own inner life.

In the first room, a small sculpted figure of a boy stood in his pajamas in front of a window with his hands on the sill. He looked to be about the same age as Matt and Mark were then – ten or eleven. Outside, night had fallen, and three windows from the adjacent building glowed with electric light. On each window Bill had painted a scene – a man talking on the telephone, an old woman with a dog, and two lovers lying naked in bed flat on their backs. The boy's room was messy, strewn with clothes and toys. Some of these things had been painted onto the floor. Others were tiny sculptures. When I moved very close to the box, I noticed that the boy was holding a needle and a spool of thread in his right hand.

In the second room of the box, the boy had gone to sleep. To his right, a paper-doll woman was entering the room through the window. The drawn figure was striking because it was crude. With her big head, short arms and knees that bent at an impossible angle, she looked like a child's drawing. One of her legs had poked itself through the opening, and I noticed right away that attached to the paper foot was a miniature loafer.

In the third scene, this curious little woman had lifted the still sleeping boy from his bed. The next square wasn't a room at all but a flat painted panel that had been attached to the front of the box. The canvas showed the woman carrying the boy through a Manhattan street, which looked to be somewhere in the Diamond District. In the painting the formerly flat woman had gained the illusion of depth. She no longer looked like a paper doll but appeared to be in three dimensions, like the child she carried. Her back was bent and her knees buckled as she stepped forward with him in her arms. Only the woman's face remained the same – two dots for eyes, a vertical line for a nose, and another horizontal slash for the mouth. Inside the fifth room, the woman had become a sculpture with the same primitive face painted on her oval head. She stood over the boy and looked down at him where he slept inside a glass box, still gripping his needle and thread. Beside her stood another boy with his eyes shut – a figure who was identical in every way to the child who was lying in the transparent coffin. The work's sixth panel was an exact copy of the fourth – stooped woman, sleeping boy, Diamond District. The first time I saw it, I looked very closely at this second painting, searching to find a distinguishing feature, some hint of difference, but there was nothing. The final scene took up the entire bottom of the box. The woman had disappeared. One of the boys, probably the second, was sitting up in bed in a room exactly like the one that began the narrative. He was smiling and had raised his arms to stretch in the well-lit room. It was obviously morning.

I first saw the piece in Bowery Two on a rainy day in late August. Bill and I were alone. The light coming through the windows that afternoon was weak and gray. When I asked Bill where he had found the unusual story, he told me he had made it up. 'There's a lot of folklore about changelings,' he said. 'Goblins steal a baby, replace it with an identical copy, and nobody can tell the difference. It's just one version of countless doubling myths, which crop up everywhere, from the walking sculptures of Daedalus and Pygmalion to Old English lore and American Indian stories. Twins, doubles, mirrors. Did I ever tell you the story about Descartes? I read it somewhere or maybe somebody told me that he always travelled with an automaton of a beloved niece who had drowned.'

'That can't be true,' I said.

'It's not, but it's a good story. The hysterics started me on all this. When they were hypnotized, Charcot's women became changelings in a way. Even though they remained in their own bodies, they were like copies of themselves. And just think of all those UFO stories about people inhabited by aliens. It's all part of the same idea – the impostor, the fake self, the empty vessel that comes to life, or a living being that's turned into a dead thing . . .'

I bent over and pointed at the loafer. 'Is the shoe another double?' I said. 'Of the one in the painting of Violet?'

For an instant Bill looked confused. 'That's right,' he said slowly. 'I used Lucille's shoe for that picture. I'd forgotten.'

'I thought it might have been intentional.'

'No.' Bill turned away from the box and picked up a screwdriver that was lying on his worktable. He turned it over in his hands. 'She's going to marry that guy she's been seeing,' he said.

'Really? Who is he?'

'A writer. He wrote that novel *Egg Parade*. He teaches at Princeton.'

'What's his name?'

'Philip Richman.'

'It doesn't ring any bells,' I said.

Bill rubbed the handle of the screwdriver. 'You know, I can hardly believe that I was married to her now. I often wonder what the hell I was doing. She didn't even like me, much less love me. She wasn't even attracted to me.'

'How can you say that, Bill?'

'She told me.'

'People say all kinds of things when they're angry. If she told you that, I'm sure it was just to hurt you. It's ridiculous.'

'She never told me directly. She told somebody else who told me.'

I remembered Lucille's and Bill's voices through the window on that spring afternoon long ago. 'Nevertheless,' I went on, 'it can't have been true. I mean, why would she have married you? It certainly wasn't for your money. You had nothing then.'

'Lucille isn't a liar. I can say that for her. She told a mutual friend – a person who's known for calling people with vicious gossip and then commiserating with them. The irony was that this time the gossip had originated with my own wife.'

'Why didn't she talk to you herself?'

'She couldn't, I suppose.' Bill paused. 'It wasn't

until I was living with Violet that I saw how bizarre my life had been with Lucille. Violet's so present, so vital. She grabs me all the time and tells me she loves me. Lucille never said that.' Bill stopped talking. 'Not once.' He looked up from the screwdriver. 'For years, day in and day out, I lived with a fictional character, a person I'd invented.'

'That doesn't explain why she married you.'

'I pressed her, Leo. She was weak.'

'No, Bill. People are responsible for what they do. She chose to marry you.'

Bill returned his eyes to the screwdriver. 'She's pregnant,' he said. 'She told me it was an accident, but he's going to marry her. She sounded happy about it. She's moving to Princeton.'

'Does she want Mark to move there with her?'

'I'm not sure. I've learned that if I insist on having him, she insists that she wants him. When I don't, she's less interested. I think she's willing to let Mark make up his mind. Violet's worried that Lucille will take Mark away from us, that something will happen. She's . . . she's almost superstitious when it comes to Lucille.'

'Superstitious?'

'Yes, I think that's the right word. She seems to think that Lucille has some vague power over us – not just when it comes to Mark, but in other ways . . .'

I didn't pursue this turn in the conversation. I told myself that Lucille deserved happiness, a new marriage, another child. She would finally escape that gloomy apartment on East Third Street. And yet beneath my good wishes lay a turbulent awareness that Lucille was someone I didn't understand.

The very last night we stayed in the house in Vermont, I woke up and saw Erica sitting on the edge of the bed. I assumed she was going to the bathroom and turned over to go back to sleep, but as I lay in bed only half awake, I heard her footsteps in the hallway. She had passed the bathroom. I followed her into the hall and saw her standing outside Matt and Mark's bedroom door. Her eyes were open as she touched the doorknob lightly with her fingers. She didn't turn it. She withdrew her hands and then waved her fingers over it the way a magician might before performing a trick. When I approached her, she looked at me. The boys used a night-light that shone through the crack at the bottom of the door, and her face was barely lit from below. I knew then that she wasn't awake and, remembering the old advice about not waking sleepwalkers, I gently took her arm to lead her back to bed. But at the touch of my hand, she cried out in a loud emphatic voice, 'Mutti!' The exclamation startled me. I dropped her arm, and she turned back to the doorknob, touching it once with her index finger and then withdrawing it instantly as if the metal were hot. I began to whisper to her. 'It's me, Erica. It's Leo. I'm going to take you back to bed.' She looked straight at me again and said, 'Oh, it's you, Leo. Where were you?' With one arm around her shoulder, I walked her down the hallway and gently pressed her onto the bed. For at least an hour, I stayed awake with my hand on her back, watching her for signs of movement, but Erica didn't stir again.

I had called my mother 'Mutti,' too, and the word opened up a chasm inside me. I thought of my mother, not when she was old but when she was young, and for a short while as I lay in bed I recovered the smell of her as she bent over me – powder and a little perfume – and I felt her breath on my cheek and her fingers in my hair as she stroked my head. *Du musst schlafen, Liebling. Du musst schlafen.* There was no window in my room in London. I picked at the peeling wallpaper of looping ivy near my bed until I had exposed a long narrow stretch of bare yellow wall.

When the Weeks Gallery showed Bill's fairy-tale boxes in September, the crash on Wall Street, less than a month away and only a few blocks south, seemed as unlikely as the end of the world. Two hundred or more people pushed their way into the gallery for the opening, and as I looked at them they seemed to merge into one large, giddy mass – a many-headed, many-limbed being driven by a will of its own. I was knocked about that night, jostled, spilled on, elbowed, and pushed into corners. Through the din of the party, I heard prices quoted – not only for Bill's boxes but for the works of other artists that had 'gone through the roof' – an expression that made me think of dollars floating over the skyline. I knew for a fact that the woman who claimed to know what a fairy-tale box was selling for had raised its price by several thousand dollars. The cost was no secret; Bernie had a list of prices in his office for anybody who was interested. The woman's inflation probably wasn't intentional. Her sentence began with 'I heard . . .' Rumor was as good as the truth anyway. As with the stock market, buzz generated reality. And yet few people in the gallery would have connected the paintings, sculptures, installations, and conceptual somethings that were flourishing in lower Manhattan to junk bonds, swollen numbers, and clanging bells on Wall Street.

The last to arrive were the first to go. Little galleries in the East Village vanished and were instantly replaced by boutiques that sold leather clothing and spiked belts. SoHo began to wilt. The established galleries withstood the shock, but they cut back on expenses. Bernie stayed open, but he had to drop the stipends he had been handing out to younger artists, and he quietly sold his private collection of master drawings from the back room. When an English collector cleaned house by dumping the works of several 'hot eighties artists,' their reputations cooled instantly, and within months their names receded into the nostalgic past and were often prefaced by the word 'remember.' Others were forgotten. The very famous survived, but sometimes without a house in Quogue or Bridgehampton.

Bill's work dropped in value, but his collectors didn't abandon him. Most of the pieces were in Europe anyway, and there he had gained a singular status because his work attracted young people not normally interested in art. In France, his gallery did a brisk business in posters of the fairy-tale boxes, and a book of reproductions was in the works. During their flush period, Violet had bought some fashionable clothes and pieces of furniture for their loft, but Bill's nonconsumerism had never wavered. 'He doesn't want anything,' Violet said to me. 'I bought a side table for the living room, and it took him a week to notice it. He would put down a book or leave a glass on it, but it was days before he suddenly said, "Is this new?"' Bill weathered the slump because he had money in the bank, and he had money in the bank because he lived in fear of his past – the grim poverty that had meant plastering and wall painting. He had been married to Lucille then, and I noticed that as time went on Bill talked about that period in his life with increasing gloom, as if in hind-sight it had grown darker and more painful than when he was actually living it. Like everyone, Bill rewrote his life. The recollections of an older man are different from those of a young man. What seemed vital at forty may lose its significance at seventy. We manufacture stories, after all, from the fleeting sensory material that bombards us at every instant, a fragmented series of pictures, conversations, odors, and the touch of things and people. We delete most of it to live with some semblance of order, and the reshuffling of memory goes on until we die.

That fall I finished my book. Six hundred pages in manuscript, it was called *A Brief History of Seeing in Western Painting*. When I'd started it, I had hoped that an epistemological rigor would carry me through, that the book would be a synthetic argument about artistic vision and its philosophical and ideological underpinnings, but as I worked, the thing grew longer, looser, more speculative, and, I believe, more honest. Ambiguities intruded that fit no schema, and I let them stand as questions. Erica, my first reader and editor, influenced both the prose and some of my clarifications, which I acknowledged, but I dedicated the book to Bill. It wasn't only an act of friendship but one of humility. Inevitably, good works of art have what I call an 'excess' or 'plethora' that escapes the interpreter's eye.

On November seventh, Erica turned forty-six. The birthday, which brought fifty into sudden view, seemed to accelerate her. She started taking a yoga class. She lunged and breathed and stood on her head and tied herself into knots on the living room floor and insisted that these tortured exertions made her feel 'wonderful.' She created a flurry at the MLA convention with her paper 'Underneath *The Golden Bowl*,' published three of

182

her finished chapters in journals, and the English department at Berkeley offered her a job at a much higher salary, which she turned down. But the steady diet of yoga, publication, and flattery suited her. Her nerves quieted. She suffered fewer headaches, and I noticed that when she was in repose her forehead no longer looked permanently wrinkled. Erica's libido soared. She grabbed my hips while I was brushing my teeth. She nibbled at my back or slid her hand down my pants in the hallway. She stripped naked in the middle of the room when I was reading, then sidled over to the bed and climbed on top of me. I welcomed these assaults and found that the night tumbles left their traces on the morning. There were many days that year when I left the house whistling.

According to Matt, Mrs Rankleham's fifth-grade class churned with intrigue. Popularity reigned as the supreme dictate for ten- and eleven-year-olds. The grade had splintered into hierarchical factions that either fought each other openly or employed more subtle cruelties reminiscent of the French court. I gathered that certain boys and certain girls were 'going together' – a vague phrase that denoted everything from sharing a slice of pizza of furtive necking. As far as I could tell, these pairings changed weekly, but Matt was never among the chosen. While he longed for insider status, I sensed that he wasn't prepared to seek it. On a day in October when I picked up Matt after school for a dentist appointment, I understood why. I recognized several girls from Matt's class whom I had known for years, girls who played pivotal roles in the dramas Matt was reporting on at dinner. They looked like women. Many inches taller than when I had last seen them, they had grown breasts. Their hips had widened. I saw lipstick gleaming on a couple of mouths. I watched them as they sashayed past Matt and several other runty boys who were throwing fish-shaped crackers at one another's heads. Approaching one of those girls required either great courage or monumental stupidity. Matt, it seemed, was possessed of neither.

He played with Mark and a couple of other friends after school. He threw himself into baseball and his drawing and the race for good grades. He puzzled over arithmetic and science, composed little essays with painstaking care and terrible spelling, and zealously pursued his at-home projects – a Bookland collage, a Spanish galleon in clay that melted in the oven, and the memorably interminable business of a solar system in papier-mâché. For a week Matt, Erica, and I labored over slimy pieces of newspaper, wrapping and pasting and measuring the dimensions of Venus and Mars and Uranus and the moon. Three times Saturn's ring slumped and had to be redone. When the project was all finished and hung from thin silver wires, Matt turned to me and said, 'I like the Earth best,' and it was true. His Earth was beautiful.

On Saturday when Mark was visiting his mother,

who now lived in Cranbury, New Jersey, with her new husband, Matt often went to visit Bill at the studio. We allowed him to walk alone to the Bowery and would anxiously wait for him to call us when he arrived. On one of those Saturdays, Matt spent six hours alone with Bill. When I asked what he and Bill had done for all that time, Matt said, 'We talked and we worked.' I waited for details, but the answer was final. A couple of times that spring Matt exploded at me and Erica for trivial offenses. When he was really out of sorts, he posted a DO NOT DISTURB sign on his door. Without the sign we might not have been aware of the brooding reveries taking place inside his room, but the message pointed to his seclusion, and whenever I passed it, Matt's defensive solitude seemed to penetrate my bones like a physical memory of my own early adolescence. But Matt's hormonal funks seldom lasted very long. Eventually he would emerge from his room, usually in buoyant spirits, and the three of us would have lively talks over dinner – which ranged in subject matter from the risqué wardrobe of an eleven-year old named Tanya Farley to American foreign policy during World War II. Erica and I adopted a parental policy of laissez-faire, rarely commenting on Matt's fluctuating moods. It seemed senseless to blame him for ups and downs he didn't understand himself.

Through Matt I recovered my own days of awe and secrecy. I remembered warm fluid on my thighs and belly that soon turned cold after the dream, the rolls of toilet paper I hid under the bed for evening bouts of masturbation, and my clandestine trips to the bathroom to flush the soiled wads, one breathless step at a time, as if those emissions from my own body were stolen goods. Time has turned my young body into a comic thing, but it wasn't funny then. I touched the three strands of pubic hair I grew overnight and examined my underarms every morning for further growth. I shuddered in arousal and then withdrew into the aching loneliness under my tender skin. Miss Reed, a person I hadn't thought of in years, returned to me as well. My dancing teacher had peppermint on her breath and freckles on her chest. She wore full-skirted dresses with thin straps over her round white shoulders, and every once in a while, during the fox-trot or the tango, a strap would fall. It will all come to Matt, I thought, and there is no way to tell the story so that it becomes easier. The growing body has its own language, and solitude is its first teacher. On several occasions in the spring, I found Matt standing in front of the *Self-Portrait* that had hung on our wall for thirteen years. His eyes traveled over the plump young Violet and onto the little taxi that rested near her pudendum, and I saw the canvas again as though for the first time – with its full erotic force.

That early painting and the others in the series began to look oracular – as if Bill had known long ago that one day Violet would carry around inside her the bodies of people who ate themselves to immensity or starved themselves to tininess. That year Violet paid regular visits to a young woman in Queens who weighed four hundred pounds. Angie Knott never left the house in Flushing where she lived with her mother, who was also obese, but not as obese as her daughter. Mrs Knott had a small business making custom curtains in the neighborhood. Angie did the books. 'After she left school at sixteen, she got fatter and fatter,' Violet said. 'But she was a fat baby and a fat little girl and her mother stuffed food into her from the beginning. She's a walking mouth, a repository for cupcakes and Fudgsicles and boxes of pretzels and mountains of sugared cereal. We talk about the fat,' Violet added, showing me Angie's picture. 'She's turned her own body into a cave where she can hide, and the strange thing is, I understand it, Leo. I mean, from her point of view, everything outside herself is dangerous. She feels safe in all that padding, even though she's in danger of getting diabetes and heart disease. She's out of the sexual marketplace. Nobody can get through all that blubber, and that's what she wants.'

There were days when Violet would leave Angie to visit Cathy, who was being treated at New York Hospital. Violet called her Saint Catherine, after Catherine Benincasa, the Dominican saint from Siena who fasted herself to death. 'She's a monster of purity,' she said, 'fiercer and more righteous than any nun. Her mind moves in these narrow

187

little channels, but it moves well in them, and she spins out arguments for starving like some hermetic medieval scholar. If she eats half a cracker, she feels sullied and guilty. She looks horrible, but her eyes shine with pride. Her parents waited way too long. They let it go. She was always such a good girl, and they just can't understand what happened to her. She's the flip side of Angie, protected not by fat but by her virginal armor. They're worried about her electrolyte balance. She could die.' Violet wrote Angie and Cathy into her book along with dozens of others. She gave them different names and analyzed their pathologies as the result of both their personal histories and the American 'hysteria' about food – which she called 'a sociological virus.' She told me that she used the word *virus* because a virus is neither living nor dead. Its animation depends on its host. I don't know whether Violet's girls found their way into Bill's new work or whether he was simply returning to an old theme, but as he continued to work on his new piece, I noticed that hunger had once again found a place in his art.

O's Journey was organized around the alphabet. Erica was the first to refer to its twenty-six boxes as 'Bill's great American novel.' He liked the phrase and began to use it himself, saying that it would take a long time to finish, like a big novel. Each box was a small freestanding twelve-inch glass cube, which allowed the spectator to view it from all sides. The characters inside the clear glass were identified by large letters that had been sewn or painted onto their chests – in the manner of Hester Prynne. O, the 'novel's' young painter-hero, bore a striking resemblance to Lazlo, except that he had red hair, not blond, and a longer nose, which I took as a reference to Pinocchio. Bill lost himself in those cubes. The studio floated with hundreds of drawings, tiny paintings, scraps of fabric for miniature clothes, notebooks filled with quotations and Bill's own musings. On a single page, I found a comment from the linguist Roman Jakobson, a reference to the Cabbalists, and a reminder to himself about a particular cartoon featuring Daffy Duck. In the drawings, O grew and shrank, depending on his circumstances. In one of my favorite sketches, an emaciated O was lying on a narrow bed, his feeble head turned toward his own painting of a roast beef.

I made regular visits to the studio that year. Bill gave me a set of keys so that I could let myself in without disturbing him. One afternoon, I found him lying on the floor staring fixedly at the ceiling. Four empty cubes and several small dolls lay scattered around him. When he heard me, Bill didn't move. I took a chair several feet away from him and waited. After about five minutes, he sat up. 'Thank you, Leo,' he said. 'I had to think through a problem with B. It couldn't wait.' But other times, I would find him sitting cross-legged on the floor, sewing small clothes or entire figures by hand, and without looking up from his work he would greet me warmly and start to talk. 'Leo, I'm glad you're here,' he said one evening. 'Meet O's mother.' He held up a tall thin plastic figure with pink eyes. 'This is O's poor mother, long-suffering, kindhearted, but a bit of a lush. I'm calling her X. Y is O's father. He's never going to appear in the flesh, you see. He's just a letter hovering in the distance or over O's head, a thought, an idea. Nevertheless, X and Y begot O. It makes sense, don't you think? X as in former, the once-was ex-wife, or X marks the spot, but also X as in a kiss at the bottom of a letter. You see, she loves him. And then there's Y, the big missing Y as in W-H-Y?' Bill laughed. The sound of his voice and his face made me think of Dan, and I asked Bill about his brother out of the blue. 'He's the same,' Bill said to me. His eyes clouded for an instant. 'He's the same.'

Every time I visited, I would find more characters lying out on the desk and on the floor. One afternoon in March, I picked up a two-dimensional figure that had been fashioned from wire and covered with a thin muslin fabric, which looked more like a transparent skin than a dress. The girl doll was on her knees with her arms raised upward in a beseeching gesture. When I saw the C pinned to her chest, I thought of Saint Catherine. 'That's one of O's girlfriends,' Bill said. 'She starves herself to death.' Only a minute later, I noticed two small fabric dolls locked in an embrace. I picked up the double figure and saw that the two little boys – one black-headed and one brown – had been attached at their waists and that each child had a letter M sewn to his chest. The blatant reference to Matthew and Mark unsettled me for a moment. I examined the two painted faces for distinguishing features, but the children were identical.

'You've put the boys in it?' I said.

Bill looked up and smiled. 'A version of them,' he said. 'They're O's little brothers.'

I carefully lowered them back to their resting place on the glass cube in front of me. 'Have you seen Mark's baby brother?'

Bill's eyes narrowed. 'Is this free association or are you divining hidden meanings in my M's?'

'I was just wondering.'

'No – I've only seen a snapshot of a red wrinkled newborn with a big mouth.'

Although *O's Journey* didn't mirror Bill's life in any of its details, I began to think of the personified letters and their movements from one cube to another as Bill's fabular autobiography – a translation of sorts from the language of the outside world into the hieroglyphs of inner life. Bill told me that by the end of the work O would disappear – not die, just vanish. In the penultimate cube, he would be only half visible – a specter of himself. In the final cube, O would be gone, but in his room the viewer would see a half-finished canvas. What Bill intended to put on that canvas, I didn't know, and I don't think he knew either.

Sometime in December of that year, there was

a real disappearance. It was a small one, but mysterious nevertheless. For his eleventh birthday I had given Matt a Swiss Army knife engraved with his initials. The knife had come with a short lecture on its responsible use, and Matt had agreed to every restriction. The most important of them was that he couldn't take it to school. Matt loved that knife. He attached it to a small chain and let it hang from his belt. 'I like to have it handy,' he said. 'It's so useful.' Its utility may have been secondary to its symbolism, however. He wore that knife the way some janitors parade their keys, as an emblem of male pride. When he wasn't checking to make sure that his weapon hadn't fallen off him, it was swinging from his belt like an extra appendage. Before he went to sleep he laid it reverently on his bedside table. And then one afternoon, he couldn't find it. He and Erica and Mark and Grace ransacked the closet and drawers and searched under the bed. By the time I returned from work, Matt was in tears and Grace had ripped off the bedsheets to see if the knife had fallen into them during the night. Was he certain that he had put it on the night table? Had he seen the knife that morning? Matt thought so, but the more he thought, the more confused he became. We searched for days, but the knife didn't turn up. I told him that if he still longed for the same knife when his twelfth birthday approached, I would buy him another one.

That year, Matt and Mark decided they wanted

to go to 'sleep-away' summer camp together. In late January, Bill, Violet, Erica, and I perused a fat book of camp listings. By February we had narrowed our choices and were dissecting the literature sent by seven camps. All our hermeneutic talents were brought to bear on the innocent brochures and xeroxed flyers. What was actually meant by 'noncompetitive philosophy'? Did it suggest a healthy lack of a winning-is-all mentality or was it an excuse for laxness? Bill studied the photographs for clues. If their style was too glossy and artificial, he was suspicious. I dismissed two camps because their literature was studded with grammatical errors, and Erica worried about the qualifications of the counselors. In the end, a camp called Green Hill in Pennsylvania won the competition. The boys liked the picture on the cover of its catalogue – twenty boys and girls with Green Hill T-shirts beaming out at the spectator from under a canopy of leafy trees. The camp had everything we had hoped for – baseball, basketball, swimming, sailing, canoeing, and an arts program that included painting, dance, music, and theater. The decision had been made. We sent off our checks.

In April, not long before the Columbia semester ended, Bill, Mark, Matthew, and I drove to Shea Stadium on a Friday evening for a Mets game. The home team came from behind and rallied to win the game in the ninth inning. Matt scrutinized every pitch and every play. After mumbling the statistics for each player aloud, he offered his analysis of the man's prospects at the plate. As the game progressed, he agonized, suffered, and rejoiced, depending on the fate of the Mets at the moment, and because his emotions ran so high, I found myself both exhausted and relieved when it was all over.

It was late when I walked into Matt's room that night with a glass of water to put on his night table. Erica had already left him. I leaned over and kissed his cheek, but he didn't kiss me back. He squinted at the ceiling for a couple of moments and then said, 'You know, Dad, I'm always thinking about how many people there are in the world. I was thinking about it between innings at the game, and I got this really funny feeling, you know, how everybody is thinking thoughts at the same time, billions of thoughts.'

'Yes,' I said. 'A flood of thoughts that we can't hear.'

'Yeah. And then I got this weird idea about how all those different people see what they see just a little different from everybody else.'

'You mean that every person has a different way of seeing the world?'

'No, Dad, I mean really and truly. I mean that because we were sitting where we were sitting tonight, we saw a game that was a little different from those guys with the beer next to us. It was the same game, but I could've noticed something those guys didn't. And then I thought, if I was sitting

194

over there, I'd see something else. And not just the game. I mean they saw me and I saw them, but I didn't see myself and they didn't see themselves. Do you get what I mean?'

'I know just what you mean. I've thought about it a lot, Matt. The place where I am is missing from my view. It's like that for everybody. We don't see ourselves in the picture, do we? It's a kind of hole.'

'And when I put that together with people thinking their zillions of thoughts – right now they're out there thinking and thinking – I get this floaty feeling.' He paused. 'On the way home in the car when we were all quiet, I thought about how everybody's thoughts keep changing. The thoughts that people were having during the game turned into new thoughts when we were in the car. That was then, but this is now, but then that now is gone, and there's a new now. Right now, I'm saying right now, but it's over before I've finished saying it.'

'In a way,' I said to him, 'that *now* you're talking about hardly exists. We feel it, but it's impossible to measure. The past is always eating up the present.' I stroked his hair and paused. 'I think I've always loved paintings for that reason. Somebody makes a canvas in time, but after it's made, a painting stays in the present. Does that make sense to you?'

'Yes,' he said. 'Definitely. I like things to last for a long, long time.' Matthew looked up at me. Then he took a breath. 'I've made up my mind, Dad. I'm going to be an artist. When I was little

I thought I would try for the Major Leagues. I'll always play ball, but that's not going to be my job. No, I'm going to have a studio right here in the neighborhood and an apartment close by, so I can visit you and Mom whenever I want.' He closed his eyes. 'Sometimes I think I'll make great big paintings, and other times I think I'll make pretty small ones. I don't know which yet.'

'You have time to decide,' I said. Matt turned onto his stomach and gripped the covers. I leaned down and kissed his forehead.

When I left Matthew's room that night, I stopped in the hallway and leaned against the wall for a couple of minutes. I was proud of my son. Like a rush of air in my lungs, the feeling grew, and then I wondered if my pride wasn't a form of reflected vanity. Matthew's thoughts echoed mine, and that night when I listened to him, I heard myself, and yet as I stood there I knew that I also admired a quality in Matthew that I didn't have. At eleven, he was bolder and more certain than I had ever been. When I told Erica about our talk, she said, 'We're lucky. We're lucky to have him. He's the best boy on earth.' And after that hyperbolic declaration, she rolled over and fell asleep.

On June twenty-seventh, the six of us crowded into a rented minivan and drove to Pennsylvania. Bill and I carried two leaden duffel bags into a cabin Matt and Mark were going to share with seven other boys and greeted their counselors, Jim and Jason. The pair reminded me of an adolescent version of Laurel and Hardy – one thin, the other rotund – both grinning broadly. We briefly met the camp director, a hairy man with a pumping handshake and a hoarse voice. We strolled around the grounds and admired the mess hall, the lake, the tennis courts, and the theater. We lingered over our good-byes. Matt threw himself into my arms and hugged me. Only at night did I get such affectionate treatment anymore, but he had clearly made an exception for that farewell. I felt his ribs through his T-shirt as he pressed himself against me, and I looked down into his face. 'I love you, Dad,' he said in a low voice. I answered him as I always did. 'And I love you, Matt. I love you.' I watched him embrace Erica, and I noticed that he found it a little hard to withdraw from his mother. Erica removed his Mets cap and stroked his hair away from his forehead.

'Matty,' she said. 'I'll embarrass you with a letter every day.'

'That's not embarrassing, Mom,' he said. He held her tightly and pressed his cheek into her collarbone. Then he lifted his chin and smiled. 'This is embarrassing.'

Erica and Violet prolonged our departure with futile reminders that Matt and Mark brush their teeth, wash themselves, and get enough sleep. When we reached the car, I turned around to look at the boys. They were standing on the wide mowed lawn beside the camp's main building. A large oak tree spread its branches over them, and behind them the afternoon sun shone on the lake, its light catching the ruffle of waves on the water's surface. Bill was driving the first leg of the trip home, and after I had taken my seat beside Violet in the back, I turned again to watch the two figures recede as the van moved down the long driveway toward the road. Matthew had raised his hand to wave at us. From that distance, he looked like a very small boy wearing clothes that were too big for him. I noticed how thin his legs were under his wide shorts and the narrow line of his neck above his billowing T-shirt. He was still holding his cap in his hand, and I saw a tuft of his hair blow up and away from his face in the wind.

TWO

Eight days later Matt died. On July fifth at about three o'clock in the afternoon, he went canoeing on the Delaware River with three counselors and six other boys. His canoe hit a rock and capsized. Matt was hurled out, hit his head on another boulder, and was knocked unconscious. He drowned in the shallow water before anybody could get to him. For months, Erica and I went over the sequence of events, looking for the guilty party. At first we blamed Matt's counselor Jason, who had been in the stern, because it was all a matter of inches. Had Jason steered two or three inches to the right, there wouldn't have been an accident. An inch to the left, the collision would have occurred, but Matt wouldn't have hit the rock in the water. We also blamed a boy named Rusty. A few seconds before the crash, he had raised himself up and out of his seat in the middle of the canoe and wiggled his buttocks at Jason. In those seconds, the counselor lost sight of the shallow rapids in front of him. Inches and seconds. When Jim and a boy named Cyrus pulled Matthew out of the river, they didn't know that he was dead. Jim performed mouth-to-mouth, blowing air in and out of Matt's still body. They flagged down a car on the road, and the driver, a Mr Hodenfield, sped across the border to the nearest hospital, in Callicoon, New York – Grover M. Hermann Community Hospital. Jim never stopped breathing into Matt. He pressed on his chest and blew air into him over and over, but at the hospital Matthew was pronounced dead. It is a strange word, 'pronounced.' He had died already, but in the emergency room, they spoke the words and it was over. The pronouncement made it real.

Erica took the telephone call late that afternoon. I was standing only a few feet away from her in the kitchen. I saw her face change, watched her clutch the counter, and heard her gasp the word 'No.' It was a hot day, but we hadn't turned on the air conditioners. I was sweating. Looking at her, I began to sweat more. Erica scribbled words on a pad. Her hand shook. She gulped for air as she listened to the voice. I knew that the call was about Matthew. Erica had repeated the word 'accident,' then written down the name of the hospital. I was ready to leave. Adrenaline surged through my body. I ran for my wallet and the car keys. When I returned to the living room with the keys in my hand, Erica said, 'Leo, that man on the telephone. That man said that Matthew is dead.' I stopped breathing, shut my eyes, and said to myself what Erica had said aloud. I said no. Nausea welled up into my mouth. My knees buckled, and I grabbed the table to steady myself. I heard the keys jangle as my hand hit the wooden surface. Then I sat down. Erica had gripped the other side of the table. I looked at her white knuckles, then up at her contorted face. 'We have to go to him,' she said.

I drove. The white and yellow lines on the black road in front of me held my complete attention. I concentrated on the lines and watched them disappear under the wheels. The sun glared through the windshield, and I squinted now and then through my sunglasses. Beside me sat a woman I hardly recognized – pale, motionless, and dumb. I know that Erica and I saw him in the hospital and that he looked thin. His legs were brown from the sun, but his face had changed color. His lips were blue and his cheeks gray. He was Matthew and he wasn't Matthew. Erica and I walked down hallways and spoke to the medical examiner and we made arrangements in the hushed atmosphere of deference that surrounds people who have just stepped into grief, but the fact was that the world didn't seem to be the world anymore, and when I think back on that week, on the funeral and the cemetery and the people who came, there is a shallowness to all of it, as though my vision had changed and everything I saw had been robbed of its thickness.

I suppose that the loss of depth came from disbelief. Knowing the truth isn't enough. My whole being refuted Matt's death, and I was always expecting him to walk through the door.

I heard him moving around in his room and coming up the stairs. Once I heard him say 'Dad.' The sound of his voice was as distinct as if he had been a foot away from me. Belief would come very slowly, and it would come sparingly, in moments that bored holes into the curious stage set that had replaced the world around me. Two days after the funeral, I was wandering around the apartment and heard noises from Matthew's room. When I looked through the door, I saw Erica lying in Matt's bed. She had curled up under his sheets and was rocking back and forth as she clutched his pillow and bit into it. I walked over to her and sat down at the edge of the bed. She continued to rock. The pillow case was wet with ragged spots of saliva and tears. I put my hand on her shoulder, but she wrenched her torso toward the wall and began to scream. Her howls rose up from deep inside her throat – hoarse and guttural. 'I want my baby! Get away! I want my baby!' I withdrew my hand. She punched the wall and beat the bed. She sobbed and bellowed out the words over and over. Her cries seemed to gouge my lungs, and I stopped breathing each time they came. As I sat there and listened to Erica, I felt afraid, not of her grief but of my own. I let her noises tear and scrape through me. Yes, I said to myself. This is true. These sounds are real. I looked at the floor and imagined myself lying on it. To stop, I thought, just to stop. I felt dry. That was the problem. I was dry as an old bone – and I envied Erica her flailing and her shouting. I couldn't find it in me, and I let her do it instead. She ended up with her head in my lap, and I looked down at her squashed face with its red nose and swollen eyes. I put four fingers on her cheek and let them run to her chin. 'Matthew,' I said to her. Then I said it again. 'Matthew.'

Erica looked up at me. Her lips were trembling. 'Leo,' she said. 'How are we going to live?'

The days were long. I must have had thoughts but I don't remember them. Mostly I sat. I didn't read or cry or rock or move. I sat in the chair where I often sit now, and I looked out the window. I watched the traffic and the pedestrians with their shopping bags. I studied the yellow cabs, the tourists dressed in shorts and T-shirts, and then after I had been sitting for hours, I would go into Matt's room and touch his things. I never picked up anything. I let my fingers move over his rock collection. I touched his T-shirts in his drawer. I laid my hands on his backpack, still stuffed with dirty clothes from camp. I felt his unmade bed. We didn't make the bed all summer, and we didn't move a single object in his room. By the time morning came, Erica had often made her way to Matthew's bed. Sometimes she remembered climbing into it in the middle of the night. Other times she didn't.

She had started walking in her sleep again, not every night, but a couple of times a week. During these ambulatory trances, Erica was always searching for something. She yanked open drawers in the

205

kitchen and dug into closets. She pulled books off the shelf in her study and peered at the bare wood where the volumes had been. One night I found her standing in the middle of the hallway. Her hand turned an invisible knob and she thrust open an invisible door and began to clutch and grab at the air. I let her look because I was afraid of disturbing her. Asleep, she had a determination she had lost in wakefulness, and when I felt her stirring beside me and sitting up in bed, I would rouse myself and dutifully stand up to follow her around the loft until the ritual searching was over. I became a nocturnal spectator, a vigilant second to Erica's unconscious roaming. There were nights when I stood in front of the door that led to the landing, worried that she might leave and take her search out into the streets, but whatever it was that she wanted to find, the thing was lost in the apartment. Sometimes she mumbled, 'I know I put it somewhere. It was here.' But she never named the object. After a while, she would give up, walk to Matthew's room, climb into his bed, and sleep until morning. During the early weeks of her wandering, I spoke to her about it, but after a while, I stopped. There was nothing left to tell her, and my descriptions of her unconscious rummaging only made her suffer more.

We didn't know how to give him up, how to be. We couldn't find the rhythms of ordinary life. The simple business of waking, retrieving the paper from outside the door, and sitting down to eat breakfast became a cruel pantomime of the

206

everyday enacted in the gaping absence of our son. And although she sat at the table with her bowl of cereal in front of her, Erica couldn't eat. She had never been a big eater, had always been thin, but by the end of the summer she had lost fifteen pounds. Her cheeks sank into her face, and when I sat across from her I could see her skull. I nagged her about eating, but my prompting was halfhearted because I tasted nothing on my plate either and had to force the food into my mouth. Violet was the one who fed us. She started cooking dinner for me and Erica the day after Matt died and didn't stop until well into the fall. In the beginning, she knocked before she entered. After that, we left the door open for her. Every evening, I would hear her steps on the stairs and see her walk in, carrying pans with tinfoil over them. Violet never said much to us in the early days after Matt's death, and her silence was a relief. She would announce the names of the foods – 'Lasagna, salad,' or 'Chicken cutlets with green beans and rice,' and then she would plop the plates on the table, uncover them, and dish out the food. By August she was staying to encourage Erica to eat. She cut up her food for her, and while Erica took hesitant bites, Violet massaged her shoulders or stroked her back. She touched me, too, but differently. She would grab my upper arm and squeeze it hard – to steady me or shake me, I don't know which.

We depended on her, and when I think back on it now, I'm aware of how hard she worked. If she and Bill were going out to dinner, she would cook for us anyway and drop off the food. When they vacationed for two weeks in August, she arrived with dinners for our freezer, labeled with the days of the week. She called us every day at ten in the morning from Connecticut to check on us and closed her conversation by saying, 'Take out Wednesday right now, and it will be defrosted by dinner time.'

Bill came to us alone. Neither Violet nor Bill ever mentioned it, but I think they did their duties separately rather than together so that Erica and I would have more hours of company. About two weeks after the funeral, Bill brought a watercolor with him that Matt had done during a visit to his studio. It was another cityscape. When Erica saw it, she said to Bill, 'I think I'll look at it later, if you don't mind. I can't now. I just can't . . .' She left us, walked down the hallway, and I heard the sound of our bedroom door closing behind her. Bill pulled up a chair next to mine, placed the watercolor on the coffee table in front of us, and began to talk. 'Do you see the wind?' he said.

I looked down at the scene.

'Look at these trees pulled hard by the wind and the buildings. The whole city is shaking with it. The picture is trembling. Eleven years old, Leo, and he did this.' Bill moved his finger across the images. 'Look at this woman collecting cans, and the little girl in the ballerina costume with her mother. Look at this man's body over here, the way he's walking, fighting the wind. And here's Dave feeding Durango . . .'

Through a window I saw the old man. He was bent over toward the floor with a bowl in his hands. Because of his stooped posture, Dave's beard hung away from his body. 'Yes,' I said. 'Dave is always there somewhere.'

'He made this picture for you,' Bill said. 'It's for you.' He picked up the watercolor and put it on my lap. I held it very carefully and studied the street with its people. A plastic bag and a newspaper were flying in the wind near the pavement and then, as I looked up, I noticed a tiny figure on the roof of Dave's building – the outline of a boy.

Bill pointed at the child. 'There's no face on him. Matt told me he wanted it like that . . .'

I brought the paper closer to my eyes. 'And his feet aren't on the ground,' I said slowly. The featureless child had something in his hand – a knife with its many blades opened like the points on a star. 'It's the Ghosty Boy,' I said, 'with Matt's lost knife.'

'It's for you,' Bill repeated. At the time, I accepted this explanation, but now I wonder if Bill didn't invent the story of the gift. He laid a hand on my shoulder. I had been afraid of this. I didn't want him to touch me and remained rigid. But when I turned to the man beside me, I saw that he was crying. Tears ran down his cheeks, and then he sobbed loudly.

After that, Bill came every day to sit with me

by the window. He came home from his studio earlier than usual, always at the same time: five o'clock. Often Bill would put his hand on the arm of my chair and leave it there until he left, about an hour later. He told me stories from his childhood with Dan and stories from when he was a young artist roaming Italy. He described his first house-painting job in New York – in a brothel where most of the customers were Hasidic Jews. He read to me from *Artforum*. He talked to me about Philip Guston's conversion, Art Spiegelman's *Maus*, and Paul Celan's poems. I rarely interrupted him, and he demanded no response. He didn't avoid Matthew as a subject. Sometimes he reported on conversations they had had at the studio. 'He wanted to know about line, Leo. I mean metaphysically, about the edges of things as you look at them, if blocks of color have lines, if painting is superior to drawing. He told me that he had dreamed several times that he was walking into the sun and that he couldn't see. The light blinded him.'

Bill would always pause after he mentioned Matt. When Erica felt strong enough to be with us, she would lie on the sofa several feet away. I know she listened, because sometimes she would lift her head and say, 'Go on, Bill.' He would always continue his monologue then. I heard everything he said, but his words sounded muffled, as if he were speaking through a handkerchief. Before he left, he would move his hand off the armchair, squeeze my arm firmly, and say, 'I'm here, Leo. We're here.' Bill came every day he was in New York for a year. When he was traveling, he called me around the same time. Without Bill, I think I would have dried up completely and blown away.

Grace stayed with us through the first week of September. Matt's death had made her quiet, but whenever she mentioned him, she called him 'my little boy.' Her grief seemed to lodge itself in her chest and the way she breathed. Her full breasts rose and fell while she shook her head. 'It can't be understood,' she said to me. 'It's outside our powers.' She got a job with another family in the neighborhood, and on the day she left us, I found myself examining her body. Matt had always loved the plenitude of Grace. He had once told Erica that when he sat on Grace's lap there were no bones sticking out to interfere with his comfort. But the woman's fullness was spiritual as well as physical. Grace eventually moved to Sunrise, Florida, where she now lives with Mr Thelwell in a condominium. She and Erica still write to each other after all these years, and Erica tells me that Grace keeps a photograph of Matt in the living room beside the pictures of her six grandchildren.

Just before Erica and I returned to work that fall, Lazlo came to visit us. We hadn't seen him since the funeral. He walked through the door with a grocery box, greeted us with a nod, and set it down on the floor. He proceeded to unwrap the object inside and then place it on the coffee table.

The blue sticks of the small sculpture had nothing to do with the anatomical works I had seen before. Fragile open rectangles rose up from a flat dark blue board. The piece looked like a toothpick city. Taped to its base was a title: *In Memory of Matthew Hertzberg.* Lazlo was unable to look at us. 'I'd better be going,' he mumbled, but before he could take a step, Erica reached out for him. She grabbed him around his narrow waist and hugged him. Lazlo's arms swung up and out. For a moment he stood with his arms extended at his sides as if hesitant about whether he should take flight or not, but then he brought them around to Erica's back. His fingers rested lightly there for a couple of seconds and then he dropped his chin onto her head. There was a momentary spasm in his face, a wrinkling around his mouth, and then it was gone. I shook Lazlo's hand, and as his warm fingers pressed mine, I swallowed hard and swallowed again, the gulps resounding in my ears like distant gunfire.

After Lazlo left, Erica turned to me. 'You don't cry, Leo. You haven't cried at all, not once.'

I looked at Erica's red eyes, her wet nose and trembling mouth. She repulsed me. 'No.' I said. 'I haven't.' She heard the repressed rage in my voice and her mouth dropped open. I turned around and stalked down the hallway. I walked into Matthew's room and stood by his bed. Then I put my fist through the wall. The Sheetrock buckled under the blow and pain shot through my hand. The pain felt good – no, more than good. For an instant, I felt intense soaring relief, but it didn't last. I could feel Erica's eyes on my back as she stood in the doorway. When I turned around to look at her, she said, 'What have you done? What have you done to Matt's wall?'

Erica and I both worked hard at our jobs, but the sameness and familiarity of our duties felt more like a reenactment than a continuation of our old lives. I recalled perfectly the Leo Hertzberg who had taught in the art history department before Matthew's death, and I found that I could impersonate him smoothly. After all, my students didn't need me. They needed him: the man who lectured, corrected papers, and held office hours. If anything, I performed my duties more scrupulously than before. As long as I didn't stop working, I couldn't be faulted, and I soon discovered that because my colleagues and students knew that my son had died, they protected me with their own walls of silent respect. I could see that Erica had adopted a similar posture. For about an hour after she came home from Rutgers, her gestures were brisk and mechanical. She insisted on staying up late to correct papers. When she spoke to her colleagues on the phone, her voice sounded like a movie parody of an efficient secretary. In her tight determined face, I saw myself, but I didn't like the reflection, and the more I looked at it, the uglier I found it.

The difference between us was that Erica's pose

collapsed daily. By the end of the summer, she stopped walking in her sleep. Instead, she would go to Matt's room and weep on his bed until she was too tired to cry anymore. Erica's misery was volatile. For months, I went to sit beside her on Matt's bed, not knowing what to expect. There were nights when she would grab me and kiss my hands and face and chest and nights when she beat my arms and pummeled my chest. There were nights when she begged me to hold her and then when I had her in my arms, she would push me away. After a while, I discovered that my responses to Erica were robotic. I performed my duties of holding her or, if she didn't want me near her, sitting silently in a chair a few feet away, but the gestures and words that passed between us seemed to evaporate immediately and leave nothing behind them. When Erica brought up Rusty or Jason, I wanted to go deaf. When she accused me of being 'catatonic,' I closed my eyes. We no longer slept in the same bed. There was no sex between us, and I didn't touch myself. I was tempted to masturbate, but the relief it promised me also seemed to threaten disintegration.

In December, Erica went to a doctor about her weight, and he directed her to another doctor who was also an analyst. Every Friday, she visited Dr Trimble in her office on Central Park West. Dr Trimble asked to see me, but I refused to go. The last thing I wanted was some stranger prodding my mind for childhood traumas and quizzing me about my parents. But I should have gone. I can see that now. I should have gone because Erica wanted me to go. My refusal became the sign of my withdrawal from her without hope of return. While Erica talked to Dr Trimble, I sat at home and listened to Bill for an hour and then, after he left, I looked out the window. My body hurt all over. Pain had settled into my arms and legs, and I suffered from a chronic stiffness in my muscles. My right hand, the one that had gone through the wall, took a long time to heal. I had broken my middle finger and the collision had left a large bump near my knuckle. This small disfigurement and my aching body were my sole satisfactions, and I would often rub the lumpy finger while I sat in my chair.

Erica drank cans of liquid sustenance called Ensure. In the evening, she took a sleeping pill. As the months passed, she became much kinder to me than she had been, but her new solicitude had an impersonal quality, as if she were tending a homeless man on the street rather than her husband. She stopped sleeping in Matt's bed and returned to ours, but I rarely joined her, choosing instead to sleep in my chair. One night in February, I woke up to find Erica covering me with a blanket. Rather than opening my eyes, I pretended that I was still asleep. When she put her lips to my head, I imagined myself pulling her toward me and kissing her neck and shoulders, but I didn't do it. At the time, I was like a man encased in a heavy suit of armor, and inside that corporeal fortress I lived with a single-minded wish: *I will not be comforted*. As perverse as it was, this desire felt like a lifeline, the only shred of truth left to me. I feel quite sure that Erica knew what I felt, and in March she announced a change.

'I've decided to accept the position at Berkeley, Leo. They still want me.'

We were eating Chinese food out of boxes. I looked up from the chicken and broccoli to study her face. 'Is this your way of saying that you want a divorce?' The word 'divorce' had a curious ring to it. I realized that it had never occurred to me.

Erica shook her head and looked down at the table. 'No, I don't want a divorce. I don't know if I'll stay there. All I know is that I can't live anymore in the place where Matt was, and I can't be here with you anymore, because . . .' She paused. 'You've gone dead, too, Leo. I didn't help. I know that. I was so crazy for a long time and I was mean.'

'No,' I said. 'You weren't mean.' I couldn't bear to look at her, so I turned my head and spoke to the wall. 'Are you sure that you want to go away? Moving is hard on people, too.'

'I know,' she said.

We were silent for a while and then she continued: 'I remember what you said about your father – the way he was after he found out about his family. You said, "He went still."'

I didn't move. I kept my eyes on the wall. 'He had a stroke.'

'Before the stroke. You said it happened before the stroke.'

I saw my father in his chair. His back was to me as he sat in front of the fireplace. I nodded before I looked at Erica. When our eyes met, I saw that she was half-smiling and half-crying. 'I'm not saying it's over between us, Leo. I want to come visit you if you'll let me. I'd like to write to you and tell you what I'm doing.'

'Yes.' I began to nod over and over, like one of those dolls whose heads are on a spring. I felt my two-day beard with both my hands and rubbed my face as I continued to nod.

'Also,' she said, 'we have to go through Matthew's things. I thought that you could sort his drawings. We can frame some and put the others in portfolios. I'll take care of his clothes and the toys. Some of them can go to Mark . . .'

That job took over our evenings, and I discovered that I was able to do it. I bought folders and storage boxes and began to organize hundreds of drawings, school art projects, notebooks, and letters that had belonged to Matt. Erica folded his T-shirts and pants and shorts very carefully. She saved his ART NOW shirt and a pair of camouflage pants that he had loved. She put the rest into boxes for Mark or for Goodwill. She gathered up his toys and separated the good ones from the junk. While Erica sat on the floor of Matt's room with cardboard boxes around her, I filed drawings at his desk. We worked slowly. Erica lingered over

Matthew's clothes, his shirts and underpants and socks. How strange they were – at once terrible and banal. One evening, I started tracing the lines of his drawings with my finger – his people and buildings and animals. I found the motion of his living hand that way, and once I had started it, I couldn't stop. On an evening in April, Erica came and stood behind me. She watched my hand moving over the page, and then she reached out and put her finger on Dave and made the rounds of the old man's body. She cried then, and I understood how much I had hated her tears, because for some reason I didn't hate them then.

Erica's imminent departure changed us. The knowledge that we would soon be separated made us both more indulgent, relieving us of a burden I still can't name. I didn't want her to go away, and yet the fact that she was going away loosened a bolt in the machinery of our marriage. It had become a machine by then, a churning repetitive engine of mourning.

That spring I was teaching a seminar on still life to twelve graduate students, and in April I taught one of my last classes. When I walked in that day, one of the students, Edward Paperno, was opening the windows in the classroom to let the warm air into the room. The sunshine, the breeze, the fact that the semester was almost over all contributed to an atmosphere of languor and fatigue. As I sat down to begin the discussion, I yawned and covered my mouth. On the table in front of me I had my notes and a reproduction of Chardin's *Glass of Water and a Coffee Pot*. My students had read Diderot and Proust and the Goncourt brothers on Chardin. They had been to the Frick to study the still lifes in that collection. We had already discussed several paintings. I began by pointing out how simple the painting was, two objects, three heads of garlic, and the sprig of an herb. I mentioned the light on the pot's rim and handle, the whiteness of the garlic, and the silver hues of the water. And then I found myself staring down at the glass of water in the picture. I moved very close to it. The strokes were visible. I could see them plainly. A precise quiver of the brush had made light. I swallowed, breathed heavily, and choked.

I think it was Maria Livingston who said, 'Are you all right, Professor Hertzberg?'

I cleared my throat, removed my glasses, and wiped my eyes. 'The water,' I said in a low voice. 'The glass of water is very moving to me.' I looked up and saw the surprised faces of my students. 'The water is a sign of . . .' I paused. 'The water seems to be a sign of absence.'

I remained silent, but I could feel warm tears running down my cheeks. My students continued to look at me. 'I believe that's all for today,' I told them in a tremulous voice. 'Go outside and enjoy the weather.'

I watched my twelve students leave the room in silence, and I noticed with some surprise that

Letitia Reeves had beautiful legs, which must have been hidden under trousers until that day. I listened to the door close. In the hallway, I heard the students break into low conversations. The sun lit the empty classroom and a wind rose up and blew through the windows and across my face. I tried not to make any noise, but I know that I did. I gulped for air and I gagged and deep ugly sounds came from my throat as I sobbed for what seemed to be a very long time.

Weeks later, I came across my calendar from 1989, the little agenda in which I had marked down appointments and events. I paged through it, pausing at Matt's baseball games, his teacher conferences, an art show at his school. When I turned to April, I noticed that I had written METS GAME in large letters on the fourteenth. Exactly one year to the day, I had broken down in class over the Chardin painting. I remembered my conversation with Matt that night. I remembered exactly where I had been sitting on his bed. I remembered his face as he talked to me and how for part of the time he had addressed the ceiling. I remembered his room, his socks on the floor, the plaid cotton blanket he had pulled up to his chest, the Mets T-shirt he had been wearing instead of pajamas. I remembered his lamp with the base designed to look like a pencil, the light it shed on the night table, and the glass of water that stood underneath it – flanked on the left by his wristwatch. I had brought hundreds of glasses of water to Matt's bedside, and after his death I had drunk many more, since I always kept a glass beside me at night. A real glass of water had not once reminded me of my son, but the image of a glass of water rendered 230 years earlier had catapulted me suddenly and irrevocably into the painful awareness that I was still alive.

After that day in the classroom, my grief took a new turn. For months I had lived in a state of self-enforced rigor mortis, interrupted only by the playacting of my work, which didn't disturb the entombment I had chosen for myself, but a part of me had known that a crack was inevitable. Chardin became the instrument of the break, because the little painting took me by surprise. I hadn't girded myself for its attack on my senses, and I went to pieces. The truth is, I had avoided resurrection because I must have known that it would be excruciating. That summer, light, noise, color, smells, the slightest motion of the air rubbed me raw with their stimuli. I wore sunglasses all the time. Every shift in brightness hurt me. Car horns ripped at my eardrums. The conversations of pedestrians, their laughter, their hoots, even the lone person singing in the street felt like an assault. I couldn't bear shades of red. Crimson sweaters and shirts, the red mouth of a pretty girl hailing a cab forced me to turn my head. Ordinary jostling on the sidewalk – a person's arm or elbow brushing my body, the jab of a stranger's shoulder,

221

sent a shudder up my spine. Wind blew through rather than over me, and I thought I could feel my skeleton rattle. Garbage baking in the streets gave me fits of nausea and dizziness, but so did the aromas of food from restaurants – smoking burgers and chicken and the pungent spices of Asian food. My nostrils took in every human odor, both artificial and real, colognes and oils and sweat and the rank, sour, and tart odors of people's breath. I was bombarded and couldn't escape.

But the worst was that during those months of hypersensitivity, I sometimes forgot Matthew. Minutes would pass when I didn't think of him. When he was alive, I had felt no need to think of him constantly. I knew that he was there. Forgetfulness was normal. After he died, I had turned my body into a memorial – an inert gravestone for him. To be awake meant that there were moments of amnesia, and those moments seemed to annihilate Matthew twice. When I forgot him, Matthew was nowhere – not in the world or in my mind. I think my collection was a way to answer those blanks. As Erica and I continued to sort through Matthew's things, I chose a few of them to put in my drawer with the photographs of my parents, grandparents, aunt, uncle, and the twins. My selection was purely a matter of instinct. I chose a green rock, the Roberto Clemente baseball card Bill had given him for his birthday one year in Vermont, the program he had designed for the fourth-grade production of *Horton Hears a Who*, and a small picture he had done of Dave with Durango. It had more humor than many of the pictures of Dave. The old man was sleeping on the sofa with a newspaper over his face while the cat licked his naked toes.

Erica moved away in early August, five days before Matt's birthday. She said she needed several weeks to settle into her apartment in Berkeley. I helped her pack up books, and we mailed them to her new address. She had to leave Dr Trimble, and I sometimes felt that she dreaded leaving her more than Rutgers, more than Bill and Violet, more than me. But Erica had the name of another doctor in Berkeley, whom she began seeing only a few days after she arrived. That morning, I carried her suitcase and walked her down the stairs and outside the building to find a taxi. It was a cloudy day but with a strong glare from the sun, and although I was protected by sunglasses, I winced from the light. After I had hailed the cab, I told the driver to turn on the meter and wait for a couple of moments. When I turned to say good-bye, Erica began to tremble.

'We've been better, you know,' I said. 'Lately.'

Erica looked down at her feet. I noticed that despite her weight gain, the skirt she was wearing hung too low around her waist. 'It's because I shook things up, Leo. You started to hate me. Now you won't.' Erica lifted her chin and smiled at me. 'We . . . we . . . we . . .' Her voice cracked and she laughed. 'I don't know what I'm saying.

I'll call you when I get there.' She fell toward me and put her arms around my back. I felt her body against mine – her small breasts and her shoulders. Her damp face was crushed into my neck. When she withdrew from me, she smiled again. The lines around her eyes wrinkled and I looked at the mole over her lip. Then I leaned forward and kissed it. She knew I had targeted the mole and smiled, 'I liked that,' she said. 'Do it again.'

I kissed her again.

When she slid into the car, I looked down at her legs, which had stayed white all summer. I had an impulse to slide my hand between her thighs and feel their skin. The warm flood of sexual feeling made me shake inwardly. I listened to the car door slam shut and stood on the side-walk while it drove up Greene Street and turned right. Now you want her – after all these months, I said to myself, and as I turned to walk back into the building, I understood how well Erica knew me.

The apartment didn't look much different. There were a few empty places on the bookshelves. Our closet in the bedroom was roomier. When all was said and done, Erica had taken very little with her. Nevertheless, as I walked through the loft and surveyed the gaps in the shelves, the empty hangers, the bare floor where Erica's shoes had been lined up only the day before, I found myself gasping for breath. For months I had been prepared for the moment of her departure, but I hadn't guessed that I would feel what I felt – cold, pinching fear.

I clutched at the rightness of it, my punishment come due. I stalked from one room to another, letting the cold anxiety squeeze my lungs. I turned on the television to hear voices. I turned it off to get rid of them. An hour passed and then another. By four o'clock I was exhausted from flying around the apartment like a terrified bird. I continued to walk from room to room, but I paced myself, going more slowly. In the bathroom, I opened the medicine cabinet and studied an old toothbrush of Erica's and a lipstick. I removed the lipstick from the shelf and opened it. I screwed it up from the bottom and examined the brownish-red shade. After lowering it and replacing its top, I walked to my desk, opened my drawer, and put the lipstick inside. I chose two other objects to keep there – a small pair of black socks and two barrettes that were lying on her night table. The absurdity of the hoarding was obvious to me, but I didn't care. The act of closing the drawer on these things that belonged to Erica soothed me. By the time Bill arrived, I was calm. He stayed longer than he usually did, however, and I'm sure he did it because he sensed that under my apparent equilibrium lay panic.

Erica called that night. Her voice sounded high and a little squeaky. 'When I put the key in the door, I felt glad,' she said, 'but when I walked inside, sat down, and looked around, I thought I'd gone completely mad. I've been watching TV, Leo. I never watch TV.'

'I miss you,' I said.

'Yes.'

That was her response. She didn't say that she missed me, too. 'I'm going to write to you. I don't like the phone.'

The first letter came at the end of the week. It was a long letter dense with domestic particulars – the spider plant she had bought for the apartment, the drizzly weather that day, her trip to Cody's bookstore, her course plans. She explained her preference for letters. 'I don't want the words to be naked the way they are in faxes or on the computer. I want them to be covered by an envelope that you have to rip open in order to get at. I want there to be waiting time – a pause between the writing and the reading. I want us to be careful about what we say to each other. I want the miles between us to be real and long. This will be our law – that we write our dailiness and our suffering very, very carefully. In letters I can only tell you about my wildness. It isn't the wildness itself, and I *am* wild and savage over Matt. Letters can't scream. Telephones can. When I got back from Cody's today, I put my books on the table and went to the bathroom, stuffed a washcloth in my mouth, and walked into the bedroom so that I could lie on the bed and scream without making too much noise. But I'm beginning to see him again, not dead but alive. For a whole year, I've only seen him dead on that gurney. Far away with only letters between us, we may begin to find our way back to each other. Love, Erica.'

I wrote back the same evening, and Erica and I embarked on the epistolary chapter of our marriage. I stuck to the bargain and didn't call her, but I wrote long and hard. I kept her informed about my work and the apartment. I told her my colleague Ron Bellinger was trying a new drug for his narcolepsy that made him a little owl-eyed but less apt to drop off in committee meetings, and that Jack Newman was still going at it with Sara. I told her that Olga, the cleaning lady I had hired, had scrubbed the stove with such ferocity that the printed words FRONT and BACK to indicate the burners had vanished into her little ball of steel wool, and I told her that I had been distraught when I understood that she was gone, really gone. She answered me, and so it went. What neither one of us could know was what the other omitted. Every correspondence is skewered by invisible perforations, the small holes of the unwritten but not the unthought, and as time went on, I hoped fervently that it wasn't a man who was missing from those pages I received every week.

Over and over again during the months that followed, I found myself on the stairs walking up to Bill and Violet's loft for dinner. Violet would call me in the early evening and ask if she should set an extra place, and I would say yes. It was hard to say with any conviction that I preferred to eat scrambled eggs or corn flakes downstairs. I let Bill and Violet take care of me, and while they took care of me, I found myself looking at them all over again. Like a man who had crawled out of a dungeon after years in murk and shadow, I was a little shocked by their vividness. Violet kissed my cheeks and touched my arms and my hands and my shoulders. Her laugh had a raucous timbre, and sometimes she made little sounds of pleasure while she ate. But I also detected lapses in her that I hadn't seen before – five or six seconds here and there when she moved inward to reflect sadly on someone or something. If she was stirring a sauce, her hand would stop, a wrinkle would form between her brows, and she would look vacantly at the stove until she caught herself and began stirring again. Bill's voice seemed both hoarser and more musical than I remembered. Age and cigarettes perhaps, but I listened to it rise and fall and to its frequent pauses with new attentiveness. I felt an added gravity in him, the almost palpable heft of a life that had grown more dense. Violet and Bill seemed a little different, as if their life together had shifted from a major to a minor key. It could have been that Matt's death had changed them, too. It could have been that because Matt had died, I saw in them what I had never seen before, or it could have been that without Matt, my vision of things would never be the same.

The only person who appeared unchanged was Mark. He had never taken up much room in my life, except as Matt's amiable sidekick, and when

Matt had died, Mark had vanished for me as well. But I began to look at him more closely during those meals we shared upstairs. He had grown a little taller, but not much. He had just turned thirteen, but he still had a soft, round, childish face, which I found remarkably sweet. Mark was a very good-looking boy, but his sweetness was separate from his beauty. It came from his facial expressions, which conveyed a perpetual, untouchable innocence, not unlike his hero of the moment – Harpo Marx. At the dinner table, Mark chuckled and clowned and made Harpo's 'googly face.' He read us passages from *Harpo Speaks* and sang 'Hail Fredonia,' from *Duck Soup*. But he also talked about his pity for New York's homeless people, the stupidities of racism, and the cruelty of chicken farmers. He never went deeply into any of these subjects, but whenever he spoke of injustice, his voice, still high and boyish, touched me with its inflections of sympathy. Airy, buoyant, and kind, Mark made me feel lighter. I began to look forward to seeing him, and when he left on the weekends to visit his mother, stepfather, and little brother, Oliver, in Cranbury, New Jersey, I discovered that I missed him.

Over winter break, a few days before they flew to Minnesota for Christmas with the Bloms, Bill and Violet threw a belated birthday party for Mark. He had turned thirteen months earlier, but for Bill the event served as a kind of secular bar mitzvah, a way

229

to acknowledge tradition without ritual. Bill and Violet sent an invitation to Erica, but she chose not to come. In a letter, she informed me that she had decided to remain in Berkeley over the vacation. For weeks I stewed over a gift for Mark. In the end I settled on a chess set, a beautiful board with carved pieces that reminded me of my father, who had taught me the game. I knew that Mark had never learned to play, and I wanted to compose the note that accompanied the present very carefully. In the first draft, I mentioned Matthew. In the second, I didn't. I wrote a third, short and to the point: 'Happy late thirteenth birthday. This gift includes lessons from the giver. Love, Uncle Leo.'

I had planned to do well at Mark's party. I had wanted to do well, but I found I couldn't. I took several trips to the bathroom, not to relieve myself but to grab the sink and hyperventilate for a couple of minutes before returning to the crowd. There must have been sixty people at the party, but I knew only a few of them. Violet rushed from one person to another and then back to the kitchen, where she gave instructions to the three waiters. Bill wandered around with a glass of wine, which he refilled often, his eyes a little red and his voice a little strained. I said hello to Al and Regina, and I greeted Mark, who looked remarkably comfortable in his blue blazer, red tie, and gray flannel pants. He grinned at me and gave me a warm hug just before he shook the hand of Lise Bochart, a sculptor in her early sixties. 'I think

230

your piece at the Whitney is really cool,' Mark told her. Lise cocked her head to one side and her face wrinkled into a big smile. Then she leaned over and gave him a kiss. Mark didn't blush or look away. He eyed her confidently, and after a couple of seconds moved on to another guest.

I had grown used to Mark and was becoming more and more fond of him, but several of Matt's old school friends were among the guests, and as I recognized them one by one, the permanent ache in my chest sharpened into pain. Lou Kleinman had grown at least six inches since I had last seen him. He stood in the corner with Jerry Loo, another buddy of Matt's, snickering over an ad for phone sex he must have picked up in the street, because it had a heel print on its upper-right-hand corner. Another boy, Tim Andersen, hadn't changed at all. I remembered that Matt had felt sorry for the stunted, pale kid who wheezed too much to play sports. I didn't talk to Tim or even look at him, but I seated myself in a chair near where he was standing. From that spot, I could hear him breathing. I had just wanted to take a look at the boy, but instead I sat with my back to him and listened to his asthmatic lungs with a sudden terrible fascination. I hung on to each noisy exhalation as proof that he was alive – frail, runty, ill, maybe – but alive. I listened to the hoarse, greedy life in him and let it torture me. There were so many other noises – one voice on top of another talking – laughing, the clink of silverware on plates, but all I wanted to hear was the noise of Tim's breathing. I yearned to get closer to him, to bend over and put my ear to his mouth. I didn't do it, but I realized that I was sitting in the chair with clenched fists, swallowing audibly to keep down a quaking misery and rage, and then Dan saved me.

Disheveled and dirty, Dan was heading toward me with long strides. He bumped a woman's elbow, spilled her wine, apologized loudly into her startled face, and then continued toward me. 'Leo!' he yelled from a distance of no more than four feet. 'They changed my meds, Leo! The Haldol was making me stiffen up like a board, and I couldn't bend.' Dan held his arms out in front of him and finished his walk toward me like Frankenstein's monster. 'Too much pacing, Leo. Too much talking to myself. So they hauled me into St Luke's for an adjustment. I read my play to Sandy. She's a nurse. It's called *Odd Boy and the Odd Body*.' He paused, leaned over, and said confidingly, 'Leo, guess what? You're in it.'

Dan was very close to me, grinning with his mouth open so that I looked directly at his badly stained teeth. I had never felt so moved by him or so grateful to be near him. For the first time, his madness felt curiously comforting and familiar.

'You put me in your play?' I said to him. 'I'm honored.'

Dan looked sheepish. 'Your character doesn't have any lines.'

'No lines?' I said. 'Just a walk-on?'

'No, Leo's lying down through the whole play.'

'Dead?' I said.

'No!' Dan boomed at me. He looked shocked. 'Sleeping.'

'Oh, I'm a sleeper.' I smiled, but Dan didn't smile back.

'No, I mean it, Leo. I've got you in here.' He tapped a finger to his temple.

'I'm glad,' I said, and I was.

After everyone else had gone home, Dan and I were sitting on the sofa several feet apart. We weren't talking, but we had staked out a place for ourselves together. The insane brother and the broken-down 'uncle' had formed a temporary alliance to survive the party. Bill seated himself between us, putting one arm around each of us, but his eyes were on Mark, who was in the kitchen picking frosting off what was left of the cake. It wasn't until that moment that I remembered Lucille. 'Shouldn't Lucille and Philip and Oliver have been here?' I said to Bill.

'They wouldn't come,' he said. 'She gave me an odd explanation. She said that Philip doesn't want Oliver in the city.'

'Why on earth not?' I said.

'I don't know,' he said, and wrinkled his forehead. That was all that was said about Lucille. Even at a distance, I realized, she had a way of stopping conversation. Her peculiar responses to ordinary talk or, in this case, a simple invitation, often left others in bewildered silence.

I was standing over Mark when he ripped the paper off my gift and saw the chessboard. He leapt up from the floor and threw his arms around my waist. It had been a long, hard birthday party, and I wasn't prepared for his excitement. I clung to him and looked over at Bill, Violet, and Dan, who were all on the sofa. Dan was sound asleep, but Bill and Violet were both smiling with tears in their eyes, and their emotion made it much harder for me to check mine. I stared hard at Dan to keep control of myself. Mark must have felt the heaving in my chest, and when he withdrew from the hug, he must have seen the spasm I felt moving across my face, but he continued to look at me happily, and for reasons difficult to articulate, I felt hugely relieved that I hadn't mentioned Matthew in my note.

Mark learned chess fast. He was a nimble and intelligent player, and his ability excited me. I told him the truth: not only did he understand the moves, but he had the unruffled demeanor necessary to play well, that calculated indifference I had never mastered but which could unnerve even a superior opponent. As my enthusiasm waxed, however, Mark's waned. I told him he should join the chess team at school, and he said that he would look into it, but I don't believe he ever did. I sensed that he was humoring me rather than pleasing himself, and I tactfully withdrew. If he wants to play, I said to Bill, he can ask. He never asked.

★　　★　　★

234

I sank into another life. My writing that year was all for Erica. I wrote no articles, no essays, had no thoughts for another book, but I told Erica everything in long letters that I sent off weekly. I wrote that my teaching had become more passionate and that I spent more time with my students. I wrote that I allowed some of them to ramble on about their private lives during office hours and that I didn't always hear what they were saying, but I recognized their need to say whatever it was and discovered that my distant but benevolent presence was met with gratitude. I wrote about my dinners with Bill and Violet and Mark. I recorded for her the titles of the books I found for Mark on silent comedy and the movie stills from *A Night at the Opera* and *Horse Feathers* I bought for him at a shop on Eighth Street, and I described his happy face when he received my gifts. I also told her that since Matt had died, *O's Journey* had taken on an afterlife that inhabited my hours alone. Sometimes when I sat in my chair in the evenings, I would see parts of the narrative in my mind – the fat figure of B with wings sprouting from her back as she straddled O, her heavy arms outstretched in orgasm and her face a parodic imitation of Bernini's Saint Theresa. I saw the two M's, O's little brothers, clinging to each other behind a door while a burglar robs the house, stealing one of O's paintings – a portrait of the two young M's. But most often, I saw O's last canvas, the one he leaves behind after he disappears. That canvas has no image, only the letter B – the mark of O's creator and the fat woman who embodied him in the work.

I didn't tell Erica that there were evenings when I returned home after dinner and I smelled Violet on my shirt – her perfume and soap and something else, her skin maybe, an odor that deepened the others and made the floral scent corporeal, human. I didn't tell Erica that I liked to breathe in that faint smell, and I didn't tell her that I tried to resist it at the same time. On some nights, I would remove the shirt and throw it into the hamper.

In March, Bill and Violet asked me if I would stay with Mark for a long weekend. They were headed for Los Angeles, where a gallery was showing *O's Journey*. Lucille was also traveling and thought it best not to burden Philip with two children. I moved upstairs with Mark. We were easy together, and Mark was helpful. He did dishes, carried out the garbage, and tidied up after himself. On Saturday night, he put on a tape and lipsynched a pop song for me. He leapt around the living room with an imaginary guitar. Gyrating madly, he affected a tortured expression and finally collapsed to the floor as he imitated the agonies of a rock 'n' roll star whose name I can't remember anymore.

As we talked, however, I noticed that Mark had absorbed little of the subjects generally taught in school – geography, politics, history – and that his ignorance had a willed quality to it. Matthew had served as a scale upon which to weigh differences among boys of his age, but then who was to say that Matt was a barometer of normality? Before he died, his brain had been loaded with information, both trivial and important, from baseball statistics to the battles of the American Civil War. He knew the names of all sixty-four flavors of his favorite brand of ice cream and could identify dozens of contemporary painters, many of whom I didn't recognize. Except for his love of Harpo, Mark's interests were more ordinary – popular music, action and horror movies – and yet he brought to these subjects the same agility of mind, the same fleet brain that had made itself felt in chess. What he lacked in content, he seemed to make up for in quickness.

Mark resisted going to bed. Every night I was with him, he lingered in the doorway of Bill and Violet's bedroom, where I was reading, as if he was unwilling to tear himself away. Fifteen, twenty, twenty-five minutes would pass as he leaned in the doorway and chatted. All three nights, I had to tell him that I was turning in and that he should do the same.

The single hitch in our weekend together was over doughnuts. On Saturday afternoon, I looked for a box of doughnuts I had bought the day before. I searched the pantry but couldn't find them. 'Did you eat the doughnuts?' I called out to Mark, who was in the next room. He walked into the kitchen and looked at me. 'Doughnuts? No.'

'I could have sworn I put them in this cupboard, and now they aren't here. It's strange.'

'Too bad,' he said. 'I like doughnuts. I guess it's one of those household mysteries. Violet always says that the house eats things when you're not looking.' He shook his head, smiled at me, and disappeared into his room. An instant later, I heard him whistling a pop song – high, sweet, and melodic.

At around three o'clock the following afternoon, I answered the telephone. A woman was screaming at me through the receiver in a piercing, angry voice. 'Your son started a fire! I want you over here right now!' I forgot where I was, forgot everything. Too shocked to speak, I breathed into the receiver once and said, 'I don't understand you. My son is dead.'

Silence.

'Aren't you William Wechsler?'

I explained. She explained. Mark and her son had started a fire on the roof.

'That's not possible,' I said. 'He's in his room reading.'

'Wanna bet?' she said loudly. 'He's standing here right in front of me.'

After confirming that Mark wasn't in his room, I walked downstairs and went to retrieve him from the building next door. When she let me into the apartment, the woman was still shaking. 'Where did they get the matches?' she screeched at me when I walked through the door. 'You're

responsible for him, aren't you? Well, aren't you?'
I mumbled yes, and then I said that boys could pick
up matches almost anywhere. What kind of fire was
it? I wanted to know. 'A fire! A fire! What does it
matter what kind?' When I turned to Mark, his face
was vacant. There was no belligerence in it – there
was nothing. The other boy, who looked to be no
more than ten years old, had wet, red eyes. Snot
leaked from his nose as he repeatedly pushed away
his bangs, which instantly fell back into his face. I
apologized weakly and led Mark home in silence.

We talked it over in Mark's room. He told me
that he had met the kid, Dirk, on the roof, and
that Dirk had already started the fire. 'All I did
was stand there and watch.'

I asked him what they had burned.

'Just some paper and stuff. It was nothing.'

I warned him that fires could quickly get out of
control. I told him that he should have let me know
that he was leaving. He listened, his eyes calmly
taking in my comments. Then he said in a voice
that was surprisingly hostile. 'That kid's mother
was crazy!'

Mark's eyes were illegible. They bore a striking
resemblance to Bill's, but they had none of his
father's energy. 'I think she was scared, not crazy,'
I said. 'She was really scared for her son.'

'I guess so,' he said.

'Mark, don't do anything like that again. It
was your job to stop it. You're a lot older than
that boy.'

'You're right, Uncle Leo,' he said. I heard conviction in his voice, and it relieved me.

In the morning, I made Mark French toast and sent him off to school. When we said good-bye, I gave him my hand, but he hugged me instead. When I put my arms around him, he felt small, and the way he pressed his cheek against me made me think of Matthew, not when my son was eleven but when he was four or five.

After Mark left, I climbed the stairs to the roof to look for remnants of the fire. I had thought that I might have to cross over to the next building, where Dirk lived, but I discovered a heap of ash and litter on the roof of our building, and I squatted down to examine it. Feeling both underhanded and a little ridiculous, I stirred the charred debris with a wire hanger that lay nearby. This had not been a bonfire, just a small conflagration that couldn't have lasted very long. I noticed a few partly burned rags and picked one up, part of an athletic sock. Green shards of a broken bottle were scattered among bits of paper, and then I saw a piece of the incompletely burned box – the empty doughnut box. I could still read a few letters on the label: ENTE.

Mark had lied to me. He had quoted Violet so smoothly. He had smiled so easily. It had never occurred to me to doubt him, but even more curious was the fact that if he had told me he had eaten the doughnuts, I wouldn't have cared. When I bought them, I had been thinking of him. I held the bit of cardboard in my hand and looked over the bleak landscape of lower Manhattan's roofs, with their rusted water towers and peeling tar. A wan sun was trying to break through the clouds and a wind had started to blow. I swept the ash and glass into an old grocery bag someone had abandoned on the roof, and as I watched my hands turn gray from the ashes, I had an unexpected feeling of guilt, as though I were somehow implicated in Mark's lie. When I left the roof, I didn't add the piece of burned box to the bag with the rest of the garbage. I walked downstairs and carefully deposited what was left of it in my drawer.

I said nothing to Bill and Violet about the fire. Mark must have been glad that I didn't mention it, must have felt he had an ally in Uncle Leo downstairs, and that's how I wanted it. The fire incident receded the way dreams often do, leaving behind it no more than a sensation of vague discomfort. I seldom thought about it, except when I opened my drawer to inspect my collection, and then I wondered why I had decided to keep that piece of cardboard.

I didn't move it, however, and I didn't throw it away. Some part of me must have felt that it belonged there.

In the fall of 1991, the University of Minnesota Press published *Locked Bodies: An Exploration of Contemporary Body Images and Eating Disorders*. As I read Violet's book, the missing doughnuts and the burned box floated back into my consciousness from time to time. The book began with simple questions: Why are thousands of girls in the West starving themselves now? Why are others gorging and vomiting? Why is obesity on the rise? Why did these once rare diseases become epidemics?

'Food,' Violet wrote, 'is our pleasure and our penance, our good and evil. Like hysteria a hundred years ago, it has become the focus of a cultural obsession that has infected huge numbers of people who never become seriously ill with eating disorders. Fanatical running, the rise of the health club and the health-food store, Rolfing, massage, vitamin therapy, colonics, diet centers, bodybuilding, plastic surgery, a moral horror of smoking and sugar, and a terror of pollutants all testify to an idea of the body as extremely vulnerable – one with failing thresholds, one that is under constant threat.'

The argument continued for almost four hundred pages. The first chapter served as a historical introduction. It ran quickly through the Greeks and the ideal bodies of their gods, lingered for a while on medieval Christianity, its female saints and cult of physical suffering and the broader phenomena of plagues and famines. It touched on neoclassical Renaissance bodies and then the Reformation's suppression of the Virgin and her maternal body. It galloped through eighteenth-century medical drawings and the dissection obsessions born of the Enlightenment and eventually made its way to hunger artists and to the starving girls of Dr

Lasègue, the physician who had first used the word 'anorexia' to describe their illness. In passing through the nineteenth and into the twentieth century, Violet noted Lord Byron's fasts and binges, J. M. Barrie's intractable self-denial, which may have stunted his growth, and Binswanger's case study of Ellen West, a tormented young altruist who died of starvation in 1930, when anorexia was still considered extremely rare.

Violet insisted that our bodies are made of ideas as much as of flesh, that the contemporary obsession with thinness can't be blamed on fashion – which is merely one expression of the wider culture. In an age that has absorbed the nuclear threat, biological warfare, and AIDS, the perfect body has become armor – hard, shiny, and impenetrable. She marshaled evidence from exercise tapes and advertisements for programs and machines, including the telling phrases 'buns of steel' and 'bulletproof abs.' Saint Catherine starved against church authority for Jesus. Late-twentieth-century girls starve for themselves against their parents and a hostile, borderless world. Emaciation in the midst of plenty shows that you are above ordinary desire, obesity that you are protected by stuffing that can ward off all attacks. Violet quoted psychologists and analysts and doctors. She discussed the widely held view that anorexia in particular is a misguided bid for autonomy among girls whose bodies are sites of rebellion for what they can't say. But private histories don't explain epidemics, and Violet made strong arguments that social upheavals lie behind eating disorders, including the breakdown of courting rituals and sexual codes, which leaves young women formless and vulnerable, and she elaborated her idea of 'mixing' – citing developmental research on 'attachment' and studies of infants and young children for whom food becomes the tangible site of an emotional battle.

A large part of the book was taken up by stories, and as I read on, I found the individual cases most absorbing. Raymond, a hugely fat seven-year-old, told his therapist that he thought his body was made of jelly and that if his skin was punctured, his insides would run out. After months of reducing the amounts of food she ingested, Berenice made a meal of a single raisin. She cut it into four pieces with a knife, sucked on the quarters for a good hour and a half, and then, when the last one had dissolved in her mouth, she declared herself 'stuffed.' Naomi went to her mother's house to gorge. Sitting at the kitchen table, she wolfed down vast quantities of food and then vomited the contents of her stomach into plastic bags, which she tied up and hid in various rooms for her mother to find. Anita had a horror of lumps in her food. She solved the problem with a liquid diet. After a while, she turned against color, too. The liquid had to be both pure and clear. Living only on water and one-calorie Sprite, she died at fifteen.

While I didn't suspect Mark of excesses like the

ones Violet recounted, I wondered if he hadn't lied about the doughnuts because he was guilty about eating them. Violet stressed that people who are rigorously honest in most ways often lie about food when their relationship to it has been tainted. I remembered the brown dish of beans and limp vegetables Lucille had cooked the evening I first met her, and in the same instant I recovered an image of her coffee table the night we were together. Lying on top of a pile of other magazines were several copies of one called *Prevention*.

Erica didn't answer my letters as promptly as she had in the beginning. Sometimes two weeks would pass before a letter arrived from her, and I sweated out the days. Her tone wasn't quite the same either. Although she wrote in a straightforward, honest way, I felt a lack of urgency in her telling. Much of what she wrote me, she must have told Dr Richter, too – her psychiatrist, pyschoanalyst, psychotherapist, whom she saw twice a week. She had also become the close friend of a young woman in her department named Renata Doppler – who, among other things, wrote dense, scholarly articles on pornography. She must have talked often to Renata as well, and I know that she called Violet and Bill regularly. I tried not to think of those telephone conversations, tried not to imagine Bill and Violet hearing Erica's voice. My wife's world had expanded, and as it grew, I guessed that my place in it had shrunk. And yet, there were a few sentences here and there to which I clung as evidence of some lingering passion. 'I think of you at night, Leo. I haven't forgotten.'

In May, she wrote to tell me that she was coming to New York for a week in June. She was going to stay with me, but her letters made it clear that the visit didn't mean a resumption of our old life. As the day approached, my agitation mounted. By the morning of her arrival, it had reached a pitch that felt something like an inner scream. The very thought that I would soon see Erica again didn't excite me as much as wound me. As I wandered around the loft trying to calm myself, I realized that I was holding my chest like a man who had just been stabbed. After sitting down, I tried to untangle that feeling of injury but couldn't do it – not fully. I knew, however, that Matt was suddenly everywhere. The loft reverberated with his voice. The furniture seemed to hold the imprint of his body. Even the light from the window conjured Matthew. It won't work, I thought to myself. It's not going to work. As soon as Erica stepped through the door, she started crying.

We didn't fight. We talked in the intimate way of old lovers who haven't seen each other for a long time but hold no grudges. One night, we ate dinner with Bill and Violet in a restaurant and Erica laughed so hard at a Henny Youngman joke Bill told about a man hiding in a closet that she almost choked, and Violet had to beat her on the back. At least once a day Erica stood in the

246

doorway of Matt's room for several minutes and looked in at what remained of it – the bed, his desk and chair, and the watercolor of the city Bill had given me and which I had framed. We made love twice. My physical loneliness had taken on shades of desperation, and when Erica leaned close to kiss me, I leapt at her. She trembled through my attack and had no orgasm. Her lack of pleasure soured my release, and afterward I felt empty. The night before she left, we tried again. I wanted to be careful with her, gentle. I touched her arm cautiously and then kissed it, but my hesitation seemed to irritate her. She lunged for me, grabbed my hips, and pinched my skin with her fingers. She kissed me hungrily and climbed on top of me. When she came, she made a small, sharp noise, and she sighed again and again, even after I had ejaculated. But under our lovemaking I felt a bleakness that couldn't be dispelled. The sadness was in both of us, and I think we pitied ourselves that night, as if we were other people looking down on the couple who lay together on the bed.

In the morning, Erica reassured me that she didn't want a divorce unless I wanted one. I said I didn't. 'I love your letters,' she said. 'They're beautiful.'

The comment annoyed me. 'I think you're glad you're leaving,' I said.

Erica moved her face close to mine and narrowed her eyes. 'Aren't *you* glad I'm leaving?'

'I don't know,' I said. 'I really don't know.'

She put her hand on my face and stroked it. 'We're broken, Leo. It's not our fault. When Matt died it was like our story stopped. There was so much of you in him . . .'

'You'd think we could at least have each other,' I said to her.

'I know,' she said, 'I know.'

After she was gone, I felt guilty because, turbulent as my feelings were, I detected in them the relief Erica had been brave enough to mention. At two o'clock in the afternoon, I drank a glass of Scotch in my chair like an old booze hound. As I told myself not to drink in the afternoon again, I felt the alcohol move into my head and then into my limbs. I leaned back into the fraying cushions of my chair and knew what had happened to me and Erica. We wanted other people. Not new people. Old ones. We wanted ourselves before Matthew died, and nothing we did for the rest of our days would ever bring those people back.

That summer I began to work on Goya's 'black paintings.' Studying his monsters and ghouls and witches kept me occupied for hours at a time during the day, and his demons helped to keep mine at a distance. But when night came, I walked through other imaginary spaces, subjunctive realms in which I saw Matt talking and drawing, and Erica near me – unchanged. These waking fantasies were pure exercises in self-torture, but around that same time Matthew started to come to me in my dreams, and when he came, he was as much there as he had been in life. His body was as real, as whole, as palpable as it had always been. I held him, spoke to him, touched his hair, his hands, and I had what I couldn't have when I was awake – the unshakable, joyous certainty that Matthew was alive.

While Goya didn't feed my gloom, his savage paintings gave new license to my thoughts – permission to open doors that in my former life I had left closed. Without Goya's ardent images, I'm not sure that Violet's piano lesson would have come surging back with such surprising force. The daydream began after I had seen Bill and Violet for dinner. Violet was wearing a pink sundress that showed her breasts. A long walk in the sun that afternoon had turned her cheeks and nose a little red, and while she talked to me about her next book, which had something to do with extreme narcissism, mass culture, pictures, instant communications, and a new illness of late capitalism, I found it hard to listen to her. My eyes kept wandering onto her flushed face and over her bare arms and onto her breasts and then to her fingers, with their pink polish. I left dinner early that evening, spent some time with the objects in my drawer, and then began leafing through a large book of Goya's drawings, starting with the ones for the *Tauromaquia*. While I admit that the artist's sketches of a bullfight have little in common with Violet's piano lesson and her encounter with

Monsieur Renasse, the loose energy of his lines and his fierce rendering affected me like an aphrodisiac. I kept turning the pages, eager for more pictures of brutes and monsters. I knew every one of them by heart, but that night their carnal fury scorched my mind like a fire, and when I looked again at the drawing of a young, naked woman riding a goat on a witches' Sabbath, I felt that she was all speed and hunger, that her crazed ride, born of Goya's sure, swift hand, was ink bruising paper. His beast runs, but his rider is out of control. Her head has fallen back. Her hair streams out behind her and her legs may not cling much longer to the animal's body. I touched the woman's shaded thigh and pale knee, and the gesture sent me to Paris.

I changed the fantasy as it suited me. There were nights when I was content to watch the lesson through a window across the street and other nights when I became Monsieur Renasse. There were nights when I was Jules peeking through a keyhole or floating magically above the scene, but Violet was always on the bench beside one of us, and one of us would always reach out and grab her finger in an abrupt, violent motion and whisper 'Jules' into her ear in a hoarse, insistent voice, and at the sound of the name, Violet's body would always tighten with desire and her head would fall back, and one of us or the other would have her right there on the piano bench, would pull up her pink dress from behind and lower the small underpants of varying colors and

250

descriptions and enter her as she made loud noises of pleasure, or one of us would drag her under a potted palm and part her legs on the floor and make raucous love to her while she screamed her way to orgasm. I released untold amounts of semen into that fantasy and inevitably felt let down afterward. My pornography was no more idiotic than most, and I knew I wasn't the only man who indulged himself in harmless mental romps with the wife of a friend, but the secret pained me nevertheless. I would often think of Erica afterward and then of Bill. Sometimes I tried to supplant Violet with another figure, a nameless stand-in who could take her place, but it never worked. It had to be Violet and it had to be that story, not of two people but of three.

Bill worked long hours on a series of autonomous pieces about numbers. Like *O's Journey*, the works took place inside glass cubes, but these were twice as large – about two feet square. He drew his inspiration from sources as varied as the Cabbala, physics, baseball box scores, and stock market reports. He took a number between zero and nine and played with it in a single piece. He painted, cut, sculpted, distorted, and broke the numerical signs in each work until they became unrecognizable. He included figures, objects, books, windows, and always the written word for the number. It was rambunctious art, thick with allusion – to voids, blanks, holes, to monotheism and the individual, to the dialectic and yin-yang, to the Trinity, the three fates, and three wishes, to the golden rectangle, to seven heavens, the seven lower orders of the sephiroth, the nine Muses, the nine circles of Hell, the nine worlds of Norse mythology, but also to popular references like *A Better Marriage in Five Easy Lessons* and *Thinner Thighs in Seven Days*. Twelve-step programs were referred to in both cube one and cube two. A miniature copy of a book called *The Six Mistakes Parents Make Most Often* lay at the bottom of cube six. Puns appeared, usually well disguised – one, won; two, too, and Tuesday; four, for, forth; ate, eight. Bill was partial to rhymes as well, both in images and words. In cube nine, the geometrical figure for a line had been painted on one glass wall. In cube three, a tiny man wearing the black-and-white prison garb of cartoons and dragging a leg iron has opened the door to his cell. The hidden rhyme is 'free.' Looking closely through the walls of the cube, one can see the parallel rhyme in another language: the German word *drei* is scratched into one glass wall. Lying at the bottom of the same box is a tiny black-and-white photograph cut from a book that shows the entrance to Auschwitz: ARBEIT MACHT FREI. With every number, the arbitrary dance of associations worked together to create a tiny mental landscape that ranged in tone from wish-fulfillment dream to nightmare. Although dense, the effect of the cubes wasn't visually disorienting. Each object, painting, drawing, bit of text, or sculpted figure found its rightful place under the glass according to the necessary, if mad, logic of numerical, pictorial, and verbal connection – and the colors of each were startling. Every number had been given a thematic hue. Bill had been interested in Goethe's color wheel and in Alfred Jensen's use of it in his thick, hallucinatory paintings of numbers. He had assigned each number a color. Like Goethe, he included black and white, although he didn't bother with the poet's meanings. Zero and one were white. Two was blue. Three was red, four was yellow, and he mixed colors: pale blue for five, purples in six, oranges in seven, greens in eight, and blacks and grays in nine. Although other colors and omnipresent newsprint always intruded on the basic scheme, the myriad shades of a single color dominated each cube.

The number pieces were the work of a man at the top of his form. An organic extension of everything Bill had done before, these knots of symbols had an explosive effect. The longer I looked at them, the more the miniature constructions seemed on the brink of bursting from internal pressure. They were tightly orchestrated semantic bombs through which Bill laid bare the arbitrary roots of meaning itself – that peculiar social contract generated by little squiggles, dashes, lines, and loops on a page.

In several pieces Bill alluded to the often tedious business of acquiring the signs we need for comprehension – a fragment of Mark's math homework, a chewed pencil eraser, and my favorite in cube nine: the figure of a boy fast asleep at a desk, his cheek only partly covering a page of algebra. It turned out that these pictures of boredom were more personal than I thought. Bill confided to me that Mark had been doing so badly in school that the headmaster had gently suggested to Bill that he consider looking elsewhere. It wasn't an expulsion, the man had emphasized, merely a bad match between student and school. Mark's high I.Q. didn't compensate for his lack of concentration and discipline. Perhaps a less rigorous curriculum would suit him better. Bill had been on the telephone with Lucille for hours about a new school, and in the end Lucille had found a place that would accept Mark, a 'progressive' institution near Princeton. The school took him with a single condition: they wanted him to repeat the eighth grade. The fall after he turned fourteen, Mark moved to Cranbury with his mother and spent his weekends in New York.

That year he grew six inches. The little boy who had played chess with me was replaced by a lanky teenager, but his temperament stayed the same. I've never seen a boy more free of adolescent heaviness than Mark. His body was as light as his spirit, his step weightless, his gestures graceful. But Bill never stopped worrying about his son's dilatory attitude in school. His school reports were erratic – A's turned to D's. His teachers used adjectives like 'irresponsible' and 'underachieving.' I eased

Bill's mind with platitudes. He's a little immature, I would say, but time will change that. I listed great men who had been lousy students and star students who'd turned into mediocrities. My pep talks usually worked. 'He'll turn it around,' Bill would say. 'Just wait. He'll find his way, even in school.'

Mark began to visit me on the weekends, usually on Sunday afternoon, before he returned to his mother's house. I looked forward to the sound of his feet on the stairs, to his knock, and to his open, untroubled face when I let him into the apartment. Often he would bring a piece of artwork to show me. He had started making small collages from magazines, some of which were interesting. One afternoon in the spring, he appeared at my door with a large shopping bag. After I let him in, I noticed that he had grown since I'd last seen him. 'I can look you straight in the eyes now. I think you're going to be even taller than your father.'

Mark had been smiling at me, but as I spoke, he looked grumpy. 'I don't want to grow anymore,' he said. 'I'm tall enough.'

'What are you, five-ten now? That's not too tall for a man.'

'I'm not a man,' he said peevishly.

I must have looked surprised, because Mark shrugged and said, 'Never mind. I don't really care.' Lifting the bag toward me, he said, 'Dad thought I should show you this.'

After sitting down on the sofa with me, Mark

pulled out a large piece of cardboard, which had been folded in half and opened like a book. The two halves were covered with pictures cut from magazine ads, all of young people. He had also cut out a few words and letters from more ads and pasted them over the images: CRAVE, DANCE, GLAM, YOUR FACE, and SLAP. I found the images a little dull, to be honest, a confusing hodge-podge of the chic and beautiful, and then I noticed the same little photograph of a baby in the middle of both pages. I looked down at the infant's fat, drooping cheeks. 'Is that you?' I said, and laughed.

Mark didn't seem to share my humor. 'There were two copies of that picture. Mom let me have them.'

To the right of one photo and to the left of the other, I noticed two more photographs, both of which had been blurred by several layers of Scotch tape. I looked more closely. 'What are these?' I said. 'Two of the same picture again, right?'

Through the Scotch tape, I made out the vague outline of a head in a baseball cap and a long thin body. 'Who is it?'

'Nobody.'

'Why is he covered up in tape?'

'I don't know. I just did it. I didn't think about it. I thought it looked good.'

'But it's not from a magazine. You must have found it somewhere.'

'I did, but I don't know who it is.'

'This part of the picture is the same on both

sides. The rest isn't. It takes a while to see it, though. There's so much going on around it, but the photos are eerie.'

'You think that's bad?'

'No,' I said. 'I think that's good.'

Mark closed up the cardboard and put it back into the bag. He leaned back on the sofa and put his feet on the coffee table in front of us. His sneakers were enormous – size eleven or twelve. I noticed that he was wearing the oversized, clownish pants favored by boys his age. We were silent for a while, and then I asked him the question that abruptly came to my mind: 'Mark, do you miss Matthew?'

Mark turned to me. His eyes were wide and he pressed his lips together for a moment before he spoke. 'All the time,' he said. 'Every day.'

I fumbled for his hand on the sofa and breathed in loudly. I heard myself grunt with emotion, and my vision blurred. When I had gotten hold of his hand, I felt him squeeze mine firmly.

Mark Wechsler was a few months shy of fifteen. I was sixty-two. I had known him all his life, but until then, I hadn't considered him a friend. All at once, I understood that his future was also mine, that if I wanted a lasting rapport with this boy who would soon become a man, I could have it, and the thought became a promise to myself: Mark will have my attention and care. I've relived that moment many times since then, but in the last couple of years, as with other events of my own life, I've started to imagine it from a third point of view. I see myself reach for my handkerchief, remove my glasses, and wipe my eyes before I blow my nose loudly into the white fabric. Mark looks on at his father's old friend with sympathy. Any informed spectator would have understood that scene. He would know that the emptiness left in me by Matthew's death could never be filled by Mark. He would have understood clearly that it wasn't a matter of one boy replacing another but a bridge built between two people over an absence they both shared. And yet, that person would have been wrong, just as I was wrong. I misread both myself and Mark. The problem is that my scrutiny of the scene from every possible angle doesn't reveal a single clue. I haven't left out words or gestures or even those emotional intangibles that pass between people. I was wrong because, under the circumstances, I had to be wrong.

The idea came to me the following week. I said nothing to Mark, but I wrote to Erica and asked her what she thought. I proposed that we allow Mark to take Matthew's room as a studio where he could work on his collages. His room upstairs was small, and he could use the extra space. The change would mean that the room where Matt had lived would not remain a mausoleum, an uninhabited, unused space for nobody. Mark, Matthew's best friend, would bring life back to it. I argued strenuously for the cause, told Erica that Mark missed Matt every day, and then said it would mean a lot to me if she gave me her permission. I told her frankly that I was often lonely and that having Mark around lifted my spirits. Erica answered me promptly. She wrote that a part of her was reluctant to let the room go, but that after thinking it over, she agreed. In that same letter, she told me that Renata had given birth to a little girl named Daisy, and that she had been made the child's godmother.

The day before Mark took over the room, I opened the door, walked inside, and sat on the bed for a long time. My enthusiasm for the change was replaced by an aching awareness that it was too late to go back on my word. I studied Matt's watercolor. It would have to stay. I decided to mention it to Mark as my only stipulation. I didn't need a memorial space for Matt, I told myself; he lived in me. But as soon as I had thought of the words, the comforting cliché turned gruesome. I imagined Matt in his coffin, his small bones and his hair and his skull under the earth, and I started to shake. The old fantasy of substitution rose up inside me, and I cursed the fact that I hadn't been able to take his place.

Mark brought paper and magazines and scissors and glue and wire and a brand-new boom box to his 'studio.' Throughout the spring, he spent an hour or so in the room every Sunday, cutting and pasting pictures onto cardboard. He rarely worked for more than fifteen minutes at a time. He was constantly interrupting himself to come out and tell me a joke, make a telephone call, or run to the corner to get 'some chips.'

Not long after Mark had settled in, Bill came to see me and asked to take a look at the room. He nodded approvingly at the magazine clippings and cardboard, the pile of notebooks and cup full of pencils and pens.

'I'm glad he has this place,' Bill said. 'It's neutral. It's not his mother's house and it's not mine.'

'He never talks about his life at Lucille's,' I said, realizing suddenly that this was true.

'He doesn't tell us anything either.' Bill paused for several seconds. 'And when I talk to Lucille, all she does is complain.'

'About what?'

'Money. I pay all of Mark's expenses, his clothes, his school, his medical bills – everything except food at her house – but just the other day, she told me that her grocery bills are sky-high because he eats so much. She actually labels the food in the refrigerator she doesn't want him to eat. She counts every penny.'

'Maybe she has to. Are their salaries low?'

Bill gave me a hard, angry look. 'Even when I didn't have two nickels to rub together, I didn't resent feeding my kid.'

By June, Mark had stopped knocking. He had his own key. Matt's nearly empty room had been transformed into a cluttered teen pad. Records,

CDs, T-shirts, and baggy pants filled the closet. Notebooks, flyers, and magazines were piled on the desk. Mark lived between rooms, coming and going as if the two lofts were all one house. Sometimes he arrived as Harpo and rushed around the living room with a horn he had bought at a yard sale near Princeton. He often kept the act going, and I would discover that he was standing beside me with his knee looped through my arm. If Mark made collages that summer, he kept them to himself. He relaxed, read a little, and listened to music I didn't understand, but then by the time it reached my ears in the living room, it was no more than a mechanical thumping that resembled the bass rhythm of a disco song – fast, steady, interminable. He came and went. For six weeks he attended a camp in Connecticut, and he spent another week with his mother on the Cape. Bill and Violet rented a house in Maine for four of the weeks Mark was at camp, and the building seemed to die. Erica decided not to visit. 'I don't want to open the wound,' she wrote. I lived alone with Goya and missed them all.

In the fall, Mark fell back into his old rhythm of weekend visits. He usually took a train from Princeton on Friday evening and made an appearance at my loft on Saturday. Often he returned on Sunday as well for an hour or so. My meals with Bill and Violet dropped off to about twice a month, and I came to rely on Mark's faithful visits as a respite from myself. Sometime in October he mentioned 'raves' for the first time – huge gatherings of young people that lasted through the night. According to Mark, finding a rave required connections with people in the know. Apparently, tens of thousands of other teenagers were also among the cognoscenti, but that didn't dampen Mark's enthusiasm. The word 'rave' was enough to sharpen his features with expectation.

'It's a form of mass hysteria,' Violet said to me, 'a revival meeting without religion, a nineties love-in. The kids work themselves up into a frenzy of good feeling. I've heard there are drugs, but I've never noticed any signs that Mark is high when he gets home. They don't allow alcohol.' Violet sighed and rubbed her neck with her hand. 'He's fifteen. All that energy has to go somewhere.' She sighed again. 'Still, I worry. I feel that Lucille . . .'

'Lucille?' I said to her.

'It's not important,' she said. 'I'm probably just paranoid.'

In November, I noticed an ad in the *Voice* for a reading Lucille was giving only six blocks away, on Spring Street. I hadn't spoken to her since Matthew's funeral, and seeing her name in print prompted an urge to hear her read. Mark had become a part-time resident of my apartment and my intimacy with him drew me toward Lucille, but I also think that my decision to go was fueled by Violet's unfinished remark and Bill's earlier comment about Lucille's stinginess. It wasn't like him to be uncharitable, and I suppose I wanted to judge for myself.

The site of Lucille's reading was a woody bar with poor lighting. As soon as I walked through the door, I looked through the gloom and saw Lucille standing near the far wall with a sheaf of papers in her hand. Her hair was tied back and her pale face was lit by a small overhead lamp that deepened the shadows under her eyes. From that distance, I thought she looked lovely – waiflike and solitary. I walked toward her. She lifted her face to mine, and after a moment she smiled stiffly without opening her mouth. When she spoke, however, her voice was even and reassuring. 'Leo, this is a surprise.'

'I wanted to hear you read,' I said.

'Thank you.'

We were both silent.

Lucille looked uncomfortable. The 'thank you' hung between us with an air of finality.

'That was the wrong response, wasn't it?' she said, and shook her head. 'I'm not supposed to say "Thank you." I should have said "It was nice of you to come" or "Thank you for coming." If you had spoken to me after the reading and said, "I like your poems," then I could have said a flat "thank you," and we would not be standing here wondering what had just happened.'

'The land mines of social intercourse,' I said. The word intercourse made me pause for a second. A bad choice, I thought.

She ignored the comment and looked down at her papers. Her hands were trembling. 'Readings are hard for me,' she said. 'I'm going to prepare for a few minutes.' Lucille walked away, sat down on a chair, and began to read to herself. Her lips moved and her hands continued to shake.

About thirty people came to listen to her. We sat at tables, and a number of the guests drank beer and smoked while she read. In a poem called 'Kitchen,' Lucille named objects, one after the other. As the list grew, it began to form a crowded verbal still life, and I closed my eyes from time to time to listen to every beat of the syllables as she read. In another poem, she dissected a sentence uttered by a nameless friend: 'You don't really mean that.' It was a witty, logical, and convoluted analysis of the intimidation inherent in such a statement. I think I smiled through every line of the poem. As she read on, I began to understand that the tone of the work never varied. Scrupulous, concise, and invested with the comedy inherent in distance, the poems allowed no object, person, or insight to take precedence over any other. The field of the poet's experience was democratized to a degree that leveled it to one enormous field of closely observed particulars – both physical and mental. I was amazed that I had never noticed this before. I remembered sitting beside her, my eyes on the words she had written, and I remembered her voice as she explained the reasoning behind a decision in her clean economical sentences, and I felt nostalgic for the lost camaraderie between us.

I bought her book, *Category*, after the reading and waited in line for her to sign it. I was the last person of seven. She wrote 'for Leo' and looked up at me.

'I would like to write something amusing but my mind is blank.'

I leaned over the table where she was sitting. 'Just put "from your friend Lucille."'

As I watched her pen move across the page, I asked her if she wanted me to find her a cab or walk her to wherever she was going. She said she was headed for Penn Station, and we stepped outside into the cold November night. The wind blew past us, bringing with it the smell of gasoline and Asian food. As we walked down the street, I looked at her long beige raincoat and saw that the worn garment was missing a button. The sight of the loose thread dangling from her open coat sparked a feeling of sympathy for her that was immediately followed by a memory of her gray dress twisted around her waist and her hair falling across her face as I held her by the shoulders and pushed her down onto the sofa.

As we walked, I said, 'I'm glad I came. The poems are good, very good. I think we should stay in touch, particularly now that I see so much of Mark.'

She turned her head and looked up at me, her face puzzled. 'You see him more than before?'

265

I stopped walking. 'Because of the room, you know?'

Lucille paused on the sidewalk. Under the street-lamp I noticed the deep lines around her mouth as she gave me a puzzled look. 'The room?'

I felt a growing pressure on my lungs. 'I've given him Matthew's room as a studio. He began to use it last spring. He comes every weekend.'

Lucille continued walking. 'I didn't know that,' she said evenly.

I began several questions in my mind, but I noticed that Lucille had quickened her step. She lifted her hand for a taxi and turned to me. 'Thank you for coming,' she said, speaking the line she had missed earlier, but only her eyes showed amusement.

'It was a pleasure,' I said, and took her hand. For an instant, I contemplated kissing her cheek, but her set jaw and compressed lips stopped me, and I squeezed her hand instead.

We were on West Broadway by then, and as I watched the cab drive north, I noticed the moon in the sky over Washington Square Park. It was still early. The crescent shape of that moon with a wisp of cloud across it replicated almost exactly the painted moon I had been looking at that afternoon in one of Goya's early witchcraft paintings. Pan, in the form of a goat, is surrounded by a circle of witches. Despite the gruesome cabal around him, the pagan god looks rather innocent with his empty eyes and goofy expression. Two of the witches offer him infants. One is a gray and emaciated child, the other plump and rosy. From the position of his hoof, it's clear that Pan wants the fat baby. As I crossed the street, I thought of Bill's witch, Violet's comments on hexed maternity, and then I wondered what she had meant to say about Lucille. I also wondered about Mark's silence. What did it mean? I imagined asking him, but the question 'Why didn't you tell your mother about Matthew's room?' had an absurd ring to it. When I turned the corner onto Greene and walked down the sidewalk toward my building, I realized that my mood had suddenly dropped and a growing sadness was following me home.

Mark's night life escalated in the following months. I heard his feet on the stairs as he leapt down them to rush out for the evening. The girls laughed and shrieked. The boys shouted and cursed in the deep voices of men. Mark's love for Harpo was supplanted by DJs and techno, and his pants grew ever wider, but his smooth young face never lost its expression of childish wonder, and he always seemed to have time for me. While we talked, he would lean against my kitchen wall and fiddle with a spatula or literally hang in my doorway with his hands on the lintel and his legs swinging. It's odd how little I've retained of what we actually said to each other. The content of Mark's conversation was usually dull and attenuated, but his delivery was superb and that's what I recall best – the earnest, plaintive tone of his voice, his bursts of laughter, and the languid movements of his long body.

On a Saturday morning in late January, my relationship with Mark took a small turn I hadn't expected. I was sitting in the kitchen reading the *Times* and drinking a cup of coffee when I heard a faint whistling noise from somewhere near the back of the apartment. I froze, listened, and heard it again. Following the sound to Matthew's room, I opened the door and discovered Mark sprawled on the bed whistling through his nose while he slept. He was wearing a T-shirt that had been torn in half and then reattached with what looked like several hundred safety pins. A slice of bare skin showed through the gap. His huge beltless pants had slipped down to his thighs, revealing a pair of underpants with the maker's name written across the elastic band. His pubic hair curled out from between his legs, and for the first time, I recognized that Mark was a man – at least physically a man – and for some reason, this truth appalled me.

I had never said he could sleep in the room, and the idea that he had arrived in the middle of the night without my permission irritated me. I glanced around the room. Mark's backpack and coat lay in a pile on the floor beside one of his sneakers. When I turned toward Matt's picture, I saw that pasted onto the glass were pictures of five pale, thin girls in short skirts and platform shoes. Over their heads were the words THE GIRLS OF CLUB

268

USA. My irritation turned to anger. I walked to the bed, grabbed Mark by the shoulders, and began to shake him. He moaned and then opened his eyes. He looked at me without recognition. 'Go away,' he said.

'What are you doing here?' I demanded.

He blinked. 'Uncle Leo.' He smiled weakly, pushed himself up on his elbows, and looked around. His mouth hung open. His face looked flaccid, moronic. 'Wow,' he said. 'I didn't think you'd be so upset.'

'Mark, this is my apartment. You have a room here to do your artwork or listen to music, but you have to ask me if it's all right to sleep here. Bill and Violet must be worried sick.'

Mark's eyes were slowly gaining focus. 'Yeah,' he said. 'But I couldn't get in upstairs. I didn't know what to do, so I came here. I didn't want to wake you up, because it was late. Besides,' he said, and cocked his head to one side, 'I know you sometimes have trouble sleeping.'

I lowered my voice. 'Did you lose your key?'

'I don't know how it happened. It must have fallen off my ring somehow. I didn't want to wake up Dad and Violet either, and I still had your key, so I used it.' Mark's eyes widened as he spoke to me. 'I probably made the wrong decision.' He sighed.

'You'd better go upstairs right now and tell your father and Violet that you're all right.'

'I'm on my way,' he said.

Before he left, Mark put his hand on my arm and looked me directly in the eyes. 'I just want you to know that you're a real friend to me, Uncle Leo, a real friend.'

After Mark left, I returned to my cold coffee. Within minutes, I regretted my anger. Mark's offense had been caused by poor judgment – nothing more. Had I ever actually said that he couldn't spend the night? The problem wasn't Mark but Matthew. The sight of Mark's mature body on my son's bed had shaken me. Was it that the six-foot boy-man had violated the invisible but sacred outlines of the eleven-year-old child whom I still imagined sleeping in that bed? Maybe, but I wasn't really angry until I saw the stickers. I had told him that the watercolor was the single object in the room that mustn't be touched. Mark had agreed with me: 'That's cool. Matt was a great artist.' Mark hadn't been thinking, I said to myself. He might be thoughtless, but he isn't malicious. Remorse shriveled my righteous anger to nothing, and I decided to walk upstairs and apologize to him immediately.

Violet opened the door. She was wearing only a long white T-shirt, probably Bill's, and I could see her nipples through the material. Her cheeks were flushed. Several sweaty strands of hair hung down in her forehead. She smiled and said my name. Bill was standing a few feet behind her, wearing a white bathrobe and smoking a cigarette. Not knowing where to look, I glanced down at the floor and said, 'I actually came up to see Mark. I wanted to tell him something.'

Bill answered. 'Sorry, Leo. He was going to come this weekend, but he decided at the last minute to stay with his mother. She's taking him and Oliver riding at some stables near there.'

I looked at Bill and then at Violet, who smiled and said, 'We're having a dissipated weekend.' She let her head fall back and stretched. The T-shirt rose up her thighs.

I excused myself. I hadn't been prepared for Violet's breasts under her shirt. I hadn't been prepared to see the faint darkness of her pubic hair under the thin white cloth or her face looking a little soft and silly after sex. Without pausing, I walked downstairs, found a razor blade, and scraped off the stickers that were covering up Matt's painting.

When I confronted Mark about lying to me the following weekend, he looked surprised. 'I didn't lie, Uncle Leo. I changed my plans with Mom. I called Dad, but they were out. I came up to New York anyway to see some friends, and then I had the key problem.'

'But why didn't you tell Bill and Violet that you were here?'

'I was going to, but it seemed kind of complicated, and I remembered that I had to get a bus back to Mom's, because I promised her that I'd take care of Ollie in the afternoon.'

I accepted the story for two reasons. I recognized that the truth is often muddled, a tangle of mishaps and blunders that converge to appear unlikely, and when I looked at Mark as he stood before me with his large steady blue eyes, I was absolutely convinced that he was telling the truth.

'I know I mess up,' he said. 'But I really don't mean to.'

'We all mess up,' I said.

The image of Violet late that Saturday morning colored my memory like a deep stain I couldn't rub out, and when I remembered her, I always remembered Bill, too, standing behind her with a cigarette, his eyes fixed on mine and his large body heavy with spent pleasure. That picture of the two of them kept me awake at night. I would lie on my bed with speeding nerves and a body that hovered over the sheets rather than settled into them. Sometimes I would get up, go to my desk, and check my drawer, emptying its contents slowly and methodically. I touched Erica's socks and studied Matt's picture of Dave and Durango. I examined my aunt and uncle's wedding picture. One night I counted the roses among the other flowers in Marta's bouquet. There were seven roses. The number made me think of Bill's cube for seven and the thick layer of dirt that covered its bottom. If you held up the cube, you could see the white number from below, not whole but in pieces, like a disintegrating body. I fingered the waxy bit of cardboard that I had saved from the fire on the roof, and then I stared down at my hands and the blue veins that stood out from the bones below my knuckles. Lucille had once called them psychic's hands, and I wondered what it would be like to penetrate the minds of others. I knew little enough about myself. I continued to examine my hands, and the longer I looked at them the more foreign they seemed, as if they belonged to another person. I felt guilty. At least that was the name I gave to the lowering ache beneath my ribs. I was guilty of greed – a rapacious longing that I fought every day – but its object wasn't clear. Violet was only a single strand in the thick knot of my desires. My guilt was bound up in the whole story. I turned to look at my painting of Violet. I walked over to it and stood in front of her image and reached out to touch the shadow of a man that Bill had painted into the canvas – his shadow, I remembered that when I first saw it, I had mistaken it for my own.

Erica wrote that she was worried about Violet. 'She's plagued by irrational fears about Mark. I think the fact that she couldn't have a child has finally caught up with her. She hates sharing Mark with Lucille. On the telephone the other day she kept saying, 'I wish he were mine. I'm afraid.' But when I asked her what frightened her, she said she didn't know. When Bill is gone on his trips to Japan and Germany, I think you should check on her. You know how much I care about her, and think of what she did for us after Matt died.'

Two nights later, Bill and Violet invited me for dinner upstairs. Mark was at his mother's, and the three of us stayed up late. The conversation moved from Goya to Violet's ongoing analysis of popular culture to Bill's new project – making a hundred and one doors that opened onto rooms – to Mark. Mark was flunking chemistry. He had pierced his lip. He lived for raves. None of this was extraordinary, but during the evening I noticed that whenever Violet talked about Mark, she couldn't finish her sentences. On every other topic, she spoke as she always did, easily and fluently, rounding off her statements with periods, but Mark made her hesitant, and her words were left hanging without ends.

Bill drank a lot that night. By midnight, he had his arms around Violet on the sofa and was declaring her the most wonderful and beautiful woman that had ever lived. Violet untangled herself from Bill's embrace and said, 'That's it. When you start in on your undying love for me, I know you've had too much. It's time to call it a night.'

'I'm fine,' Bill said. His voice was thick and grumpy.

Violet turned to him. 'You are fine,' she said, trailing her finger along his unshaven cheek. 'Nobody is finer than you.' I watched the motion of her hand as she smiled at him. Her eyes were as steady and clear as I had ever seen them.

Bill softened under her touch. 'A last toast,' he said.

We lifted our glasses.

'To the people dearest to my heart. To Violet, my beloved and indomitable wife, to Leo, my closest and most loyal friend, and to Mark, my son. May he weather the harrowing years of adoleshence.'

Violet smiled at the slur.

Bill continued. 'May we always be a family as we are now. May we love each other for as long as we live.'

That night there was no piano lesson. When I closed my eyes, the only person I saw was Bill.

I didn't visit the Bowery until the following fall. Bill drew and planned but didn't start the construction of his doors until September. It was a Sunday afternoon in late October. The sky was cloudy and the weather had turned very cold. After I turned my key in the lock of the steel door, I stepped into the dingy, darkened hallway and heard the noise of a door opening to my right. Startled by the sound of life from long-abandoned rooms, I turned and noticed two eyes, a pair of white eyebrows, and the dark brown nose of a man from between several chains. 'Who's that?' he boomed at me in a voice so deep and rich I expected an echo.

'I'm a friend of Bill Wechsler's,' I said, and immediately wondered why I had bothered to explain my presence to this stranger.

Instead of answering me, he shut the door fast. A loud rattle and two clinks followed his disappearance. As I climbed the stairs, wondering about the new tenant, I saw Lazlo leaving and took note of his orange vinyl pants and pointed black shoes. When we met, he drawled out a cool, 'Hey, Leo,' smiled at me, and I saw his teeth. One front tooth overlapped the other slightly, not an unusual feature, but in that instant, I knew that I had never seen his teeth before. Lazlo paused on a step.

'Read your views book,' he said. 'Got it from Bill.'

'Really?'

'It was great, man.'

'Why, thank you, Lazlo. I'm very flattered.'

Lazlo didn't move. He looked down at the step. 'Thought I'd take you out to eat sometime, you know.' He paused, moved his head up and down and beat a brief rhythm on his orange thigh as if an inaudible jazz tune had suddenly interrupted his speech. 'You and Erica helped me out.' Five more beats to his thigh. 'You know.'

The muttered 'you know' seemed to stand in place of 'Would that be all right?' I said that I would be delighted to have dinner with him. Lazlo said, 'Cool' and continued down the stairs. On the way, he patted the railing and moved his head to the beat of that same music, which must have been playing somewhere in the invisible corridors of his mind.

'What's up with Lazlo?' I said to Bill. 'First he smiled at me and then he invited me to dinner.'

'He's in love,' Bill said. 'He's madly, passion-ately in love with a girl named Pinky Navatsky. She's a great-looking dancer who performs with a company called Broken. A lot of shaking and contortion and sudden violent kicks. Maybe you've read about them.'

I shook my head.

'His work's getting better, too. He's com-puterized those sticks. They move now, and I think the stuff is interesting. He's in a group show at P.S. 1.'

'And the stentorian voice on the first floor?'

'Mr Bob.'

'I didn't know those rooms had been rented.'

'They're not. He's squatting. He hasn't been here long. I don't know how he got in, but he's in now. He introduced himself to me as 'Mr Bob.' We've got a deal that I keep him a secret from the landlord. Mr Aiello almost never comes in from Bayonne anyway.'

'Mad?' I said.

'Probably. Doesn't bother me. I've lived with crazy people all my life, and he needs a roof. I gave him some old kitchen stuff and Violet packed up a blanket and some dishes and a hot plate she had from her apartment. He likes Violet. Calls her "Beauty."'

The studio had become a vast construction zone, crowded with materials, which made it look smaller than it really was. Doors of varying sizes lay in piles near the window along with stacks of Sheetrock.

Sawdust and lumber scraps covered the floor. In front of me, however, were three oak doors of different heights attached to small rooms that were no wider or higher than the doors, although their depths seemed to vary.

'Try the middle one,' Bill said. 'You have to go inside and close the door behind you. You're not claustrophobic, are you?'

I shook my head.

The door was only five feet five inches tall, which meant that I had to bend down to enter the space. After pulling the door shut behind me, I found myself hunched over in a plain white box, about six feet deep, with a glass ceiling for light and a cloudy mirrored floor. At my feet, I noticed what appeared to be a small pile of rags. Standing was so uncomfortable that I kneeled down to examine the rags, but when I touched them, I discovered that they were made of plaster. At first I saw only the murky reflection of my own gray, beaky face staring up at me, but then I noticed that there was a hole in the plaster. I put my cheek to the mirror and looked into it. A splintered image of a child had been painted onto the underside of the plaster, which was then reflected onto the mirror. The little boy seemed to float in the mirror – his arms and legs detached from his torso. It wasn't a picture of violence or war, but something dreamlike and weirdly familiar – an image I couldn't look at without also seeing my own muzzy face. I closed my eyes. When I opened them again, the mirror looked watery, uterine, the boy more distant, and I realized that I didn't want to see it anymore. I felt a little dizzy and then nauseated. I stood up too quickly, hit my head on the ceiling, and grabbed the door-knob. It stuck. Suddenly, I desperately needed to get out of that place. After I gave it a fierce tug, the door opened and I nearly fell onto Bill.

'Are you okay?' he said. 'You're sweating.'

Bill had to help me to a chair. I stammered out my embarrassment and apology as I breathed deeply and wondered what had happened to me behind the door. We were silent for at least a minute while I recovered from my bout of faintness. I thought again about the reflection under that clump of plaster. Maybe it had been more like a pile of bandages. The boy had seemed to float in an oily, heavy liquid, his body in pieces. He would never emerge intact.

I spoke breathlessly. 'Matt. Drowning. I didn't understand it until now.'

When I looked up at Bill, he looked startled. 'I had no intention . . .'

I interrupted him. 'I know that. It just hit me that way.'

Bill placed his hands on both my shoulders and squeezed them for a moment. Then he walked over to the one clear space near the window and looked out. He was silent for several seconds before he said, 'I loved Matthew, you know.' He spoke very quietly. 'That year before he died, I understood what he was and what was in him.' Bill moved his hand to the pane.

I rose from the chair and walked toward him.

'I envied you,' he said. 'I wished . . .' He paused and breathed through his nose. 'I still wish that Mark were more like him, and I feel bad for wishing it. Matt was open to everything. He didn't always agree with me.' Bill smiled at the memory. 'He argued with me. I wish Mark . . .'

I said nothing. After another short pause, he continued talking. 'It would've been so much better for Mark if Matthew had lived. For all of us, of course, but Matt felt the ground under his feet.' Bill looked down at the Bowery. I saw gray in his hair. He's aging fast now, I thought. 'Matt wanted to grow up. He would've become an artist. I believe that. He had the talent. He had the need. He had the lust for work.' Bill rubbed his hair. 'Mark's still a baby. He has great gifts, but somehow he's not equipped to use them. I'm afraid for him, Leo. He's like Peter Pan in exile from Never-Never-Land.' Bill was silent for several seconds. 'My memories of being a teenager don't help me. I never liked crowds. Fads didn't interest me. If everybody loved it, I wasn't interested. Drugs, flower power, rock 'n' roll. It wasn't for me. I was looking at icons, copying Caravaggio and seventeenth-century drawings. I wasn't even a good rebel. I was against the war. I marched in protests, but the truth was, a lot of the rhetoric grated on me. All I really wanted to do was paint.'

Bill turned toward me and lit a cigarette, cupping his hands around the match as though he were outside in a wind. He pressed his lips together and said, 'He lies, Leo. Mark lies.'

I looked at Bill's pained face. 'Yes,' I said. 'I've sometimes wondered about that.'

'I catch him in little lies, lies that don't make any sense. I sometimes think he lies just to lie.'

'It might be a phase,' I said.

Bill looked away from me. 'He's been lying for a long time. Ever since he was a little boy.'

Bill's frank statement jarred me. I hadn't been aware of a history of lying. He had lied about eating the doughnuts and he had probably lied to me the morning after he slept in Matt's room, but I knew nothing of more lies.

'At the same time,' Bill said, 'he has a good heart. He's a gentle soul, my son.' He waved the cigarette at me. 'He likes you, Leo. He told me that he feels free with you, that he can talk to you.'

I went to stand by Bill at the window. 'I like seeing him. These last few months, we've talked quite a bit.' I turned toward the street. 'He's listened to my stories. I've listened to his. You know, he told me that when he was living in Texas, he used to pretend that Matt was there with him. He called him "Imaginary Matt." He said he used to have conversations with "Imaginary Matt" in the bathroom before he went to school.' I looked out at the roofs across the Bowery and then down at a man lying on the sidewalk, his feet in two brown paper bags.

'I didn't know that,' he said.

I stood beside him until he finished the cigarette. His eyes were distant. 'Imaginary Matt,' he said once and then fell silent for a while. He stubbed out the cigarette beneath his foot and turned back to the window. 'Of course,' he said, 'my father thought I was crazy, thought I'd never make a living.'

I left Bill soon after that. At the bottom of the stairs, I opened the door to the street and heard the voice of Mr Bob again, this time from behind me. Resonant and beautiful, its round bass tones forced me to listen, and I stopped on the threshold. 'May God shine down upon you. May God shine down upon your head and your shoulders and your arms and legs and upon your whole body with radiant beneficence. May he save you and keep you in his mercy and goodness from the shattering ways of Satan. God go with you, my son.' I didn't turn around, but I felt quite sure that Mr Bob had delivered his benediction through a tiny crack in the door. Outside I squinted in the glare of the sun as it pushed its way through the clouds, and by the time I turned onto Canal Street, I realized that the squatter's strange blessing had lightened my step.

The following January, Mark introduced me to Teenie Gold. About five feet tall and seriously underweight, Teenie had white skin that was tinged with gray beneath her eyes and on her lips. A shock of blue colored her otherwise platinum hair, and a gold ring glittered in her nose. She was wearing a shirt with pink teddy bears on it that looked as if it might once have belonged to a two-year-old. When I offered her my hand, she took it with an air of surprise, like a stranger performing a bizarre greeting ritual on a remote island. Once she had retrieved her limp hand from me, she stared at the floor. While Mark ran to find something he had left in Matt's room, I asked Teenie polite questions, which she answered in short, anxious fragments, without once raising her eyes. Her school was Nightingale. She lived on Park Avenue. She wanted to be a fashion designer. When Mark returned, he said, 'I'll get Teenie to show you some of her drawings. She's amazingly talented. Guess what, it's Teenie's birthday today.'

'Happy birthday, Teenie,' I said.

She stared at the floor and moved her head back and forth as her face turned red, but she didn't answer.

'Hey,' Mark said. 'That reminds me. When's your birthday, Uncle Leo?'

'February nineteenth,' I said.

Mark nodded. 'Nineteen thirty, right?'

'Right,' I said, a little baffled, but before I could say anything, they disappeared out the door.

Teenie Gold left an odd impression on me – something wistful and eerie, akin to the feeling I'd once had in London after strolling past hundreds of dolls in the Bethnal Green Museum of Childhood. Part baby, part clown, part woman with a broken heart, Teenie looked damaged, as if her neuroses had written themselves onto her body. Although Mark had begun to look a little absurd in his teen getup – the big pants, the little gold stud that gleamed from under his bottom lip, the platform sneakers he had taken to wearing that elevated him to a massive six foot five – his poise and open, friendly manner contrasted sharply with Teenie's lowered gaze and thin, tense body.

In themselves, clothes are unimportant, but I observed that Mark's new friends cultivated a wan, undernourished aesthetic that reminded me of the way the Romantics had glorified tuberculosis. Mark and his friends had an idea of themselves, and illness played a role in that idea, but I couldn't name the sickness. Drawn faces, thin, pierced bodies, colored hair, and platform shoes seemed innocuous enough. After all, stranger fads had come and gone. I remembered the stories of young men who threw themselves out of windows in yellow jackets after reading *Werther*. A rage for suicide. Goethe came to detest the novel, but in its day the book stormed the ranks of the young and vulnerable. Teenie inspired thoughts of faddish deaths not only because she looked sicker than Mark's other friends, but because I had begun to understand that in that circle, looking unwell was considered attractive.

★   ★   ★

284

I saw very little of Bill and Violet that spring. I still shared the occasional dinner with them upstairs, and Bill telephoned me from time to time, but the life they were living took them away from me. They went to Paris for a week in March for a show of the number pieces and from there they travelled to Barcelona, where Bill lectured to students at an art school. Even when they were at home, they often left for the evening to attend dinners and openings. Bill hired two more assistants, a whistling carpenter named Damion Dapino to help build the doors and a gloomy young woman named Mercy Banks to answer his mail. Bill regularly turned down invitations to teach, discuss, lecture, or sit on panels all over the world, and he needed Mercy to pen his 'no thank yous.'

One afternoon while I was waiting in line at the Grand Union, I paged through a copy of *New York* magazine and found a small picture of Bill and Violet at an art opening. Bill had his arm around his wife and was looking down at her as Violet smiled into the camera. The photograph was evidence of Bill's changing status, a glimmer of fame even in his critical hometown. It had been under way for a long time – that slide into the third person that had turned his proper name into a salable commodity. I bought the magazine. At home, I cut out the picture and put it in my drawer. I wanted the picture there, because the photo's small dimensions imitated the proportions of distance – two figures standing very far away from me. I had never put anything to remind me of Bill and Violet in the drawer before that, and I understood why. It was a place to record what I missed.

Despite its morbid qualities, I didn't use my drawer for grief or self-pity. I had begun to think of it as a ghostly anatomy in which each object articulated one piece of a larger body that was still unfinished. Each thing was a bone that signified absence, and I took pleasure in arranging these fragments according to different principles. Chronology provided one logic, but even this could change, depending on how I read each object. Were Erica's socks the sign of her leaving for California or were they really a token of the day Matt died and our marriage began to fail? For days I worked on possible time tables and then abandoned them for more secret, associative systems, playing with every possible connection. I put Erica's lipstick beside Matt's baseball card one day and moved it near the doughnut box on another. The link between the latter two objects was delightfully obscure but plain once I noticed it. The lipstick conjured Erica's colored mouth, the doughnut box Mark's hungry one. The connection was oral. I grouped the photograph of my twin cousins, Anna and Ruth, with the wedding picture of their parents for a while, but then I shifted it to sit beside Matt's play program on one side and the photo of Bill and Violet on another. Their meanings depended on their placement, what I thought of as a mobile syntax. I played this game only at night before I went to bed. After a couple of hours, the intense mental effort required to justify moving objects from one position to another made me tired. My drawer proved to be an effective sedative.

The first Friday in May, I was awoken from a deep sleep by noises in the stairwell outside my apartment. I turned on the light and saw that the clock read four-fifteen. I stood up and walked into the living room, and as I neared the door I heard someone laugh from the landing and then the distinct sound of a key turning in my lock.

'Who's there?' I said in a loud voice.

Someone screeched. I opened the door and saw Mark dart away from the threshold. I stepped into the hallway. The light on the landing must have burned out, because it was dark, and the only illumination came from the floor above. I noticed that Mark had two companions with him. 'What's going on, Mark?' I said, squinting at him. He had moved toward the wall and I couldn't see his face clearly.

'Hi,' he said.

'It's four o'clock in the morning,' I said. 'What are you doing here?'

One of the others stepped forward – a ghostly figure of uncertain age. In the dim light his complexion looked very pale, but I couldn't tell if it was caused by ill health or an application of theater makeup. The man's step was tremulous, and when I looked down at his feet, I saw that he was wearing very high platform shoes. He waved a small hand in my direction. 'Uncle Leo, I presume,' he whined in a falsetto, and then giggled. His lips looked blue, and I noticed that his hands were shaking as he spoke. The man's eyes, however, were sharp, even vigilant, and they didn't leave mine. I forced myself to meet his gaze. After a couple of seconds, he looked down, and I turned my eyes to the third person, who was sitting on the steps. This boy looked very young. Had he not been with the other two, I would have guessed his age as not more than eleven or twelve. A delicate, feminine person with very long eyelashes and a small pink mouth, he was clutching a green purse on his knees. The clasp had come open, and inside I saw a jumble of tiny cubes – red, white, yellow, and blue. The boy was carrying around Lego blocks. He yawned loudly.

A girl's voice came from above me, 'Poor guy, you're tired.' I looked up and saw Teenie Gold at the top of the stairs.

She was wearing wings made of ostrich feathers that shook as she came down the stairs, one wobbly foot at a time. She held out her skinny arms like a high-wire walker, seemingly oblivious to the railing within inches of her hand. She stared down, her chin tucked onto her chest.

'Do you need help, Teenie?' I said, and stepped into the hallway.

The pale man backed away from me nervously, and I saw him finger something in his pants pocket.

I turned to Mark again, who looked at me with wide eyes. 'Everything's okay, Leo,' he said. 'Sorry we woke you.' Mark's voice sounded different – lower, or perhaps it was just his inflection that had changed.

'I think we should talk, Mark.'

'I can't. We're on our way out. Gotta go.' He stepped away from the wall and I glimpsed his T-shirt for half a second before he turned away. Something was written on it – ROHYP . . . He started down the stairs. The white man and the child loitered after him. Teenie was still making her way down the stairs toward me. I pulled the door shut, locked it, and hooked the chain, something I rarely bothered with. And then I did something I'd never done. I clicked off the light and moved my feet as if I were returning to bed. How authentic this ruse was I have no idea, but I put my ear to the door and heard the pale man say loudly, 'No K tonight, huh, M&M?'

The irony wasn't lost on me. I had turned myself into a spy, had listened through a door only to discover that I was eavesdropping on a language I didn't understand. The name M&M turned me cold, however. I knew full well that it might have been a nickname for one of them, taken from the candy by the same name, but Bill's two childish figures from *O's Journey* had also been M's, and the possible reference made me uneasy. Then I heard a rumble, followed by a gasp from the stairs, and I rushed into the hallway to see what had happened.

Teenie was lying on the landing below me. I walked down the steps and helped her to her feet. She didn't look at me once while I took her by the arm and led her down the stairs. Ridiculous shoes seemed to be an adolescent requirement. Teenie was wearing black patent-leather Mary Janes with absurdly high heels, shoes that would have been a challenge to walk in stone-cold sober, and Teenie was three sheets to the wind. As I held her arm, she swayed from her hips, first in one direction, then the other. At the bottom of the steps I opened the door for her. I had no key and was wearing my pajamas, which prevented me from going any farther. When I looked up toward Grand Street, I saw Mark and his two cohorts standing at the end of the block.

'Are you going to be okay, Teenie?' I said, looking down at her.

She nodded at the sidewalk.

'You don't have to go with them,' I said suddenly. 'You can come back in with me, and I'll call you a car.'

Without looking up, she shook her head no. Then she started to walk toward them. I remained standing in the doorway to watch her. She reeled first to the right and then to the left, zigzagging her way down the block toward her three friends – a small winged creature with buckling ankles who would never fly.

The following morning, I called Bill. I hesitated before I did it, but the incident had left me uneasy. For a sixteen-year-old, Mark seemed to have unbridled freedom, and I began to think that Bill and Violet were overly permissive. But it turned out that Bill hadn't known that Mark was in the city. He thought that he was arriving on the train from his mother's early that afternoon. Lucille was under the impression that he was spending the night with one of his classmates in Princeton. When Mark arrived that afternoon, Bill telephoned and asked me to come upstairs.

Mark stared at his knees while Bill and Violet questioned him about lying. He claimed it was all 'a mix-up.' He hadn't lied. He thought he was going over to Jake's house, but then Jake decided to go to New York to see a friend, and he went with him. Where was Jake last night, then? Bill wanted to know. Leo hadn't seen Jake in the hallway. Mark said that Jake had gone off with some other people. Bill told Mark that lying undermined trust and that he had to stop. Mark vehemently denied that he had lied. Everything he had said was true. Then Violet mentioned drugs.

'I'm not stupid,' Mark said. 'I know drugs screw you up. I saw a documentary on heroin once, and it really freaked me out. I'm just not into that.'

'Teenie was high last night,' I said, 'and that pale fellow was shaking like a leaf.'

'Just because Teenie's messed up doesn't mean I am.' Mark looked directly at me. 'Teddy shakes because it's part of his act. He's an artist.'

'Teddy who?' Bill said.

'Teddy Giles, Dad. You must have heard of him. He does performances and sells these really cool sculptures. He's been written about in lots of magazines and everything.'

When I looked at Bill, I thought I saw a flicker of recognition pass across his face, but he made no comment.

'How old is Giles?' I asked.

'Twenty-one,' Mark said.

Violet said, 'Why were you trying to get into Leo's apartment?'

'I wasn't!' Mark sounded desperate.

'I heard the lock turn, Mark,' I said.

'No! That was Teddy. He didn't have a key. He turned the doorknob because he thought it was our apartment upstairs.'

I looked Mark directly in the eyes and he looked back at me. 'You didn't use my key last night?'

'No,' he said. There was no hesitation in him.

'What did you want in our apartment, then?' Violet said. 'You didn't come home until an hour ago.'

'I wanted my camera to take pictures.'

Bill rubbed his face. 'For the rest of the month, you'll stay put while you're here.'

Mark's jaw fell open in disbelief. 'But what did I do?'

Bill sounded tired. 'Listen, even if you hadn't lied to me and to your mother, you need to do your schoolwork. You'll never graduate if you don't start studying. Also,' he said, 'I want you to return Leo's key.'

Mark stuck out his bottom lip and pouted. The expression on his soft young face reminded me of a disgruntled two-year-old who had just been told that another bowl of ice cream wasn't forthcoming. At that moment his head with its infantile features and his long, growing body seemed to be at odds with each other, as if the top of him hadn't caught up with the bottom.

I asked Mark about Teddy Giles the following Saturday afternoon when he came to see me. Despite the fact that he was grounded, I didn't notice any change in Mark's mood. I did notice that he had dyed his hair green, but I decided not to say anything about it.

'How's your friend Giles?' I said.

'He's fine.'

'You said he was an artist?'

'He is. He's famous.'

'Is he?'

'At least with kids. But he's got a gallery now and everything.'

'What's the work like?'

Mark leaned against the wall in the hallway and yawned. 'It's cool. He cuts things up.'

'What things?'

'It's hard to explain.' Mark smiled to himself.

'Last week you said that he was shaking because it was part of his act. I didn't understand that.'

'He's into looking frail.'

'And the little boy? Who was he?'

'Me?'

'No, not you. You're not a little boy, are you?'

Mark laughed. 'No, that's his name, Me.'

'Is it an Asian or Indian name?' I said.

'No, it's M-E, like "me." I'm "me."'

'His parents gave him a first-person pronoun for a name?'

'Nah,' Mark said. 'He changed it. Everybody just calls him Me.'

'He looks about twelve,' I said.

'He's nineteen.'

'Nineteen?'

'Is he Giles's lover?' I asked pointedly.

'Wow,' Mark said. 'I didn't expect you to ask me something like that, but no, they're just friends. If you really want to know, Teddy's bi, not gay.'

Mark studied me for a moment before he continued. 'Teddy's brilliant. Everybody admires him. He grew up really poor in Virginia. His mother was a prostitute, and he didn't know who his dad was. When he was fourteen, he ran away from home and wandered around the country for a while. Then he came to New York and started working as a busboy at the Odeon. After that, he got into art – performances. For a guy who's only twenty-four, he's done a lot, you know.' I remembered that Mark had said Giles was twenty-one, but I let it go. He paused for a couple of seconds and then looked me in the eyes. 'I never met anybody more like me. We talk about it all the time, how we're the same.'

Two weeks later, at one of Bernie Weeks's opening dinners, Teddy Giles came up again. It had been a long time since I had been out with Bill and Violet, and I had looked forward to that dinner, but I was seated between Bernie's date for the evening, a young actress named Lola Martini, and Jillian Downs, the artist whose show had just opened, and I didn't get much chance to speak to either Bill or Violet. Bill was on the other side of Jillian and they were deep in conversation. Jillian's husband, Fred Downs, was talking to Bernie. Before Giles came up, Lola had been telling me about her career on Italian television as a game-show hostess. Her wardrobe for the job had consisted of bikinis that related to the game's fruit theme. 'Lemon yellow,' she said, 'Strawberry red, lime green, you get the picture.' She pointed to her head. 'And I had to wear these fruit hats.'

'Carmen Miranda style,' I said.

Lola looked at me blankly. 'The show was pretty stupid, but I learned Italian, and it got me a couple of film roles.'

'Without fruit?'

She laughed and adjusted her bustier, which had been sinking slowly for about half an hour. 'No fruit.'

When I asked her how she knew Bernie, she said, 'I met him last week in this gallery – the Teddy

Giles show. Oh my God, it was so disgusting.' Lola made a face to indicate her revulsion and lifted her bare shoulders. She was very young and very pretty, and when she talked, her earrings shook against her long neck. She pointed her fork at Bernie and said loudly, 'We're talking about that show where we met. Wasn't it disgusting?'

Bernie turned toward Lola. 'Well,' he said. 'I'm not going to disagree with you, but he's made quite a stir. He started out performing in clubs. Larry Finder saw him and brought the work into the gallery.'

'But what's the work like?' I said.

'It's bodies all cut up – women and men and even kids,' Lola said as she wrinkled her forehead and stretched her lips to telegraph her distaste. 'Blood and guts all over the place, and then they had photographs from this show he did in some club – spurting an enema. I guess it was red water, but it looked like blood. Oh my God, I had to cover my eyes. It was soooo gross.'

Jillian looked at Bill. She raised her eyebrows. 'You know who's taken Giles under his critical wing?'

Bill shook his head.

'Hasseborg. He wrote this long article about him in *Blast*.'

A brief look of pain crossed Bill's face.

'What did he say?' I asked.

'That Giles exposes the celebration of violence

296

in American culture,' Jillian said. 'It's Hollywood horror deconstructed – something like that.'

'Jillian and I went to the show,' Fred said. 'I thought it was pretty hokey, thin stuff. It's supposed to be shocking, but it's not really. It's tame when you think of the artists who've really gone the distance. That woman who has plastic surgery to change her face to look like a Picasso or a Manet or a Modigliani. I always forget her name. You remember when Tom Otterness shot that dog?'

'Puppy,' Violet said.

Lola's face fell. 'He shot a little puppy?'

'It's all on tape,' Fred explained. 'The little guy's bouncing all over the place and then bang.' He paused. 'But I guess it had cancer.'

'You mean it was sick and going to die?'

Nobody answered Lola.

'Chris Burden had himself shot in the arm,' Jillian volunteered.

'The shoulder,' Bernie corrected. 'It was his shoulder.'

'Arm, shoulder.' Jillian smiled. 'Same area. Schwarzkogler, now there's radical art.'

'What did he do?' Lola asked.

'Well, for one thing,' I said to her, 'he sliced his penis lengthwise and had the whole thing photographed. Pretty gruesome and bloody.'

'Wasn't there another guy who did the same thing?' Violet said.

'Bob Flanagan,' Bernie said. 'But it was nails. He hammered nails into it.'

297

Lola's mouth dropped open. 'That's sick,' she said. 'I mean mentally sick. I don't think that's art. That's just sick.'

I turned to look at Lola's face, with its perfectly plucked eyebrows, little nose, and gleaming mouth. 'If I picked you up and put you in a gallery, you'd be art,' I said to her. 'Better art than a lot I've seen. Prescriptive definitions don't apply anymore.'

Lola moved her shoulders. 'You're saying that anything's art if people say it is? Even me?'

'Exactly. It's perspective – not content.'

Violet leaned forward and rested her elbows on the table. 'I went to the show,' she said. 'Lola's right. If you take it seriously at all, it's horrible. At the same time it feels like a joke – a one-liner.' She paused. 'It's hard to tell whether it's purely cynical or whether there's something else in it – a sadistic pleasure behind hacking up those fake bodies . . .'

The conversation drifted away from Giles again and onto other artists. Bill continued to talk to Jillian. He didn't participate in the lively dispute on the best bread in New York that followed or in the discourses on shoes and shoe stores that somehow came after that, which led to Lola lifting up her long leg to display a sandal with stiletto heels by a designer with a very curious name I forgot instantly. On the walk home, Bill was silent. Violet linked arms with both of us.

'I wish Erica were here,' she said.

I didn't answer her for a moment. 'She doesn't want to be here, Violet. I don't know how many times we've planned visits. Every six months she writes to say she's coming to New York, and then she backs down. Three times I had plane tickets to California, and each time she wrote to say she couldn't see me. She wasn't strong enough. She told me she's living a posthumous life in California and that's what she wants.'

'For someone who isn't alive, she's written a lot of articles,' Violet said.

'She likes paper,' I said.

'She's still in love with you,' Violet said. 'I know.'

'Or maybe she's in love with the idea of me on the other side of the country.'

At that moment Bill stopped walking. He let go of Violet, looked up at the night sky, spread his arms, and said loudly, 'We know nothing. We know absolutely nothing about anything.' His loud voice carried down the street. 'Nothing!' He boomed the word again with obvious satisfaction.

Violet reached for Bill's hand and tugged at him. 'Now that we've settled that, let's go home,' she said. He didn't resist her. Violet held his hand as he shuffled down the block with his head lowered and his shoulders hunched. I thought he looked like a child being led home by his mother. Later, I wondered what had provoked Bill's outburst. It might have been the talk about Erica, but then again, it might have been rooted in what had been

299

revealed earlier: Mark happened to have chosen a friend whose staunchest supporter was the man who had written the cruelest review of his father's work to date.

Bill found Mark a summer job through an acquaintance of his, another artist named Harry Freund. Freund needed a crew of workers for a large art project in Tribeca about New York's children, which was being funded by both private and public money. The enormous, impermanent work was to be part of a celebration in September for the 'Month of the Child.' The design included huge flags, some Christo-like wrappings of lampposts, and blown-up drawings by children from every borough. 'Five days a week, nine to five, physical labor,' Bill said to me. 'It'll be good for him.' The job started in the middle of June. While I sat with my coffee in the morning and began the day's work of puzzling out another couple of paragraphs on Goya, I would hear Mark running down the stairs on his way to work. After that, I would move to my desk to write, but for a couple of weeks I found myself distracted by thoughts of Teddy Giles and his work.

Before his show closed at the Finder Gallery at the end of May, I went to see it. Lola's description hadn't been off the mark. The show resembled the aftermath of a massacre. Nine bodies made of polyester resin and fiberglass lay on the gallery floor, dismembered, ripped open, and decapitated.

What appeared to be dried blood stained the floor. The instruments of the simulated torture were displayed on pedestals: a chain saw, several knives, and a gun. On the walls hung four huge photographs of Giles. In three he was performing. He wore a hockey mask in the first and held a machete. In the second he was in drag, dolled up in a blond Marilyn wig and evening gown. In the third, he sprayed his enema. The fourth photograph presumably showed Giles as 'himself.' He was sitting on a long blue sofa in ordinary clothes with a television remote control in his left hand. His right hand appeared to be massaging his crotch. He looked pale, calm, and not nearly as young as Mark had said he was. I would have guessed that Giles was at least thirty.

The show repulsed me, but I also found it bad. In the name of fairness, I had to ask myself why. Goya's painting of Saturn eating his son was just as violent. Giles used classic horror images presumably to comment on their role in the culture. The remote control was an obvious allusion to television and videos. Goya, too, borrowed from standard folk images of the supernatural that were immediately recognizable to anyone who saw his work, and they were also meant as social commentary. So why did Goya's work feel alive and Giles's dead? The medium was different. In Goya, I felt the physical presence of the painter's hand. Giles hired craftsmen to cast his bodies from live models and then fabricate them for him. And yet, I had admired other artists who had their work made for them. Goya was deep. Giles was shallow. But then sometimes shallowness is the point. Warhol had devoted himself to surfaces – to the empty veneers of culture. I didn't love Andy Warhol's work, but I could understand its interest.

The summer before my mother died, I'd traveled alone in Italy and made the journey in Piedmont to Varallo to see the *sacro monte* and the chapels above the town. In the Chapel of the Massacre of the Innocents I saw the figures of weeping mothers and murdered babies with real hair and clothes, and their effect on me was wrenching. When I walked through the Finder Gallery and looked at Giles's polyurethane victims, I shuddered but felt little connection to them. It may have been partly due to the fact that the figures were hollow. There were a number of artificial organs, hearts, stomachs, kidneys, and gall bladders lying among the mess of bodies, but when you peered into a severed arm, there was nothing inside it.

Nevertheless, explaining Giles's art wasn't easy. When I read Hasseborg's article in *Blast*, I saw that he had taken the simple route – arguing that the act of moving horror images from the flat screen into the three dimensions of a gallery forced the viewer to rethink their meaning. Hasseborg ran at the mouth for several pages, his prose roiling with hyperbolic adjectives: 'brilliant,' 'riveting,' 'astounding.' He quoted Baudrillard, panted over Giles's shifting identities, and then in one long and final grandiloquent sentence, pronounced him 'the artist of the future.'

Henry Hasseborg also reported that Giles had been born in Baytown, Texas, not Virginia, as Mark had told me, and in Hasseborg's version of Giles's life, the artist's mother wasn't a prostitute but a hardworking waitress devoted to her son. Giles was quoted as saying, 'My mother is my inspiration.' As the weeks passed, I came to believe that although Hasseborg was right about the fact that Giles reproduced the gruesome images of horror flicks and cheap violent porn, he was wrong about their effect on the viewer – at least in my case. They criticized nothing and they revealed nothing. The work was simulacra excreted from the culture's bowels – sterile, commercial feces meant purely for titillation. And although I was biased against Hasseborg, I began to feel that he had fallen for Giles because the man's work was the visual embodiment of his own voice – that smirking, cynical, joyless tone he usually adopted in his articles about art and artists. Of course, Hasseborg wasn't alone. He had many compatriots who wrote just like him – although with less intelligence – other cultural journalists who had adopted the slick palaver of the moment. It's a language I've come to hate, because it admits no mystery and no ambiguity into its smug vocabulary, which arrogantly suggests that everything can be known.

★　　★　　★

Although I didn't judge Giles's work hastily, I did judge it, and Mark's attraction to those vacuous scenes of slaughter and to the man who had created them worried me. Every time Giles gave his birthplace and age, he said something different. Hasseborg wrote that Giles was twenty-eight. No doubt Giles wanted to obsfucate his background, perhaps to create a mystique about himself, but his prevarications couldn't be good for Mark, who, at the very least, was in the habit of bending the truth too often.

Late one morning in early July, I ran into Mark on West Broadway. He was crouched on the sidewalk petting a cocker spaniel and talking to the animal's owner. He put his face close to the dog's snout and spoke to it in a low, friendly voice. When I greeted him, he jumped up and said, 'Hi, Uncle Leo.' Turning to the dog, he said, 'Bye, Talulah.' I asked him why he wasn't at work.

'Harry doesn't need me until noon today,' he said. 'I'm on my way there now.'

As Mark and I walked down the street together, a young woman stuck her head out of a clothing store and waved at Mark. 'Hi, Marky. What's up, honey?'

'Darien,' Mark called back. He smiled sweetly at her, lifted a hand, and wiggled his fingers. The wave struck me as out of character, but when I looked over at Mark, he grinned broadly at me and said, 'She's really nice.'

Before we reached the end of the block, Mark was accosted again, this time by a younger boy.

He came running from across the street, yelling, 'The Mark!'

'The Mark?' I muttered aloud.

Mark turned to me and lifted his eyebrows as if to say, People will call you anything.

The boy ignored me. Breathing heavily from his run, he looked up at Mark. 'It's me, Freddy. Remember? From Club USA?'

'Sure,' Mark said. He sounded bored.

'There's this really cool photo show opening tonight around the corner. I thought you might like to go.'

'Sorry,' Mark said in the same laconic voice. 'Can't.'

I watched Freddy press his lips together in an unsuccessful attempt to hide his disappointment. Then he lifted his chin and smiled up at Mark. 'Another time, okay?'

'Sure, Freddy,' Mark said.

Freddy ran back to the other side of the street, scooting within inches of a passing taxi. The driver pressed on the horn, and the noise blared in the street for two or three seconds.

As Mark watched Freddy's close call, he slouched on one hip and lowered his shoulders in a posture I supposed was meant to look nonchalant. Then he turned to me, straightened his spine, and threw back his shoulders. When our eyes met, he must have seen a trace of confusion on my face, because he hesitated for half a second. 'Gotta run, Uncle Leo. I don't want to be late for work.'

I checked my watch. 'You'd better hurry.'

'I will.' Mark sprinted down the block, his huge pants waving like two flags on either side of his ankles, the elastic and several inches of his underpants in full view. The pants were so long that the bottoms had frayed and torn along the inner seams. I stood for a few moments and watched him run. His figure grew smaller and smaller, and then he turned a corner.

As I made my way home, I realized that two narratives about Mark had unfolded inside me – one on top of the other. The superficial story went something like this: Like thousands of other teenagers, Mark had hidden parts of his life from his parents. No doubt he had experimented with drugs, slept with girls, and maybe, I had begun to think, a couple of boys. He was intelligent but a very poor student, which suggested an attitude of passive rebellion. He had lied to his parents. He had failed to tell his mother about his room in my apartment and had once slept there without my permission. Another time, he had hoped to sneak back into that room at four in the morning. He was attracted to the violent content of Teddy Giles's art, but then so were countless other young people. And finally, like so many children his age, he tried on various personas to discover which one suited him. He behaved one way with his peers and another way with adults. This version of Mark's story was ordinary, one tale like a million others of a normal, bumpy adolescence.

The other story was similar to the one that lay above it, and its content was identical: Mark had been caught lying. He had formed a friendship with an unsavory person I privately called 'the ghost,' and Mark's body and voice changed depending on whom he was speaking to at the moment. But this second narrative lacked the smoothness of the first. It had holes in it, and those gaps made the story difficult to tell. It didn't rely on a larger fiction about teenage life to fill in its ragged openings but left them gaping and unanswered. And unlike the reassuring tale above it, it didn't begin when Mark was thirteen, but at some unknown and earlier date that sent me hurtling into the past rather than the future, and it came in the fractured form of isolated pictures and sounds. I remembered little Mark walking through our door when Lucille lived upstairs, his head hidden under a rubber fright mask. I saw his father's portrait of him with a lamp shade on his head – a small body hovering in the nowhere of that canvas – and then I heard Violet hesitate, breathe, and leave her sentence unfinished.

I repressed those underground images and stuck to the coherent story on the surface. It was both more comfortable and more rational. After all, I had become a creature of mourning. Matthew's absence had made me unusually alert to nuances in Mark's character that might turn out to be of little importance. I had lost faith in predictable stories. My son was dead, and my wife lived in self-imposed exile. But I told myself that just because my own life had been rocked by accident didn't mean that other people didn't have lives that plodded along a prescribed course, becoming over the years rather like what they had expected all along.

That summer Bill came back to me. He called almost every day, and I followed the progress of the doors as they were made on the Bowery. Although Bill put in long hours at the studio, he had more time for me, and I sensed that his desire to see me was partly the result of a new optimism he felt about Mark. Worry always took the form of retreat in Bill, and over the years I had come to recognize the outward signs of his withdrawal. His expansive gestures vanished. His eyes focused on an object across the room but failed to register the thing he was seeing. He chainsmoked cigarettes and kept a bottle of Scotch under his desk. I was sensitive to Bill's internal weather, to the intense pressure that built up inside him and then stormed quietly. Those tempests usually began and ended with Mark, but while they were raging, Bill found it hard to talk to me or anyone else. Violet may have been an exception. I don't know. I felt that Bill's inner tumult wasn't fury against Mark for his lying and irresponsibility but rather a seething anger and doubt he turned on himself. At the same time, he was eager to believe that the winds were changing, and he seized on every nuance in his son's behavior as a sign of better days to come. 'He's stuck with the job,' Bill said to me, 'and he really enjoys it. He's stopped seeing Giles and that club bunch and is hanging out with kids his own age. It's a big relief to me, Leo. I knew that he was going to find some direction in his life.' Because Violet was out doing research for her book, I saw her much less than either Bill or Mark, and not seeing her helped me to repress her imaginary twin – the woman I took to bed in my mind. Erica talked to Violet regularly, however, and she wrote that Violet was better, less anxious, and that she, too, felt a new determination in Mark that was connected to his job for Freund. 'She told me that Mark is genuinely moved by the fact that the project is about children. She thinks it struck a chord with him.'

Mr Bob was still in residence on the Bowery, and every time I went to visit Bill, he regarded me through his chained door with suspicion, and every time I left, he blessed me. I knew that Mr Bob made full-bodied appearances for Bill and Violet, but I never saw more than a fraction of his brooding face. Although Bill didn't talk about it, I understood that the old man had become his dependent. Bill left groceries at the bottom of the stairs for Mr Bob, and once I saw a note on Bill's desk written in a tiny neat hand: '*Crunchy* not smooth peanut butter!' But as far as I could tell, Bill had simply accepted his downstairs neighbor as an obligatory presence in his life. He shook his head and smiled when I mentioned the old squatter, but he never complained about what I suspected were Mr Bob's growing demands.

In the middle of August, Bill and Violet asked if I would let Mark stay with me for two weeks while they vacationed on Martha's Vineyard. Mark couldn't abandon his job, and they felt uncomfortable leaving him in the apartment alone. I agreed to take him in and gave Mark another key. 'This,' I said to him, 'is a sign of trust between us, and I'd like you to hold on to it, even after these two weeks are over.' He held out his hand and I lowered the key into his palm. 'You understand me, don't you, Mark?'

He looked at me steadily and nodded. 'I do, Uncle Leo.' His bottom lip trembled with emotion, and we embarked on our two weeks together.

Mark spoke warmly about his work for Freund, about the large colored flags he had helped mount, about the other young men and women who worked alongside him – Rebecca and Laval and Shaneil and Jesus. Mark lifted and climbed and hammered and sawed, and by the time he quit for the day, he said, his arms ached and his legs felt wobbly. When he returned home at around five or six, he often needed a nap to recover. Around eleven o'clock at night, he went out and usually didn't return until morning. 'I'm staying with Jake,' he would say, and leave a telephone number. 'I'll be at Louisa's house. Her parents said I could sleep in the guest room.' Another number.

He wandered in at between six and eight in the morning and would sleep until work. His schedule changed daily. 'I don't have to be in until noon,' he would say, or 'Harry doesn't need me today,' and then he would drop into a coma until four in the afternoon.

Sometimes, his friends came to my door to retrieve Mark for a night out. Most of them were short white girls, dressed in baby clothes with pigtails in their hair and glitter on their cheeks. One evening, a brunette came to the door with a pacifier hanging on a pink ribbon around her neck. With voices to match their infantile clothing, Mark's girlfriends cooed and piped and twittered in high, thin tones suffused with misplaced emotion. When I offered them soft drinks, they breathed out their lilting thank-yous as if I had just offered them immortality. Although Mark had played tough for Freddy, he didn't swagger or act bored with the girls. With Marina, Sissy, Jessica, and Moonlight (the daughter of glassblowers in Brooklyn), his tone was invariably gentle and earnest. When he bent down to talk to them, his handsome face softened with feeling.

One night when Mark was out with friends, I had dinner with Lazlo and Pinky at Omen on Thompson Street. Pinky was the one who first brought up the story of the dead cats. Although I had met Pinky Navatsky several times, I had never spent much time with her until that evening. She was a tall girl in her early twenties, with red

311

hair, gray eyes, a significant, slightly hooked nose, which gave her an air of substance, and a very long neck. Like many dancers, she had a permanent turnout that affected her walk, which was a little ducklike, but she held her head like a queen at her coronation, and I loved to watch her move her arms and hands while she talked. When she gestured, she often used the whole limb, moving her arm from her shoulder. At other times she would bend her elbow and open her hand toward me in a single sure sweep. Her movements weren't at all affected. She simply had a relation to her own musculature that for most of us is unthinkable. Just before she mentioned the cats, she leaned toward me, turned her palms over so they faced the ceiling, and said, 'Last night I had a dream about the murdered cats. I think it was that picture in the *Post*.'

When I said that I knew nothing about murdered cats, Pinky explained that the flayed, skewered, and dismembered animals had been discovered around the city, nailed to walls, hanging from doorways, or simply lying in the middle of an alley, sidewalk, or subway platform.

Lazlo informed me that the animals were all partly dressed, wearing diapers, baby outfits, pajamas, or training bras, and they had all been signed with the letters S.M. Those letters may have started the rumors that Teddy Giles was responsible. Giles called his drag persona the 'She-Monster,' initials that coyly but not very subtly also referred to sadomasochism. Although

312

Giles had denied all responsibility for the cats, Lazlo said that he had kept ambiguity and shock alive by calling the animal corpses 'guerrilla art at its furious best.' Giles had also said he envied the artist and hoped he had been an inspiration to the unnamed 'perpetrator/creator.' Finally, he had given his blessing to all future 'copycats.' These comments drove animal-rights organizations to screeching outrage, and Larry Finder had come to work one morning to find the words ACCESSORY TO MURDER scrawled in red paint on the gallery door. I had missed the furor in the papers and the clip that had made the local television news.

Lazlo chewed thoughtfully and took long breaths through his nose. 'You're out of it, did you know that, Leo?'

I admitted that I was.

'Lazlo,' Pinky said, 'not everybody's like you, always checking out everything all the time. Leo has other things to think about.'

'No offense,' Lazlo said to me.

After I had made it clear to both of them that I wasn't the least bit upset by the comment, Lazlo continued, 'Giles'll say anything if he thinks it'll be hyped.'

'It's true,' Pinky said. 'He might not have a thing to do with those cats.'

'Do Bill and Violet know about this?'

Lazlo nodded. 'But they think Mark's not seeing Giles.'

'And you know that he is.'

'We saw them together,' Pinky said.

'At the Limelight last Tuesday.' After a vigorous inhalation through his nose, Lazlo said, 'I hate to tell Bill, but I'll do it. The kid's in over his head.'

'Even if Giles isn't murdering cats,' Pinky said, leaning across the table, 'he's creepy. I'd never seen him before, and it wasn't his makeup or clothes that got me, it was something in his eyes.'

Before we said good-bye, Lazlo slipped me an envelope. I had gotten used to these parting gifts. He left them for Bill, too. Usually he typed up a quotation for me to think about. I had already been treated to Thomas Bernhard's spleen: 'Velázquez, Rembrandt, Giorgione, Bach, Handel, Mozart, Goethe . . . Pascal, Voltaire, all of them such inflated monstrosities,' and to a quote from Philip Guston I particularly liked: 'To know and yet how not to know is the greatest puzzle of all.' That night I opened the envelope and read: '*Kitsch* is always in the process of escaping into rationality. Hermann Broch.'

I asked myself if the dead cats were meant to be a form of kitsch, a thought that led to ruminations on animal sacrifice, the chain of being, ordinary slaughterhouses, and finally to pets. I remembered that as a little boy Mark had kept white mice, guinea pigs, and a parakeet named Peeper. One day the cage door had fallen on Peeper's neck and killed him. After the accident, Mark and Matt had paraded around our loft with a shoe box that held the stiff little corpse, singing the only song they

314

knew that would function as a dirge: 'Swing Low, Sweet Chariot.'

When Mark returned from work the next day, I couldn't bring myself to mention either Giles or the cats, and at dinner he had so much to tell me about his day, I never found a good opening for the subject. That morning he had helped mount his favorite blown-up drawing, by a six-year-old girl in the Bronx – a self-portrait with her turtle, which looked very much like a dinosaur. In the afternoon, his friend Jesus had fallen off a ladder but was saved by a huge pile of canvas flags that were piled beneath him on the ground. Before Mark left for the night, he retreated to the bathroom and I heard him whistling. He put a telephone number on the table with a name beside it. Allison Fredericks: 677–8451. 'You can reach me at Allison's,' he said.

After Mark was gone, a vague suspicion began to churn inside me. I listened to Janet Baker singing Berlioz, but the music didn't drive away the uneasiness that constricted my lungs. I studied the name and telephone number Mark had left on the table. After twenty minutes of hesitation, I picked up the telephone and called. A man answered. 'I'd like to speak to Mark Wechsler,' I said.

'Who?'

'He's a friend of Allison's.'

'There's no Allison here.'

I looked at the number. Maybe I had dialed

wrong. Very carefully I punched in the numbers again. The same man answered and I hung up.

When I confronted Mark about the wrong number the following morning, he looked puzzled. He dug into his pocket, produced a number, and laid it beside the little piece of paper he had written on the night before. 'I see what I did.' He spoke in a bright, clear voice. 'I reversed these two numbers. Look here. 'It's four eight, not eight four. I'm sorry. I guess I was in a hurry.'

His innocent face made me feel foolish. Then I confessed that I had been feeling upset because of Lazlo's story about seeing him with Giles and because of the cat rumors.

'Oh, Uncle Leo,' he said. 'You should've talked to me right away. I ran into Teddy when I was out with some other friends, but we're not really close anymore. I have to tell you something, though. Teddy likes to shock people. It's his thing, but he wouldn't hurt a fly. I mean that. I've seen him carry flies out of his apartment like this.' Mark cupped his hands. 'Those poor cats. It just makes me sick. You know, I've got two cats at Mom's, Mirabelle and Esmeralda. They're like my best friends.'

'The rumor probably got started because Giles's work is so violent,' I said.

'But that's all fake!' Mark said. 'I thought Violet was the only person who didn't know the difference.' Mark rolled his eyes.

'Violet doesn't know the difference?'

'Well, she *acts* like it's real or something. She

316

never even lets me watch horror movies. What does she think? I'm going to go out and cut somebody because I saw it on TV?'

Mark looked very pale during the second week of our time together, but then he must have been exhausted. Friends of his phoned all day and half the night, asking for Mark, Marky, and The Mark. In order to get any work done, I stopped answering the telephone and listened to the messages later in the day. On Tuesday, at around two o'clock in the morning, I was awakened from a deep sleep by the phone and heard a man's deep voice say, 'M&M?' 'No,' I said, and then, 'Do you mean Mark?' I heard a click and the line went dead. The steady calls, Mark's erratic comings and goings, his things scattered around the apartment had all started to confuse me. I wasn't used to living with another person anymore, and I found that I misplaced some things and lost others. My pen vanished for a couple of days and then I found it behind a sofa cushion. A kitchen knife disappeared. I couldn't find my silver letter opener, which had been a present from my mother. As I sat at my desk, I was often distracted by unfocused worry about Mark.

One afternoon, I stood up from my desk and walked to Matt's room. Stacks of records and CDs rose from the floor. Flyers littered the shelves. Advertisements with names like Starlight Techno and Machine Paradise were plastered to the walls.

Sneakers lay everywhere. He must have owned twenty pairs. Pants, sweaters, socks, and T-shirts had been strewn on the bed, over the chair, and in heaps on the floor. Some of them still had store tags clinging to their necks or waistlines. I walked into the room and picked up a videotape lying on the desk: *Killers Unleashed.* I had never seen the movie but had read about it. It was based on the true story of a boy and girl who first murder their parents and then cross the country on a rampage of theft and homicide. A respected director had filmed it, and the movie had caused some controversy. I put it down and noticed an unopened box of Legos lying only inches away. Its cover featured a merry little policeman, one stiff arm raised in a salute. On the desk I noticed gum wrappers, a green rabbit's foot, keys to somewhere, a curly straw, old Star Wars figures, stickers of a cartoon dog, and, oddly enough, several broken pieces of dollhouse furniture. I also found a xeroxed flyer, which I picked up and read. It had been typed entirely in capital letters:

Why are you at this event? the rave scene is not just about techno. It's not just about drugs. This scene is not just about fashion. It is something special about unity and happiness. it is about being yourself and being loved for it. It should be a harbor from our society. but our scene right now is disintegrating. We don't need fronts and attitudes in our scene. The outside world is tough enough. Open your hearts and let the good feelings flow. Look around

318

you, pick a person, ask them their name, and make a friend. Eliminate boundaries. Open your hearts and minds. Ravers unite and keep our scene alive!

Around the edges of the paper in hand-drawn letters the nameless author had written little slogans by hand: 'You gotta be real!' 'Be yourself!' 'Be happy!' 'Group hugs!' and 'You're beautiful!'

There was something pitiful about the flyer's crudely written idealism, but the sentiments expressed were nothing if not pure. The text made me think of the flower children who long ago had become adults. Even in the sixties, I had been too old to believe that 'eliminating boundaries' was of much use in the world. After carefully replacing the flyer, I looked up from the desk and studied Matt's watercolor. It should be dusted, I thought. Then I looked through the window of Dave's apartment and examined the figure of the old man for a couple of minutes and wondered what Matthew would have been like at sixteen. Would he too have gone to raves and dyed his hair green or pink or blue? Hours after I had left the room, I remembered that I had planned to dust the watercolor, but by then I had lost the will to return to the chaotic room, with its litter, garish signs, and pathetic little manifesto.

The last days of my cohabitation with Mark were marred by a clutching distress that came over me as soon as he left the apartment but was then instantly dispelled as soon as I saw him again. I had begun to feel that Mark's physical presence had an almost magical quality. While I was looking at him, I always believed him. The frank sincerity in his face instantly banished all my doubts, but once he was out of view, the dull anxiety would rise up again. On Friday evening he emerged from the bathroom, and I noticed green glitter on his white face and neck.

'I'm worried about you, Mark. You're exhausting yourself. I think a quiet night at home would do you good.'

'I'm okay. I'm just hanging out with my friends.' Mark reached over and patted my arm. 'Really, we just listen to music and watch movies and stuff. The thing is, I'm young now. I'm young and I want to have fun and experiences now when I'm young.' He looked at me with sympathy, as if I were the living embodiment of the adage 'too little, too late.'

'When I was your age,' I said to him, 'my mother gave me a piece of advice that I've never forgotten. She said, "Don't do anything you don't really want to do."'

Mark's eyes widened.

'She meant that if your conscience holds you back, if it muddles the purity of your desire, if it gives you mixed feelings, don't do it.'

Mark nodded soberly and then continued to nod several times. 'That's smart,' he said. 'I'm going to remember that.'

★ ★ ★

Saturday night, I went to bed knowing that Mark would be leaving the next day. The knowledge of Bill and Violet's imminent return affected me like a sleeping pill, and not long after Mark left the house, at around eleven, I fell asleep. Sometime during the course of the night, I had a long dream that began as an erotic adventure with Violet, who didn't look like herself, and then turned into a dream in which I was walking down long corridors in a hospital, where I found Erica in one of the beds and discovered that she had given birth to a baby girl. The child's paternity was in question, however, and just as I was kneeling by Erica's bed and telling her that I didn't care who the father was, that I would be the father, the baby disappeared from the hospital ward. Erica was strangely indifferent to the missing child, but I felt desperate, and suddenly I was the one lying in the hospital bed, and Erica was sitting beside me pinching my arm in a gesture that was supposed to comfort me but didn't. I woke up with the peculiar sensation that someone really was pinching my arm. I opened my eyes and jerked up in surprise. Mark was leaning over me, his head only inches from my face. He lurched backward and began to walk toward the door.

'Good God,' I said. 'What are you doing?'

'Nothing,' he whispered. 'Go back to sleep.' He had reached the doorway to my bedroom, and the ceiling lamp in the hallway lit his profile. His lips looked very red as he turned away from me.

My arm was still stinging. 'Did you want to wake me?'

Mark spoke without turning around. 'I heard you yell in your sleep and I wanted to make sure you were okay.' His voice sounded deliberate, mechanical. 'Go back to sleep.' He disappeared, closing the door softly behind him.

I turned on the lamp beside my bed and looked down at my forearm. There was a haze of red on it. The color, which looked like the traces of a pastel crayon, had matted some of the hairs. I brought the arm closer to my face and noticed a circular pattern of tiny irregular indentations like pock marks gouged into my skin. The word that came to mind made me breathe faster: teeth. I looked at the clock. It was five o'clock in the morning. I put my finger to the red again and saw that it wasn't crayon but something less waxy and softer – lipstick. I got out of bed, walked to the door, and locked it. After I returned to bed, I listened to Mark shuffling around the room across the hall. I stared at my arm and scrutinized the marks. I went so far as to bite my own arm rather gently and then compare the ridges in my skin. Yes, I said to myself, he bit me. The inflamed circle notched into my arm faded very slowly, despite the fact that the pressure hadn't broken the skin or drawn blood. What could it possibly mean? I realized that it hadn't occurred to me to run after Mark and demand an explanation. For two weeks, I had been wobbling between trust and dread when it came to Mark, but my worries had never veered toward suspicions of madness. This sudden, inexplicable, thoroughly irrational act threw me completely off balance. What on earth would he have to say to me when I saw him later in the day?

I woke and slept and slept and woke for hours. By the time I crawled out of bed and lumbered toward the coffee machine around ten, Mark was sitting at the table with a bowl of cereal.

'Boy, you slept late,' he said. 'I got up early.'

I grabbed the bag of coffee from the refrigerator and began spooning its dark contents into the filter. An answer seemed impossible. While I waited for the coffee, I stared at Mark, who was shoveling a colored cereal with marshmallows into his mouth. He crunched happily on the repellent concoction and gave me a smile. All at once, I felt that I was the one who had gone insane overnight. I looked at my arm. There was no trace of the bite. It happened, I said to myself, but maybe Mark doesn't remember it. Perhaps he had been drugged or even asleep. Erica had held conversations with me while she walked in her sleep. I brought my cup of coffee over to the table.

'Uncle Leo, you're shaking,' Mark said. His limpid blue eyes looked concerned. 'Are you okay?'

I removed my trembling hand from the tabletop. The question in my throat – Do you remember coming into my room and biting my arm last night? – refused to form itself on my lips.

He put down his spoon. 'Guess what?' he said.

'I met a girl last night. Her name is Lisa. She's really pretty, and I think she likes me. I'm going to introduce you to her.'

I picked up my coffee cup. 'That's nice,' I said. 'I'd like to meet her.'

In the second week of September, Bill ran into Harry Freund on White Street. Bill asked Harry about the unveiling of the children's project, which was only a week away, and then asked how Mark had been as a worker. 'Well,' Freund said, 'the week he worked for me, he was great, but then he disappeared. I haven't seen him since.'

Bill quoted and requoted Freund's words to me, as if to reassure himself that the man had actually said them. Then he said, 'Mark must be crazy.'

I was stupefied. Every day for two weeks Mark had come home and described his days at work to me in elaborate detail. 'It's so great that the project's about kids, especially poor kids who don't have anybody to speak for them.' That's what he had said to me. 'But how did Mark explain it?' I asked Bill.

'He said the job for Harry was boring, that he didn't like it, so he left and got another one. He worked at some magazine called *Split World* as a gofer, and he made seven dollars an hour instead of minimum wage.'

'But why didn't he just tell you?'

'He kept mumbling that he thought I wouldn't like it if he quit.'

'But all those lies,' I said. 'Doesn't he know that it's much worse to lie than it is to get another job?'

'I kept telling him that,' Bill said.

'He needs help,' I said.

Bill fumbled with his cigarettes. Extracting one, he lit it and blew the smoke away from me. 'I had a long talk with Lucille,' he said. 'Actually, I did most of the talking. She listened to me, and then after I had been ranting for a while, she volunteered a piece of information she had plucked from some article in a parenting magazine. The author had said that a lot of teenagers lie, that it's part of maturing. I told her that this wasn't just lying. This was an Academy Award-winning performance. This was completely nuts! She didn't answer me, and I stood there with the telephone in my hand, shaking with anger, and then I hung up on her. I shouldn't have done it, but it's like she doesn't understand the magnitude of this thing at all.'

'He needs help,' I said again. 'Psychiatric help.'

Bill pressed his lips together and nodded slowly. 'We're looking for a doctor, a therapist, someone. It won't be the first one, Leo. He's been in therapy before.'

'I didn't know that.'

'He saw a man in Texas, a Dr Mussel, and then he saw someone in New York for a year. The divorce, you know. We thought it would help . . .' Bill covered his face with his hands, and I saw his shoulders tremble for a moment. He was sitting in my chair by the window. I was seated beside him and had grabbed his forearm as a gesture of comfort. As I watched the smoke move upward from the cigarette that hung loosely between his two fingers, I remembered Mark's earnest face when he told me about Jesus taking a fall.

Lies are always double: what you say coexists with what you didn't say but might have said. When you stop lying, the gap between your words and inner belief closes, and you continue on a path of trying to match your spoken words to the language of your thoughts, at least those fit for other peoples' consumption. Mark's lie had departed from ordinary lying because it required the careful maintenance of a full-blown fiction. It got up in the morning, went to work, came home, and reported on its day for nine long weeks. Looking back on my fourteen days with Mark, I saw that the lie had been far from perfect. If Mark had been working outdoors all summer, he wouldn't have been white as an eggshell; he would have been tan. Also, his schedule had changed a little too often and a little too conveniently. But spectacular lies don't need to be perfect. They rely less on the liar's skill than on the listener's expectations and wishes. After Mark's dishonesty was exposed, I understood how much I wished that what he had told me had been true.

After his lies were exposed, Mark looked like a slightly compressed version of his former self. He gave off an attitude of generalized sorrow – head

326

down, shoulders slumped, and wide hurt eyes –
but when asked directly why he had manufactured
the deception, he could only answer in a dull voice
that he thought his father would be disappointed
if he quit the job. He agreed that lying had been
'dumb' and said he was 'embarrassed' about it.
When I said that the stories he had fed me about
the job effectively annihilated all our conversations,
he vehemently insisted that he had lied only about
the job but not about anything else. 'I care about
you, Uncle Leo. I really do. I was just stupid.'

Bill and Violet grounded him for three months.
When I asked Mark if Lucille was also punishing
him, he gave me a surprised look and said, 'I didn't
do anything to her.' He added that Princeton was
'boring' anyway. Nothing 'good' ever happened
there, so whether he was grounded or not mattered
little when it came to the pursuit of fun. He was
sitting on my sofa when he said this, resting his
elbows on his knees while he cupped his chin in his
hands. He jiggled his knees idly and stared straight
ahead. All at once, I found him repugnant, shallow,
alien. But then he turned his face to me, his eyes
large with pain, and I pitied him.

I didn't see Mark again until well into October,
when he was given a one-night reprieve to attend
his father's opening of the one hundred and one
doors at the Weeks Gallery. The smallest door
was a mere six inches tall, which meant that the
viewer had to lie on the floor to open it and

look inside. The largest door rose to twelve feet, nearly touching the gallery's ceiling. The crowded opening was noisy, not only with conversation but with the sound of doors shutting. People stood in line to enter the large ones and took turns peering into the smaller ones.

Each space was different. Some were figurative, others abstract, and some had three-dimensional figures and objects behind them, like the one I had first seen of the boy who floated in a mirror under a mound of plaster. Behind one door the viewer found that three side walls and the floor were all paintings of the same Victorian room, each rendered in a radically different style. Behind another, the walls and floor were painted to look like more doors, each one bearing a DO NOT ENTER sign. One little room had been painted entirely in red. A tiny sculpture of a woman was seated on the floor, her chin raised in laughter. She was holding her stomach in an effort to control her hilarity, and when you looked closely, you could see glistening polyurethane tears on her cheeks. A life-sized figure of a baby, wearing a diaper, wept on the floor behind one of the tall doors. Another door, only a foot and half high, opened onto a green man whose head grazed the ceiling of the little room. He was holding a wrapped gift in his outstretched hands with a large tag on it that said FOR YOU. Some of the figures behind the doors were flat, like color photographs. Others were canvas cutouts, still others cartoons. In one, a two-dimensional black-and-white cartoon man made love to a three-dimensional woman who seemed to have walked out of a Boucher painting. Her frilly skirts were lifted and her supernaturally pale and flawless thighs were parted to allow entrance for the man's absurdly large paper penis. One interior resembled an aquarium with acrylic fish that swam behind thick plastic. Numbers and letters appeared on other walls, sometimes in human positions. A number 5 sat on a small chair at a table with a teacup. A huge letter B lay on a bed on top of the covers. Behind other doors, the viewer discovered only one part of a person – the latex head of an old man with thinning hair who grinned up at you after you opened the door, or a little woman with no arms and legs clenching a paintbrush between her teeth. Behind one door there were four television screens, all black. Except for their size, the doors were identical from the outside. They were made of stained oak with brass knobs, and the outer walls of all the rooms were white.

When I looked at Bill that evening, I felt relieved that he had nearly finished the project before Freund's revelation. The attention he was given at the opening appeared to hurt him, as if every warm congratulation were another dagger in his gut. He had always been shy of publicity and crowds, but on other occasions I had seen him deflect pointed questions with a joke or avoid small talk by conducting a long conversation with someone he liked. That evening, he looked poised for another abrupt exit to Fanelli's. But Bill stayed. Violet, Lazlo, and I all checked on him regularly. Once, I heard Violet whispering to him that he should slow down on the wine. 'Sweetheart,' she said, 'you'll be completely sloshed before dinner.'

Mark, on the other hand, looked well. His confinement had probably increased his eagerness for any form of social life, and I watched him as he chatted with one person after another. While he was talking to someone, he was all attention. He leaned forward or bent his head as if to hear better, and sometimes he narrowed his eyes as he listened. When he smiled, his eyes never strayed from the other person's face. The technique was simple, its effect powerful. A woman in an expensive black suit patted his arm. An older man I recognized as one of Bill's French collectors laughed at something Mark said, and then a few seconds later, he gave Mark a hug.

At around seven o'clock, I saw Teddy Giles enter the gallery with Henry Hasseborg. Giles was thoroughly transformed from the last time I had seen him. He wore a pair of jeans and a leather jacket and had no makeup on his face. I watched him smile at a woman and then turn to Hasseborg and begin to talk, his face sober and intent. I started to worry that Bill would see them, and just as I was entertaining the ridiculous idea of standing in front of them to block Bill's view, I heard a child yell, 'No! No! I want to stay in here with the moon! No, Mommy, no!' I turned toward

330

the sound of the voice and saw a woman on all fours outside one of the doors, conducting a conversation with the small person inside. The child was happily ensconced behind a door with a space just large enough to hold him or her. 'People are waiting, darling. They want to see the moon, too.'

Behind that door were many moons – a map of the moon, a photograph of the moon, Neil Armstrong lifting a foot on the moon, van Gogh's moon in *Starry Night*, discs and slivers in white and red and orange and yellow, and fifty other renditions of the moon, including one made of cheese and another as a crescent with eyes, a nose, and a mouth. As I watched the mother reach inside for what turned out to be a kicking, wailing little girl, I turned to look for Giles and Hasseborg and couldn't find them. I walked quickly around the gallery. When I passed the child, who was now tearfully muttering the word 'moon' in her mother's arms, I guessed that she was no more than two and a half. 'We'll come back,' the mother said as she stroked her daughter's dark head. 'We'll come back and visit the moon.'

I turned toward Bernie's office door and saw Giles and Mark leaning against it. Mark was much taller than Giles and had to bend over to listen to him. A big woman wearing a shawl was standing in front of me and blocked part of my view, but I leaned to one side and caught what appeared to be an exchange of a small object between them. Mark slipped his hand into his pocket and grinned happily. Drugs, I thought. I marched toward them, and Mark raised his chin to look at me. He smiled, pulled his hand out of his pocket, and said brightly, 'Look what Teddy gave me? It belonged to his mom.'

Mark opened his palm and showed me a small round locket. He opened it, and inside were two tiny photos.

'That's me when I was six months old, and that's me when I was five,' Giles said as he pointed from one picture to the other. He held out his hand. 'You may not remember me. Theodore Giles.'

I shook his hand. He had a firm grip.

'I actually have another party tonight,' he said briskly. 'It was very nice to see you again, Professor Hertzberg. I'm sure we'll meet again.'

As he strode off toward the door with long confident steps, I turned back to Mark. The change in Giles's demeanor, the saccharine gift of a locket with baby pictures of himself, the return of the mysterious mother, prostitute, waitress, or God-knows-what mingled to create such confusion in my mind that I gaped at Mark.

He smiled at me. 'What's the matter, Uncle Leo?'

'He's completely different.'

'I told you it was an act. You know, part of his art. That's the real Teddy.'

Mark looked down at the locket. 'I think this is the nicest present I ever got. What a sweet guy.' He paused for several seconds as he stared at the floor. 'I wanted to talk to you about something,' he said. 'I've been thinking. I'm grounded, but I was hoping I could still come and visit you on Saturdays and Sundays like I used to.' He hung his head. 'I miss you. I wouldn't be leaving the building, and I don't think Dad and Violet would mind if we ask them.' He bit his lip and his forehead wrinkled. 'What do you think?'

'I think it can be arranged,' I said.

That fall was quiet. Paragraph by paragraph the Goya book inched ahead. I looked forward to a trip to Madrid that summer and to the long hours I would spend at the Prado. I worked closely with Suzanna Fields, who was writing her thesis on David's portraits and their relation to revolution, counterrevolution and the role women had played in both. Suzanna was a grave, shuffling girl with wire-rimmed glasses and a severe haircut, but over time I came to find her plain round face with its thick eyebrows rather attractive. Of course, deprivation had made many women attractive to me. On the streets, in the subway, in coffee shops and restaurants, I studied women of all ages and all shapes. As they sat and sipped their coffee or read their newspapers and books or hurried on their way to an appointment, I stripped them slowly in my mind and imagined them naked. At night, Violet still played the piano in my dreams.

The real Violet was listening to her collection of tapes – hundreds of hours of people answering the same questions: 'How do you see yourself?' and 'What do you want?' When I was at home during the day, their voices came through the ceiling from Violet's study. I could rarely hear what they were saying, but I heard mumbles and whispers, laughter, coughs, stammers, and every once in a while the throaty noise of sobs. I also heard the sound of the tape rewinding and understood that Violet was playing the same sentence or phrase over and over again. She had stopped talking to me about her book, and Erica reported that Violet had become a little mysterious about its content with her, too. All Erica knew for certain was that Violet had rethought her project completely. 'She doesn't want to talk about it yet,' Erica wrote to me. 'But I have a feeling the change in the book has something to do with Mark and his lies.'

Mark remained under house arrest every weekend until the first week in December. Bill and Violet allowed him to visit me when he was in New York, and he came faithfully every Saturday for a couple of hours. On Sunday he would turn up again for a short talk before he returned to Cranbury. In the beginning, I was wary of Mark and a little severe with him, but as the weeks passed I found it hard to stay angry. When I openly doubted his word, he looked so hurt, I stopped asking whether I could believe him. Every Friday he saw Dr Monk, an M.D. and psychotherapist, and I felt those weekly talks steadied and sobered him. I also met Mark's girlfriend, Lisa, and the simple fact that Lisa cared about Mark softened me toward him. Although all of Mark's friends were welcome to visit him, Teenie, Giles, and the strange boy called Me never came to Greene Street, and Mark never mentioned them – nor did he wear the locket Giles had given him. Lisa came. Seventeen, pretty and blond, Lisa was an enthusiast. She flapped her hands at the sides of her face when she talked about her vegetarianism, global warming, or a species of tiger that was nearly extinct. When the two of them visited me, I noticed that Lisa would often reach out and touch Mark's arm or take his hand in hers. These gestures reminded me of Violet, and I wondered if Mark had felt their likeness. Lisa was obviously in love with Mark, and when I thought of the injured Teenie, I rejoiced at his improved taste. Lisa's 'life goal,' as she called it, was to become a teacher for autistic children. 'My younger brother's autistic,' she said, 'and Charlie's been doing much better since he started this music-therapy program. The music kind of unblocks him.'

'She's very moral,' Mark said to me on the Saturday in December that marked the last day of his punishment. 'When she was fourteen, she got involved with drugs for a while, but then she went into a program and has been clean ever since. She doesn't even have a beer. She doesn't believe in it.'

As I nodded at the nobility of her abstinence, Mark volunteered information about their sex life, which I could have done without. 'We haven't had intercourse yet,' he said. 'We both think it should be planned, you know, talked about before. It's a big thing, and you can't just rush into it.'

I didn't know what to say. 'Rush' is a word that pretty much covered every initial sexual encounter I had ever had in my life, and the fact that these two young people felt it necessary to deliberate over sex made me feel a little sad. I have known women who withdrew from me at the last moment and women who regretted their passion the next morning, but a precoital committee meeting had never been a part of my experience.

Mark continued to visit every Saturday and Sunday into the spring. He arrived punctually at eleven on Saturday and often accompanied me on my ritual errands, to the bank, to the grocery store and the wine shop. On Sundays he always returned for a good-bye. I was touched by Mark's loyalty and heartened by his news about school. He told me proudly about the 98s he was receiving on his vocabulary quizzes, a paper on *The Scarlet Letter* he had 'aced,' and more about Lisa, the ideal girl.

In March, Violet called me late one afternoon and asked if she could come down and talk to me alone. Her request was so unusual that when she arrived, I said, 'Are you all right? Has anything happened?'

'I'm fine, Leo.' Violet sat down at my table, motioned for me to sit opposite her, and said, 'What do you think of Lisa?'

'I like her very much,' I said.

'So do I.' Violet looked down at the table. 'Do you ever get the feeling that there's something wrong with it?'

'With it? Lisa, you mean?'

'No, with Mark and Lisa. With the whole thing.'

'I think she's really in love with Mark.'

'I do, too,' she said.

'Well?'

Violet put her elbows on the table and leaned toward me. 'Did you ever play that game when you were a kid: 'What's wrong with this picture?' You would look at a drawing of a room or a street scene or a house, and when you started to look at it closely, you would see that a lamp shade was upside down or a bird had fur instead of feathers or a candy cane was sticking out of an Easter display? Well, that's how I'm feeling about Mark and Lisa. They're the picture, and the longer I look at them, the more I feel like there's something out of whack, but I don't know what it is.'

'What does Bill think?'

'I haven't said anything to him. He's had such a terrible time. He couldn't work after Mark's lie about the job, and now he's just coming back to himself. He's impressed with Mark's improvement, with Lisa, the therapy with Dr Monk. I don't have the heart to mention something that's just a gut feeling.'

'It's very hard to trust someone who lied in such

a spectacular way,' I said. 'But I haven't noticed any obvious lies, have you?'

'No.'

'Then I think he deserves the benefit of the doubt.'

'I hoped you would say that. I've been so afraid that something's happening.' Violet's eyes filled with tears. 'At night I lie awake worrying about who he is. I think he hides so much of himself that it scares me. For a long time, Leo. I mean, since Mark was a kid . . .' She didn't finish.

'Tell me, Violet,' I said. 'Don't stop.'

'Every once in a while, not, not always, just now and then, I talk to him, and I get this weird feeling that . . .'

'That . . .' I prompted.

'That I'm talking to somebody else.'

I narrowed my eyes. Violet was hunched over the table. 'It's made me awfully shaky, and Bill, well, Bill's had to fight his way out of a depression. He has great hopes for Mark, great hopes, and I don't want him to be disappointed.' She let the tears fall, and she started to shake. I stood up, walked around the table, and put my hand on her shoulder. She shuddered once and stopped crying very suddenly. She thanked me in a whisper, and after that, she hugged me. For hours afterward, I felt her warm body against me and her wet face on my neck.

On the third Saturday in May, I walked to the bank much earlier than usual. The end of the semester and the sunny weather lured me outside. The morning sun and the still-empty streets buoyed my spirits as I headed north toward the Citibank above Houston Street. There was no line at the bank, and I walked directly to the cash machine to take out my money for the week. When I removed my wallet from my pocket and opened it, I couldn't find my bank card. Befuddled, I tried to think when I had last used it. The Saturday before. I always replaced my card. Turning to the machine's screen with its sign that said, 'May I help you?' I started thinking about the word 'I' in that sentence. Did the automated teller deserve that pronoun? The thing sent messages and performed operations. Was that all that was needed to claim the privilege of the first person? And then, as if the answer had been given to me by the text on the screen, I knew. The clear wounding truth hit me suddenly, and it hit me hard. I always left my wallet and keys by the telephone in the hallway when I was at home. This habit prevented me from having to search through various jackets and coats before I left for work. I remembered Mark asking, 'When's your birthday, Uncle Leo?' 21930. My pin number. Mark had never observed my birthday. How many times had he accompanied me to the bank? Many times. Didn't he always leave me to go to the bathroom or visit Matt's room, passing my billfold, which was laid out in full view? Several people had entered the bank, and a line had formed behind me. A woman gave me a questioning look as I stood ogling my open wallet. I rushed past her and half-ran, half-walked home.

Once inside my apartment, I yanked out my bank records and removed my checks. I rarely bothered to look closely at either of them. When statements arrived in the mail, I filed the papers and forgot about them until tax time. My checking account was untouched, but a Day-to-Day Savings Account where I had kept $7,000 in fees from articles and the small advance I had received for my Goya book had all but disappeared. It was the money I had saved for Spain. I had told Mark about my trip, had even mentioned the account. All that remained of it was $6.31. Withdrawals had been made from all over the city since December, some from banks I had never heard of, often during the wee hours of the morning, and all of the recorded dates were Saturdays.

I called Bill and Violet but heard only Bill's soft voice telling me to leave a message. I asked them to call me immediately when they came in. Then I called Lucille, whom I hadn't spoken to since her reading. As soon as she answered the phone, I launched into the story. When I finished talking, she was silent for at least five seconds. Then, in a small, toneless voice, she said, 'How can you be sure it was Mark?'

I raised my voice. 'The pin number. He asked about my birthday! Most people use their birthdays! And the dates! The dates all correspond to his visits. He's been robbing me blind for months!

I can go to the police! Mark's committed a crime. Don't you understand?'

Lucille was silent.

'He's stolen nearly seven thousand dollars from me!'

'Leo,' Lucille said firmly. 'Calm down.'

I was not calm, I told her, and I didn't want to be calm, and if for some reason Mark arrived at her house without paying his regular visit to mine first, she was to seize the card immediately.

'But what if he didn't take it?' she said in the same unruffled voice.

'You know he did!' I howled, and I slammed the receiver into its cradle. I regretted my anger at Lucille almost immediately. She hadn't stolen money from me. She didn't want to condemn Mark without real proof. What seemed clear to me wasn't obvious to her, and yet when Lucille's cool, detached voice met my anger, it was like throwing gasoline on a fire. Had she expressed shock, pity, even dismay, I wouldn't have yelled.

Less than an hour later, Mark knocked at my door. When I opened it, he smiled at me and said, 'Hi. How's it going?' Then he paused and said, 'What's the matter, Uncle Leo?'

'Give me my card,' I said to him. 'Give me my card right now.'

Mark squinted at me with a puzzled expression. 'What are you talking about? What card?'

'Give me my ATM card right this minute,' I

said, 'or I'll get it myself.' I waved my fist in his face, and he took two steps backward.

He looked very surprised. 'You're crazy, Uncle Leo. I don't have your card. Even if I did, what would I do with it? Calm down.'

Mark's handsome face and startled eyes, his dark curls and relaxed, unresponsive body seemed to invite violence. I grabbed him by his silver Lurex sweater and pushed him against the wall. Four inches taller, forty years younger, and certainly stronger than I was, Mark let me push him up against the wall and pin him there. He said nothing. His body was as limp as a rag doll's.

'Take out the card right now,' I grunted at him through clenched teeth, 'and hand it over. I swear if you don't, I'll beat you bloody.'

Mark continued to look at me with an expression of blank amazement. 'I don't have it.'

I shook my fist in his face. 'This is your last chance.'

Mark reached for his back pocket, and I let go of him. He pulled out a wallet, opened it, and slipped out my blue card. 'I was tempted to take your money, Uncle Leo, but I swear I didn't use it. I didn't take a penny.'

I backed away from him. The boy is mad, I thought. A sensation of awe passed through me, old awe, the awe of childhood fears, of monsters and witches and ogres in the dark. 'You've been stealing from me for months, Mark. You've taken almost seven thousand dollars of my money.'

Mark blinked. He looked uncomfortable.

'It's all recorded. Every withdrawal is on paper. You stole my card on Saturday after I had gone to the bank and then returned it Sunday morning. Sit down!' I yelled.

'I can't sit. I told Mom I would come home early today.'

'No,' I said. 'You're not going anywhere. You've committed a crime. I can call the police and have you arrested.'

Mark sat down. 'The police?' he said in a small puzzled voice.

'You must have known that, stupid and absentminded as I am, eventually I would find out. I mean, this isn't a few quarters.'

Mark turned to stone before my eyes. Only his mouth moved. 'No,' he said. 'I didn't think you'd find out.'

'You knew that money was for my trip to Madrid. What did you think would happen when I went to take it out to pay for my airline tickets and the hotel?'

'I didn't think about that.'

I couldn't believe it. I refused to believe it. I badgered, pushed, and interrogated him, but he only gave me the same dead answers. He was 'embarrassed' that I had discovered the theft. When I asked him if he had used the money for drugs, he told me with apparent candor that he could get drugs for free. He bought things, he said. He went to restaurants. Money goes fast, he explained to me. His answers struck me as outlandish, but I now believe that the frozen person sitting on that chair was telling me the truth. Mark knew that he had stolen money from me, and he knew that it had been wrong to do it, but I am also convinced that he felt no guilt and no shame. He could offer no rational explanation for the stealing. He was not a drug addict. He wasn't in debt to anyone. After an hour, he looked at me and said flatly, 'I took the money because I like having money.'

'I like having money, too,' I screamed at him. 'But I don't rob my friends' bank accounts to get it.'

Mark had nothing more to say on the subject. He didn't stop looking at me, however. He kept his eyes on mine, and I looked into them. Their clear blue irises and shining black pupils made me suddenly think of glass, as if there were nothing behind those eyes and Mark were blind. For the second time that afternoon, my anger changed to awe. What is he? I asked myself – not who, but what? I looked at him and he looked at me until I turned away from those dead eyes, walked to the telephone, and called Bill.

The next morning Bill offered me a check for seven thousand dollars, but I refused it. I told him it wasn't his debt. I said that Mark could pay me back over the years. Bill tried to push the check into my hand. 'Leo,' he said, 'please.' His skin looked gray in the light from my window, and he smelled strongly of cigarettes and sweat. He was wearing the same clothes he had had on the night before when he came downstairs with Violet and they listened to the story. I shook my head. Bill started to pace. 'What have I done, Leo? I talk to him and talk to him, but it's like he doesn't get it.' Bill paced. 'We've called Dr Monk. We're all going to see her again. She wants Lucille there, too. She also asked to see you alone, if you wouldn't mind. We're cracking down on him. He can't go out. No telephone calls. We're going to escort him everywhere – pick him up at the train, walk him home, take him to the doctor. When school's over, he'll live here, get a job, and start paying you back.' Bill stopped walking. 'We think he's been stealing from Violet, too, from her purse. She doesn't keep track of her money. It took her a long time to catch on, but . . .' He stopped. 'Leo, I'm so sorry.' He shook his head and held out his hands. 'Your trip to Spain.' He closed his eyes.

I stood up and put my hands on both his shoulders. 'You didn't do it, Bill. It wasn't you. Mark stole from me.'

Bill dropped his chin to his chest. 'You'd think that if you really love your child, these things couldn't happen.' He looked up at me, his eyes fierce. 'How did this happen?'

I couldn't answer him.

★ ★ ★

Dr Monk was a short plump woman with frizzy gray hair, a soft voice, and economical gestures. She began the interview with a simple statement. 'I'm going to tell you what I told Mr and Mrs Wechsler. Children like Mark are difficult to cure. It's very hard to get through to them. After a while, their parents usually give up on them, and they go out into the world alone, where they either pull themselves together, land in prison, or die.'

Her bluntness shocked me. Prison. Death. I muttered something about trying to help him. He was still young, still young.

'It's possible,' she said, 'that his personality isn't fixed yet. You understand that Mark's problems are characterological.'

Yes, I thought. It's a question of character. Such an old word – character.

I talked about my anger, about feeling betrayed and the uncanny effect of Mark's charm. I mentioned the fire and the doughnuts. Through the window in the room I could see a small tree that had begun to leaf. The broken knots on its long branches would later become large blooms. I had forgotten the name of the tree. I looked at it in silence after telling her about the friendship between Matt and Mark and continued to stare at it, searching for its identity as though its name were important. Then it came to me: hydrangea.

'You know,' I said to her, 'I think that before his death, Matthew withdrew from Mark. When I remember it now, they were very quiet with each

346

other in the car on the way to camp, and then in the middle of the ride, Matt said loudly, "Stop pinching me." It seemed so ordinary then – boys irritating each other.' The pinch led to the bite, and when I finished the story, Dr Monk raised her eyebrows and her eyes sharpened.

She didn't say anything about the bite, and I kept talking. 'I told Mark about my father's family,' I said. 'I hardly remember them. I never even met my cousins. They died in Auschwitz-Birkenau. My Uncle David survived the *lager* but died during the march out of the camp. I told him about my father's death from a stroke. When he listened to me, his face was so serious. I think there might have been tears in his eyes . . .'

'It isn't something that you tell many people.'

I shook my head and looked at the hydrangea tree. I felt lost to myself at that moment, as though another person were speaking. I kept my eyes on the tree, and there was something red in my mind, very red through a window.

'Do you know why you chose to tell Mark?'

I turned to her and shook my head.

'Did you tell Matthew?'

My voice shook. 'I told Mark much more. Matt was only eleven when he died.'

'Eleven is very young,' she said gently.

I began to nod, and then I wept. I cried in front of a woman I didn't know at all. After I left her, I wiped my face in her small neat bathroom with its bountiful supply of Kleenex and imagined all the

347

people who had been there before me, wiping away their tears and snot beside the toilet. When I walked outside the building on Central Park West, I looked across at the trees that had burst into full leaf and had a sensation of ineffable strangeness. Being alive is inexplicable, I thought. Consciousness itself is inexplicable. There is nothing ordinary in the world.

A week later, Mark signed a contract in front of me, Violet, and Bill. The document was Dr Monk's idea. I think she hoped that by agreeing to conditions laid down in black-and-white, Mark would be drawn into an understanding that morality is finally a social contract, a consensus about basic human laws, and that without it, relations among people degenerate into chaos. The paper read like an abbreviated, individualized version of the Ten Commandments:

> I will not lie.
> I will not steal.
> I will not leave the house without permission.
> I will not talk on the telephone without permission.
> I will repay in full the money I stole from Leo out of my allowance money, the money I will earn this summer, next year, and into the future.

I still have my copy among my papers. At the bottom is Mark's signature scrawled in a childish hand.

Every Saturday throughout the summer, Mark arrived at my door with his payment. I didn't want him in my apartment, so he remained in the hallway while he opened the envelope and counted the bills into my hand. After he was gone, I recorded the amount in a small notebook I kept on my desk. Mark paid me from the earnings he made as a cashier at a bakery in the Village. Bill walked him to work every morning, and at five o'clock Violet picked him up. Every day she asked his boss how Mark was doing, and the response was always the same. 'He's doing fine. He's a good kid.' Mr Viscuso must have pitied Mark for having such an over-protective mother. Other than his family, me, and his coworkers, the only person Mark saw was Lisa. She came to visit him two or three times a week, often carrying a book under her arm for Mark to read. Violet told me that these volumes usually came from the pop-psychology shelves of local bookstores and were filled with prescriptions for 'inner peace' that included exhortations to the reader such as 'Learn to love yourself first' and 'Fight the underground beliefs that keep you from being your best, happiest self.' Lisa had signed on to the cause of Mark's reformation, and she spent many hours with him explaining the path to enlightenment. According to Violet, when Mark wasn't working, eating, or communing with Lisa about the tranquillity of his soul, he was sleeping. 'That's all he does,' she said, 'sleep.'

In late August, Bill flew to Tokyo to prepare for a show of the doors. Violet stayed home with Mark. At nine o'clock on the Thursday morning after Bill left, Violet came downstairs to my apartment wearing her bathrobe. 'Mark's gone,' she said as she walked into the kitchen. She poured herself a cup of coffee and sat down at the table with me.

'He left through the window, took the fire escape to the roof, and then walked down the stairs to the front door. I thought the roof door was locked, but when I checked this morning, I found it open. I think he's been doing it all along, but usually he comes back before morning. He sleeps and sleeps because he's exhausted from being out all night. I never would've known,' she said quietly, 'but the phone rang at around two o'clock last night. I don't know who it was. Some girl. She wouldn't tell me her name, but she asked me if I knew where Mark was, and I said he was sleeping and I wouldn't wake him. She said, "The hell he is. I just saw him." There was a lot of noise in the background, probably a club. Then she said that she wanted to help me out. "You're his mother," she said. "You ought to know." It's funny, I didn't say I wasn't his mother. I just listened. Then she said she had to tell me something.' Violet took a big breath and sipped the coffee. 'It might not be true, but the girl said that Mark is with Teddy Giles every night. She

350

said, "The She-Monster's out of its cave," but I didn't know what she was talking about. I tried to interrupt her, but she just rushed on, saying that Giles had bought a boy in Mexico.'

'Bought?' I said.

'That's what she said, that the boy's parents sold him to Giles for a few hundred dollars and that after that, the boy fell in love with Giles, that Giles dressed him up as a girl and took him everywhere for a while. Her story was pretty confused, but she said that one night they had a fight and Giles cut off the boy's little finger. Giles then took the boy to an emergency room and had the finger sewn back on, but not long after that, the kid, Rafael, disappeared. She said that there are rumors going around that Giles murdered him and threw his body into the East River. "He's a maniac," she said. "And he's got his claws in your kid. I just thought you oughta know." Those were her exact words. Then she hung up.'

'Have you told Bill?'

'I've tried. I left messages at his hotel, but not urgent ones. What's the poor guy going to do from Tokyo?' Violet looked thoughtful. 'The problem is, I'm afraid.'

'Well, if any of this is remotely true, you have reason to be. Giles is a frightening person.'

Violet opened her mouth as if to speak, but then she closed it. She nodded and turned her head away from me, and I admired her neck and profile. She's still beautiful, I thought, maybe more beautiful now that she's older. She and her face have a new harmony that didn't used to be there when she was young.

Mark showed up at his mother's house the following Sunday. According to Bill and Violet, he insisted that he had never left the house before, declared the story about Rafael 'total B.S.' and explained that he had run off to see some friends because he had been 'bored.' A week later, he was back at his mother's house, going to school. Every Friday, either Bill or Violet picked him up at the train, took him on the subway to Dr Monk's for his therapy, waited for him, and then escorted him back to Greene Street. His imprisonment at home continued.

In the months that followed, Mark's behavior fell into a recognizable pattern I began to call 'the rhythm of dread.' For weeks at a time, he appeared to do well. He produced A and B work in school, was cooperative, helpful, and kind, and paid me weekly out of his allowance money. Bill and Violet reported that their long talks with him about trust, honesty, and abiding by the contract seemed to be helping him 'stay on track.' He unburdened himself to Dr Monk, who was pleased with his 'progress.' And then, just at the moment when the people around him had been lulled into a feeling of cautious optimism, Mark would burst into flames. In October, Violet found his bed empty in the middle of the night and all the cash in her purse missing. He reappeared Sunday morning. In

November, his stepfather, Philip, noticed a large dent in his car before he went to work. In December, Bill took Mark to lunch in the neighborhood. After they had ordered hamburgers, Mark excused himself to go to the bathroom; he showed up three days later at Lucille's. In February, Mark's history teacher found him vomiting in the boys' toilet, a litre of vodka in his backpack and Valium pills in his pocket.

Every incident played itself out according to the same master script. First, the unhappy discovery; second, the injured person's explosion; third, Mark's reappearance and fervent denials. Yes, he had absconded, but he hadn't really done anything wrong. He had walked around the city. That was all. He needed to be alone. He hadn't taken Philip's car out in the middle of the night. If there was a dent in the door, somebody else must have stolen the station wagon. Yes, he had run from the house that night, but he hadn't stolen money. Violet was mistaken. She must have spent it or miscounted. Mark's indignant assertions of his innocence were astoundingly irrational. Only when he was presented with positive proof did he admit guilt. In hindsight, Mark's actions were nauseatingly predictable, but not one of us was looking back then, and although his behavior ran in cycles, we weren't clairvoyant. The day of an uprising couldn't be foretold.

Mark had become an interpretive conundrum. It seemed to me that there were two ways to read his behavior, both of which involved a form of dualism. The first was Manichaean. Mark's double life resembled a pendulum that swung between light and dark. A part of him truly wanted to do well. He loved his parents and his friends, but at regular intervals he was overwhelmed by sudden urges and acted on them. Bill firmly believed in this version of the story. The other model for Mark's behavior might be compared to geological layers. The so-called good impulses were a highly developed surface that largely disguised what lay underneath. Every so often, the restless, quaking forces below would make a sudden volcanic push toward the surface and erupt. I began to think that this was Violet's theory, or more precisely that this was the theory she feared.

However one chose to read them, Mark's outbursts of delinquency exacted a cruel vengeance on Violet and Bill. At the same time, by stealing my money, Mark had brought his father and stepmother even closer to me. We were all victims, and the taboos that had existed before Mark's theft were now toppled. The anxieties Bill and Violet had once left unspoken in the name of protecting Mark became part of our conversations. Violet raged against his betrayals and then she forgave him, only to rage and forgive again. 'I'm on a love-hate roller-coaster,' she said. 'It's always the same ride, over and over again.' And yet, despite her frustration, Mark became Violet's crusade. I noticed that lying on her desk along with several other volumes was a book called *Deprivation and Delinquency* by D. W. Winnicott. 'We're not going to lose him,' she told me. 'We're going to fight.' The problem was that Violet's frenzied battles were fought against an invisible enemy. She armed herself with passion and information, but when she rushed forward for the attack, she found nothing on the field of battle but an agreeable young man who offered no resistance.

Bill wasn't a soldier, and he didn't read a single book on teenage disturbances. He languished. Every day he looked older, grayer, more hunched, and more distracted. He reminded me of a large wounded animal whose powerful body was steadily shrinking. Violet's bouts of fury at Mark kept her vigorous. If Bill felt anger, it was turned against himself, and I watched as he slowly, steadily gnawed at his own flesh. It wasn't the content of Mark's crimes that hurt Bill – the fact that he ran off, mixed vodka with Valium, snitched his stepfather's car, or even that he lied and stole. All this could have been forgiven under other circumstances. Bill would have been far more accepting of open rebellion. Had Mark been an anarchist, he would have understood. Had he argued for his own hedonism or even run away from home to live his life according to his own daft ideas, Bill would have let him go. But Mark did none of these things. He embodied everything Bill had fought long and hard against: shallow compromise, hypocrisy, and cowardice. When he talked to me, Bill seemed more confused by his son than anything else. He told me in an amazed voice that when he had asked Mark what he most wanted from life, the boy had replied with apparent candor that he wanted people to like him.

Bill went to his studio every day, but he didn't work. 'I walk over there,' he said, 'and I hope that something will come to me, but it doesn't. I read the box scores from spring training. Then I lie down on the floor and invent ball games in my head, the way I used to when I was a kid. The games go on and on. I do the play-by-play, and then I sleep. I sleep and dream for hours, and then I stand up and go home.'

I couldn't offer Bill much more than my presence, but I gave him that. There were days when I left work and went straight to the Bowery. There we would sit on the floor and talk until dinnertime. Mark wasn't our only subject. I complained about Erica, whose letters to me always managed to keep some small hope for us alive. We told stories from our childhoods and talked about paintings and books. Around five, he allowed himself to open a bottle of wine or pour himself a Scotch. In the woozy hours that followed, the light of the lengthening days shone through the window over our heads, and Bill, enlivened by the alcohol, quoted Samuel Beckett or his Uncle Mo with his finger pointed at the ceiling. He declared his love for Violet with wet, pink eyes and reaffirmed his hopes for Mark in spite of everything. He roared over bad jokes, dirty limericks, and silly puns. He railed against the art world as a paper tower of dollars and marks and yen and told me in solemn tones that he was dried up, finished as an artist. The doors had been a swan song 'to all that.' But a minute later, he would say that he had been thinking a lot about the color of wet cardboard. 'It's beautiful on the streets after a rain, lying loose in a gutter or tied up in those neat bundles with string.'

They were afternoons of drama – the drama of Bill, who never bored me, because when I was near him I felt his weight. The man was heavy with life. So often it's lightness that we admire. Those people who appear weightless and unburdened, who hover instead of walk, attract us with their defiance of ordinary gravity. Their carelessness mimics happiness, but Bill had none of that. He had always been a stone, massive and hulking, charged from within by magnetic power. I was pulled toward him, more than ever before. Because he was suffering, I gave up my defenses and my envy. I had never examined that feeling, had never admitted to it, but I did then. I had envied him – potent, stubborn, lustful Bill, who had made and made and made until he felt that the making was over. I had envied him Lucille. And Violet. And I had envied him Mark, if only because the boy had lived. The truth was bitter, but Bill's pain brought a new frailty to his character, and that infirmity had made us more equal.

Violet joined us at the Bowery one evening in early March with a brown bag of Thai food that we ate on the floor. We gobbled down the dinner like three starved refugees and then stayed in the studio and talked and drank into the night. Violet crawled onto the mattress and lay on her back and spoke to us from that position. After a while, we all found a spot on the bed – Violet in the middle, Bill and I on either side of her – three contented drunks who kept up a piecemeal conversation. At around one o'clock in the morning, I said I had to go home or I'd never get to work tomorrow. Violet grabbed Bill's arm and then mine. 'Five more minutes,' she said. 'I'm happy tonight. I haven't been happy like this for a long, long time. It's so good to be forgetful and free and stupid.'

Half an hour later, we were walking on Canal Street toward Greene. Our arms were still linked, and Violet was still between me and Bill. She sang us a Norwegian folk song – something about a fiddler and his fiddle. Bill joined in the chorus, his voice deep and loud and flat. I sang, too, imitating the sounds of the meaningless words as we marched home. While she was singing, Violet lifted her chin and her face caught the light of the streetlamps above us. The air was cold but clear and dry, and as she hugged my arm tightly, I could feel the lift in her step. Before she launched into the second verse, she took a big breath and smiled at the sky, and then, as I continued to look down at her, I saw her close her eyes for a couple of seconds to blind herself to everything but the swelling happiness that sounded in our voices. We all felt it that night – the return of joy for no reason. When I closed my door after saying good night to Bill and Violet, I knew that by morning the feeling would be gone. Transience was part of its grace.

For months, Lazlo kept his ears open. I don't know exactly where he picked up his information. He roamed the galleries, and he and Pinky were often out at night. All I know is that when the gossip and rumors flew, they seemed to fly in Lazlo's direction. The tall thin young man with the notable hair, garish clothes, and big black glasses took in far more than he let out. Ideal spies are supposed to be inconspicuous, and yet I came to regard Lazlo as the perfect sleuth. His brilliant exterior was like a beacon in New York's crowds of black-clad people, but that very bright-ness made him unsuspicious. He, too, had heard stories about a boy's disappearance and rumbles about a murder, but Lazlo believed that the talk was part of Teddy Giles's underground publicity machine, which manufactured the ghoulish tales to increase his status as the art world's latest enfant terrible. There was other talk that worried Lazlo more – that Giles 'collected' young people, both boys and girls, and that Mark was a favored object. Giles was said to lead small groups of kids on forays into Brooklyn and Queens where the bands committed meaningless acts of vandalism or broke into basements and stole objects like teacups and sugar bowls. According to Lazlo's sources, the teenagers disguised themselves before these outings, changing the color of their skin and hair. Boys went as girls and girls as boys. There were stories of cruel harassments of homeless people in Tompkins Square Park, of overturning their shopping carts and stealing their blankets and food. Lazlo also heard peculiar reports about 'branding' – some form of body marking unique to Giles's inner circle.

Whether any of this actually happened was difficult to know. All that could be verified with any certainty was that Teddy Giles was rising as an art star. A recent sale to an English collector of a work called *Dead Blonde in a Bathtub* for a huge sum gilded his reputation by making him not only controversial but expensive. Giles had coined a new phrase, 'entertainment art,' which he brandished in every interview. He made the old argument that the distinctions between high and low art had disappeared, but then he added that art was no more and no less than entertainment – and that entertainment value was measured in dollars. Critics embraced these comments either as the clever height of irony or as the dawn of truth in advertising – the ushering in of a new era that admitted that art, like everything else, ran on cash. Giles gave interviews in various personas. Sometimes he dressed as a woman, delivering his comments in an absurd falsetto. At other times, he wore a suit and tie and sounded like a broker discussing his deals. I understood why people were fascinated by Giles. His voracious desire for attention forced him to reinvent himself regularly. Change is news, and he delighted the press in spite of the fact that his art was constructed from images that had long established themselves as trite conventions in more popular genres.

In late March, Bill started working again. The new project began with a woman and her baby on Greene Street. I saw her, too, from the window of Bill and Violet's loft, but I would never have guessed that she would be responsible for a whole new direction in Bill's work. There was nothing extraordinary about what we saw, but I've come to believe that Bill wanted exactly that – the everyday in all its dense particularity. For this he turned to film, or rather video. I was conservative enough to feel that an artist of such technical brilliance betrayed his talent by turning to the video camera, but after I saw the tapes, I changed my mind. The camera liberated Bill from the debilitating weight of his own thoughts by sending him into the streets, where he found a thousand children and the visual fragments of their unfolding life stories. He needed those children for his own sanity, and through them he would begin to compose an elegy about what all of us who live long enough have lost – our childhoods. Bill's lament would be unsentimental. There was no room in his work for the Victorian haze that continues to obscure our notions of childhood. But most important, I think he found a way to address his anguish about Mark without Mark.

We saw the woman early on a Sunday afternoon, after Mark had already been sent off on the train to Cranbury. Bill and I were standing near the window when Violet walked up behind Bill and put her arms around his waist. She pressed her cheek into his sweater, moved beside him, and pulled his arm over her shoulder. For a minute, the three of us watched the pedestrians below in silence. A cab pulled up, the door opened, and a woman in a long brown coat emerged with a child on her hip, several packages over both arms, and a stroller. We watched as she moved the child from one hip to the other, dug in her purse, extracted a bill, paid the driver, and then unfolded the stroller with her left hand and right foot. She lowered the heavily dressed baby into the contraption and fastened a belt around its middle. In the same instant, the child began to cry. The woman squatted on the sidewalk, removed her gloves, stuck them hastily into her pockets, and began to search a large quilted bag. She dug out a pacifier and popped it into the infant's mouth. Then she loosened the strings that tied the hood of the child's snowsuit, started jiggling the stroller with one hand, and leaned close to the baby's face. She smiled and began to talk. The baby leaned back in the stroller, sucking hard, and closed its eyes. The woman glanced at her watch, stood up, hung her four bags over the handlebars, and began pushing the stroller up the street.

When I turned from the window, Bill was still watching the woman. He didn't say a word about her that afternoon, but while we ate Violet's frittata and talked about whether Mark would pass his last semester's classes and manage to graduate from high school, I sensed the deflection in Bill. He listened to what Violet and I were saying and he answered us, but at the same time he remained aloof, as if some part of himself had already left the apartment and was walking down the sidewalk.

The following morning, he bought a video camera and started working. For the next three months, he left early in the morning and stayed out well into the afternoon. When he finished filming, he walked to the studio and sketched until dinner. After eating, he often returned to his notebooks, drawing far into the night. But he spent every minute of the weekends with Mark. According to Bill, the two of them talked, watched rented movies, and then talked again. Mark had become Bill's handicapped child, someone who had to be nursed like an infant, someone who could never leave his sight. In the middle of the night, Bill checked on his son to make sure he hadn't climbed out the window and disappeared. His paternal vigilance, once a form of punishment, became a means of preventing the inevitable rampage, one he feared would tear the boy to pieces.

Although Bill had recovered his energy through the new project, his excitement had a manic edge. When I looked at him, I felt that his eyes hadn't regained their old focus so much as taken on a fervid gleam. He slept very little, lost several pounds, and shaved even less often than was usual for him. His clothes stank of smoke, and late in the day, his breath smelled of wine or Scotch. Despite his intense schedule, I saw him often that spring, sometimes every afternoon. He would call me at home or at my office. 'Leo, it's Bill. How about a stop on the Bowery?' I said yes even on the days when it meant that I would be up late with papers or lecture preparations, because something in his voice on the telephone communicated his need for company. When I walked in on him at work, he always stopped to pat my back or take me by the shoulders and shake them as he told me about the children on a playground he had seen that afternoon and captured on tape. 'I'd forgotten how loony little kids are,' he said. 'They're completely dotty.'

One afternoon in the middle of April, Bill suddenly started talking about the day he'd returned to Lucille to give their marriage one more chance.

'When I walked through the door, the first thing I did was crouch down and tell Mark that I was never going away again, that we were all going to live together.' Bill turned his head and studied the bed he had made for his son years ago. It was still standing in a far corner of the room not far from the refrigerator. 'And then I betrayed him. I told him the usual rot – that I loved him but couldn't live with his mother anymore. The day the fifth letter came and I walked out the door, he started to scream 'Dad!' I heard him from the landing. I heard him all the way down the stairs, and I heard him in the street when I was walking away. I'll never forget his voice. He sounded like he was being killed. It's the worst thing I've ever heard.'

'Little children can cry like that over a candy bar or bedtime – anything.'

Bill turned to me. His eyes were narrowed and when he spoke his voice was low but incisive. 'No, Leo. That's just it. It wasn't that kind of crying. It was different. It was horrible. I can still hear it in my ears. No, I chose myself over him.'

'You don't regret it, do you?'

'How can I? Violet's my life. I chose to live.'

On the afternoon of May seventh, I didn't go to visit Bill. He didn't call me, and I stayed at home. When the phone rang, I was rereading a letter I had received from Erica a few hours earlier in the mail. The sentences I had been pondering were: 'Something has happened to me, Leo. I've taken a step, not in my mind that's always been racing ahead of me, but in my body, where the pain has made it impossible for me to move, to go anywhere except in circles around Matt. I realized that I want to see you. I want to get on a plane and come to New York and visit. I understand if you don't want to see me, if you're fed up. I don't blame you if you are, but I'm telling you what I want.' I didn't doubt Erica's sincerity. I doubted that her conviction would hold. At the same time, after I had read the words again, I thought she might really make the trip. The thought made me nervous, and when I lifted the receiver, I was still distracted by thoughts of Erica's possible decision to visit.

'Leo?'

The person on the line was speaking in an odd half whisper, and I didn't recognize the voice. 'Who's calling?'

For a second, no one answered. 'Violet,' she said in a louder voice. 'It's Violet.'

'What's the matter?' I said. 'What's happened?'

'Leo?' she said again.

'Yes, I'm here,' I said.

'I'm at the studio.'

'What's the matter?'

Again she didn't answer me. I heard her breathe into the receiver and then I repeated the question.

'I found Bill on the floor . . .'

'Is he hurt? Have you called an ambulance?'

'Leo.' Violet was whispering now, slowly, methodically. 'He was dead when I found him. He's been dead for a while. He must have died soon after he came in, because he still had his jacket on and the camera was on the floor beside him.'

I knew she had to be right but I said, 'Are you sure?'

Violet took a long breath. 'Yes,' she said. 'I'm sure. He's cold, Leo.' She had stopped whispering, but as Violet continued to talk in that foreign, uninflected voice, her composure frightened me. 'Mr Bob's been here, but now he's gone. I think I hear him praying.' She pronounced every word carefully, enunciating each syllable as if she were working hard to say her piece exactly right. 'You see,' she continued, 'I went to the train to pick up Mark, but he gave me the slip. I called the studio and left a message. I thought Bill was still out but that he'd be back by the time I got there. I was so pissed off at Mark, so furious, I needed to see Bill. It's funny, my anger doesn't mean anything now. I don't care. Bill didn't answer the buzzer, so I let myself in. I think that I must have cried out when I saw him, and that's why Mr Bob came up, but I don't remember that. I want you to come here, Leo, and help me call whoever it is you're supposed to call when somebody dies. I don't know why, but I can't do it. And then when you've done it, I want to be alone with him again. Do you understand what I'm saying?'

'I'm coming right now.'

Through the window of the taxi, I saw the familiar streets and signs and crowds on Canal Street, and while I saw everything with uncommon clarity, I felt that these sights didn't belong to me anymore, that they weren't tangible and that if the cab stopped and I stepped out, I wouldn't be able to grasp any of it. I knew the feeling. I had had it before, and I continued to feel it as I walked into the building and heard Mr Bob praying behind the door of the old locksmith shop. His voice didn't boom with the same Shakespearean resonance I had grown used to. He droned indistinctly in a chant that rose and fell and grew fainter as I neared the top floor and began to hear another voice – Violet's half whisper coming from inside the room a few steps above me. The door to the studio was standing ajar, but not fully open. Violet's low voice continued speaking, but I couldn't make out her words. I stopped behind the door, and for an instant I hesitated, because I knew that I would see Bill in the room. It wasn't fear I felt as much as an unwillingness to cross over into the inviolate strangeness of the dead, but the sensation was brief, and I pulled the door wide open. The lights were off and the late-afternoon sun filled the windows and cast a hazy light on Violet's hair. She was sitting cross-legged on the floor at the far end of the room, near the desk. She had Bill's head in her lap and was bent over him, talking in the same barely audible voice she had first used with me on the telephone. Even from that distance, I could see that Bill was dead. The stillness of his body couldn't be mistaken for repose or sleep. I had seen that inexorable quiet in my parents and in my son, and when I looked across the room at Bill, I knew right away that Violet was holding a corpse.

She didn't hear me enter, and for a few seconds

I didn't move. I stood in the doorway of the large familiar room and looked at the many rows of canvases against the wall, the boxes stored on shelves above it, the portfolios filled with thousands of drawings that were piled high below the windows, the familiar sagging bookshelves, the wooden crates of tools. I took it all in, and I noticed the specks of dust hovering in the dimming sunlight that fell in three long rectangular blocks to the floor. I began walking toward Violet, and at the sound of my footsteps, she lifted her chin and her eyes met mine. For a fraction of a second, her face contorted, but she covered her mouth with her hand and when she removed it, her features were once again calm.

I stopped beside Violet and looked down at Bill. His eyes were open and empty. There was nothing behind them, and their vacancy hurt me. She should close them, I thought to myself. She should close his eyes. I lifted my hands in a meaningless gesture.

'You see,' she said, 'I don't want them to take him away, but I know they have to. I've been here for a while.' She narrowed her eyes. 'What time is it?'

I looked at my watch. 'It's five-ten.'

Bill's expression was serene. It showed no sign of struggle or pain, and his skin looked younger and smoother than I remembered, as though death had stolen years from his face. He was wearing a blue work shirt stained with spots of what may have been grease, and seeing those dark flecks on his breast pocket made me shake. I felt my mouth move suddenly, and a small involuntary noise came from me – a grunt that I quickly suppressed.

'I came at about four,' Violet was saying. 'Mark got out of school early today.' She nodded. 'Yes, I was here at four.' Then she looked up at me and said fiercely, 'Do it! Go call!'

I walked to the telephone, looked down at it, and dialed 911. I didn't know any other number. I gave them the address. I think he had a heart attack, I said, but I don't know. The woman said they would send police officers. When I protested, she said that it was procedure. They would stay until the medical examiner arrived and determined the cause of death. When I hung up the phone, Violet looked at me harshly and said, 'Now I want you to go, so I can be with him. Wait downstairs for the people to come.'

I didn't wait downstairs. I seated myself on the step just outside the room, and I left the door ajar. As I sat there, I noticed a large crack in the wall I had never seen before. I put my fingers to it and let them run down the fissure as I waited and listened to the sound of Violet whispering to Bill, telling him things I didn't try to understand. I also heard Bob chanting downstairs, and I heard the noise of the traffic outside and impatient drivers honking their horns on the Manhattan Bridge. There was very little light on the stairway, but the steel door below me that led to the street was illuminated by a dull shine that must have come from a lamp inside Bob's rooms. I put my head in my hands and I breathed in the familiar smell that came from the studio – paint, mildewed rags, and sawdust. Like his father, I thought, he dropped dead, fell to the ground and died, and I wondered if Bill knew when the pains or spasm hit that his death was coming. For some reason, I imagined that he did and that his placid face meant that he had accepted that his life had come to an end. But that might have been a lie I was telling myself to soften the picture of his corpse on the floor.

I tried to re-create the conversation I'd had with him the day before about editing the videotapes. He had said that he planned to begin in a couple of months and was explaining the machine to me, the process of cutting. When it had become obvious that I understood very little, he had laughed and said, 'I'm boring you to death, aren't I?' But it wasn't true. I hadn't been bored at all, and I had said as much. Nevertheless, while I was sitting there on the step, I worried that I hadn't been adamant enough, that perhaps when I had said good-bye to him the day before, there had been a small unspoken cleft between us, seen only as a hint of disappointment in Bill's eyes. Perhaps he'd sensed my reservations about his sudden enthusiasm for video and had felt a little hurt. I knew that it was silly to focus on this insignificant exchange at the very end of a frienship that had lasted for twenty years, but the memory stung me nevertheless, and with it came a keen awareness that I would never be able to speak to him again about the tapes or anything else.

After a while, I realized that Violet had stopped talking. I didn't hear Mr Bob either. Disturbed by the silence, I stood up and looked through the door into the room. Violet had lain down beside Bill and put her head on his chest. One of her arms had disappeared under his torso and the other arm was looped around his neck. She looked small next to him, and she looked alive, even though she wasn't moving. The light had changed during the minutes I had been gone, and although I could still see both of them, their bodies were now in shadow. I saw the outline of Bill's profile and the back of Violet's head, and then I saw her lift her arm from around his neck and move it to his shoulder. While I watched, she began to stroke his shoulder over and over again, and while she did it, she rocked herself against his large motionless body.

In these last years, there have been times when I wished I hadn't witnessed that moment. Even then, while I was looking at the two of them lying together on the floor, the truth of my own solitary life closed over me like a large glass cage. I was the man in the hallway, the one who looked on at a final scene being played out inside a room where I had spent countless hours, but I wouldn't allow myself to step across the threshold. And yet, now I am glad that I saw Violet clinging to the minutes she had left with Bill's body, and I must have known that it was important for me to look at them, because I didn't turn my head away, and I didn't return to the step. I stood in the doorway and watched over them until I heard the buzzer and let in the two young officers who had come to perform their peculiar duty – hanging around until another official came and pronounced Bill dead of natural causes.

THREE

My father once told me a story about getting lost. It happened the summer after he had turned ten in the countryside near Potsdam, where his parents had a vacation house. He had spent every summer there since he was born and knew the woods and hills and meadows surrounding that house by heart. My father made a point of telling me that just before he walked off into the woods he had been quarreling with his brother. David, who was then thirteen, had pushed his younger brother out of the room they shared and locked the door, shouting that he needed privacy. After the fight, my father ran off, hot with anger and resentment, but after a while his temper cooled, and he began to enjoy moving through the trees, stopping to examine the tracks left by animals, and listening to the sounds of the birds. He walked and walked, and then, all at once, he no longer knew where he was. He turned around and tried to retrace his steps, but not a single clearing, rock, or tree seemed familiar to him anymore. Finally, he made his way out of the woods and found himself on a hill looking down at a house and a meadow. He saw a car and a garden, but he recognized nothing. Several seconds passed before he understood that the view was of his own house and garden and his family's dark blue automobile. When he told me the story, he shook his head and said that he had never forgotten the moment, that for him it illustrated the mysteries of cognition and the brain. He called it uncharted territory and followed up the story with a lecture on neurological devastations that leave their victims unable to recognize anything or anyone.

Years after my father died, I had a similar experience in New York. I was meeting a colleague who teaches in Paris for a drink in the bar of his hotel, and after asking a clerk for directions, I found myself walking down a long shining corridor with a marble floor. A man in an overcoat was striding toward me. Several seconds passed before I realized that the man I had taken for a stranger was my own reflection in a mirror at the end of the hall. Such brief intervals of disorientation aren't uncommon, but they interest me more and more, because they suggest that recognition is far more feeble than we suppose. Only a week ago, I poured myself what I imagined was a glass of orange juice, but it was milk. For several seconds, I couldn't say that it was milk I had tasted, only that the juice was disgusting. I like milk very much, but it doesn't matter. All that matters is that I expected one thing and got another.

The bewildering estrangement of such moments,

when the familiar turns radically foreign, isn't merely a trick of the brain but a loss of the external signposts that structure vision. Had my father not lost his way, he would have recognized his family's house. Had I known there was a mirror in front of me, I would have seen myself immediately, and had I identified the milk as milk, it would have tasted like itself. During the year that followed Bill's death, I continually found myself at a loss – either I didn't know what I was seeing or I didn't know how to read what I saw. Those experiences have left their traces in me as a nearly perpetual disquiet. Although there are times when it vanishes altogether, usually I can feel it, lurking beneath the ordinary activities of my day – an inner shadow cast by the memory of having been completely lost.

It is ironic that after spending years thinking through the historical conventions of painting and how they influenced perception, I found myself in the position of Dürer drawing a rhinoceros from hearsay. The artist's famous creature bears a strong resemblance to the real animal, but he got a number of crucial bits wrong, as did I when it came to reconstructing the people and the events that were a part of my life that year. My subjects were human, of course, and therefore notoriously difficult to get right, perhaps impossible, but I made a number of errors that were grave enough to qualify as a false picture.

The difficulty of seeing clearly haunted me long before my eyes went bad, in life as well as in art. It's a problem of the viewer's perspective – as Matt pointed out that night in his room when he noted that when we look at people and things, we're missing from our own picture. The spectator is the true vanishing point, the pinprick in the canvas, the zero. I'm only whole to myself in mirrors and photographs and the rare home movie, and I've often longed to escape that confinement and take a far view of myself from the top of a hill – a small 'he' rather than an 'I' travelling in the valley below from one point to another. And yet, remove doesn't guarantee accuracy either, although sometimes it helps. Over the years, Bill had become a moving reference for me, a person I had always kept in view. At the same time, he had often eluded me. Because I knew so much about him, because I had been close to him, I couldn't bring the various fragments of my experience with him into a single coherent image. The truth was mobile and contradictory, and I was willing to live with that.

But most people aren't comfortable with ambiguity. The job of piecing together a picture of Bill's life and work began almost immediately after his death with an obituary in the *New York Times*. It was a rather long and muddled article that included, among more flattering statements, a quotation from an excoriating review in the same newspaper. It labeled Bill a 'cult artist' who had mysteriously attracted large followings in Europe, South America, and Japan. Violet hated the article.

She railed against the writer and the paper. She shook the page in my face and said that she recognized the photograph of Bill but couldn't find him anywhere in the seven paragraphs that had been devoted to him, that he was missing from his own obituary. It didn't help to remind her that most journalists are merely conduits of received opinion, and it's the rare obituary writer who can turn out something other than a dull summary pieced together from equally witless articles on the man or woman in question. But as the weeks went on, Violet was comforted by the letters that came to her from all over the world, written by people who had seen Bill's work and found something in it to take away for themselves. Many of them were young, and many of them weren't artists or collectors but ordinary people who had somehow stumbled onto the work, often only in reproduction.

The incidents of blindness to art that is later pronounced 'great' are so frequent in history that they have become clichés. Van Gogh is now worshiped as much for his martyrdom to the cause of 'No Recognition in His Lifetime' as for his paintings. After hundreds of years in obscurity, Botticelli was reborn in the nineteenth century. The change in their reputations was simply a matter of reorientation, a new set of conventions that made understanding possible. Bill's work was complicated and cerebral enough to threaten art critics, but it also had a simple, often narrative power that engaged the untrained eye. I believe that *O's Journey*, for example, will last, that after the faddish jokes and winking absurdities that crowd the galleries have had their day in the sun, they'll wither like so much before them, and the glass boxes with their alphabetical characters will stand. It's impossible to know whether I'm right, but I hold fast to the belief, and so far, I haven't been proved wrong. In the five years since his death, Bill's reputation has grown stronger.

He left a lot of work behind him, including much that had never been shown. Violet, Bernie, and several gallery assistants began the task of organizing the canvases, boxes, sculptures, prints, drawings, notebooks, as well as the incomplete tapes that had been part of Bill's last project. In the early stages of the sorting, Violet asked me to come along, because she 'needed someone to lean on.' In a month, the cluttered storehouse of a man's life was transformed into a spare, eerie room with a desk and chair, mostly empty shelves, and crates illuminated by the changing sunlight nobody could take away. There were discoveries: delicate drawings of Mark as a baby, several paintings of Lucille that none of us had known existed. In one, she is writing in a notebook, and although part of her face is hidden, the intent focus she is giving to the words on the page is clear from her eyes and forehead. Written in longhand across the middle of the canvas are the large words 'It cried and cried.' The script cuts Lucille through the chest

382

and shoulders and seems to exist on another plane from the one she occupies. The canvas was dated October 1977. There was also a drawing of me and Erica that Bill must have done from memory, because we hadn't posed for it and I had never seen it. We are sitting together on Adirondack chairs outside the Vermont house. Erica is leaning toward me and has placed her hand on the arm of my chair. As soon as she found the drawing, Violet gave it to me, and I took it to the framers the very next day. Erica had come and gone by then. The New York trip she had imagined – a trip she had hinted might result in a reconciliation between us – had become instead a miserable journey to bury a friend. We never did get around to talking about ourselves. I hung Bill's drawing on the wall near my desk and looked at it often. In the quick lines that were Erica's hand, Bill seemed to have caught my wife's tremulous fingers, and looking at the sketch, I would invariably remember how she had shaken at his funeral, how her whole body had vibrated with a slight but visible palsy. I would remember taking her cold hand and clasping it between both of mine, and I would remember that despite my firm hold on her, the quiver, generated from somewhere deep in her nerves, did not stop.

Whenever an artist dies, the work slowly begins to replace his body, becoming a corporeal substitute for him in the world. It can't be helped, I suppose. Useful objects, like chairs and dishes, passed down from one generation to another, may briefly feel haunted by their former owners, but that quality vanishes rather quickly into their pragmatic functions. Art, useless as it is, resists incorporation into dailiness, and if it has any power at all, it seems to breathe with the life of the person who made it. Art historians don't like to speak of this, because it suggests the magical thinking attached to icons and fetishes, but I have experienced it time and time again, and I felt it in Bill's studio. When the art movers came and carried out the meticulously packed and carefully labeled crates and boxes as Violet, Bernie, and I watched, I was reminded of the two men from the funeral home who had put Bill's body into a vinyl bag and hauled it out of the same room two months earlier.

Although I knew better than most people that Bill himself and Bill's art were not identical, I understood the need to grant an aura to the work he had left behind him – a kind of spiritual halo that resists the harsh truths of burial and decay. When Bill's coffin was lowered into the ground, Dan rocked back and forth beside the grave. He folded his arms across his chest, bent forward from his waist, and then threw himself backward, over and over again. Like an Orthodox Jew at his prayers, he seemed to find comfort in the physical repetition, and I rather envied him his freedom. But when I walked over to him and looked into his face, it was ravaged and his eyes were wild and staring. Later that day on Greene Street, Violet gave Dan a tiny canvas that Bill had done of the letter *W* with a real key set into it. Dan put it under his shirt and hugged the little painting throughout the afternoon. It was warm, and I worried that he was sweating all over it, but I knew why he was holding the object next to his skin. He wanted no separation between himself and the little painting, because somewhere in the wood and canvas and metal he imagined that he was touching his older brother.

I brought Bill back to life in my dreams. He would come walking through my door or appear beside my desk, and I would always say to him, 'But I thought you were dead,' and he would say, 'I am. I just came back for a talk,' or 'I'm here to check on you – to make sure you're all right.' In one dream, however, when I asked him the same question, he said, 'Yes, I'm dead. I'm with my son now.' I began to argue with him. 'No, I said, Matthew is my son. Mark is your son,' but Bill wouldn't admit to it, and in the dream I was furious and woke up tormented by the misunderstanding.

Even after most of Bill's work had been taken from the studio, Violet continued to go to the Bowery every day. She told me she was taking care of odds and ends, sorting through Bill's personal things, mostly letters and books. I often saw her leaving the building in the morning with a heavy leather bag over her shoulder. She didn't return until six, sometimes seven o'clock at night, and when she did, she often had dinner with me. I cooked for her, and even though my culinary skills were inferior to hers, she always thanked me vociferously. I began to notice that for about half an hour after she arrived at my apartment, Violet looked strange. Her eyes had a glassy look, an oblique, shiny expression that alarmed me, especially in the first few minutes after she had stepped through the door. I didn't comment on it, because I could barely put what I was seeing into words. Instead I made small talk about the food or a book I was reading, and very slowly her face began to look more familiar and more present, as if she were returning to the here and now. Although I had heard Violet crying a couple of times since Bill died, had listened to her anguished sobs coming through the ceiling of my bedroom at night, she didn't greive in front of me. Her strength was admirable, but it had a brittle, determined air about it that every once in a while made me uncomfortable. I guessed that her toughness was Blomian – a Scandinavian trait inherited from a long line of people who had believed in suffering alone.

It may have been that same pride that caused Violet to ask Mark to come and live with her. She told Lucille that starting in July he could stay with her and find work in the city. Mark had managed to graduate from high school, but he hadn't applied to college, and his future lay in front of him like a great unmapped wilderness. When I asked Violet whether she was in any shape to take care of Mark, she bristled at me, saying that Bill would have wanted her to do it. She narrowed her eyes and pressed her lips together to indicate that she had made her decision and no further discussion was wanted.

The night before Mark moved in with her, Violet didn't return from the studio. She had called me in the morning to say that she wanted to take me out to dinner in the neighborhood. 'Don't buy food,' she said. 'I'll be home by seven.' At eight o'clock, I called her. The line was busy. Half an hour later, it was still busy. I walked to the Bowery.

The door to the street was wide open, and when I looked through it, I saw Mr Bob's entire person for the first time. A man of uncertain age, he had a rounded spine and thin legs, which contrasted sharply with his muscular arms. He was sweeping the hallway and nudged a thick pile of dust past my feet onto the sidewalk. 'Mr Bob?' I said.

Without raising his head to look at me, he glowered at the floor.

'I got worried about Violet,' I said. 'We were supposed to have dinner.'

The man didn't answer me and he didn't move. I stepped around him and began to climb the stairs.

'Watch your step,' he boomed.

Just as I reached the top, he added, 'Watch your step with Beauty!'

The door to the studio was also open, and I

drew a breath before I walked through it. The only light in the room came from a lamp on Bill's desk that illuminated a stack of papers lying beneath it. Although I had seen the naked loft in daylight, the evening murk seemed to enlarge the barren space, because my eyes didn't take in its perimeter. At first, I saw nobody, and then, as I looked toward the windows, I thought I saw Bill step into the blurry light that came from outside. As I looked at the apparition, I stopped breathing. Bill's withered ghost was standing in front of the pane smoking a cigarette. He had his back to me – baseball cap, blue work shirt, black jeans. I walked toward him, and at the sound of my steps, the deformed shrunken Bill turned around and he was Violet. I had never seen Violet smoke. She was holding the cigarette between her thumb and index finger the way Bill used to hold his butts when there was little left but the filter. She walked toward me.

'What time is it?' she said.

'It's after nine.'

'Nine?' she said, as if she were trying to fix the number in her thoughts. 'You shouldn't have come.' She let the cigarette fall and stepped on it.

'We were going to have dinner.'

Violet squinted at me. 'Oh yes.' She looked confused. 'I forgot.' After a few seconds, she said. 'Well, you're here.' She looked down at herself and stroked the sleeve of Bill's shirt with one hand. 'You look worried. Don't worry. I'm all right. The day after Bill died, I came back here. I wanted to look around alone. His clothes were lying in the corner, and I found the carton of cigarettes on the desk. I put them away in the cupboard above the sink. I told Bernie that everything in there was personal, that he couldn't touch it. After Bernie was finished organizing the art, I started coming again. It's my work now – to come here and stay. One afternoon, I went to the cupboard and took out his pants and shirt and the cigarettes. At first, I just looked at them and touched them. His other clothes are still at home, but most of them are clean, and because they're clean, they're dead. These have paint on them. He worked in these clothes, and then after a while, I didn't want to just touch them anymore. It wasn't enough. I wanted his clothes on me, touching my body, and I wanted to smoke the Camels. I've been smoking one a day. It helps.'

'Violet,' I said.

She acted as if I hadn't spoken, and looked around the room. I noticed a single open box on the floor and tubes of paint lined up in rows. 'I feel comforted here,' she said.

Matt's drawing of Jackie Robinson was still hanging on the wall not far from Bill's desk. I thought of asking about it, but I didn't.

Violet leaned toward me and put her hand on my arm. 'I was afraid he would die,' she said. 'I never told you or anybody else, because we're all afraid that people we love are going to die. It doesn't mean much really. But I began to think he wasn't well. He breathed too hard. He couldn't sleep. Once, he told me that he didn't like to close his eyes, because he thought that he might die in the night. After Mark stole your money, he'd sit up late and drink whiskey instead of coming to bed. I'd find him dozing on the sofa at three o'clock in the morning with the television still on. I'd pull off his shoes and his pants and cover him up out there or I'd get him into our bed.' She glanced at the floor for a moment. 'He was in bad shape, gloomy all the time. He talked about his father a lot. He talked about Dan's illness and how he had tried to help him, but nothing had worked. He started thinking about the child we never had together. Sometimes he said we should adopt a baby, but then he said it was too risky. He'd tried to be a good father, but he must have done it all wrong. When it was really bad, he would quote every mean sentence anybody had ever written about him. He had never seemed to care much about that stuff before, but it added up, Leo. Reviewers roughed him up pretty bad. Their spite seemed to come from the fact that there were other people who were so fanatically devoted to his work, but he forgot all the good things that had happened to him.' Violet stared across the room and stroked her arm again. 'Except me. He never forgot me. I would whisper in his ear, "Come to bed now," and he would put his hands on my face and kiss me. He was usually still a little drunk, and he'd say, "My darling. I love you so much" and other mushy things. The last few months were better. He seemed happy with the kids and his videotapes. I really thought the filming would keep him alive.' Violet turned her head to the wall. 'Every day it gets a little harder for me to go home. I just want to stay here and be with him.'

Violet took the pack of Camels out of Bill's shirt pocket. She lit a cigarette, and as she shook out the match, she said. 'I'm going to have one more today.' She blew a long stream of smoke out of her mouth. After that, we didn't speak to each other for at least a minute. My eyes had adjusted to the darkness, and the room seemed brighter. I studied the tubes of oil paints on the floor.

Violet broke the silence. 'There's something I want you to hear. It's on the answering machine. I listened to it the same day I found the clothes.' Violet walked to the desk and pressed the button on the machine several times. A girl's voice said, 'M&M knows they killed me.' That was all.

For a second, I heard Bernie's voice begin another message, then Violet turned off the machine. 'Bill heard it the day he died. The light wasn't blinking. He must have listened to the message when he came in.'

'But it's nonsense.'

Violet nodded. 'I know, but I think it's the same girl who called me that night about Giles. He couldn't have known that, because he didn't

391

talk to her.' She looked up at me and put her hand on mine. 'They call Mark M&M, did you know that?'

'Yes.'

Violet began to squeeze the top of my hand. She gripped it hard and I could feel her shaking.

'Oh, Violet,' I said.

My voice seemed to break her. Her lips quivered, her knees buckled, and she fell into me. I put my arms around her as she grabbed me around my waist and pressed her cheek against my neck. I removed the baseball cap and kissed her head once, just once. While I held her shuddering body and listened to her sobs, I smelled Bill – cigarettes, turpentine, and sawdust.

In Mark, mourning looked like deflation. His body reminded me of a squashed, airless tire that needed pumping up. He seemed unable to raise his chin or lift his hand without tremendous effort. When he wasn't working at his job as a clerk in a local bookstore, he was lying on the sofa wired to his Walkman or wandering sluggishly from one room to another, eating crackers from the box or gnawing at a Twinkie. He nibbled, munched, and gobbled all day and throughout the evening, leaving a trail of cellophane, plastic, and cardboard behind him. Dinner held little interest for him. He would pick at the meal and then leave most of the food on his plate. Violet never said a word to Mark about his eating habits. I guess she had decided that if

Mark wanted to chew his way through the loss of his father, she wasn't going to stop him.

Despite the fact that Violet didn't eat much dinner either, sharing the evening meal became a habit that lasted well into the following year. Preparing food was an important ritual that defined the day for all three of us. I bought the food and did most of the cooking. Violet chopped the vegetables, and Mark managed to keep himself upright long enough to stack the dishes in the dishwasher. After that chore was over, he would often lie on the sofa and watch television. Violet and I would sometimes join him, but after a couple of weeks the moronic sitcoms and garish dramas, which featured rapists and serial killers, began to annoy me, and I either excused myself and went downstairs or read quietly in a corner of the big room.

From my chair I made a study of the two of them. Mark held Violet's hand or rested his head on her chest. He draped his legs over hers or curled up on the sofa close to her. If his gestures hadn't been so infantile, I might have found them unseemly, but when Mark snuggled into his stepmother, he looked like a gigantic toddler exhausted from a long day at nursery school. I interpreted his clinging to Violet as another response to Bill's death, even though I had seen him lean on both his father and Violet in much the same way earlier. When my father died, I worked hard to play the man with my mother, and after a while the performance began to seem real, and then it was real. About a year after his death, I came home from school and found my mother sitting in the living room of our apartment. She was slumped over in the chair with her hands on her face. When I walked over to her, I could see that she had been crying. Except for the day my father died, I had never heard or seen my mother weep, and when she lifted her red swollen face toward me, she looked like a stranger, as if she weren't my mother at all. Then I saw the photo album sitting beside her on a table. I asked her if she was all right. She took my hands and answered me first in German, then in English. '*Sie sind alle tot*. They are all dead.' She reached out for me and laid her cheek just above my belt and I remember that the pressure of her head pushed the buckle into my skin and pinched me. It was an awkward embrace, but I remained standing and was relieved that she didn't cry. She hugged me very tightly for a minute or so, but during that time I felt unusually lucid, as though I had suddenly gained a commanding focus of everything in the room and everything beyond it. I squeezed my mother's shoulders to make her understand that I would protect her, and when she withdrew from me, she was smiling.

I was eighteen then, an authority on nothing and no one, a boy who could study hard but who floundered from one day to the next. Nevertheless, my mother had read my intention to be worthy of more and better, and it was all in her face – pride, sorrow, and a touch of amusement at my fit of manliness. I wondered if Mark would be able to shake off his torpor and console Violet, but the truth was, I didn't understand what lay beneath his lethargy. He was needy but not demanding, and his constant fatigue looked more like boredom than the paralysis of someone who has suffered a trauma. I sometimes wondered whether he really understood that his father wasn't coming back. It seemed possible that he had hidden that truth somewhere inside him where it wasn't available to his conscious thoughts. His face was so untouched by grief, it made me think that perhaps he had developed an immunity to very idea of mortality.

In the weeks following the night Violet broke down in the studio, she spoke more openly about her sadness, and her body began to look less rigid. She continued to walk to the Bowery every morning, and although she didn't talk about what she did there, she told me, 'I'm doing what I have to do.' I felt quite sure that when she arrived at the studio, she dressed herself in Bill's clothes and smoked her daily cigarette and did whatever else it was that she did in that room to observe her husband's death. I believe that while she was away Violet mourned intensely and deliberately, but once she came home to Mark, she did her best to take care of him. She picked up after him, washed his clothes, and cleaned the apartment. In the evenings when I looked at her as she sat beside him in front of the television, I could tell she wasn't watching the show. She simply wanted to be near him. While she stroked Mark's head or arm, Violet would often turn away from the TV altogether and look off into a corner, but she rarely stopped touching him, and I began to think that despite his childish dependency, she needed him as much as he needed her, perhaps more. On a couple of occasions, they fell asleep on the sofa together. Because I knew that Violet sometimes couldn't sleep at all, I didn't wake them. I stood up quietly and left the room.

I didn't forget that Mark had stolen my money, but after Bill died the theft seemed to belong to another era, to a time when Mark's criminal behavior took up more room inside me. The truth was that my rage had already been dissipated by Bill's suffering. He had done penance instead of Mark, had taken on the guilt as if it were his own. Through his self-flagellating atonements, Bill had managed to turn my missing $7,000 into his paternal failure. I hadn't wanted his contrition. I had wanted an apology from Mark, but he had never come to me and asked for forgiveness. He had made his weekly payments, delivered in increments of ten, twenty, or thirty dollars, but when Bill was no longer there to supervise the transaction, the money stopped coming, and I couldn't bring myself to ask for it. So when Mark showed up at my door one Friday in early August and handed me a hundred dollars, I was surprised.

Mark didn't sit down after he gave me the bills;

he leaned against my table and looked at the floor. I waited for him to say something, and after a long pause he looked up at me and said, 'I'm going to pay you back every penny. I've been thinking about it a lot.'

Again he was silent, and I decided not to help him out by responding.

'I want to do what Dad would want,' he said finally. 'I can't believe I'm never going to see him again. I didn't think he'd die before I changed.'

'Changed?' I said. 'What are you talking about?'

'I've always known that I would change. You know, do the right thing and go to college and get married and everything, that Dad would be proud of me and we could forget all the bad stuff that happened and go back to the way we used to be. I know I hurt him, and it bothers me now. I can't sleep sometimes.'

'You're always sleeping,' I said.

'Not at night. I lie in bed and think about Dad and it gets to me. He was the best thing in my life. Violet's really nice to me, but she's not like Dad. He believed in me and he knew that deep down I have a lot of good in me and it made all the difference. I thought I was going to have time to prove myself.'

Mark's eyes began to leak tears. They ran down his cheeks in two continuous clear streams. He didn't make any noise and his expression didn't change. I realized that I'd never seen anyone cry quite like that. He didn't sniffle or sob, but he produced a lot of liquid. 'Dad loved me a lot,' he said.

I nodded at Mark then. Up until that moment, I had kept my distance, maintaining the hard, suspicious attitude I had learned to adopt with him, but I could feel myself beginning to weaken.

'I'm going to show you,' he said in a loud determined voice. 'I'm going to show you because I can't show Dad, and you're going to see . . .' He dropped his head to his chest and squinted through his tears at the floor. 'Please believe me,' he said, his voice shaking with emotion. 'Please believe me.'

I stood up from my chair and walked over to him. When he lifted his head to look at me, I saw Bill. The resemblance came suddenly, a flare of recognition that called up the father in the son. The likeness caught me off guard, and during the seconds that followed it, I felt the loss of Bill in my body, as a pain in my gut that rose into my chest and lungs and seemed to choke off my breath. Both Mark and Violet had greater claims on Bill, and I had hidden my own pain out of deference to them, had suppressed the depths of my unhappiness even from myself, and then, like a revenant, Bill had appeared in Mark for an instant and vanished. Suddenly, I wanted him back and I was enraged that I couldn't have him. I wanted to pummel Mark with my fists and shout at him to return Bill. I felt that the kid had the power to do it, that he was the one who had worn his father to death, killed him with worry and anguish and fear, and now it was time to reverse the story and bring Bill to life again. These were insane thoughts, and I knew just how unhinged they were as I stood in front of Mark and realized that he had been telling me that he was guilty and wanted everything to be different from now on. I had a hundred dollars in my hand. He shook his head back and forth, repeating the refrain, 'Please believe me.' When I looked down, I saw that his sneakers had small pools of tears between the laces and the toes. 'I believe you,' I said in a voice that sounded peculiar, not because it was filled with emotion but because its tone was flat and normal and didn't begin to represent what I was feeling. 'Your father,' I said to him, 'was more to me than you can possibly know. He meant the world to me.' It was a stupid, banal phrase, but when I uttered it, the words seemed invigorated by a truth I had been keeping to myself for some time.

Mark's disappearance the following weekend had the quality of reenactment. He told us that he was going to visit his mother. Violet gave him money for the train and sent him off alone. The following morning, she discovered that $200 was missing from her purse and called Lucille, but Lucille knew nothing about the weekend visit. Three days later, Mark reappeared on Greene Street and heatedly denied that he had taken the money. While Violet cried, I stood beside her and played the role of disappointed father in Bill's absence, which didn't take any acting on my part, because only a week earlier I had believed that Mark meant what he said. I began to wonder if it wasn't exactly such moments that set him off, that in order to enact a betrayal, he had to first convince whomever it was of his unwavering sincerity. Like a machine of perfect repetition, Mark was driven to do what he had done before: lie, steal, vanish, reappear, and finally, after recriminations, fury, and tears, reconcile with his stepmother.

Proximity and belief are closely connected. I lived close to Mark. That immediacy and contact flooded my senses and played on my emotions. When I was only inches away from him, I inevitably believed at least a part of what he was saying. To believe nothing would have meant complete withdrawal, exile not only from Mark but from Violet, and I organized my days around the two of them. While I read and worked and shopped for dinner, I anticipated the aura of the evening – the food, Violet's strange, ecstatic face when she returned from the studio, Mark's chatter about DJs and techno, Violet's hand on my arm or shoulder, her lips on my cheek when I said good night, and the smell of her – that mixture of Bill's scents with her own skin and perfume.

For me and maybe for Violet, too, Mark's lapse into his old pattern and the punishment Violet imposed – another grounding – had the remote quality of bad theater. We saw what was happening, but the story and the dialogue were so stilted and familiar, it made our emotions seem a little absurd. I suppose that was the problem. It wasn't that we stopped feeling pained by Mark's crimes but that we recognized that our pain had come from the lowest kind of manipulation. Yet again, we had been duped by the same old dreary plot. Violet tolerated Mark's treachery because she loved him, but also because she didn't have the strength to confront the meaning of his fresh betrayals.

Three weeks later, Mark disappeared again. This time he took a Han horse from my bookshelf and Violet's jewelry box. In it were pearls from her mother and a pair of sapphire and diamond earrings Bill had given her on their last anniversary. The earrings alone were worth almost five thousand dollars. I don't know how he managed to squirrel the horse out of my apartment. It wasn't very large, and he could have done it on a number of occasions when I wasn't watching him, but I didn't notice that it was missing until the morning after he left. This time Mark didn't show up after a couple of days. When Violet called the bookstore to ask if they had seen him, the manager told her he hadn't been there in weeks. 'One day he didn't come in. I tried calling, but the telephone number he gave us didn't work, and when I looked up William Wechsler, the number was unlisted. I hired somebody else.'

Violet waited for Mark to return. Three days passed, then four, and with each passing day Violet seemed to diminish. Early on, I thought her shrinking was an illusion, a visual metaphor that expressed our shared anxiety about Mark's absence, but on the fifth day, I noticed that Violet's pants were hanging loosely around her middle and that the familiar roundness of her neck and shoulders and arms was gone. That evening at dinner, I insisted that she try to get some food into her, but she shook her head at me and her eyes filled with tears. 'I've called Lucille and all his school friends. Nobody knows where he is. I'm afraid he's dead.' She stood up, opened a kitchen cabinet, and began to remove every cup and dish from it. For two nights after that, I watched Violet clean cupboards, wash floors, scrape dirt from under the stove with a knife, and bleach the loft's bathrooms. On the third evening, I walked upstairs with a bag of groceries for our dinner, and when she answered the door, Violet was wearing rubber gloves and had a pail of soapy water in her hand. I didn't say hello. I said 'Stop. Stop cleaning. It's over, Violet.' After giving me a surprised glance, she put down the pail. Then I walked over to the phone and called Lazlo in Williamsburg.

Within half an hour, he buzzed from the front door. When Violet pressed the intercom and heard Lazlo's voice, she made a noise of astonishment. The clogged bridges, traffic jams, and lazy subway lines that slowed travel for every other inhabitant of New York didn't seem to hinder Lazlo Finkelman. 'Did you fly?' Violet asked him when she opened the door. Lazlo smiled faintly, strode into the room, and sat down. Just looking at Lazlo had a soothing effect on me. His familiar hairdo, big black glasses, and long poker face inspired me even before he said he would look into Mark's disappearance. 'Keep track of your hours,' Violet said to him. 'And I'll add on the extra money when I pay you at the end of the week.'

Lazlo shrugged.

'I mean it,' she said.

'I get around anyway,' he said. He followed this vague statement by saying to Violet, 'Dan said I should tell you he's writing you a play.'

'He told me he calls you,' Violet said. 'I hope he's not bothering you too much.'

Lazlo shook his head. 'I've got it down to one poem a day.'

'He reads you poems over the telephone?' I said.

'Yup, but I told him I could only deal with one a day. I had to ward off inspiration overload.'

'You're very kind, Lazlo,' Violet said.

Lazlo squinted behind his glasses. 'No.' He lifted a finger toward the ceiling and I recognized Bill's gesture. 'Sing loudly,' Lazlo said, 'Into the dead face. Bang hard on the deaf ears. Jump up and down on the corpse and wake it up.'

'Poor Dan,' Violet said. 'Bill won't wake up.'

Lazlo leaned forward. 'Dan told me that it was a poem about Mark.'

Violet looked at him steadily for a couple of seconds and then lowered her eyes.

After Lazlo left, I made dinner. While I prepared the food, Violet sat quietly at the table. Every now and then, she would smooth back her hair or touch her arm, but when I put the plates of food on the table, she said, 'Tomorrow morning I'm going to call the police. He's always come back before.'

'Worry about that tomorrow,' I said. 'Right now you have to eat.'

Violet looked down at her food. 'Isn't it funny? All my life I've worked hard not to get too fat. I used to eat when I was sad, but now it just won't go down anymore. I look at it, and it's gray.'

'It's not gray,' I said. 'Look at that nice pork chop – a lovely Castilian brown – beside those attractive green beans – the color of dark jade. Now, ponder the brown and green in relation to the pallor of the mashed potatoes. They aren't quite white, but tinged by the faintest of yellows, and I put the tomato slice near the beans for color – a clear red to brighten the plate and give pleasure to your eyes.' I moved into the chair beside her. 'But the visual satisfaction, my dear, is only the beginning of the feast.'

Violet continued to look glumly at her plate. 'And after writing a whole book on eating disorders,' she said.

'You're not listening to me,' I said.

'Yes, I am.'

'Then relax. We're here to have dinner. Have some wine.'

'But you're not eating, Leo. Your food is getting cold.'

'I can eat later.' I reached for her glass and brought it to her mouth. She took a small sip. 'Look here,' I said, 'your napkin's still on the table.' With the pretentious flourish of a waiter, I grabbed the napkin by one corner, waved it open, and let it fall to her lap.

Violet smiled.

I leaned across her plate, picked up her knife and fork, cut a small piece off the pork chop, and then added a bit of mashed potatoes to the bite.

'What are you doing, Leo?' she said.

As I lifted the fork off the plate, she turned to me and I saw two wrinkles form between her eyebrows. When her mouth quivered for an instant, I thought she might cry, but she didn't. I brought the food to her lips, nodded at her as she hesitated, and then she opened her mouth like a small child and I gave her the meat and potatoes.

Violet let me feed her. I worked very slowly, making sure that she had plenty of time to chew and swallow, that she was allowed a pause between forkfuls and took drinks of the wine. I think my scrutiny made her eat more decorously than usual, because she chewed slowly with her mouth closed, revealing her small overbite only when her lips parted to take in the morsel. We were both silent for the first few minutes, and I pretended that I didn't see her glistening eyes or hear the noise she made every time she swallowed. Her throat must have been small and tight from anxiety, because she gulped rather loudly and then blushed at the sound. I starting talking to distract her – mostly nonsense, a chain of culinary free associations. I talked about a lemon pasta I had eaten in Siena under a sky full of stars and the twenty different kinds of herring Jack had ingested in Stockholm. I talked about squids and their indigo ink in a Venetian risotto, the underground business of sneaking unpasteurized cheese into New York, and a pig I had once seen in the south of France snuffling while truffling. Violet didn't say a word, but her eyes cleared and the corners of her mouth showed signs of amusement when I began telling her about a maître d' in a local restaurant who tripped and fell over a small elderly woman as he ran to greet a movie actor who had just walked through the door.

In the end, only the tomato was left on the plate. I pierced it and brought it to Violet's mouth, but as I slid the gelatinous red slice between her teeth, a few seeds and their juice escaped and ran down her chin. I grabbed her napkin and began gently dabbing her face with it. Violet closed her eyes, leaned her head back a little, and smiled. When she opened her eyes she was still smiling. 'Thank you,' she said. 'The meal was delicious.'

The next day, Violet filed a missing-persons report with the police department, and although she didn't mention the theft to the person on the telephone, she did say that Mark had disappeared before. She tried calling Lazlo, but he wasn't home, and then late that same afternoon after spending only a couple of hours at the studio, Violet invited me upstairs to listen to the sections of her tapes that were connected to Teddy Giles. 'I have this feeling that Mark is with Giles,' she said, 'but his number is unlisted and the gallery won't give it to me.' As we sat in her study and listened, I noticed that Violet's drawn face tightened with interest and her gestures had a quickness I hadn't seen in weeks.

'This is a girl who calls herself Virgina,' Violet said. 'With a long second *i*, like "virgin" and "vagina."'

A young female voice began to speak in midsentence. '. . . a family. That's how we think of it. Teddy's like the head of the family, you know, 'cause he's older than us.'

Violet's voice interrupted her. 'How old is he exactly?'

'Twenty-seven.'

'Do you know anything about his life before he came to New York?'

'He told me the whole story. He was born in Florida. His mom died, and he never knew his dad. He was raised by his uncle, who beat him up all the time, so he ran away to Canada, where he worked as a mailman, and after that he came here and got into clubs and art.'

'I've heard several versions of his life story,' Violet's voice said.

'I know this is the real one on account of the way he told me. He was like really sad about his childhood.'

Violet mentioned the rumor about Rafael and the chopped finger.

'I heard that, too. I don't believe it, though. This kid we call Toad – he's got acne real bad – was spreading that around. You know what else he said? He said that Teddy killed his own mother, pushed her down the stairs, but nobody found out, because it looked like an accident. That's the kind of stuff Teddy says to keep up his She-Monster act, but he's a super-gentle guy, really. Toad's pretty stupid, and how's Teddy going to kill somebody who died before he was even born?'

'His mother couldn't have died *before* he was born.'

Silence. 'No, I guess I mean right when he was born, but the point is, Teddy's sweet. He showed me his collection of salt and pepper shakers – soooo cute. Oh my God, little animals and flowers and these two teeny-weeny guys playing guitars with holes in their heads for the salt and pepper . . .'

Violet stopped the tape and moved it forward. 'Now I want you to listen to this boy named Lee. I don't know much about him, except that he's on his own. He might be a runaway.' She pressed PLAY, and Lee started talking. 'Teddy's for freedom, man. That's what I appreciate about him – he's for self-expression, for the higher consciousness. He's going against all that normalcy shit and

408

telling it like it is. Our society is bullshit and he knows it. His art gives me a rush. It's real, man.'

'What do you mean by real?' Violet asked him.

'I mean real, honest.'

Silence.

'I'll tell you something,' Lee continued. 'When I had nowhere to go, Ted took me in. Without him, I would've been pissing in the streets.'

Violet moved the tape forward. 'This is Jackie.' I heard a man's voice. 'Giles is a pig, honey, a liar and a fake. And I tell you this from firsthand knowledge. Artifice is my life. This gorgeous body didn't come cheap. I've made myself into myself, but when I say he's fake, I mean fake on the inside. I mean that little creep has got a falsie where his soul ought to be. *She-Monster* – what a load of B.S.' Jackie's voice rose into a dynamic falsetto. 'That She-Monster act is ugly and it's cruel and it's stupid, and I tell you, Violet, I'm shocked, really shocked that that fact isn't crystal clear to anybody with a single brain cell in his or her head.'

Violet stopped the machine. 'That's all there is about Teddy Giles. It doesn't get us very far.'

'Did you ever ask Mark about that weird message on the tape?'

'No.'

'Why not?'

'Because I knew if there was anything in it, he wouldn't tell me, and I didn't want him to feel that the tape was connected to Bill's heart attack.'

'You think it was?'

'I don't know.'

'Do you think Bill knew something that we don't?'

'If he did, he found out that same day. He wouldn't have kept it from me. I'm sure of that.'

I didn't have to feed Violet that night. We cooked together in my apartment for a change, and she finished all her pasta. After I poured her a second glass of wine, she said, 'Did I ever tell you about Blanche Wittmann? I think her real name was Marie Wittmann, but she's usually called Blanche.'

'I don't think so, but it rings a bell.'

'They called her 'the Queen of the Hysterics.' She was featured in Charcot's demonstrations of hysteria and hypnosis. They were very popular, you know. All of fashionable Paris came to watch the ladies chirp like birds, hop around on one leg, and get lanced by pins. But after Charcot died, Blanche Wittmann never had another hysterical attack.'

'You're saying that she had them for him?'

'She adored Charcot and wanted to please him, so she gave him what he wanted. In the newspapers she was often compared to Sarah Bernhardt. After the master died, she didn't want to leave the Salpêtrière. She stayed on and became a radiology technician. Those were the early days of X-rays. She died of the poisoning. One by one she lost her limbs.'

'Is there some reason for this story?' I said.

'Yes. Trickery, deception, lying, and susceptibility to hypnosis were supposedly, symptoms of hysteria. That's like Mark, isn't it?'

'Yes, but Mark isn't paralyzed or having fits, is he?'

'No, but that's not how we want him to behave, is it? Charcot wanted the women to perform, and they did. We want Mark to seem to care for other people, and when he's with us, that's how he appears. He gives us the performance he thinks we want.'

'But Mark isn't hypnotized, and I really don't think we can call him a hysteric.'

'I'm not saying that Mark is hysterical. Medical language keeps changing. Illnesses overlap. One thing mutates into another. Hypnosis merely lowers a person's resistance to suggestion. I'm not sure Mark has all that much resistance to begin with. What I'm saying is something very simple. It's not always easy to separate the actor from his act.'

The following morning, Lazlo called Violet. He had spent two long nights in clubs, going from the Limelight to Club USA to the Tunnel, where he had picked up bits of contradictory information. The consensus was, however, that Mark was travelling with Teddy Giles, who was in either Los Angeles or Las Vegas. Nobody was really sure. At three in the morning, Lazlo had bumped into Teenie Gold. Teenie had implied that she had a lot to say but refused to say it to Laz. She told him that the only person she would talk to now that Bill wasn't around was 'Mark's Uncle Leo.' She was prepared to tell me 'the whole story' if I arrived at her house tomorrow at four P.M. By the time I heard about it, 'tomorrow' had become today, and at three-fifteen, armed with an address on East Seventy-sixth Street and Park Avenue, I set off on my peculiar mission.

After I was announced, a doorman led me through the posh lobby toward an elevator, which opened automatically at the seventh floor. A woman, who I guessed was Filipino, opened the door for me, and I looked through the foyer into a vast apartment that seemed to have been decorated almost entirely in powder blue with gold accents. Teenie appeared from behind a door that led to a hallway, took a few steps in my direction, stopped, and looked down at the floor. The expensive ugliness seemed to swallow her up, as if she were too small for the space.

'Susie,' Teenie said, turning to the woman who had opened the door. 'This is Mark's uncle.'

'Nice boy,' Susie said. 'Very sweet boy.'

Without looking up, Teenie said, 'Come on. We'll talk in my room.'

Teenie's room was small and messy. Except for the yellow silk curtains on the window, her sanctuary had little in common with the rest of the apartment. Shirts, dresses, T-shirts, and underwear were strewn over an upholstered chair,

412

and behind it I saw her wings partially crushed by a pile of magazines that had been thrown on top of them. Jars, bottles, and small cases of makeup littered her desk, along with lotions, creams, and a few schoolbooks. When I looked at a shelf, I noticed a small new box of Legos, still in its plastic covering, exactly like the one I had come across in Mark's room.

Teenie sat down on the edge of her bed and examined her knees as she pushed her bare feet into the carpeting.

'I'm not sure why you wanted to talk to me, Teenie,' I said.

In a small, high voice, she said, 'It's because you were nice to me that time when I fell.'

'I see. We're worried about Mark, you know. Lazlo found out he might be in Los Angeles.'

'I heard it was Houston.'

'Houston?' I said.

Teenie continued to examine her knees. 'I was in love with him,' she said.

'Mark?'

She nodded vigorously and sniffed. 'I thought so, anyway. He told me all kinds of things that made me feel all wild and free and crazy-like. It was good for a while. I really thought he loved me, you know?' She eyed me for half a second and then looked down again.

'What happened?' I said.

'It's over.'

'But it's been over for quite some time, hasn't it?'

413

'We've been really tight on and off for two whole years.'

I thought of Lisa. That was when Mark was seeing Lisa. 'But we haven't seen you,' I said.

'Mark said his parents wouldn't let me visit.'

'That wasn't true. He was grounded, but friends could visit him.'

Teenie shook her head back and forth, and I saw a big tear roll down her right check. Teenie must have shaken her head for twenty seconds while I encouraged her to speak. Finally, she said, 'It started out like a game. I was going to get a tattoo on my stomach that said 'The Mark.' Teddy was joking around and he said he'd do it for me, but then . . .' Teenie lifted up her shirt and I saw two small scars that formed an *M* and a *W*, one on top of the other, so the bottom of the M met the top of the W to form a single character.

'Giles did that to you?'

She nodded.

'And Mark? Was Mark there?'

'He helped. I was screaming, but he held me down.'

'My God,' I said.

Tears ran down her face as she reached for a stuffed rabbit on her bed and began to stroke its ears. 'He isn't what you think. He was so sweet to me in the beginning, but then he started to change. I gave him this book called *Psycholand*. It's about this rich guy who flies all over the world in his private plane, and in every city

414

he kills somebody. Mark read it about twenty times.'

'I saw some reviews of that book. I understood that it was a kind of parody, a social satire.'

Teenie raised her eyes momentarily to give me a blank look. 'Yeah, well,' she continued, 'it started to creep me out, you know, and sometimes when he spent the night here, he'd start talking to me in this really weird voice. It wasn't his regular voice, you know, but a put-on voice. He'd just go on and on, and I'd tell him to stop, but he wouldn't, and I'd put my hand over his mouth, and still he wouldn't stop. And then he got me into all this trouble with my parents 'cause he stole my dad's codeine pills, the ones he takes for his bad shoulder, and they thought it was me, and I didn't dare tell them it was Mark, 'cause by then I was afraid of him. He kept saying he didn't take them, but I know he did, and kids are saying that him and Teddy go out at night and rob people just for fun. Sometimes they take money, but other times they just take something stupid, like their tie or scarf or belt or something.' Teenie shuddered through her tears. 'I thought I was in love with him.'

'Do you think the rumors about the robberies are true?'

Teenie shrugged. 'I'd believe anything now. Are you going to Dallas to look for him?'

'I thought you said Houston.'

'I think it's Dallas. I don't know. Maybe they're back already. What day is it?'

'Friday.'

'They're probably back.' Teenie started chewing on the nail of her little finger. She appeared to be thinking. She removed the finger from her mouth and said, 'He might be at Giles's house, but he's probably at the *Split World* offices. Sometimes kids sleep there.'

'I need the addresses, Teenie.'

'Giles lives at 21 Franklin Street on the fifth floor. *Split World* is on East Fourth.' She stood up and began to rummage in a drawer. She produced a magazine and handed it to me. 'The street number's in there.'

On the cover of the magazine there was a lurid picture of a young man, supposedly dead or dying, his head propped up against a toilet. His slashed wrists rested on his thighs as he sat in a brilliant pool of blood.

'Charming photo,' I said.

'They're all like that,' she said in a bored voice. Then she raised her chin and looked at me for at least three seconds. After she had looked down, she continued, 'I'm telling you all this 'cause I don't want any more bad stuff to happen. That's what I said to Mark's dad when I called him.'

For an instant I held my breath, then with deliberate calm I said, 'You spoke to Mark's father? When was that?'

'It was a pretty long time ago. The next thing I heard was that he died. That was pretty sad. He seemed like a nice man.'

'You called him at home?'

'No, at his office, I think.'

'Where did you get that number?'

'Mark gave me all his numbers.'

'Did you tell Mark's father about the cut on your stomach?'

'I think so.'

'You think so?' I tried to keep the irritation out of my voice.

Teenie pushed the carpet hard with her toes. 'I was pretty upset and I was high, too.' She pushed harder. 'Maybe you can find a hospital for him. Both Mark and Teddy should probably be in a hospital somewhere.'

'Were you the one who left a message with Bill saying that Giles had killed you?'

'He didn't kill me. He hurt me. I told you.'

I decided not to ask her anything more about the message. After talking to her, I felt sure that the voice I had heard on Bill's machine didn't belong to Teenie. 'Where are your parents?' I asked her.

'My mom's at some charity meeting thing for cancer and my dad's in Chicago.'

'I think you should talk to them. That was an assault, Teenie. You could go to the police.'

She didn't move. She began to shake her platinum head back and forth and fixed her gaze on her desk as though she had forgotten I was there.

I took the magazine and walked out of the room. When I opened the front door to leave, I heard water running and the sound of a woman singing to herself. It must have been Susie.

On my way downtown in a taxi, the bathetic tones of Teenie's confession lingered in my ears, especially her refrain, 'I thought I was in love with him.' Her skinny little body, her lowered gaze, the jumble of makeup and feminine paraphernalia around her had depressed me. I pitied Teenie, pitied the small ruined figure in a vast pale blue apartment, and yet I wondered about the phone call. Had Bill's heart stopped after he heard the story about Mark holding her down? Had she even mentioned it? The truth was I found it hard to imagine Mark restraining her, because the scar had been too neat. Could she have been cut so cleanly if she were struggling? Teenie's stories about *Psycholand* and the stolen codeine pills were more believable, however, and I began to speculate on Mark's drug use and its possible role in lifting whatever inhibitions he may have had when it came to lying and stealing. Apparently, Teenie retained a few scruples, a dim moral code that condemned what she called 'bad stuff,' but the badness of that stuff seemed to be determined by its effect on her rather than its lack of adherence to broader ethical sanctions. She couldn't remember her conversation with Bill because she had been drugged, and by her own lights, this made her amnesia both natural and excusable. Teenie belonged to a subculture where the rules were lax and permission was broad, but as far as I could tell, it was also surprisingly bland. If Mark and Teenie were any indication, these kids had little fervor. They weren't Futurists glorifying the aesthetics of violence or anarchists advocating liberation from the reigns of law. They were hedonists, I suppose, but even the taking of pleasure seemed to bore them.

When I looked up at the narrow building on East Fourth Street between Avenues A and B, I knew that I could walk away, that I could choose not to know anything more about these overgrown children and their small, sad lives. I chose to press the buzzer, chose to yank open the door on the first floor of that old tenement building, and chose to walk down the hallway, and I well understood that I was moving in the direction of something ugly. I was also aware that the ugliness pulled me toward it. I wanted to see what it was, to get close to it and examine it. The tug was morbid, and by giving in to it, I felt that the loathsome thing I was looking for had already stained me.

I didn't plan to lie, but when the somnambulant young woman behind the desk raised her eyes to me, eyes that were shielded by red glasses with wings, and when I saw twenty *Split World* covers on the wall behind her, one of which featured Teddy Giles with blood dripping from his mouth and a spoon that held what looked like a human finger, I lied spontaneously. I told her I was a journalist for the *New Yorker* who was researching small alternative magazines for an article. I asked the young woman if she would explain *Split World* to me – its raison d'être. I looked into the brown eyes behind the red wings. They were dull.

'I don't know what you mean.'

'What the magazine is about, why it exists.'

'Oh,' she said, pondering the question. 'Are you going to quote me? The name is Angie Roopnarine. R-O-O-P-N-A-R-I-N-E.'

I took out my pen and notebook and inscribed Roopnarine in large letters on the paper. 'For example,' I continued. 'Why the name? What's the split?'

'I don't know. I just work here. You should probably talk to somebody else, only nobody's here right now. They're out at lunch.'

'It's five-thirty in the afternoon.'

'We don't open until noon.'

'I see.' I pointed to the picture of Teddy Giles. 'Do you like his art?'

She craned to look at the cover. 'It's all right,' she said.

I plunged into the heart of the matter. 'They say he has an entourage, isn't that right? Mark Wechsler, Teenie Gold, a girl who calls herself Virgina, and a boy named Rafael who seems to be missing.'

Angie Roopnarine's body grew suddenly tense. 'That's part of your article?'

'I'm focusing on Giles.'

She squinted at me. 'I don't know what you

want. You seem kinda wrong to be writing about this stuff.'

'The *New Yorker* hires a lot of oldsters,' I said. 'You must know Mark Wechsler anyway,' I said. 'He worked here last summer.'

'Well, I can tell you, you've got that wrong. He never *worked* here. He hung around, okay? But Larry never paid him.'

'Larry?'

'Larry Finder. He owns the magazine and a lot of others.'

'The gallery owner?'

'It's no secret.' The telephone rang. '*Split World*,' Angie sang into the phone, her voice suddenly animated.

I nodded at her, mouthed a thank-you, and escaped. On the street, I took a deep breath to quiet the anxiety that had clamped itself around my lungs. Why lie? I said to myself. Had I lied out of some misguided impulse to protect myself? Maybe. Although I didn't construe my posing as a huge moral lapse, I felt both ridiculous and compromised as I walked westward away from the building. Discoveries about Mark had a tendency to fall into the negative category. He had not worked for Harry Freund last summer. He had not worked for Larry Finder at *Split World* either. Mark's life was an archaeology of fictions, one on top of the other, and I had only just started to dig.

*   *   *

Violet had left several urgent messages on my machine for me to come upstairs as soon as I returned home. When she opened the door, she looked pale, and I asked her if she was okay. Instead of answering me, she said, 'I have something to show you.'

She led me to Mark's room, and when I looked through the door, I saw that Violet had turned the place inside out. The closet door was open, and although clothes were still hanging inside, the shelves were bare. The floor was thick with papers, flyers, notebooks, and magazines. I also saw a box of toy cars, another with bent postcards, letters, and broken crayons. The drawers in Mark's desk had been removed and were lying in a row beside the boxes. Violet bent over one of them, picked up a red object, and handed it to me. 'I found it inside a cigar box wrapped in masking tape.'

It was Matthew's knife. I looked down at its silver initials, M.S.H.

'I'm sorry,' Violet said.

'After all these years,' I said, and began to tug at its corkscrew. When I had pulled it out, I moved my finger down its spiral blade and remembered Matt's desperation. 'I always put it on the night table, always!' I must have been very tired, because a part of me seemed to levitate then, and I had the most peculiar sensation of having floated to the ceiling. I felt as though I were looking down on the room, on Violet, on myself, and on the knife that I held in my hand. This curious division between earth and air, between the elevated me and the me on the ground didn't last very long, but even after it was over, I felt far away from everything in that room, as if I were looking at a mirage.

'I remember the day Matt lost it,' Violet was saying in a deliberate voice. 'And I remember how upset he was. It was Mark who told me, Leo, Mark who said how awful it was that the knife was missing. He was so sympathetic, so sad for Matt. He told me how he had looked for it everywhere.' Violet's eyes were wide and her voice trembled. 'Mark was eleven years old then. He was eleven.' I felt her grab my arm and then the tight grip of her fingers. 'You understand that it isn't the stealing that's so terrible or even the lying. It's the pretense of compassion, so perfectly modulated, so believable, so authentic.'

I put the knife in my pocket then, and although I had heard what she said and had understood it, I didn't know how to respond, and instead of answering I stood very still, my eyes on the wall, and after a couple of seconds, I thought of the taxi in Bill's self-portrait – that toy he had given to Violet to hold when he painted her. The image of the taxi and Matt's knife had something in common, and I groped to articulate the similarity between them. The word 'pawn' came to me, and yet it wasn't quite right. Some form of exchange inked the picture of a toy car with the real object that was hidden in my pocket. The connection had nothing to do with knives or automobiles.

The knife was like the painted car because it too had become intangible – not a real thing anymore. It didn't matter that I could reach into my trousers and retrieve it. Through the machinations of a child's dark needs and secrets, a switch had been made. The present I had given Matt on his eleventh birthday no longer existed. In its place was something else, a sinister copy or facsimile, and as soon as I had thought this, my thinking came full circle. Matt had made his own double of the knife in the painting Bill had given to me. He had sent the Ghosty Boy up to the roof with his stolen prize, where the moon shone down on his empty face and lit the opened knife that he held in his hand.

After I told Violet about Teenie and *Split World*, I walked downstairs and spent the evening alone. It took me a while to find a place for the knife in the drawer, but in the end I decided to push it far to the back, away from the other objects. When I closed the drawer, I realized that the thing had helped to harden me to my task. I was no longer just looking for Mark. I wanted something more – exposure. I wanted to fill in the features of that missing face.

A couple of hours after Violet left home for Bill's studio, I was pressing a buzzer that read T.G./S.M. at 21 Franklin Street. To my surprise, I was immediately let in. A short, muscular boy wearing only a pair of shorts opened the steel door to Teddy Giles's fifth-floor loft. When the door was fully opened, I saw the boy's tanned body from every angle, and I saw myself, because all four walls of the entryway were mirrors.

'I'm here to see Teddy Giles,' I said.

'I think he's asleep.'

'It's very important,' I said.

The boy turned around, opened a mirror that turned out to be also a door, and vanished. To my right was a large room with an immense orange sofa and two voluminous chairs – one turquoise, the other purple. Everything in the room looked new: the floors, the walls, the light fixtures. As I studied the room, I realized that the phrase 'new money' didn't begin to cover what I was looking at. These furnishings were the product of instant money – a few big sales converted into real estate so fast that the agents, lawyers, architect, and contractor must have found themselves breathless. The apartment smelled of cigarette smoke and, more vaguely, of garbage. A pink sweater and several pairs of women's shoes lay on the floor. There were no books in that room, but there were hundreds of magazines. Glossy art and fashion periodicals were stacked in tall piles on the single coffee table. More were spread out on the floor, and I noticed that some of their pages had been marked with yellow and pink Post-its. On the far wall were three enormous photographs of Giles. In the first, he was dressed as a man and was dancing with a woman who reminded me of Lana Turner in *The Postman Always Rings Twice*.

In the second, he was in female persona, wearing a garish blond wig and a silver evening gown that hugged his artificial breasts and padded hips. In the third picture, Giles appeared to have gone to pieces by some visual trick and was eating the flesh of his own severed right arm. While I was studying the now familiar images, Giles appeared from behind the mirrored door. He was wearing a red silk Japanese kimono that looked authentic. The heavy silk made a noise as he walked toward me. He smiled. 'Professor Hertzberg,' he said. 'To what do I owe this pleasure?'

Before I could answer, he continued. 'Sit down.' He made a sweeping gesture with his hand toward the living room. I took the large turquoise chair and lowered myself into it. I tried leaning back, but the chair's porportions put me into a nearly reclining position, so I perched on its edge.

Giles seated himself in its purple twin, which was a little too far away for comfortable conversation. In order to compensate for the awkward distance, he leaned toward me, and the material of his robe parted to reveal the white skin of his hairless chest. He eyed a pack of Marlboros on the round table between us and said, 'Do you mind if I smoke?'

'Go ahead,' I said.

His hand trembled as he lit the cigarette, and I felt suddenly glad that he wasn't closer to me. From my position about five feet away from him, I was able to examine the overall effect of Teddy Giles. His features were bland and regular. He had light

426

green eyes with pale lashes, a small nose that was a little flat, and colorless lips. It was the robe that gave his nondescript face its character. The stiff and elaborate kimono turned Giles into the very picture of a depraved fin de siècle fop. Against the red material his skin took on an almost corpselike pallor. Its large sleeves emphasized his thin arms, and its likeness to a dress enhanced his sexual ambiguity. It was hard to say whether he was consciously cultivating this image of himself for my benefit or whether he had settled into it as one of his several personas. Nodding at me, he said, 'Now, what can I do for you?'

'I thought you might know where Mark is. He's been gone for ten days, and his stepmother and I are worried.'

He answered without any hesitation. 'I've seen Mark several times in the last week. He was here last night, as a matter of fact. I had a little gathering, but he left with some people. Are you telling me he hasn't been in touch with' – he paused – 'with Violet? Isn't that his stepmother's name?'

I recounted Mark's thefts and his disappearance while Giles listened. His light green eyes never left my face except when he turned his head to avoid blowing the cigarette smoke in my direction.

Then I said, 'I heard he was travelling with you, somewhere out West – for a show,'

Giles shook his head very slowly, his eyes still fixed on mine. 'I was in L.A. for a couple of days, but Mark wasn't with me.' He appeared to be thinking. 'Mark was devastated by his father's death. Of course, you know that. We had several long talks about it, and I honestly believed that I helped him . . .' After a pause, he added, 'When he lost his father, I think he lost part of himself.'

It was hard to say what I had been expecting from Giles, but it wasn't compassion for Mark. As I sat there, I began to wonder if I hadn't shifted a portion of my anger and frustration at Mark onto this artist whom I didn't know at all. My Teddy Giles was a figment, a man constructed from rumor and hearsay and a couple of articles in newspapers and magazines. I looked across the room at the photograph of Giles as a woman.

He noticed my glance. 'I'm aware that you disapprove of my work,' he said flatly. 'Mark has said as much, not only about you but about his stepmother. I'm aware that his father didn't have much use for it either. It's the content that upsets people, but I use violent material because it's ubiquitous. I'm not my work. As an art historian, you should be able to make that distinction.'

I tried to answer carefully. 'I suppose that part of the problem is that you yourself have confused the issue, have promoted the idea that you can't be cut off from what you do – that you yourself are, well, dangerous.'

He laughed. There was contentment, pleasure, and charm in that laugh. I also noticed how small his teeth were – like two rows of baby teeth. 'You're right,' he said. 'I use myself as an object. I recognize that it's not new, but nobody's quite done what I do either.'

'With horror clichés, you mean?'

'Exactly. Horror is extreme, and extremes are purging. That's why people watch the films or come to see my work.'

I had a strong feeling of repetition. Giles had said this before. He had probably said it a thousand times.

'But clichés are deadening, aren't they?' I said. 'By their very nature they kill meaning.'

He smiled at me, a little indulgently. 'I'm not interested in meaning. I have to tell you, I don't think it's very important anymore. People don't care about it, really. Speed is important. And pictures. The quick take for short attention spans. Ads, Hollywood movies, the six o'clock news, yes, even art – it all comes down to shopping. And what *is* shopping? It's walking around until a desirable something pops up and you buy it. Why do you buy it? Because it catches your eye. If it doesn't, you click to another channel. And why does it catch your eye? Because something about it gives you a little rush. It might be a sparkle or a glow or a bit of gore or a bare ass. It doesn't matter. It's the rush that counts – not the something. It's circular. You want the rush again, so you go looking for it. You plunk down your dollars and buy again.'

'But very few people buy art,' I said.

'True, but sensational art sells magazines and newspapers, and the buzz brings collectors, and collectors bring money, and round and round it goes. Does my honesty shock you?'

'No. I'm just not sure that people are quite as shallow as you pretend.'

'But you see, I don't think there's anything *wrong* with shallow.' He lit another cigarette. 'I'm far more offended by all the pious pretensions people have about how *deep* they are. It's a Freudian lie, isn't it – that there's this big unconscious blob in everybody.'

'I think notions of human depth probably pre-date Freud,' I said. I could hear the dry academic take hold in my voice. Giles was boring me, not because he was stupid but because there was some-thing detached in his tone, a remote and practiced cadence that made me tired. He was looking at me, and I thought I sensed disappointment from him. He had wanted to entertain me. He was used to journalists who rose to the bait, who found him clever. I changed the subject. 'I spoke to Teenie Gold yesterday,' I said.

Giles nodded. 'I haven't seen her in months. How is Teenie?'

I decided not to mince words. 'She showed me a scar on her stomach – Mark's initials – which she said . . .' I stopped and looked at Giles.

He was listening attentively. 'Yes?'

'She said you cut the letters into her skin while Mark held her down.'

Giles looked more than surprised. 'Oh my God,' he said. 'Poor Teenie.' He shook his head sadly and blew smoke upward. 'Teenie cuts herself. She has scars all over her arms. She's tried to stop, but she can't. It makes her feel good. She once told me it makes her feel real.' He paused, tapped the ash off his cigarette, and said, 'We all like to feel real.' He crossed his legs, and a naked knee appeared from between the folds of the elaborate robe. I glanced down at his calf and noticed razor stubble. Giles had confirmed my own doubts about Teenie's story, and yet I wondered why she would manufacture such an elaborate tale. Teenie was far from clever. 'I'm sure Mark will call me,' Giles continued. 'Maybe even today. What if I have a talk with him and ask him to get in touch with you and let you know where he is? I think he'll listen to me.'

I stood up. 'Thank you,' I said. 'If you do that, we'd be very grateful.'

Giles stood up too. He smiled at me, but his lips looked strained. 'We-e?' he said, turning the word into two chanted syllables.

His tone unnerved me, but I answered him steadily. 'Yes,' I said. 'He can call either me or Violet.' I began to walk in the direction of the door. In the entryway, I was met with myriad reflections again from all sides – my own in blue oxford shirt and khaki pants, Giles's in the brilliant red kimono and the garish colors of the furniture in the vast room behind us, all of it fractured by the mirrored panels. With the unctuous 'We?' reverberating in my ears, I grabbed a knob, turned it, and opened

431

the door, but instead of the elevator, I found myself looking down a narrow hallway. Hanging on the wall at its dead end, I saw a painting I recognized, one Bill had painted of Mark when he was two years old. The little boy was laughing madly as he held a lamp shade on top of his head like a hat, and he was naked except for a paper diaper so heavy with urine or feces that it had sunk low on his hips. I didn't move. The image of the little boy seemed to float toward me. I made a surprised noise. Behind me Giles said, 'Wrong door, Professor.'

'That's Bill's,' I said.

'Yes, it is,' Giles said.

'What's it doing here?'

'I bought it.'

'From whom?' I said.

'From the owner.'

I turned to him suddenly. 'From Lucille? You bought it from Lucille?' I knew as well as anyone that paintings circulate – move from owner to owner, languish in dark rooms, reappear, are sold and resold, stolen, destroyed, restored for better or for worse. A painting may resurface anywhere, and yet the sight of that canvas in this place appalled me.

'I'm thinking of using it,' Giles said. He was standing very close to me. I could feel his breath on my ear. Instinctively, I pulled my head away.

'Using it?' I echoed. I began to walk toward the painting.

'I thought you were leaving,' Giles said from

behind me. There was a note of amusement in his voice, and as soon as I heard it, I fumbled inwardly, dropped further into confusion. Giles's lilting 'We?' had started it. Whatever advantage I had had during our conversation disappeared in that hallway. My own feeble repetition 'Using it?' sounded like a scoff aimed at myself, a self-inflicted jeer I couldn't repair with a witty retort. All I could see was the painted child in front of me with his wild expression of glee and manic pleasure.

I am still muddling over what happened to me then and the exact sequence of events, but I know I had a sensation of enclosure and then of dread. Teddy Giles was hardly imposing, but he had managed to intimidate me with a couple of cryptic comments that suggested worlds, whole worlds, and it seemed to me that Bill was somehow at the center of all of them, that it didn't matter that he was dead. The mostly unarticulated combat between me and Giles was over Bill, and my sudden awareness of this turned into near panic. Then, just as I reached the painting, I heard a toilet flush. The sound of the toilet brought with it a belief that I had heard other sounds earlier and that my reaction to the painting had only partly blotted them out. I stopped to listen. Gagging noises came from behind a door, then a low hoarse cry for help. I yanked open the door directly in front of me and saw Mark lying on the floor of a bathroom, its walls covered with tiny green glass tiles. He was slumped on the floor near the bathtub with his mouth open and his eyes closed. His lips had turned blue. The sight of Mark's blue mouth made me suddenly calm. I moved forward and felt my shoe slip for a second. After I caught my balance, I noticed a pool of vomit at my feet. I knelt beside Mark and grabbed his wrist as I looked down at his white face. My fingers moved upward on his clammy skin, searching for his pulse. Without turning around, I said to Giles, 'Call an ambulance.' When he didn't answer me, I looked back at him.

'He'll be all right,' he said.

'Go to the phone,' I said, 'and dial 911 right now before he dies here in your apartment.'

Giles disappeared down the hallway. My fingers kept searching. He had a weak pulse, and when I looked down at his face, I saw that it was dead white. 'You're going to live, Mark,' I whispered to him, and then again, 'You're going to live.' I put my ear to his mouth. He was breathing.

He opened his eyes, and I felt a rush of happiness. 'Mark,' I said. 'I have to get you to a hospital. Don't sleep. Don't close your eyes.' I put my arm under his head to cushion it and looked down at him. He closed his eyes. 'No,' I said emphatically. I began to tug him upward. He was heavy, and as I pulled on him, my pants leg slid in the vomit on the floor. 'Listen to me,' I said sternly. 'Don't sleep.'

Mark looked at me narrowly. 'Fuck you,' he said. I grabbed him under his arms and began to pull him out of the bathroom, but he resisted. With an abrupt motion he reached for my face, and I

434

felt his nails dig into my cheek. The sudden pain shocked me, and I dropped him. His head thudded on the tiles and I heard him groan. A long glistening thread of saliva dripped from his open mouth down his chin, and then he threw up again, spewing ocher liquid onto his gray T-shirt.

The vomiting saved Mark's life. According to Dr Sinha, who treated him in the emergency room at New York Hospital, Mark had overdosed on a combination of drugs that included an animal tranquilizer that went by the name Special K on the streets. By the time I spoke to Dr Sinha, I had done my best to clean my pants in the men's room, and a nurse had given me a bandage for the three bloody stripes on my right cheek. As I stood in the hospital corridor, I could still smell vomit, and the large wet spot on my pants was turning cold in the air-conditioned hallway. When the doctor said 'Special K,' I remembered Giles's voice in the hallway: 'No K tonight, huh, M&M?' Over two years had passed between the time I first heard those words and the moment they were decoded for me. I found it ironic that while I had lived in New York for almost sixty years, my translator must have arrived in this country far more recently. He was a very young man with intelligent eyes who spoke the musical English of Bombay.

Three days later, Violet and Mark boarded a plane for Minneapolis. I wasn't present when Violet gave

Mark the ultimatum in the hospital, but she told me that after she threatened to cut him off without a cent, he had agreed to go to Hazelden – a drug-rehabilitation clinic in Minnestoa. Violet was able to place Mark at Hazelden quickly by calling an old friend of hers from high school who held an important position at the clinic. While Mark was in treatment, Violet planned to stay with her parents and visit him weekly. Addiction went far to explain Mark's behavior, and the simple act of giving his problem a name eased some of my fears. It was a little like shining a flashlight into a dark corner and identifying every speck and fluff of dust that fell inside the orb of light as a single entity. Lying, stealing, and absconding all became symptoms of Mark's 'disease.' From this point of view, Mark was only twelve steps away from freedom. Of course, I knew it wasn't that easy, but when Mark woke up in the hospital after his ordeal, he had become somebody new – a boy with a bona fide illness, who could be treated in a clinic where the experts knew all about people like him. He didn't want to go at first. He said he wasn't a drug addict. He took drugs, but he wasn't addicted. He also said he hadn't stolen Violet's jewelry or my horse, but as anyone will tell you, denial is part of the 'addiction profile.' The diagnosis also opened the door to renewed sympathy for Mark. Beset by terrible cravings, he had had little control over his actions and deserved another chance. But every pat solution, every convenient name has its overflow, the acts or feelings that resist interpretation – Matt's stolen knife, for example. As Violet had said, 'Mark was eleven.' Drugs had not been part of his life when he was eleven.

But the child inevitably haunts the adult, even when that former self is no longer recognizable. Bill's portrait of his puckish two-year-old in a dirty diaper had wound up in the apartment where his eighteen-year-old came close to dying. No longer a mirror of anyone, the canvas had become a disturbing specter of the past – not only Mark's but its own. Lucille told Violet that she had sold the painting through Bernie five years earlier. A telephone call to Bernie revealed that he knew nothing about Giles. He had dealt with a woman named Susan Blanchard, who was a reputable adviser to several well-known collectors in the city. Bernie said the buyer was a man named Ringman, who had also bought one of the fairy-tale boxes. Violet was annoyed that Lucille and Bernie hadn't mentioned the sale to Bill. 'He had the right to know,' she said. 'Morally.' But Lucille hadn't wanted Bill to know and had asked Bernie not to mention it. 'I felt sorry for Lucille,' Bernie said to Violet. 'And it was her painting to sell.'

Violet blamed Lucille for the roaming canvas. I didn't. It was a great relief to me that Lucille hadn't sold the painting directly to Giles, and I felt quite sure that she had needed the money from the sale. But for Violet, one story merged into another. Lucille had sold a portrait of her own son to the highest bidder and she hadn't bothered to come visit him in the hospital. Lucille had called him instead, and according to Mark, she'd never even mentioned the overdose. Violet thought Mark was lying, called Lucille, and asked her outright. Lucille confirmed that she hadn't talked to Mark about his near death from drugs. 'I didn't think it would be productive,' she said. What had she talked about, then? Violet had wanted to know. Lucille said that she had given him news about Ollie's day camp and the two cats and what she was cooking for dinner and had wished him luck. Violet was incensed. When she told me the story she trembled with irritation. My feeling was that Lucille had made a conscious decision not to speak of what had happened, that she had weighed the decision carefully and had come to the conclusion that going over that territory would do neither Mark nor her any good. I think every word she uttered to him had been deliberate. I suspected, too, that after she hung up, she went over the talk in her mind and may even have chided herself about what she had said and revised the conversation after the fact. Violet believed that any mother who didn't hop the next train and come running to her son's bedside was 'unnatural,' but I knew that self-consciousness and uncertainty paralyzed Lucille. She was stuck in the mud of her own internal debates, the pros and cons and logical conundrums that made almost any action on her part impossible. Just making the telephone call to

438

the hospital had probably taken a good deal of courage.

The difference between Lucille and Violet was one of character, not knowledge. Violet's confusion about Mark was as great as Lucille's. What Violet didn't question, however, was the strength of her own feeling for him and her need to act on it. Lucille, on the other hand, felt powerless. Bill's two wives had become Mark's two mothers, and while the marriages had come one after the other, Lucille's motherhood and Violet's adopted motherhood had coexisted for years and now had outlived Bill's death. The two women were the surviving poles of a man's desire, bound together by the boy he had fathered with only one of them. I couldn't help but feel that Bill was still playing a crucial role in the story that was unfolding before me, that he had created a fierce geometry among us, and that it lived on. Again, I found hints in the painting that hung in my apartment: the woman who left and the one who fought and stayed; the strange little car in the plump Violet's lap – a thing that wasn't itself and wasn't a symbol either, but a vehicle of unspoken wishes. When Bill painted that canvas he had been hoping for a child with Lucille. He had told me that himself. I started to study the painting again, and the longer I looked at it, the more I began to feel that Mark was there in the canvas, too, hiding in the body of the wrong woman.

⋆　　⋆　　⋆

Violet and Mark were gone for two months. During that time I took in their mail, watered the three plants upstairs, and listened to the answering machine for messages on which I could still hear Bill's voice telling the callers to wait for the beep. I also checked in on the Bowery loft once a week. Violet had made a special request that I look in on Mr Bob. It turned out that not long after Bill died, Mr Aiello, the landlord, had discovered the squatter, and after striking a deal with him, Violet was now paying extra rent for the dilapidated room downstairs. Mr Bob's new status as official resident of 89 Bowery had made him both proprietary and officious. During my visits, he trailed behind me and sniffed loudly to express his disapproval. 'I'm taking care of everything,' he would say. 'I've swept.' Sweeping had become Mr Bob's calling, and he swept obsessively, often brushing the backs of my feet with the broom as though I were leaving a trail of dust behind me. And while he swept, he declaimed, his grandiose words rising and falling for full dramatic effect.

'It won't settle, I tell you. It has said a resounding no to eternal sleep, and all day and far into the night I am forced to listen to the doleful sound of its feet pacing up there under the roof, and last night when I had swept away the last tidbits, crumbs, and what-have-yous of my long day's work, I spied it on the stairs – the spitting image of Mr W. himself, but bodiless of course – a mere astral puff of what he once was, and that discarnate, spiritized phantasma

440

reached out its arms in a gesture of indescribable sorrow and then it covered its poor blind eyes, and I discerned that it was looking for her, for Beauty. Now that she's gone, the ghost is disconsolate. Mind my words, because I've seen it before and I'll see it again. My knowledge of spirit doings comes firsthand. When I had my business (I worked with fine antiques, you know), I had experience of several pieces that had been *penetrated*. You are aware of that expression and its meaning in this particular instance – *penetrated*. One Queen Anne dresser formerly owned by a petite, elderly lady in Ditmas Park, Brooklyn. Beautiful home, that was, with a turret, but Mrs Deerborne's essence or, shall we say, her animus, the shadowy wraith of what she once had been, was still fleet, still quick. It fluttered like a bird inside that fine piece of furniture, a timorous presence within the drawers. Let us just say they rattled. Seven times I sold the Anne, reluctantly, ever so reluctantly, and seven times the buyers returned it to me. Seven times I took it back, no questions asked, because I had the knowledge of it. It was her son who tortured her. He was unmarried, unsettled, a bad sort who drifted, and I don't think the old lady could bear to leave him like that with no position in life. William Wechsler, a.k.a. Mr W., has unfinished business, too, and Beauty knows it, and that's why she's been coming every day until now. I hear her singing to him and talking to him to help him sleep. She'll be back to him soon now. His ghost

441

can't do without her. It's more restless, flighty, peevish than ever before, and she's the only one who can quiet him – or rather it. And I'll tell you why. She takes succor in her trials from the angels. You understand me! They drop down! They drop down! I am the witness. I have seen her coming out the door, and I have seen the fiery mark of the seraphim on her face. She is touched, touched by the burning fingers of the heavenly host.'

Mr Bob's monologues plagued me. They never stopped. It wasn't his mishmash of religion and the occult that irritated me as much as the tone of bourgeois superiority that inevitably crept into his narratives about possessed tables, highboys, and secretaries, which usually included a condemnation of 'drifters,' 'losers,' and 'bums.' Bob had added Bill and Violet to the cast of characters in his muddled lore, because he wanted them for himself. Legends can live and breathe only on verbal terrain, and so Bob talked and talked to keep his Mr W. and his Beauty secure in a world of his own making. There they could climb his celestial heights or fall into his demonic ditches without any interference from me.

And yet, I would have liked to be alone as I walked up to the studio, unlocked the door, and looked into the big room and the little that remained there of Bill. I would have liked to study the chair with Bill's work clothes draped over it, the ones I had seen Violet wearing. I would have liked to let the light of the tall windows, brilliant

442

with sun or darkening with the evening, fall over me in silence, would have liked to stand quietly and inhale the smell of the room, which hadn't changed at all. But it wasn't possible. Bob was the building's resident hobgoblin, its sniffing, sweeping, tirading, self-appointed mystical concierge, and there wasn't a thing I could do about it. Nevertheless, I continued to wait for his blessing when I walked through the front door: 'O Lord, lift up the soul of thy tattered servant who walketh out into the pedestrian hubbub of thine city that he may not be sorely tempted by the demons of Gotham, but will make his way straight and true toward thy heavenly light. Bless him and keep him and let thy great beaming countenance shine down upon him and give him peace.'

I didn't believe in the old man's ghosts or angels, but as the summer wound down, Bill haunted me more rather than less, and without mentioning it to anyone, I began taking notes and organizing material for an essay about his work when I should have been finishing the book on Goya. The essay was launched one afternoon when I was paging through the catalogue of *O's Journey*, and the hero's initial, which signified both the presence of the letter and the absence of the number, summoned other works by Bill that turned on appearance and disappearance. After that, I spent every morning with Bill's catalogues and slides and began to understand that it was a book I was writing, one organized

443

not by chronology but by ideas. It wasn't simple. There were many works that fell into more than one of my original categories – into both Disappearance and Hunger, for example. But I discovered that Hunger was actually a subset of Disappearance. The distinction might seem academic, but the more I studied the images, the color, the brush strokes, sculptures, and inscriptions, the more I felt that their ambiguities were all part of the idea of vanishing. The body of work Bill had left behind him formed the anatomy of a true ghost, not because every work of art by a man now dead is his trace on the world but because Bill's work in particular was an investigation of the inadequacy of symbolic surfaces – the formulas of explanation that fall short of reality. At every turn, the desire to locate, stop, pinpoint through letters or numbers or the conventions of painting was foiled. You think you know, Bill seemed to be saying in every work, but you don't know. I subvert your truisms, your smug understanding and blind you with this metamorphosis. When does one thing cease and another begin? Your borders are inventions, jokes, absurdities. The same woman grows and shrinks, and at each extreme she defies recognition. A doll lies on her back with the sign of an outdated diagnosis over her mouth. Two boys become each other. Numbers in stock reports, numbers preceded by dollar signs, and numbers burned into an arm. I had never seen the work more clearly, and at the same time I floundered inside it, choked by doubt and something else – a smothering intimacy. There were days when my work took on the qualities of a tormenting mistress whose bouts of passion were followed by inscrutable coldness, who screamed for love and then slapped my face. And like a woman, the art led me on, and I suffered and enjoyed it. Sitting at my desk with a pen in my hand, I wrestled with the hidden man who had been my friend, a man who had painted himself as a woman and as B, a fat, lusty fairy godmother. But the struggle made me unusually vivid to myself, and as the summer days drew to an end, I felt very alive in my solitude.

Violet called regularly. She told me about Hazelden – a retreat I confused with the sanatoriums of my early childhood. My mother's parents, whom I had never known, had both died of tuberculosis in 1929 after long confinements at Nordrach, a sanatorium in the Black Forest. I imagined Mark lying on a chaise longue near a lake that sparkled in the sun. The fantasy was probably false – a mixed picture taken from my mother's stories and my memory of reading Thomas Mann's *The Magic Mountain*. The crucial thing, I realized, was that whenever I thought about Mark at the time, he wasn't moving. He was frozen like a person in a snapshot, and this stasis was all that mattered. I felt that Hazelden had put him on hold. Like a benevolent prison, it reined in his mobility, and I understood that what I feared most in Mark were his disappearances and subsequent roaming. Violet said she was encouraged by Mark's progress. Every Wednesday, she went to the family meetings, and she prepared herself by reading about the twelve steps. She said that Mark had had a bumpy start, but that he had slowly begun to reveal himself as the weeks went on. She talked about the other patients, or 'peers,' as the inmates were called at Hazelden, especially about a young woman named Debbie.

The summer ended. Classes started, and with them I lost my daily rhythm of writing the book on Bill. I continued to work on it, however, often in the evenings after reviewing my lecture notes. In late October, Violet called to say that she and Mark would be home the following week.

A couple of days after I spoke to Violet, Lazlo appeared at my door. One glance at him told me that he had bad news. I had learned to read Lazlo's body rather than his face for clues. His shoulders sloped, and when he stepped into the room, he walked slowly. When I asked him what had happened, he told me about the painting in Giles's upcoming show. The story was only a rumor then, one of those floating bits of gossip that Lazlo seemed to snatch from thin air, but a week later, the show opened and we knew it was true. Teddy Giles had used the painting of Mark in his new exhibition. The scandal revolved around the fact that the valuable canvas had been destroyed. A figure of a murdered woman, missing one arm and a leg, had been pushed through Bill's painting of his son. Her head protruded through one side of the canvas, choking her at the neck. The rest of her maimed body stuck out on the other side. The force of the piece relied on the fact that an original work of art, owned by Giles, was now as mutilated as the mannequin.

The news excited the art world. If you owned a painting, it wasn't illegal to harm it. You could use it for target practice if you wanted to. I remembered Giles's warning: 'I'm thinking of using it.' It had made no sense to me. Use had nothing to do with art. It was by nature useless. Once the show opened, it was the only work in the show that anybody discussed. The others were similar to Giles's earlier pieces – the hacked hollow bodies of women, a couple of men, and several children; bloody clothes; severed heads; guns. Nobody seemed to care. What excited everyone – outraging some and pleasing others – was that here was an act of genuine violence. It wasn't simulated but real. The bodies were fake, but the painting was authentic. Even more titillating was the fact that Bill's work was expensive. There was considerable musing over whether the presence of the painting – in spite of the damage – raised the price of the piece as a whole. It was hard to know what Giles had actually paid for the portrait of Mark. Several high prices were quoted, but I suspect they came from Giles himself – a notoriously unreliable source.

Violet returned to an uproar. Several journalists

called to get her statement. Wisely, she refused to speak to them. It wasn't long before the trail led to Mark and his association with Giles. A gossip columnist in a downtown free paper speculated on the connection between them, hinting that Giles and 'Wechsler the Younger' were lovers, or had been lovers. One reviewer referred to the piece as 'art rape.' Hasseborg climbed on board, arguing that the desecration renewed the possibility of subversion in art. 'With one shot, Theodore Giles has sent a bullet through all the pieties that surround art in our culture.'

Neither Violet nor I visited the show. Lazlo went with Pinky and took a surreptitious Polaroid, which he brought back to me and Violet. Mark was staying with his mother for several days before returning to New York. Violet said that when she'd told Mark about the painting, he had been perplexed. 'He seems to think that Giles is really a good guy and he can't understand why he would do this to his father's work.' After Violet examined the little photo, she laid it on the table but said nothing.

'I hoped it was a copy,' Lazlo said. 'But it's not. I was very close to it. He used the real painting.'

Pinky was sitting on the sofa. I noticed that even while sitting, her long feet were turned out in first position. 'The question is,' she said, 'why Bill's work? He could have bought any painting for the same money and wrecked it. Why that portrait of Mark? Because he knows him?'

Lazlo opened his mouth, closed it and opened it again. 'The word is Giles knows Mark because he was . . .' He hesitated. 'Fixed on Bill.'

Violet leaned forward. 'Do you have any reason to believe that?'

Through his glasses I saw Lazlo's eyes narrow slightly. 'I heard he has a file on Bill that goes back to before he knew Mark – clippings, catalogues, photos.'

None of us said a word. The idea that Giles had cultivated the son because of the father had dimly occurred to me in the hallway the day I found Mark in the bathroom, but what did Giles want? Had Bill still been alive, the ruined painting would have hurt him, but Bill was dead. Did Giles want to wound Mark? No, I thought to myself, I'm asking the wrong questions. I remembered Giles's face when we talked, his apparent sincerity about Mark, his comments about Tennie. 'Poor Teenie. Teenie cuts herself.' I remembered the sign on her skin – the connected M's, or the M attached to the W. M&M. Bill's M's – the boys, Matthew and Mark. *No K tonight, huh, M&M?* The changeling. I had been writing about this idea – copies, doubles, multiples of one. Confusions. I suddenly remembered the two identical male figures in Mark's collage with the two baby pictures. What was the story Bill had once told me about Dan? Yes. Dan was in the hospital after his first breakdown. Bill had had long hair then, but he'd cut it. When he went to visit Dan, Bill arrived in the ward with short

449

hair. Dan took one look at him and said, 'You cut my hair!' That happens with schizophrenics, Bill had told me. They make pronominal mistakes. And with aphasics. My thoughts weren't orderly. I saw Goya's Saturn eating his son, the photograph of Giles gnawing at his own arm, then Mark's head jerking backward from my arm as I woke up in bed. The telephone message: *M&M knows they killed me*. No. *M&M knows they killed Me*. The boy in the hallway with the green purse. Me. They called him 'Me.'

'Are you okay, Leo?' Violet said.

I looked at her and then I explained.

'Rafael and Me are the same person,' Violet said.

'You mean the kid they say was killed by Giles?' Pinky said.

The conversation that followed quickly meandered into the outlandish. We made forays into Rafael's purported slavery, Mark's possible love affair with Giles, Teenie's exquisite mutilation, and the dead cats that had been strung around the city. Lazlo mentioned Special K and another drug called Ecstasy. The little pills were also sometimes called E's, another letter in the growing alphabet of pharmaceuticals. But the single hard fact we had was my fleeting glimpse of a boy in the hallway early one morning whom Mark had called 'Me.' Over the telephone an unknown girl had relayed a rumor to Violet about a possible murder and a boy named Rafael, but who was to say that the story wasn't pure

450

fabrication? At the time, however, my imagination was running freely, and I proposed the possibility that Giles was behind the phone calls to both Violet and Bill. 'He gives interviews in different voices,' I said. 'Maybe Giles is the girl on the telephone.' Violet disagreed, saying the voice wasn't a falsetto. When Pinky mentioned voice-altering devices that could be attached to telephones, Violet started to laugh. Her laughter soon turned into high staccato shrieks, and then the tears began to run down her face. Pinky stood up, knelt in front of Violet, and put her arms around her neck. Lazlo and I sat and watched as the two women rocked each other in a long embrace. At least five minutes passed before Violet's tearful laughter subsided into small gasps for breath and convulsive sniffs. 'You're worn out,' Pinky said to Violet as she stroked her head. 'You're all worn out.'

By then, two months had gone by without a letter from Erica. On the day before Mark returned to New York, I broke our pact and called. I don't think I was expecting her to be there. I had planned a little speech for the answering machine instead, and when she picked up the telephone and said, 'Hello,' I gagged for a moment. After I identified myself, she didn't speak, and that interval of silence made me suddenly angry. I told her that our friendship, marriage, rapport – whatever the hell it was – had become a sham, a false, stupid, dead nothingness, and I was sick and tired of

451

the whole business. If she had met somebody else, I deserved to know. If she had, I wanted to be free of her, wanted to leave her behind me for good.

'There's nobody else, Leo.'

'Why haven't you answered my letters?'

'I've started fifty letters and thrown them away. I feel like I'm always explaining and analyzing myself, blah, blah, blah. Even with you. I'm sick of my own interminable need to put it all down and pick it apart. When I do, it looks like the worst kind of sophism, like clever lies, like excuses for myself.' Erica sighed heavily, and with that familiar sound my anger disappeared. Once it was gone, I realized that I missed it. Spite has focus, a keenness that sympathy lacks, and I was sorry to find myself back in that diffuse emotional territory.

'I've been writing so much, Leo, it's been hard to write to you. It's Henry James again.'

'Oh,' I said.

'I love them, you know.'

'Who?'

'His characters. I love them because they're so complicated, and while I'm working on them and their suffering, I forget myself. I've thought of calling – it was stupid of me not to call. I'm really sorry.'

By the end of the conversation, Erica and I had decided to call each other as well as write. I told her to send me the book whenever she felt she was ready, and I told her that I loved her. She said she loved me, too. There wasn't anybody else. There would never be anybody else. After I hung up the phone, I understood that we would never be free of each other. It gave me no joy. I didn't want to let go of Erica, and yet I rebelled against our stubborn connection. We had been pulled apart by absence, but that same absence had shackled us together for life.

I had made the phone call at my desk, and after a couple of minutes I opened the drawer and examined my hoard of things. They looked odd to me – that curious collection of memorabilia that included thin black socks, burned cardboard, and a thin square cut from a magazine. I looked at Violet's face in the photograph, and then at Bill, whose eyes were on his wife. His wife. His widow. The dead. The living. I picked up Erica's lipstick. My wife and her beloved characters in a dead man's books. Only fictions. But we all live there, I thought to myself, in the imaginary stories we tell ourselves about our lives, and then I picked up Matt's picture of Dave and Durango.

Mark looked better. His blue eyes had a new directness, and he had gained a few pounds during his months away. Even his voice seemed to have more resonance and conviction. His days consisted of job hunting in the morning, Narcotics Anonymous meeting in the afternoon, and appointments with a man who had become his sponsor. Alvin was a former heroin addict who couldn't have been more than thirty. He was a tidy, polite man with light brown skin, a close-cropped beard, and eyes that burned with feverish determination. Alvin was a resurrected man, a Dostoyevskian character who had crawled up from the underground to lend his support to a comrade in need. His body was a rigid block of purpose, and just looking at him made me feel languid, superfluous, and ignorant. Like thousands of others, Mark's sponsor had 'hit bottom' and then decided to change his life. I never learned Alvin's story, but Mark told me and Violet countless others he had gathered up at Hazelden, sordid tales of desperate need that led to lies, abandonments, betrayals and sometimes violence. Each story had a name attached to it – Maria, John, Angel, Hans, Mariko, Deborah. Mark was clearly interested in the stories, but he focused on their grim details rather than on the people who had made them happen. Perhaps he saw their actions as mirrors of his own degradation.

Violet was hopeful. Mark attended meetings every day, spoke to Alvin often, and was working as a busboy at a restaurant on Grand Street. Following the rules of the program, Violet had told him she was finished with punishments, but he couldn't live with her unless he was 'clean.' It was that simple. In the middle of the month, Mark knocked on my door one evening at around eleven o'clock at night. I was already in bed but still awake. When I opened the door, he was standing

454

in the hallway. I told him to come in. He walked to the sofa but didn't sit down. He glanced at the painting of Violet, looked in my direction and then down at his shoes. 'I'm sorry,' he said. 'I'm sorry for hurting you.'

I stared at him and tightened the sash of my bathrobe as if that tug would help keep in my emotions.

'I was on drugs,' he continued. 'They messed me up, but I'm responsible for all of it.'

I didn't answer him.

'You don't have to forgive me, but it's important that I ask you. It's part of the steps.'

I nodded.

Mark's face was quivering.

He's nineteen years old, I said to myself.

'I wish everything was different, that it was the way it was before.' He looked at me for the first time. 'You used to like me,' he said. 'We had good talks.'

'I don't know what those talks really meant, Mark,' I said. 'You've lied so much . . .'

He interrupted me. 'I know, but I've changed.' There was a moan in his voice. 'And I told you things I never told anybody else. I meant them. I really did.'

The desperation seemed to come from inside him, from deep within his chest. Was the sound new? Had I ever heard this tone before? I didn't think so. Very tentatively I put my hand on his shoulder. 'Time will tell,' I said. 'You have a chance to turn things around, to live in a different way. I believe you can do it.'

He moved closer to me and looked down into my face. He seemed immensely relieved. He let out a long breath, and then he said, 'Please.' Mark spread his arms for a hug. I hesitated but then relented. He leaned toward me and lay his head on my shoulder and he embraced me with an intensity and warmth that reminded me of his father.

Early in the morning on December 2, Mark disappeared. That same day Violet received a letter from Deborah – the girl Mark and Violet had befriended at Hazelden. It was almost midnight when Violet came downstairs with the letter in her hand, seated herself on the sofa and read it to me.

Dear Violet,
I wanted to write you and tell you that I'm doing all right. Every day is a big fight with the not drinking and everything but I'm getting along with my mom's help. She's trying not to yell at me so much after what we said in the family meetings. She knows it gets me down. When it's really bad I think about the singing I heard from the sky that night at Hazelden and those voices from heaven that told me I was a child of God and that he loves me just for that. I know that some of the others thought I was bonkers

when I said I wasn't Debbie no more. But in the family meeting I could tell that you were understanding of me. I had to be Deborah after I heard them singing. You are a real good person and Mark is lucky to have you for a stepmom. He told me about how you helped him through withdrawal when he was shaking and barfing so bad before you came to Minnesota. I always wished I had somebody like that for me. I've been asking everybody to pray for me, so I hope that you can pray for me too. Merry, merry Xmas and a great new year!

LUV,

Deborah

P.S. I get my cast off next week.

When Violet was finished reading, she lay the paper on her lap and looked up at me.

'You never told me that Mark had withdrawal symptoms,' I said.

'I didn't tell you because he didn't have them.'

'Why would Deborah write that, then?'

'Because he told her that he did.'

'But why would he do that?'

'I think he wanted to fit in, be more like the others. I mean, Mark has a drug problem, but he was never physically dependent on drugs. It probably made it easier to explain all the lying and stealing he did if he pretended he was a hard-core addict.' She paused for several seconds.

'By the end, they all loved him – the counselors, the other patients, everybody. They made him a group leader. Mark was a star. Nobody liked Debbie much. She dresses like a tart and has a bad complexion. She's twenty-four years old and has been in detox three times already. She almost drowned once. She got so drunk she fell into a lake. Another time she drove off the road and smashed into a tree and had her license revoked. Before she landed in Hazelden, she came home smashed, fell down the stairs in her mother's house, and broke her leg in five places. She's got a cast up to here.' Violet pointed to her thigh. 'Well, she stole from her mother and lied to her, just like Mark. She turned tricks for a while. Her mother's had it. She just kept screaming at Debbie – "You're a big baby. It's just like I've had a crying, puking baby for twenty-four years. You're not a companion to me at all. My whole life is taking care of you." Then the mother cried and Debbie cried, and I cried. I sat in that chair and sobbed my guts out for poor Debbie and her poor mother.' Violet gave me an ironic smile. 'I didn't know them from a hole in the wall. Well, sometime during the second month, Debbie had her vision and turned into Deborah.'

'The singing,' I said.

Violet nodded. 'She came back to the next family meeting shining like a light bulb.'

'That can wear off, you know. It usually does.'

'Yes, but she believes in her story and in the words she uses to tell it.'

'And Mark doesn't. Is that what you're saying?'

Violet stood up. She pressed her hands into her forehead and began to pace. I tried to remember if Violet had paced before Bill died. I watched her take several steps and turn. 'Sometimes I think he doesn't understand what language is. It's like he never figured out symbols – the whole structure of things is missing. He can speak, but he just uses words as a way to manipulate other people.' Violet took out a cigarette and lit it.

'You're smoking a lot now,' I told her.

She inhaled the Camel and waved her hand in a dismissive gesture. 'It's more than that. Mark doesn't have a story.'

'Sure he does,' I said. 'We all do.'

'But he doesn't know what it is, Leo. At Hazelden they kept asking him to talk about himself. In the beginning he would mumble a few things about the divorce – his mother, his father. The counselor prodded him. What do you mean? Explain. And he said, 'Everybody keeps telling me that it has to be the divorce, so it must be.' That made them angry. They wanted him to feel – to tell his story. So he started to talk, but when I think about it, he never said much of any significance. But he did cry. That made them happy. He gave them what they wanted – feeling, or the appearance of it. But a story is about making connections in time, and Mark's stuck in a time warp, a sick repetition that just shuttles him back and forth, back and forth.'

'You mean the way he went from one parent to another?'

Violet stopped pacing. 'I don't know,' she said. 'Lots of kids go between their divorced parents, and they don't turn out like Mark. It can't be that.' She turned her back to me and walked to the window. I looked at her body as she stood with the cigarette burning near her thigh. She was wearing old blue jeans that didn't fit her anymore. I studied the gap of bare skin between her short sweater and the waistband of her pants. After a moment, I stood up and walked toward the window. The cigarette had an acrid chemical smell, but behind the smoke I breathed in Violet's perfume. I wanted to touch her shoulder, but I didn't. We stood in silence and looked into the street. It had stopped raining, and I watched as fat drops of water broke and slid down the pane. To my right, I could see plumes of white smoke rising from a hole in the street on Canal.

'All I know is that nothing he says can be believed. I don't mean just now. I mean nothing he's ever said. Some of it must have been true, but I don't know what.' Violet was looking into the street with narrowed eyes. 'Do you remember Mark's parakeet?'

'I remember the funeral,' I said.

Only Violet's lips moved. The rest of her seemed to have frozen in place. 'It broke its neck in the cage door.' Several seconds passed before she spoke again in the same low voice. 'All his little animals died – the two guinea pigs, the white mice, even the fish. Of course they often do, small pets like that. They're frail . . .'

I didn't answer her. She hadn't asked me a question. The smoke from the manhole was beautiful in the light of the street lamps, and we watched as it billowed upward like some infernal cloud of our own blooming suspicion.

The telephone call from Mark three days later became the catalyst for the strangest journey of my life. When Violet came downstairs to tell me about the call, she said, 'Who knows if it's true, but he said he's in Minneapolis with Teddy Giles. He said that he saw a gun in Giles's bag and he's afraid that Giles is going to kill him. When I asked him why, he said that Teddy told him he had murdered that boy they called 'Me' and thrown his body into the Hudson River. Mark said he knows that it's true. I asked him how, but he said he couldn't tell me. I asked him why he lied when we confronted him with the rumors, why he didn't go to the police, and he said he was afraid. Then I asked him why he went off with Giles if he was afraid of him. Instead of answering the question, he started talking about two detectives who had been asking questions at the Finder Gallery and in the clubs about the night the boy disappeared. He thinks Giles might be running from the police. He wants money for a plane ticket home.'

'You can't send him money, Violet.'

'I know. I said I'd arrange to have a ticket waiting

461

for him at the airport. He said he doesn't have enough money to get to the airport.'

'He could change the ticket,' I said. 'And use it to go somewhere else.'

'I've never been close to anything like this, Leo. It feels unreal.'

'Do you have a gut feeling about whether he's lying or not?'

Violet shook her head slowly. 'I don't know. For a long time I've been afraid there was something underneath . . .' She took a breath. 'If it's true, we have to get Mark to the police.'

'Call him back,' I said. 'Tell him I'll meet him and fly back with him to New York. It's the only way to make sure he gets here.'

Violet looked startled. 'What about your classes, Leo?'

'It's Thursday. I don't have another class until Tuesday. It won't take me four days.'

I insisted that it was my job to retrieve Mark, that I wanted to do it, and in the end Violet agreed to let me go. But even while I was speaking, I knew that my reasons for going were murky. The idea that I was behaving rashly excited me, and that thrilling picture of myself carried me through all the arrangements. I packed while Violet called Mark and told him to meet me in the lobby of the hotel at midnight – an hour after my plane arrived – and advised him to stay in public places until then. I threw a shirt, underwear, and a pair of socks into a small canvas bag as if I routinely flew off to midwestern cities to lasso wayward boys. I hugged Violet good-bye – more confidently than usual – and instantly found a cab on the street to take me to the airport.

As soon as I took my seat on the airplane, the spell began to wear off. I felt like an actor who leaves the stage and suddenly loses the adrenaline that kept him sailing through his performance as someone else. While I studied the camouflage pants of the young man in the seat next to me, I felt more quixotic than heroic, older rather than younger, and I asked myself what I was flying toward. Mark's story was bizarre. A body dumped in the river. Detectives asking questions. A gun in a suitcase. Weren't these the familiar elements of crime fiction? Didn't Giles play with these conventions in his art? Wasn't it very likely that I had become a pawn in some conceptual 'murder piece' Giles had dreamed up? Or was I giving Giles credit for more intelligence than he actually had? I remembered the round-faced boy in the hallway gripping a plastic purse filled with Lego blocks and had the sudden absurd thought that I had left home to face a possible murderer unarmed. I owned no weapons except kitchen knives anyway. Then I thought of Matt's Swiss Army knife lying in my drawer at home. As I continued to hold the image of the knife in my mind, I found it increasingly unpleasant. I remembered the young Mark down on his hands and knees in Matt's room. I saw him sliding underneath the bed, and then, after a couple of moments, reappearing, his wide blue eyes looking up at me. 'Where could it have gone? It must be here somewhere.'

The lobby of the Minneapolis Holiday Inn was a vast room with a glass elevator, an enormous curved reception desk, and a distant ceiling ornamented with an undulating piece of thin metal in an ugly shade of maroon. I looked for Mark but didn't see him. The café to my right was dark. I sat down and waited until twelve-thirty. Then I used the house telephone to call room 1512, but no one answered. I didn't leave a message. What would I do if Mark didn't show? I walked over to a clerk behind the desk and asked if I could leave a message for one of the guests, Mark Wechsler.

I watched the man's fingers press the letters into the computer. He shook his head. 'We don't have a guest by that name.'

'Try Giles,' I said. 'Teddy Giles.'

The man nodded. 'Here it is. Mr and Mrs Theodore Giles in room 1512. If you'd like to leave a message, the house phone is over there.' He moved his head to the left.

I thanked him and and returned to my seat. Mr and Mrs? Giles is in drag, I thought. Even if the entire business was a scam, wouldn't Mark have met me to keep it going? As I considered my next move, I saw a very tall young woman out of the corner of my eye. She was crossing the lobby and walking quickly toward the door. Although

I couldn't see her face, I noticed that she had the confident, self-conscious gait of a beautiful girl. I turned around to look at her. She was wearing a long black coat with a fur collar and boots with low heels. When she entered the revolving door to the street, I glimpsed the side of her face for an instant and had the uncanny sensation that I knew her. Her long blond hair moved in the wind as the door turned. I stood up. I felt sure I knew that woman. I strode toward the door as fast as I could and noticed a green-and-white taxi waiting outside. The door to the backseat opened, and at the same moment the car's interior light illuminated a man's face in the backseat. It was Giles. The woman slid in beside him. The car door slammed, and with that sound I knew what I had seen – Mark. The young woman was Mark.

I rushed into the cold night air, waved my arms at the moving taxi, and shouted 'Stop!' It drove out of the entrance and turned onto the road. There were no other cabs, and I turned around and walked back inside.

After getting a room for the night, I left a letter with the clerk. 'Dear Mark,' I wrote. 'You seem to have changed your mind about returning to New York. I will be here until tomorrow morning. If you want a ticket home, call me in my room – 7538. Leo.'

The room had green carpeting, two queen-sized beds with floral orange and green spreads, a window that couldn't be opened, and a gigantic television set. The colors depressed me. Because I had promised to call Violet even if it was very late, I picked up the phone and dialed her number. She answered after one ring and listened in silence as I told her what had happened.

'You think it was all a lie?' she said.

'I don't know. Why would he tell me to come all the way out here?'

'Maybe he felt trapped and couldn't figure out how to get out of it. Will you call me in the morning?'

'Of course.'

'You know that I think you're a wonderful man, don't you?'

'I'm glad to hear that.'

'I don't know what I'd do without you.'

'You'd do just fine,' I said.

'No, I wouldn't, Leo. You've held me together.'

After a pause of a couple of seconds, I said, 'It goes both ways.'

'I'm glad you think that,' she said softly. 'Try to sleep.'

'Good-night, Violet.'

'Good-night.'

Violet's voice left me agitated. I raided the minibar, retrieved a tiny bottle of Scotch, and turned on the television. A man was lying dead in the street. I turned the channel. A woman with tall hair was advertising a chopping machine. A huge telephone number hung over her head. I waited for a call from Mark, drank another Scotch, and fell asleep near the end of *The Invasion of the Body Snatchers*, when Kevin McCarthy is running blindly on the highway at night as trucks loaded with the transforming pods screech past him. By the time the telephone rang, I had been asleep for hours and was dreaming about a blond man whose pockets were filled with tiny pills that moved in his palms like white worms when he held them out to show me.

I looked at the clock. It was after six.

'Teddy here.'

'Put Mark on.'

'Mrs Giles is asleep.'

'Wake him up,' I said.

'She asked me to give you this message. Are you ready? This is it: Iowa City. Got that? The Holiday Inn, Iowa City.'

'I'll come down to your room,' I said. 'I just want to see Mark for a couple of minutes.'

'She's not in the hotel. She's here. We're at the airport.'

'Mark is going with you to Iowa? What's in Iowa?'

'My mother's grave.' Giles hung up.

The Iowa City airport was deserted. A dozen travellers in parkas rolled their suitcases through the halls, and I wondered where all the people had gone. It turned out that I had to call for a taxi and then wait in an icy wind for twenty minutes before it came. The woman at the check-in counter in Minneapolis had refused to tell me whether Theodore Giles and Mark Wechsler had been among the passengers who'd left on the seven o'clock plane that morning, but the departure time matched Giles' call. When I'd telephoned Violet from the airport, she had told me to come home, but I had said no, I wanted to go on. I looked out the cab window and wondered why. Iowa was flat and brown and bleak. Its drab, mostly treeless expanse was varied only by dirty patches of unmelted snow that lay beneath a huge overcast sky. In the distance I saw a farm, its gray silo jutting up from the plain, and I thought of Alice and her seizure in the hayloft. What did I hope to find here? What would I say to Mark? My legs and arms ached. My neck had a crick in it that made it painful to turn. In order to look out the window, I had to shift my whole body, which put pressure on my lower back. I hadn't shaved, and that morning I had noticed a stain on my pants leg. You're an old wreck, I said to myself, and yet there's something you want from all this – some idea of yourself – some redemption. The word 'redemption' had come to me for a reason, but I didn't understand it. Why did I feel that a corpse was always lying under my thoughts? A boy I didn't know, a boy I had seen only once. Could I even describe him accurately? Had I come to Iowa for Rafael, whose name was also 'Me'? I couldn't answer my own questions. It wasn't a new experience. The longer I ponder something, the more it seems to evaporate, rising like steam from a cave in my mind.

The Iowa City Holiday Inn smelled dank and moist, exactly like the swimming pool at the YMHA where I had taken swimming lessons not long after I came to live in New York. As I examined the obese woman with crinkly yellow hair behind the desk, I remembered the resounding echoes of the diving board when I bounced on it and the feel of my bathing suit sliding down my legs in the dim light of the locker room. The odor of chlorine saturated the lobby, as if the unseen pool had leaked into every wall and carpet and upholstered chair. The woman was wearing a turquoise sweater with large pink and orange flowers knit into it. I wondered how to frame my question. Did I ask for two young men or a pale, thin man and a tall blond woman? I decided to use their names.

'I've got Wechsler,' she said. 'William and Mark.'

I looked at the floor. The names hurt me. Father and son.

'Are they in their room?' I asked her. My eyes settled on a pin she was wearing above her enormous right breast. It said MAY LARSEN.

'They went out an hour ago.'

As she leaned toward me, I could see that May Larsen was curious. Her watery blue eyes had an alert, shrewd glint I pretended not to see. I asked for a room.

469

She examined my credit card. 'They left you a message.' She handed me my room key and an evelope. I moved away from her to read it, but I felt her eyes on me as I opened the paper.

Dear Uncle Leo,
   Now we're all here. Me 1, Me 2, Me 3.
Off to the cemetery.
   Lots of Luv,
   The She-Monster & Co.

It was May Larsen who told me that she had overheard Mark and Giles say they were going shopping, and she was the one who gave me directions to the mall only blocks away. I should never have left the hotel, but the prospect of sitting in the lobby, perhaps for hours, under Mrs Larsen's vigilant eyes seemed impossible. I wandered out into a small walking street, an area that had been renovated according to new American standards of quaintness. I looked at its attractive benches, small naked trees, and a shop that advertised cappuccinos and lattes and espressos. At the end of that street I took a left and soon found the mall. When I walked through the door, I was greeted by a mechanical Santa Claus sitting on top of a display case. He bent forward and gave me a stiff wave.

I'm not sure how long I was in that place, strolling among the racks of limp dresses and colored shirts and plump down jackets that looked much warmer than my own wool coat. The tinsel and fluorescent lights seemed to shudder above me as I peeked into one store after another. Every one was a familiar franchise with outlets in every other city and town in America. New York City has these shops, too, and yet as I moved from the Gap to Talbots to Eddie Bauer, expecting to spot Mark and Teddy behind every towering pile of merchandise, I felt like a foreigner again. The chain stores that shine in the empty plains of middle America are swallowed whole in New York City. In Manhattan their clean logos must compete with the fading ads of a thousand dead businesses that never took down their signs, with the noise and smoke and litter in the streets, and with the conversations and shouts of people who speak in a hundred different languages. In New York only the obviously violent person stands out – the bum smashing bottles against a wall, the screaming woman with an umbrella. But that afternoon as I saw myself reflected in one mirror after another, my features looked suddenly alien. Surrounded by the inhabitants of Iowa, I looked like a gaunt Jew wandering through a mob of overfed Gentiles. And during this bout of an incipient persecution complex, I had other thoughts of graves and their stones, of Giles's dead mother, of the pronominal pun – Me too/Me 2 – and of Mark parading as a woman in a blond wig. All at once, I felt exhausted. My lower back ached, and I looked for the exit to the street. I hobbled past a plastic bin overflowing with bras, felt nauseated, and had to stop. For an instant I tasted vomit in my mouth.

After I had eaten a tough steak and a basket of french fries, I returned to the hotel, and May Larsen handed me another note:

Hey Leo!
New locale: the Opryland Hotel. Nashville.
If you don't come, I'm going to send Mark to my mother's.
Your friend and admirer,
T.G.

There are nights when I'm still wandering the hallways of the Opryland Hotel, still taking elevators to a new level and walking through jungles that grow under an arching glass roof. I pass through miniature villages that are meant to resemble New Orleans or Savannah or Charleston. I cross bridges with water running underneath them, and I ride escalators up and down and then up again, and I am always on the lookout for Room 149872 in a wing called the Bayou. I cannot find it. I have a map and I study the lines the young woman at the desk drew to help me find my way, but I can't understand them, and my bag with next to nothing in it grows heavier and heavier on my shoulder. The pain in my back moves up my spine, and everywhere I walk I hear country music. It's piped in from mysterious crevices and corners, and it never stops. The phantasmagoric interior of that hotel can never be separated from what happened to me there because its nonsensical architecture echoed my state of mind. I lost my bearings and, with them, the landmarks of an internal geography I had counted on to guide me.

I had missed the last plane out of Iowa City and ended up spending the night. In the morning I flew back to Minneapolis and boarded another plane for Nashville that afternoon. I told myself and I told Violet over the telephone that it was the threat to Mark implied in Giles's note that forced me to continue the chase. And yet I knew that my methods had been ridiculous. I could have seated myself outside Mark and Giles's hotel room in Minneapolis and waited for them to return. In Iowa City I could have done the same. Instead, I had left a note in one place and idly toured a mall in another. I had behaved as if I hadn't wanted to find them. Moreover, at every turn Giles had seemed delighted by my pursuit. Both his telephone conversation and his note had artfully combined the sinister with the flirtatious. Giles didn't seem to be worried about the police. If he was, why would he announce his every move? And Mark seemed to be in no danger from Giles. He had willingly jumped on one plane after another with his friend, or lover.

By the time the young woman behind the long desk at the Opryland Hotel was tracing the map of its myriad wings with a green pen and welcoming me for the third time to 'the biggest hotel in the world,' I had already thought myself into a hole. Another hour and a half passed before I finally located my room with the help of an older man in a green uniform whose name tag designated him only as 'Bill.' William is a common name, and yet the four letters on his chest jarred me when I saw them.

I left a written message for Mark at the desk and another on his voice mail. After that, I decided to walk however many miles necessary to his room and wait for him and Giles to return. But the very thought of journeying once again through that interminable landscape of restaurants and boutiques sickened me. I didn't feel well. It wasn't just my back that hurt me. I hadn't slept very much, and a dull but persistent headache hung like a weight in my temples.

As I walked past the endless rows of shops, with their overdressed dolls and plush bears, I lost hope. It hardly seemed to matter anymore whether I found Mark, and I wondered if Giles had known that his message would catapult me into a maze of artifice beyond anything I had ever experienced. As I trudged on, I looked into a store at masks of Laurel and Hardy, a rubber replica of Elvis Presley, and several mugs embossed with Marilyn Monroe, her skirt flying.

Only a minute later, I spotted Mark and Giles on an escalator coming up from the floor below me. Instead of calling out to them, I retreated behind the pillar of a small Georgia mansion to

474

watch them. I felt both cowardly and silly, but I wanted to observe them together. Both of them were wearing men's clothes. They were smiling at each other and looked relaxed, like two normal young men out on a lark. Mark's hip jutted out as he stood on the moving step, and I heard him talking to Giles. 'Those dogs were pretty wild, and did you check out the ass on the salesman? It was a mile wide, man.'

It wasn't what Mark said that made me catch my breath. It was that the register, the cadence, the tone of his voice were all unfamiliar to me. For years I had seen in Mark the shifting colors of a chameleon, had known that he changed according to the circumstances in which he found himself, but at the sound of that unknown voice, the disquiet that had been lurking in me for so long seemed to find its horrible confirmation, and while I shrank from it, I also felt a tremor of victory. I had proof that he was really somebody else. I stepped out from behind the pillar and said, 'Mark.'

The two turned around and stared at me. They looked genuinely surprised. Giles recovered first, strode toward me, and stopped only inches from where I was standing. He brought his face close to mine, and without thinking I moved my head away from the intimate gesture. But as soon as I had done it, I felt I had made a mistake. Giles grinned. 'Professor Hertzberg,' he said. 'What brings you to Nashville?' He put out his right hand, but I didn't take it. He kept his pale face very close to me as I searched for an adequate reply, but nothing came. Giles had asked the question I had been asking myself. I didn't know why I had come to Nashville. I looked at Mark, who was standing three or four feet behind Giles.

Giles continued to examine me. He tilted his head to the side, waiting for an answer, and I noticed that he kept his left hand in his pocket as he fingered something inside it. 'I have to talk to Mark,' I said. 'Alone.'

Mark's head drooped. I noticed that he was standing with his toes turned inward, like an unhappy child. His knees sagged for an instant before he caught himself and straightened up. I guessed that he was drugged.

'I'll let the two of you talk, then,' Giles said cheerfully. 'As you may well imagine, this hotel is a rich source of inspiration for my work. So many artists forget the fertile landscape that is commerce in America. I still have a lot to peruse.' He smiled, waved, and began to walk down the hallway.

It has been four years since I talked to Mark at the Opryland Hotel. We seated ourselves at a small red metal table with a large white heart on it in a café called the Love Corner. I've had years to digest what he told me, but I'm still not sure what to make of it.

Mark lifted his chin and looked at me with an expression I recognized. His eyes were wide with innocent sorrow, and his lip protruded in the pout he had been using since early childhood. I wondered if his repertoire of facial expressions had narrowed. Either he was losing his gift for variation or drugs were interfering with his performance. I stared at the mask of regret and shook my head.

'I don't think you understand, Mark,' I said. 'It's too late for that face. I heard you on the escalator. I heard your voice. It's not the one I know, and even if I hadn't heard it, I've seen that expression a thousand times before. It's the one you put on for the grown-ups you've hurt, but you're not three years old anymore. You're a man. That puppy-dog face is inappropriate. No, it's worse than that. It's pathetic.'

Mark looked surprised for a half a second. Then, as if on command, his expression changed. He withdrew his lip, and suddenly his face looked more mature. Altering his expression so quickly was a blunder on his part, and I felt a sudden advantage.

'It must be hard,' I said, 'to juggle so many faces, so many lies. I'm sorry for you – concocting that story about the gun and a murder just so Violet would send you money. How stupid do you think she is? Did you really imagine that she would wire you money after all you've done?'

Mark lowered his eyes and looked at the table. 'It's not a story.' He spoke to me in the voice I knew.

'I don't believe you.'

Mark raised his eyes but not his chin. The blue irises were liquid with feeling. I recognized that look, too. I had fallen for it again and again. 'Teddy told me he did it – that he killed him.'

'But this was all long before you were at Hazelden. Why did you run off with Teddy now?'

'He asked me to come, and I was afraid to say no.'

'You're lying,' I said.

Mark shook his head vigorously. 'No!' There was a little shout in his voice. Three tables away from us, a woman turned her head toward the sound.

'Mark,' I said, keeping my voice very low, 'do you understand how berserk you sound? You could have come back with me from Minneapolis. I was there to take you home.' I paused. 'I saw you in the wig, saw you get into the taxi with him . . .' I stopped when Mark smirked and shrugged his shoulders.

'What are you smiling about?'

'I don't know. You're acting like I'm a queen or something.'

'Well, what's it all about? Are you telling me that you and Teddy aren't lovers?'

'It's just for kicks. It's nothing serious. I'm not gay – only with him . . .'

I studied Mark's face. He looked a little embarrassed, nothing more. I leaned toward him. 'What kind of a person goes off with someone he thinks is a murderer, claiming to be afraid of him, and then has a few kicks on the side?'

Mark didn't answer me.

478

'That man destroyed one of your father's paintings. Doesn't that bother you? A portrait of you, Mark.'

'It wasn't me,' he said in a sulky voice. His eyes had gone blank.

'Yes, it was,' I said. 'What are you talking about?'

'It didn't look like me,' he said. 'It was ugly.'

I was silent. Mark's antipathy to the portrait blew like a breeze through me. It changed things. I wondered if it had affected Giles's motives. He must have known how Mark felt.

'Mom kept it in the barn all wrapped up. She didn't like it either.'

'I see,' I said.

'I don't get why it's such a big deal. Dad made lots of paintings. That was just one—'

'Just imagine how he would have felt,' I said.

Mark shook his head. 'He wasn't even around.'

The word 'around' set me off. Looking into Mark's shallow, dead eyes and hearing that moronic euphemism for his father's death made me furious. 'That painting was better than you are, Mark. It was more real, more alive, more powerful than you have ever been or will ever be. You are the thing that's ugly, not that painting. You're ugly and empty and cold. You're something your father would hate.' I was breathing loudly through my nose. My rage overwhelmed me. I made an effort to gain control of it.

'Uncle Leo,' Mark simpered, 'that's mean.'

I swallowed. My face was shaking. 'It's never-theless true. As far as I can tell, it's the only thing that is true. I have no idea if anything you've said is true, but I know your father would be ashamed of you. Your lies don't even make sense. They're not rational. They're stupid. The truth is easier. Why not tell the truth for once?'

Mark was calm. He seemed fascinated by my anger. Then he said, 'Because I don't think people will like it.'

I grabbed Mark's right wrist and began to squeeze. I put all my strength into that grip, and as I looked into his startled eyes, I felt glad. 'Why don't you try the truth now?' I said.

'That hurts,' he said.

His passivity amazed me. Why didn't he shake me off? Keeping up the pressure, I grunted at him, 'Tell me now. You've been faking it for years, haven't you? I've never really seen you, have I? You stole Matt's knife and then pretended to search for it, pretended to be sorry he lost it.' I grabbed Mark's other wrist and gripped it so hard a pain flashed through my neck. I stared at his Adam's apple, at his soft, red lips and slightly flattened nose that I realized was identical to Lucille's. 'You betrayed Matt, too.'

'You're hurting me,' he moaned.

I gripped him harder. I hadn't known I had it in me. I realized that I was panting for breath, but only because I heard myself gasp out the words, 'I want to hurt you.' I felt a lifting sensation inside my head, an intense pleasure of emptiness and freedom. I remembered the phrase 'blind with rage' and thought to myself, that's wrong. I saw every nuance of pain in his face and each one made me feel drunk.

'Let go of him, now.' The man's voice startled me. I dropped Mark's wrists and looked up.

'I don't know what's going on here, but I'm going to call security and have you thrown out if you don't stop right now.' The man had a bulbous nose and pink skin and was wearing an apron. 'It's all right,' Mark said. He had chosen his innocent look for the occasion. I saw his mouth tremble. 'I'm okay now, really.'

The man looked at Mark's face and then put his hand on Mark's shoulder. 'Are you sure?' he said. After that, he turned to me. 'If you lay a hand on that kid again, I'll come over here and knock your head off. Do you understand?'

I didn't speak. My eyes felt as if they had sand in them, and I stared down at the tabletop. My arms hurt. When I tried to sit up straight, a searing pain moved up my spine. I had somehow managed to throw my back out clutching Mark's wrists. I could hardly move. Mark, on the other hand, looked fine. He started to talk.

'Sometimes I think there's something wrong with me, that maybe I am crazy. I don't know. I want people to like me, I guess. I can't help it. Sometimes I get confused, like when I've met two different people in two different places and then

I meet them at the same party or something, and I don't know how to act. It's pretty confusing. I know you think I didn't like Matt, but you're wrong about that. I liked him a lot. He was my best friend. I just wanted the knife. It wasn't personal or anything. I just took it. I don't know why, but I like stealing. Sometimes when we were little and we'd have a fight about something, Matt would get all sad and he'd start crying and say, "I'm so sorry, Mark. Forgive me! Forgive me!" He talked like that. It was kind of funny. But I remember that I wondered why I wasn't like that. I didn't feel sorry.'

I tried to adjust myself so that I could look at him. I was hunched over but managed to lift my eyes toward his face. He continued to talk in a tone as vacant as his expression. 'There's a voice inside my head. I hear it, but nobody else does. People wouldn't like it, so I use other voices for them. Teddy knows about me, because we're the same. He's the only one, but even with him it's not that voice, not the one in my head.'

I pulled my hands back from the table. 'What about Dr Monk?' I said.

Mark shook his head. 'She thinks she's smart, but she's not.'

'Everything between us,' I said, 'has been a sham.'

Mark squinted at me. 'No, you just don't understand. I've always liked you, always, since I was a little kid.'

482

I couldn't really nod. I wondered how I would stand up. 'I don't know if anything happened to that boy or not, but if you think something did, if you really believe he's dead, you have to go to the police.'

'I can't,' he said.

'You have to, Mark.'

'Me's in California,' Mark blurted out. 'He ran off with another guy. Teddy wanted to fool you and he got me to go along with it. There's no murder. It was all a big joke.'

Well before he had finished speaking, I believed him. It was the only thing that made sense. The boy wasn't dead. He was alive in California. The cruelty of the story combined with my own gullibility shamed me, and my whole body felt hot. I moved my arms onto the table and tried to heave myself up and out of the chair. A shooting pain burned through my neck and down the middle of my back. There would be little dignity in my exit. 'Are you coming back to New York?' I said to Mark. 'Or are you staying here? Violet is finished with you if you don't come back. She wanted you to know that. You're nineteen. You can fend for yourself.'

Mark looked at me. 'Are you okay, Uncle Leo?'

I couldn't stand up. My body was wrenched to one side and my neck stuck out at an angle that must have made me look like a large injured bird.

Giles was suddenly in front of me, and I had the eerie sensation that he had been near us all along.

483

'Let me give you a hand,' he said. He sounded genuinely concerned and that frightened me. A second later, he took hold of my elbow. In order to prevent him from touching me, I would have had to shake my arm and realign my whole body. I couldn't do it. 'You should see a doctor,' he went on. 'If we were in New York, I'd call my chiropractor. He's great. Once I screwed up my back dancing, if you can believe it.'

'We'll take you to your room, Uncle Leo. Won't we, Teddy?'

'No problem.'

It was a long, painful walk. Every step I took sent a jab of pain from my thigh to my neck, and because I couldn't lift my head, I saw very little of what was around me. With Teddy on one side and Mark on the other, I felt vaguely threatened. They led me forward with a display of courtesy and solicitude that made me think of actors who had been asked to improvise a scene with a crippled mute. Giles did most of the talking, carrying on a monologue about chiropractors and acupuncturists. He recommended Chinese herbs and Pilates, then moved from alternative medicine to art, mentioning his collectors, recent sales, and a feature article on him somewhere. I knew that his chatter wasn't really idle, that he was moving toward a turn, and then he took it. He brought up Bill's canvas.

I closed my eyes, hoping to block out his words, but he was saying that he hadn't meant to hurt anyone, that he wouldn't 'dream' of it, that it had come to him as an inspiration, as an avenue of subversion as yet unexplored in art. He sounded just like Hasseborg. I think his choice of words might have been nearly the same as the critic's. As he talked, I thought he gripped my arm a little more tightly. 'William Wechsler,' he said, 'was a remarkable artist, but the canvas I bought was a minor work.' I was glad I couldn't look at him. 'In my piece, I really think it transcended itself.'

'That's rot,' I said. I was nearly whispering. We had turned down the long corridor that led to my room, and its emptiness unsettled me more. A soda machine glowed in the dim hallway. I didn't remember passing it earlier and wondered how I had managed to miss that large incandescent object so close to my door.

'What you fail to understand,' Giles continued, 'is that my work, too, has a personal side to it. William Wechsler's portrait of his son, my own M&M, Me 2, Mark the Shark, is now part of a very special tribute to my own late mother.'

I decided not to speak. All I wanted was to get away from them. I wanted to throw my wracked body into my room and slam the door behind me.

'Mark and I share the same regard for our mothers. Did you know that?'

'Teddy,' Mark said, 'forget it.' His tone was gruff.

I was looking down at the carpet. They had

stopped walking and I heard a soft click. Teddy was putting a card in a door.

'This isn't my room,' I said.

'No, it's ours. Ours is closer. You can stay here. We've got two beds.'

I took a breath. 'No, thank you,' I said as Giles began to push on the door. As the door moved, I anticipated seeing a room like mine, but instead I looked through the opening and saw that something was terribly wrong. The room smelled of smoke – not cigarette smoke but of something that had been burned. From the hallway I saw only part of the room, but the carpeted floor in front of me was strewn with refuse – a room-service tray littered with cigarette butts, a half-eaten hamburger that had drooled ketchup onto the carpet. Lying beside the tray were a woman's bikini underpants and a badly burned sheet that had been crumpled into a ball. I could see the ragged brown and ocher marks left by the fire, but there were also what looked like blood spots all over it, deep red stains that closed my throat when I saw them. Lying across the crumpled sheet were the coils of a pale nylon rope and, not far from the rope, a black revolver. I'm quite sure of what I saw, although my glimpse of that bizarre still life had the quality of a hallucination even while I was looking at it.

Giles tugged on my arm. 'Come on in and have a drink.'

'No,' I said. 'I'll find my room.' I dug my heels into the carpet.

'Come on, Uncle Leo,' Mark whined at me.

I straightened up, moving my spine through ratcheting pain and then shook my arm loose from Mark's hand. My lips were quivering. I moved back from the door, shuffled to the other side of the hallway, and leaned against the wall for a moment before I started to lope away, but Giles leapt toward me and flung out his arm. 'Just working through a few new ideas,' he said, pointing into the room. I had hunched over again. I simply couldn't endure standing erect. He leaned over me and whispered, 'But Professor, aren't you curious about me?' Then Giles put his fingers on my head. I could feel his hand on my scalp, felt him playing with strands of my hair, and when I looked him in the eyes, he smiled. 'Have you ever thought of using a little color?' he said. I tried to shake my head, but he grabbed me on either side of my face, pressing the sides of my glasses into my skin, and then he slammed my head against the wall. I grunted with pain.

'I'm so sorry,' he said. 'Did I hurt you?'

Giles didn't let go of me. He continued to squeeze my head with his hands. I flailed, lifted my knee to jab him, but the motion caused new pain. I gasped and felt my knees buckle under me. I was sliding down the wall, and I panicked. Moving my eyes to Mark's face, I said his name, which came like a wail from my throat. I called on him loudly and desperately, lifting my hands toward him, but he stood frozen in front of me. I couldn't read his face. In the same moment, a door opened beside me and a woman stepped out. Giles pulled me upward and began to pat me tenderly. 'You'll be all right,' he said. 'Should I call a doctor?' Then he backed quickly away from me and smiled at the woman in the doorway. As soon as he was out of the way, Mark moved toward me. He was talking fast under his breath. 'Go back to your room now. I'll go home with you tomorrow. I'll meet you in the lobby at ten. I want to go home.'

The woman was pretty and slender with puffy blond hair that fell into her eyes. Behind her I saw a little girl of about five years old with brown braids. She was holding her mother around the thighs.

'Is everything all right out here?' she asked.

Giles was pulling closed the door to the room, but I saw her eyes dart through the crack for an instant. Her lips parted and then she examined Mark, who took a step backward. She looked at me. 'That's not your room, is it?'

'No,' I said.

'Are you sick?' she said.

'I've thrown out my back,' I panted. 'I need to rest, but I've had some difficulty finding my room.'

'We took a wrong turn, ma'am,' Giles said. He smiled warmly at her.

The woman examined Giles, her jaw locked. 'Arnie!' she yelled without budging from the door.

I looked at Mark. His blue eyes met mine. He

blinked. I read the blink as a yes. Yes, I will meet you tomorrow.

Arnie led me back to my room. He matched his wife, I thought, at least physically. He was young, with a strong build and an open face. As I walked and tried to control my shaking body, Arnie held my arm. I noticed that his touch was unlike either Mark's or Teddy's. In his tentative fingers, I felt his reserve toward me – that ordinary deference for another person's body that is usually taken for granted but that had been lost to me only minutes earlier. Several times he asked me if I wanted to stop and rest, but I insisted on continuing without a pause. It wasn't until he had helped me into my room and I saw my reflection in the large mirror beside the bathroom door, that I was able to interpret the extent of his kindness. My hair had been pushed to the wrong side of my head, and a piece of it was standing up like a stiff gray stalk. My hunched and twisted body had aged me terribly, turning me into a shriveled old man of at least eighty, but it was my face that shocked me. Although the features in the mirror resembled mine, I resisted claiming them. My cheeks appeared to have collapsed into my three-day beard, and my eyes, pink from exhaustion, had an expression that made made me think of the small terrified animals I had seen so often on Vermont roads in the headlights of my car. Appalled, I turned away and made an attempt to replace the inhuman stare I had seen in the mirror with a man's gaze and to thank Arnie for his kindness. He was standing near the door with his arms folded beneath the words HOLY CROSS LITTLE LEAGUE which ran across the front of his blue sweatshirt. 'Are you sure you don't want a doctor or at least an ice pack or something?'

'No,' I said. 'I can't thank you enough.'

Arnie lingered for a moment in front of the door. His eyes met mine. 'Those punks were harassing you, weren't they?'

I could only nod. His pity was nearly beyond what I could bear at that moment.

'Well, good night,' he said. 'I hope your back's better in the morning.' Then he shut the door.

I left the bathroom light on. Because I couldn't lie flat, I propped myself up with pillows and plied myself with Scotch from the minibar. That muted the worst of the pain, for a short time anyway. All night I had motion sickness. Even when the spasms in my back woke me and I remembered where I was, I felt that the bed was moving, moving against my will, and whenever I slept, I was still moving in a dream – on a plane or a boat or a train or an escalator. Waves of nausea coursed through me, and my intestines churned as though I had been poisoned. In the dreams, I boarded one vehicle after antoher and listened to the sound of my heart pounding like an old clock, and it wasn't until I woke that I understood that the muscle was silent. When I opened my eyes and tried to shake off that sickening illusion of movement, consciousness brought Giles's fingers to my hair and his hands tightening around my face. The humiliation burned me, and I wanted to expel the memory, to force it out of my chest and lungs, where it had lodged itself like a fire in my body. I wanted to think, to turn to what had happened and make sense of it. I began to ponder what I had seen in the room – the sheet, the rope, the gun, the leftover food. It had looked like a crime scene, but even while I was seeing it, even while I was staring into the room, I had intimated a hint of the fake. The gun might have been a toy. The blood, colored water – all of it a setup. But then Giles's touch came back to me. That had been real. A sore lump had formed at the back of my head where my skull had hit the wall.

And Mark? All night his face had come and gone before me, and I knew that his last words had given me hope. People imagine that hope has degrees, but I think not. There is hope and there is no hope. His words gave me hope, and crumpled up in that bed I heard them again and again in my mind. 'I'll go home with you tomorrow.' He had hidden that statement from Giles, and this fact opened another possible interpretation of his acts. Some part of his damaged person wanted to go home. Weak and vacillating, Mark had been infected by the stronger personality of Giles, who had an almost hypnotic power over him, but there was another place inside him, the place Bill had always insisted was there – a room where he held on to those who loved him and whom he loved. I had called out to him, and he had answered me. A tormented combination of hope and guilt carried me into the morning. I had said a terrible thing to Mark when I'd spoken to him about his father's painting. At the time, I had believed it, but I suffered from the conviction that my comparison had been monstrous. A thing should never be measured against a person. Never. I take it back, I said to him in my mind. I take it back. And then, as if it were a footnote to my thoughts, I remembered that I had read somewhere, perhaps it was in Gershom Scholem, that in Hebrew 'to repent' and 'to return' are the same word.

But Mark didn't come to meet me in the lobby at ten o'clock, and when I called his room, no one answered. I waited a full hour for him. The man who sat on a bench in that lobby had made Herculean efforts to look presentable. He had shaved, holding his head sideways to prevent further injury to his back. He had vigorously rubbed the stain on his pants leg with soap and water, despite the excruciating jerks the cleaning gave his spine. He had combed his hair, and when he sat down on that bench to wait, he had contorted his body into a position he imagined might look normal. He scanned the lobby. He hoped. He revised his earlier interpretation of preceding events, made another one, and then another. He deliberated on several possibilities until he lost hope and hauled his miserable body into a cab, which drove him to the airport. I felt sorry for him, because he had understood so little.

Three mornings after I returned to New York, I was moving easily around my apartment, thanks to Dr Huyler and a drug called Relafen. At about the same time, two plainclothes detectives came to Violet's door asking for Mark. I didn't see them, but as soon as the policemen were gone, Violet came downstairs to tell me about their visit. It was nine o'clock in the morning, and Violet was wearing a long white cotton nightgown with a high neck. When I first saw her, I thought she looked a little like an old-fashioned doll. She began to talk to me, and I noticed that her voice fell into the half whisper she had used when she'd called me from the studio the day Bill had died.

'They said that they just wanted to ask him some questions. I said that Mark had been travelling with Teddy Giles and that the last place I knew he had been was Nashville. I said that he had had problems, that he might not call me at all, but if he was in touch, I would tell him they wanted to talk to him' – Violet took a breath – 'in connection with the murder of Rafael Hernandez. That was all. They didn't ask me any questions. They said "Thank you," and then they left. They must have found his body. It's all true, Leo. Do you think I should call them and tell them what we know? I didn't say anything.'

'What do we know, Violet?'

She looked confused for a moment. 'We don't really know anything, do we?'

'Not about the murder.' I listened to the word as I said it. So common. The word was everywhere all the time, but I didn't want it to come easily from me. I wanted it to be difficult to say, more difficult than it was.

'There's the message on Bill's machine that says Mark knows. I never erased it. Do you think he knows?'

'He said he did, but then he changed his story and said the boy was in California.'

'If he knows and he stays with Giles, what does it mean?'

I shook my head.

'Is it a crime, Leo?'

'Just knowing, you mean?'

She nodded.

'I suppose it depends on how you know, if you have any real evidence. Mark might not believe the story at all. He might really think that the kid ran away . . .'

Violet was shaking her head back and forth. 'No, Leo. Remember, Mark mentioned that two detectives were asking questions at the Finder Gallery. That was when Giles left town. Isn't there some law about aiding a fugitive?'

'We don't know that there's a warrant for Giles's arrest. We don't know that the police have any evidence at all. To be honest, Violet, we don't even know that Giles killed that boy. It's unlikely but possible that he might be bragging about a murder he didn't commit – simply because he knew about it. That would make him culpable, but in a different way.'

Violet looked past me and over at the painting of herself. 'Detective Lightner and Detective Mills,' she said. 'A white man and a black man. They didn't look young, and they didn't look old. They weren't fat, and they weren't thin. They were both very nice, and they didn't seem to expect anything from me. They called me Mrs Wechsler.' Violet paused and turned back to me. 'It's funny, since Bill died I like being called that by strangers. There's no Bill anymore. There's no marriage anymore, and I never changed my name. I've always been Violet Blom, but now his name is something I want to hear over and over again, and I like answering to it. It's like wearing his shirts. I want to cover myself in what's left of him, even if it's only his name.' Violet's voice carried no emotion. She was just explaining the facts.

A few minutes later, she left me to go upstairs. An hour after that, she knocked on my door again and explained that she was on the way to the studio, but she wanted to give me copies of Bill's tapes to watch when I had the time. Bernie had been dragging his feet, she said, because he had so much to look after, but he had finally handed over copies of the videos. 'Bill didn't know what the work was going to look like. He talked about building a big room for watching the tapes, but he kept changing his mind. He was going to call it *Icarus*. I know that, and that he made lots of drawings of a boy falling.'

Violet looked down at her boots and chewed on her lip.

'Are you okay?' I said.

She lifted her eyes and said, 'I have to be.'

'What do you do in the studio all day, Violet? There's not much left there.'

Violet's eyes narrowed. 'I read,' she said in a fierce voice. 'First I put on Bill's work clothes and then I read. I read all day. I read from nine in the morning until six at night. I read and read and read until I can't see the page anymore.'

The first images on the screen were of new-borns – tiny beings with distorted heads and frail, squirming limbs. Bill's camera never left the infants. Adults were present as arms, chests, shoulders, knees, thighs, voices, and occasionally a large face that intruded into the lens and came close to the baby. The first child was asleep in a woman's arms. The little creature had a large head, thin blue-red arms and legs, and was dressed in a checkered suit and an absurd little white bonnet that tied under its chin. That infant was followed by another strapped to a man's chest. His dark hair stuck straight up like Lazlo's, and his black eyes turned toward the camera in dumbfounded amazement. Bill followed along as the children rode in carriages, slept in Snuglis, lolled on a parental arm, or had seizures of desperate weeping on a shoulder. Sometimes the mostly unseen parents or nannies delivered monologues on sleeping habits, nursing, breast pumps, or spitting up as the traffic rumbled and screeched behind them, but the talk and noise were incidental to the moving pictures of the small strangers – the one who turned his bald head away from his mother's breast, leaking milk from the sides of his mouth; the dark-skinned beauty who sucked an invisible breast in her sleep and then appeared to smile; the alert baby whose blue eyes moved up toward its mother's face and gazed at her with what looked like profound concentration.

As far as I could tell, the only principle that guided Bill was age. Every day he must have gone out and looked for children a little older than the day before. Gradually his camera left infants and turned to older babies, who sat up, chirped, squealed, grunted, and put every loose object they could reach into their mouths. A big baby girl sucked on her bottle as she twined her mother's hair around her fingers in a swoon of contentment. A little boy howled as his father dislodged a rubber ball from between his gums. A baby sitting on a woman's lap reached toward an older girl sitting inches away from him and began swatting her knees. An adult hand appeared and smacked the baby's arms. It couldn't have been very hard, because the baby reached out and did it again, only to be smacked again. The camera moved back for a moment and showed the woman's tired, vacant face before it zoomed in on a third child sleeping in her stroller and held for a few seconds on her dirty cheeks and the two translucent ribbons of snot that ran from her nose to her mouth.

Bill filmed children crawling at high speed in the park and other children walking and falling and then pulling themselves up to walk again, tottering forward like old drunks in a bar. He recorded a little boy standing somewhat unsteadily beside a large, panting terrier. The child's whole body shuddered with excitement as he held his hand near the dog's snout and let out small joyous ejaculations – Eh! Eh! Eh! Another child, with fat knees and a protruding belly, was seen standing in a bakery. She looked upward and uttered a few incomprehensible syllables, which were then answered by an invisible woman, 'It's a fan, sweetheart.' With her neck craned and her lips moving, the child stared fixedly at the ceiling and began to chant the word 'fan,' repeating it over and over in a high, awestruck voice. An apoplectic two-year-old kicked and screamed on the sidewalk beside her squatting mother, who was holding an orange. 'But darling,' the woman said over the howls, 'this orange is exactly like the one Julie got. There's no difference.'

When the children he was filming reached the ages of three and four, I heard Bill's voice for the first time. Speaking over the image of an unsmiling little boy, he said, 'Do you know what your heart does?' The child looked straight into the camera, put his hand on his chest, and said gravely, 'It puts blood inside. It can bleed and live.' Another boy held up a juice box, shook it, and turned to the woman sitting beside him on a park bench. 'Mommy,' he said, 'my drink lost its gravity.' A blond child with nearly white pigtails ran in circles, jumped up and down, stopped suddenly, turned her flushed face to the camera, and said in a clear, precocious voice, 'Happy tears is sweating.' A little girl in a filthy tutu and crooked tiara bent close to a friend who was wearing a pink skirt on her head. 'Don't worry,' she whispered in a conspiratorial voice. 'It checked out. I called the man and we can be wedding girls.' 'What's your doll's name?' Bill asked a neatly dressed little girl with cornrows in her hair. 'Go ahead,' said a woman's voice. 'You can tell him.' The little girl scratched her arm and held the doll toward the camera by one leg. 'Shower,' she said.

The anonymous children came and went, aging by increments as Bill watched them, his camera lingering on their faces as they explained to him how things worked and what they were made of. One girl told Bill that caterpillars turned into raccoons, another that her brain was made of metal with eyedrops in it, a third that the world started with a 'big, big egg.' After a while, some of his subjects seemed to forget he was there. One boy stuck his finger into his nose and dug happily, retrieving a couple of crusts, which he promptly ate. Another, his hand deep in his pants, scratched his balls and sighed with pleasure. A small girl was seen bending down beside a stroller. She began to make cooing noises and then she grabbed the cheeks of the baby who was strapped into the seat. 'I love you, you little dumpling,' she said, pinching and shaking the cheeks. 'You honeybun,' she added fiercely as the baby began to sob from the pressure of her fingers. 'Stop that, Sarah,' said a woman. 'Be nice.' 'I was nice,' Sarah replied, her eyes narrowed and her jaw locked.

Another girl, slightly older, about five, stood beside her mother on a sidewalk somewhere in midtown. The two were seen from behind as they looked into a store window. After a few seconds, it was clear that Bill was most interested in the girl's hand. The camera followed it as it roved her mother's back, moving north toward the shoulder blades, then south toward the buttocks. Up and down, up and down, that small hand idly caressed the maternal back. He also filmed a boy stopped on the sidewalk, his small face screwed up in tight belligerence, a sparkle of tears showing in the corners of his eyes. A woman seen from the neck down stood beside him, her body tensed with rage. 'I'm fed up!' she bellowed at him. 'I've had it with you. You're acting like a little shit and I want you to stop!' She leaned over, grabbed the boy by the shoulders, and began to shake him. 'Stop! Stop!' The tears fell down his

500

cheeks, but the boy's expression remained stiff and unyielding.

There was a resolute, pitiless quality to the tapes, a dogged desire to look and look hard. The camera's focus remained close and tight as the children grew taller and more articulate. A boy named Ramon, who told Bill that he was seven, explained that his uncle collected chickens – 'Anything with a chicken on it, he buys it. His whole basement is chickens.' A plump boy, probably eight or nine, in wide jean shorts glowered at a taller boy in a baseball cap who was holding a box of candy. In a sudden fit of anger, the shorter boy said, 'Shit on you,' and pushed his adversary violently to the ground. Pieces of candy flew as the boy on the ground started crowing in triumph, 'He said the S word! He said the S word!' A pair of adult legs ran into the frame. Two little girls in plaid uniforms sat on cement steps and whispered to each other. A foot away, a third girl in the same uniform turned her head to look at them. Bill caught the child's profile. As she watched the others, she swallowed hard several times. The camera moved through the crowd of school-children and recorded a boy, with a mouthful of gleaming braces, as he removed his backpack and slammed it against the shoulder of the kid next to him.

The longer I watched, the more mysterious I found the pictures in front of me. What had started as ordinary images of children in the city became over time a remarkable document of human particularity and sameness. There were so many different children – fat, thin, light, dark, beautiful children and plain children, healthy children and children who were crippled or deformed. Bill had filmed a group of kids in wheelchairs who were lowered from a bus that had been designed with a lift to bring the chairs to street level. As she rolled her chair off the mechanism, a chubby girl of about eight straightened herself up and gave Bill a mocking royal wave. He filmed a boy with a scar on his upper lip who first smiled crookedly and then made a farting noise with his mouth. He followed another boy whose indeterminable illness or birth defect had left him with ballooning cheeks and a missing chin. He wore a respirator of some kind as he chugged along on his short legs beside his mother. The differences among the children were startling, and yet, in the end, their faces mingled. Above all, the tapes revealed the furious animation of children, the fact that when conscious they rarely stop moving. A simple walk down the block included waving, hopping, skipping, twirling, and multiple pauses to examine a piece of litter, pet a dog, or jump up and walk along a cement barrier or low fence. In a schoolyard or playground, they jostled, punched, elbowed, kicked, poked patted, hugged, pinched, tugged, yelled laughed, chanted, and sang, and while I watched them, I said to myself that growing up really means slowing down.

Bill died before the children reached puberty. A

few girls showed signs of breasts coming beneath their T-shirts or the blouses of their school uniforms, but most of the kids hadn't even started to change. I suspect that he had meant to go on, that he wanted to film more and more children until a moment came when the figures on the screen could no longer be distinguished from adults. After the last video ended and I had turned off the television, I felt exhausted and a little raw from the parade of bodies and faces, the sheer volume of young lives that had passed in front of me. I imagined Bill on his peripatetic adventure as he sought out kids and more kids to answer some craving in himself. What I had seen was unedited and crude, but when strung together the fragments had formed a syntax that might be read for possible meaning. It was as if Bill intended the many lives he documented to merge into a single entity, to show the one in the many or the many in the one. Everyone begins and ends. Throughout the tapes I had thought of Matthew, first as a baby, then as a toddler, and finally as a boy who had been left in childhood forever.

Icarus. The connection between the children on the tapes and the myth remained oblique. But Bill had chosen the title for a reason. I remembered Brueghel's painting, with its two figures – the father and the falling boy, whose wings are melting in the sun. Daedalus, the great architect and magician, had made those wings for himself and his son to escape from their tower prison. He warned Icarus about flying too close to the sun, but the boy refused to listen and plummeted into the sea. Nevertheless, Daedalus isn't an innocent figure in the story. He had risked too much for his freedom and, because of it, he had lost his son.

Neither Violet nor I nor Erica in California, who now knew the whole story, doubted that the police would find Mark and question him. It was just a matter of time. After the visit from Detectives Lightner and Mills, I had lost all sense of what was possible for Mark and what was impossible, and without that barrier I lived in dread. The incident in the hallway in the Nashville hotel didn't recede. Every night my helplessness came back to me. Giles's hands. His voice. The shock of my head hitting the wall. And Mark's eyes, which had nothing behind them. I heard myself call out for him, saw my arms reach toward him, and then I was waiting on the bench in the lobby for no one. I had related most of the facts to Violet and Erica, but I had kept my voice even, my description cold, and I hadn't told them about Giles touching my hair. Over time, that gesture had become unspeakable. It was much easier just to say that he had slammed my head into the wall. For some reason the violence was preferable to what had come before it. I found it hard to sleep, and sometimes after lying awake for hours I would go to check the locks on my door, even though I knew that I had bolted them shut and secured the chain.

The only fact that could be determined absolutely from the newspapers was that the broken and decayed body of a boy named Rafael Hernandez had been found in a suitcase that had washed up somewhere near a Hudson River pier, and that identification had been made through dental records. The rest was printed gossip. *Blast* ran a long article with pictures of Teddy Giles and the headline JUST KIDDING? According to the journalist, Delford Links, people in both the art world and the club scene had known of Rafael's disappearance for some time. The day after the boy disappeared, Giles had made several telephone calls to friends and acquaintances, claiming that he had just done 'a real one.' That same evening, he had gone out to Club USA wearing clothes that appeared to have dried blood all over them and had careened around the club announcing that the She-Monster had 'committed the ultimate work of art.' Not a single person had taken Giles seriously. Even after the body had been found, most people associated with Giles refused to accept the possibility that he had actually murdered someone. A seventeen-year-old boy named Junior was quoted: 'He was always saying stuff like that. He must have told me fifteen different times that he had just killed somebody.'

Hasseborg was also quoted: 'The danger inherent in Giles's work is that it attacks every one of our sacred cows. His work isn't limited to sculptures or photographs or even performances. His personas are also his art – a spectacle of shifting identities that includes the psychopathic killer, who is, after all, a celebrated, mythical character. Turn on your TV. Go to the movies. He's everywhere. But to suggest that this persona is anything more than that is an outrage. The fact that Giles knew Rafael Hernandez hardly makes him guilty of his murder.'

On the Sunday evening after I returned from Nashville, Violet and I were having dinner upstairs when Lazlo buzzed the front door. Lazlo's expression was usually sober, but when we opened the door for him, I thought his face looked almost sad. 'I found this,' he said, and handed it to Violet. The article came from the gossip column in the downtown paper *Bleep*. Violet read it aloud: 'Rumors are flying about a certain Bad Boy on the art scene and the body of his thirteen-year-old ex-toy and part-time E dealer that bobbed up in the Hudson. One of B.B.'s ex-*girlfriends* claims that there's a witness – yet another one of B.B.'s many A.C./D.C. exes. Could the plot get any thicker? Stay tuned . . .'

Violet looked at Lazlo. 'What does this mean?' she said.

Lazlo was silent. Instead of responding to Violet's question, he handed her a business card. 'He's married to my cousin,' Lazlo said. 'Arthur's a real good guy – a criminal attorney. He used to work in the D.A.'s office.' Lazlo paused. 'Could be you won't need him.' Lazlo didn't move. I couldn't even see him breathe. Then he said, 'Pinky's waiting for me.'

Violet nodded, and we watched Lazlo walk to the door and close it very gently behind him.

We didn't talk for several minutes. It was dark outside, and it had started to snow. I watched the white motion through the window. Lazlo knew things, and Violet and I both understood that he had left the card for a reason. When I turned from the window and looked at Violet, she was so pale that her skin looked transparent, and I noticed a rash on her neck. Beneath her lowered eyes were faint purple shadows. I knew what I was seeing: dry grief, grief grown old and familiar. It enters your bones and lives there, because it has no use for flesh, and after a while you feel that you're all bone, hard and dessicated, like a skeleton in a classroom. She fingered the little card and looked up at me.

'I'm afraid of him,' she said.

'Of Giles?' I said in a dull voice.

'No,' she said, 'I'm talking about Mark. I'm afraid of Mark.'

Violet and I were sitting together on the sofa upstairs when his key turned in the lock. Before we heard the sound, Violet had been laughing at something I'd said, something I've forgotten now, but I remember that her laugh was still in my ears when Mark stepped through the door. He looked sad, a little sheepish, and very mild, but the sight of him turned me cold.

'I have to talk to you,' he said. 'It's important.'

Violet's body had gone rigid. 'Then talk,' she said. Her eyes never left his face.

He walked toward us, moved around the table, and leaned down to embrace Violet.

She pulled away from him. 'No, don't. I can't,' she said.

Mark looked startled and then hurt.

In a low, steady voice, Violet said, 'You lie to me, you rob and betray me, and now you want a hug? I told you I didn't want you back.'

He stared at her in disbelief. 'What am I supposed to do? The police want to talk to me.' He took a breath, then stepped backward. His arms hung limply at his sides. 'I know Teddy did it,' he said. He narrowed his eyes. 'I saw him that night.' Mark sat down at the other end of the table. He let his head fall forward. 'He was all bloody.'

'You saw him?' Violet said loudly. 'Who? What do you mean?'

'I went to see Teddy. We were going out. He opened the door and he was all covered in blood. At first I thought it was a joke, you know, a trick.' Mark blinked, then looked at us steadily. 'But then I saw him – Me – on the floor.'

I felt as if my brain were rising inside my head. 'You knew that he was dead?'

Mark nodded.

Violet's voice was steady. 'What happened then?'

'He said he'd kill me if I said anything, and I left. I was scared, so I took the train to Mom's.'

'Why didn't you go to the police?'

'I told you. I was too scared.'

'You didn't seem scared in Minneapolis,' I said. 'Or Nashville. You seemed to enjoy Giles's company. I waited for you, Mark, but you never came.'

Mark's voice rose. 'I had to go along. I couldn't get away. Don't you see? I had to do it. It wasn't my fault. I was afraid.'

'You have to talk to the police now,' Violet said.

'I can't. Teddy will kill me.'

Violet stood up. She disappeared and returned a few moments later. 'You have to talk to the police now,' she said. 'Or they'll come and get you. Call this number. The detectives left it for you.'

'He needs a lawyer, Violet,' I said. 'He can't go without a lawyer.'

I was the one who called Lazlo's cousin's husband, Arthur Geller, and it turned out that he was expecting the call. When Mark went in to the police station to speak to the police the next day, he would have an attorney by his side. Violet told Mark that she would pay his legal bills. Then she corrected herself, 'No. Bill will pay. It's his money.'

Violet let Mark sleep in his room that night, but she told him that after that he would have to find somewhere else to live. Then she turned to me and asked if I would sleep on the sofa. She said, 'I don't want to be alone with Mark.'

509

Mark looked aghast. 'That's stupid,' he said. 'Leo can sleep at home.'

Violet turned to him. She lifted her palms toward his face as though she were warding off a blow. 'No,' she said sharply. 'No. I'm not going to stay alone with you. I don't trust you.'

By posting me as night sentry on the sofa, Violet wanted to make it clear that life was not going on as usual, but my presence wasn't enough to break the spell of the everyday. The hours that followed Mark's arrival were disquieting, not because anything happened – but because nothing did. I listened to the sound of him brushing his teeth and to his voice wishing me and Violet good night in a curiously cheerful tone and then to his shufflings in his room before he settled down to sleep. The sounds were ordinary, and because they were ordinary I found them terrible. The simple fact that Mark was in the apartment seemed to alter everything in it, to transform the table and chairs, the night-light in the hallway, and the red sofa where I had made a temporary bed. Most unsettling was the fact that the change could be felt but not seen. It was as though a veneer had settled over everything, a banal mask that clung so tightly to the hideous form beneath it that it couldn't be pried off.

Long after the whole building was quiet with sleep, I lay awake listening to the noises from outside. 'He has a good heart, my son.' Bill had been standing at the window looking down onto the Bowery when he said those words, and I know that he had believed them, but years before, in the fairy tale he called *The Changeling*, he had told a story of substitution. I remembered the stolen child lying in his glass coffin. Bill knew, I thought. Somewhere inside him, he knew.

In the morning, Mark went off with Arthur Geller and spoke to the police. The following day, Teddy Giles was arrested for the murder of Rafael Hernandez and held without bail on Rikers Island while he waited to go to trial. You would think that the dramatic entrance of a witness would have ended the case. But Mark hadn't seen the murder. He had seen a bloody Giles and the dead body of Rafael. It was important, but the D.A. wanted more. The law has to muddle along with facts, and there were few facts. The case was mostly talk – gossip, rumors, and Mark's story. There was little evidence to be gotten from the corpse, because the police hadn't found a whole body in the suitcase. The boy had been cut into pieces, and after months of decaying under water, those fragments of bone, sodden tissue, and teeth had revealed his identity – nothing more. We did find out from the newspapers that Rafael Hernandez wasn't Mexican, and he hadn't been bought by Giles. When he was four, his parents, who were both addicts, had deserted him and an infant sister. The little girl had died of AIDs when she was two years old. Rafael had run away from his third foster family, somewhere in the Bronx, and found his way into the clubs, where he met Giles. He had turned tricks. He had sold Ecstasy to willing buyers and at thirteen had made a pretty good living. Otherwise the boy was a cipher.

Giles's arrest turned the perception of his work inside out. What had been seen as a clever commentary on the horror genre began to look like the sadistic fantasies of a murderer. The peculiar insularity of the New York art scene had often made obvious work seem subtle, stupid work intelligent, and sensational work subversive. It was all a matter of how the art was 'pitched.' Because Giles had become a sort of minor celebrity, embraced by critics and collectors, his new designation as possible felon was both embarrassing and intriguing to the world he had left so abruptly. During the first month after his arrest, art magazines, newspapers, and even the television news picked up the story of the 'art murder.' Larry Finder issued a statement in which he said that in America a person is innocent until proven guilty, but that if Giles was found guilty of the crime, he would vociferously condemn the act and would no longer represent him.

In the meantime, however, prices for the work went up, and Finder did a brisk business selling Teddy Giles. Buyers wanted the work because it now seemed that it mimicked reality, but Giles, who freely gave interviews from Rikers, mounted a defense that was just the opposite. In an interview for *DASH*, he argued that it was all a hoax. He had staged a murder in his apartment for the benefit of his friends, using artificial blood and a realistic replica of Rafael to do it. He had known that Rafael was leaving, going to visit an aunt in California, and he had used the trip to perpetrate an elaborate 'art joke.' Rafael Hernandez had been murdered, but Giles insisted that he hadn't done it. He cited the fact that his 'fabricators' had known about his plan. Maybe one of them had committed the murder to frame him. Giles seemed to know that the police case rested on the shoulders of a nameless friend, a friend who had arrived that day and looked through the doorway into his apartment. Could the friend swear that the blood he had seen was real blood, that the body on the floor wasn't a fake? Perhaps the most curious aspect of the case was that Giles was able to produce an artificial corpse. Pierre Lange told the journalist that he had cast a simulation of Rafael's body on the Tuesday before he disappeared. Giles had instructed him about the injuries to the body, as he always did, and then he had worked with police and morgue photos to give the damage the appearance of believability. Of course, he added, the bodies were always hollow. Blood and sometimes crushed internal organs were added for effect, but he did not reproduce tissue or muscle or bone. According to the article, the police had impounded the faux corpse.

The case lasted for eight long months. Mark

camped out in the apartment of 'a friend' – a girl named Anya, whom we never met. Violet spoke regularly to Arthur Geller on the telephone, and he sounded reasonably confident that Mark's testimony at the trial would result in a conviction. She spoke to Mark once a week, but she said their conversations were forced and mechanical. 'I don't believe a word that comes out of his mouth,' she said. 'I often wonder why I talk to him at all.' On some evenings, Violet would speak to me while she looked out the window. Then she would stop talking and her lips would part in an expression of disbelief. She never cried anymore. Her dread seemed to have frozen her. She would stop moving for seconds at a time and become as inert as a statue. But at other times she was jumpy. The smallest noise would make her start or gasp. After she recovered from the momentary shock, she would rub her arms repeatedly as though she were cold. On the nights when she felt nervous, she would ask me to stay on the sofa, and I would bed down in the living room with Bill's pillows and the comforter from Mark's bed.

I can't say whether Violet's anxiety was the same as mine. Like most emotions, that vague form of fear is a crude lump of feeling that relies on words for definition. But that inner state quickly infects what is supposedly outside us, and I felt that the rooms of my apartment and Violet's, the streets of the city, even the air I breathed stank of a diffuse, allencompassing threat. Several times I thought I spotted Mark on Greene Street, and each time my heart raced until I discovered that it was some other tall, dark-haired boy in baggy pants. I didn't believe that I was in any danger from Mark. My trepidation seemed to come from something much larger than either him or Teddy Giles. No single person could contain it. The danger was invisible, mutable, and it spread. To be frightened of something so opaque makes me sound mad, as unbalanced as Dan, whose bouts of paranoia could turn an innocent pat on his arm into an attempt on his life, but insanity is a matter of degree. Most of us partake of it in one way or the other from time to time, feel its insidious tug and the lure of collapse. But I wasn't flirting with craziness then. I recognized that the anxiety tightening at my throat wasn't rational, but I also knew that what I feared lay beyond reason, and that nonsense can also be real.

In April, Arthur told Violet the story of the lamp. For a while the case turned on that lamp, and yet its significance for me has little to do with police work or how the charges were resolved in the end. After combing the area around Giles's apartment, the police had spoken to a woman who owned a design store on Franklin Street. Arthur couldn't explain why it had taken them so long to find her, but Roberta Alexander had identified both Giles and Mark as the two young men who had been in her store in the early evening on the day of the murder. The problem was timing. According to Ms

Alexander, they had come into the store *after* Mark said he had fled Giles's apartment and gone to the train station, where he sat on a bench in stunned distress for several hours before he finally took the train to Princeton. Mark and Teddy had bought a table lamp. Ms Alexander had the bill of sale with the date, and she was sure of the time, because she had been preparing to close her shop at seven. She had noticed nothing unusual about either Giles or Mark. In fact, she had found them both unusually polite and affable, and they hadn't haggled over the price. They had handed over $1,200 in cash.

According to Arthur, the D.A. had started to doubt Mark's story even before he knew about the lamp purchase. As he talked to more people in Giles's circle, he discovered that Mark had lied to most of them about one thing or another. A defense attorney would have little trouble proving that Mark was a habitual liar. Arthur knew that if one fact wobbled, others were likely to follow, and that one by one his facts might turn into fictions and his eyewitness into a suspect. Mark swore that his story had been perfect, with the sole omission of the lamp. Teddy had left the apartment with him, and he had gone along out of fear. He knew that it didn't look good, and that's why he hadn't mentioned it. Yes, he had waited for Teddy to change his clothes, and yes, they had returned to the apartment to drop off the lamp, but everything else was true. Lucille had already vouched for the fact that Mark had arrived at her house that same evening – around midnight.

Mark understood that fear and cowardice in a person who discovers a murder might be met with sympathy. Casually buying a lamp with the perpetrator after seeing the body of his victim would not. Nobody could vouch for Mark's time of arrival at the loft on Franklin Street, and just as Arthur had feared, the D.A. began to suspect that he might have been interviewing an accomplice rather than a witness after the fact. We all did. Arthur began to prepare Violet for Mark's possible arrest, but I think it was unnecessary. Violet had long suspected that Mark hadn't told the full truth about the murder, and instead of showing signs of shock, she told me that she pitied Arthur. Mark had fooled him, the way he had fooled us all. 'I warned him,' she said, 'but he believed Mark anyway.' Whether Mark had helped Giles kill Rafael or had merely arrived on the scene once the murder was over, his presence in the store on Franklin Street and the purchase of that expensive lamp put an end to whatever feeling I had left for him. I knew that by some definition both Teddy Giles and Mark Wechsler were insane, examples of an indifference many regard as monstrous and unnatural; but in fact they weren't unique and their actions were recognizably human. Equating horror with the inhuman has always struck me as convenient but fallacious, if only because I was born into a century that should have ended such talk for good. For me, the lamp became the sign not of the inhuman but of the all-too-human, the lapse or break that occurs in people when empathy is gone, when others aren't a part of us anymore but are turned into things. There is genuine irony in the fact that my empathy for Mark vanished at the moment when I understood that he had not a shred of that quality in himself.

Violet and I both waited for something to happen, and while we waited, we worked. I wrote about Bill and then rewrote what I had written. Nothing I came up with was any good, but the quality of my thought and prose was secondary to the fact that I was able to continue doing it. Violet read at the studio. She often returned with headaches and sore eyes, and she coughed from all the cigarettes she had smoked. I started making sandwiches for her to take to the Bowery and asked her to promise that she would eat them. I believe that she did, because she didn't lose any more weight.

Months passed, and Arthur had nothing new to report except that the D.A. was still looking for something or someone to tighten his case. Violet and I spent most of that hot summer together. A little restaurant opened on Church Street, below Canal, and we would meet there for dinner two or three times a week. One night, a couple of minutes after she arrived, Violet left the table to go to the toilet and the waiter asked me if I'd like to order a drink for my wife. When Violet spent two weeks in Minnesota in July, I called her every day. At night

I worried that she would fall fatally ill or that she might decide to stay in the Midwest and never come back. But when Violet returned, we went on living in a state of suspense, wondering if the case would ever come to an end. The newspapers had dropped the story. Mark had left Anya and was living with another girl, named Rita. He informed Violet that he was working in a flower shop and gave her the name of the place, but Violet never bothered to call and check on whether it was true or not. It didn't seem all that important.

And then, in late August, a boy named Indigo West came forward. Like a deus ex machina, he dropped from heaven and freed Mark from suspicion. He claimed to have witnessed the murder through the hallway door in Giles's apartment. Apparently, Indigo was only one of many people who had keys to Giles's apartment. He had arrived at about five o'clock in the morning and wandered into one of the bedrooms. He slept most of the next day and woke to the sound of glass breaking in the front room. When he went to see what was happening, he said that he saw Giles with an axe in one hand and a broken vase in the other, standing over Rafael, who had already lost an arm. A large plastic dropcloth lay on the floor and was covered with blood. According to Indigo, Rafael was tied up and his mouth was taped. If he wasn't dead, he was almost dead. Unseen and unheard by Giles, Indigo ran back to the bedroom and hid under the bed, where he threw up. He lay absolutely still for at least an hour. He said he heard Giles walking around, and once he heard him just outside the bedroom door. When the telephone rang, Giles answered it, and not long after that, he heard Giles talking to someone in the hallway and recognized the voice as Mark's. He distinctly overheard Mark say that he was hungry, but the rest of the conversation was too low for him to hear. When the door slammed and all noises stopped, he waited for several minutes, crawled out from under the bed, and ran out of the building. He said he went to Puffy's and ordered a coffee from a waitress with blue hair.

Indigo was a seventeen-year-old heroin addict, but Arthur said that he repeated his story without variation over and over again, and although the police hadn't found a single blood stain in Giles's apartment, they had noted a stain on the carpet under the bed where Indigo had spent the night, and the waitress at Puffy's, who had had blue hair at the time, remembered him. She had noticed him particularly because he had been shaking and crying over his espresso. When confronted with Indigo West, Teddy Giles accepted a plea bargain. The charges against him were reduced to aggravated manslaughter and he was sentenced to fifteen years in prison. Indigo West had been given immunity for his testimony, and neither he nor Mark was charged with anything. For a week the papers carried articles on the end of the case, and then it vanished from the spotlight. Arthur guessed that the D.A. didn't want to risk going to trial with two witnesses of dubious character. Indigo West had already served a sentence for drug possession in a juvenile correctional institution. The boy was a mess, but I believe that he was an honest mess.

Nevertheless, there was a magical quality to his appearance. When I discovered that Lazlo was the person who had found Indigo, my astonishment diminished somewhat. With Arthur's blessing, Lazlo had pursued his own leads, which included talking to the gossip columnist who had printed the story of a witness. The columnist didn't know Indigo, but his stepdaughter had heard through a friend that a kid who spent every Thursday night at the Tunnel had heard through someone else that there was a third person who had seen the murder. The rumor chain led to Indigo West, whose real name was Nathan Furbank. The question was, Why had Lazlo been able to locate a witness when the police had not? I couldn't help but attribute that success to the prodigious qualities of the Finkelman eyes, ears, and nose.

During the case, Violet had called Lucille regularly to give her news. Sometimes they spoke amicably, but more often than not Violet wanted something from Lucille that Lucille wouldn't or couldn't give her. Violet wanted Lucille to acknowledge the extremity of what had happened to Mark. She wanted animal pain, anguish, and desperation, but Lucille would only say that she was 'worried' and 'deeply concerned' about him. After Giles was sentenced, Lucille became even more tranquil. During her conversations with Violet, she blamed Mark's problems on drugs. The drugs had muted his feelings and his reactions. The most important thing was for him to stay off drugs. Lucille's defense of Mark wasn't unreasonable; Mark's drug use had always been a muddled issue. But while Lucille labored to stay soft-spoken and polite, Violet inevitably grew more and more upset.

One evening in late November, the telephone rang a few minutes after Violet and I had finished eating dinner. From the restrained tone of Violet's voice, I instantly knew that Lucille was on the other end of the line. Mark had stayed briefly with his mother and stepfather after the case was over. He'd then moved into a house with friends and found a job in a veterinary clinic. Lucille calmly told Violet that Mark had filched cash from one of his housemates and then stolen his car. He hadn't gone to work and he hadn't been seen for three days. Violet kept her temper. She told Lucille there was nothing either of them could do, but when she hung up the phone, her face was flushed and her hand was trembling.

'I think Lucille means well,' I said to Violet.

Violet looked at me for several seconds, then she started yelling. 'Don't you know that she's only half alive! Part of her is dead!' Her pale face and the broken cry in her voice shocked me, and I couldn't find an answer. She grabbed my upper arms and began to shake me, snarling through her teeth. 'Don't you know that she was slowly killing Bill? I saw it right away. And Mark, my boy. He was my boy, too. I loved them. I loved them. She didn't. She can't.' Her eyes opened as if she were suddenly afraid. 'Remember? I asked you to take care of Bill.' She shook me harder as her eyes filled with tears. 'I thought you understood! I thought you knew!'

I looked down at her. Her fingers had loosened their grip, but she was still hanging on to me, and I could feel the weight of her body tug at my arms for an instant before she let go. She was breathing hard from her rage, which was quickly turning into sobs. I listened to her cry loudly, and the noise caused a contraction in my chest, as if it were my own grief that I was hearing, or as if hers and mine were one and the same. She bent over, covering her face with her hands. I reached out for her and pulled her into my arms. The pressure in my lungs seemed unbearable. Her face was pressed into my neck, and I could feel her breasts against me and her arms hugging me tightly. My hand moved to her hip, and I let my fingers press the bone beneath it while I clutched her harder.

'I love you,' I said. 'Don't you understand that I love you. I'll take care of you, be with you forever. I would do anything for you.' I tried to kiss her. I grabbed her face and pressed it into mine, tilting my glasses in the process. She gave a small cry and pushed me away.

Violet was looking at me with startled eyes. She lifted her hands as if she were pleading for something and then she lowered them. When I looked at her standing there near the turquoise table with a piece of hair falling onto her forehead, I thought I had never seen anyone so beautiful. She was my hold on the world, what I suffered over and loved, and I knew in that instant that I was losing her, and the knowledge turned me cold. I sat down at the table, folded my hands, and stared at them without saying a word. I felt her eyes on me as she stood in the middle of the room. I heard her breathing, and a couple of seconds later, the sound of her footsteps coming toward me. When I felt her fingers touching my head, I didn't look up at her. She said 'Leo' several times, and then her voice cracked. 'I'm sorry. I'm really sorry. I, I didn't mean to push you away, I . . .' She knelt on the floor beside me and said, 'Please talk to me. Please look at me.' Her voice was hoarse and choked. 'I feel so bad.'

I spoke to the table. 'I think it's better that we say nothing. It was ridiculous of me to think that you might return my feelings, when I know better than anybody what you and Bill were to each other.'

'Turn your chair around,' she said, 'so I can see you. You must talk to me. You must.'

I resisted her request, but after a couple of seconds my stubbornness seemed so childish that I obeyed. Without getting up, I shifted the position of the chair, and once I was facing her I saw that tears were running down her cheeks and she was pressing her fist against her mouth to steady herself. She swallowed, moved her hand away from her face, and said, 'It's so complicated, Leo, much more complicated than you think. There's nobody like you. You're good, you're generous . . .'

I lowered my eyes and began to shake my head.

'Please, I want you to understand that without you . . .'

'Don't, Violet,' I said. 'It's all right. You don't have to make excuses for me.'

'I'm not. I want you to understand that even before Bill died, I needed you.' Violet's lips were trembling. 'There was an obtuse side to Bill – a hidden, unknowing, unknowable core that he let out in his work. He was obsessed. There were times when I felt neglected, and it hurt.'

'He adored you. You should have heard the way he talked about you.'

'And I adored him back.' She pressed her hands together so hard her arms began to shake, but her voice sounded a little more composed. 'The fact is, my own husband was less accessible to me than many other people. There was always something I couldn't get to in him, something remote, and I wanted that thing I could never have. It kept me alive and it kept me in love, because whatever it was, I could never find it.'

'But you were such good friends,' I said.

'The best of friends,' she said, and took hold of both my hands. I felt her squeeze them. 'We talked about everything all the time. After he died, I kept saying to myself, "We were each other." But knowing and being are two different things.'

'Always the philosopher,' I said. The comment had an edge to it, and Violet reacted to my hint of cruelty by withdrawing her hands.

'You're right to be angry. I've taken advantage of you. You've cooked for me and taken care of me and stayed with me, and I've just taken and taken and taken . . .' Her voice grew louder and her eyes filled with more tears.

Her distress made me guilty. 'That's not true,' I said.

She was nodding at me. 'Oh, yes it is. I'm selfish, Leo, and I have something cold and hard in me. I'm full of hate. I hate Mark. I used to love him. Of course, I didn't love him right away, but I learned to love him slowly, and then later to hate him, and I ask myself, Would I hate him if I had given birth to him, if he were my son? But the really terrible question is this: What was it that I loved?'

Violet was silent for a few seconds, and I studied my hands, which were resting on my knees. They looked old, veiny, and discolored. Like my mother's hands when she got old, I thought.

'Remember when Lucille took Mark to Texas with her, and then she decided she couldn't handle having him and sent him back to us?'

I nodded.

'He was really difficult, always acting up, but after she came to visit at Christmas and left again, he really went nuts. He pushed me, hit me, screamed at me. He wouldn't go to sleep. Every night, he threw a fit. I was nice to him, but it's hard to like someone who's awful to you – even when it's just a six-year-old kid. Bill decided that Mark missed his mother too much, that he had to go back to her, and they flew to Houston. I think it was a fatal mistake, Leo. I understood that not long ago. A week later, Lucille called Bill and told him that Mark was 'perfect.' That was the word she used. It meant obedient, cooperative, sweet. A couple of weeks later, Mark bit a little girl in school on the arm so hard that she bled, but at home he was no trouble at all. By the time he came back to New York, the furious little wild man had disappeared for good. It was like somebody had cast a spell on him and turned him into a docile, agreeable replica of himself. But that was the thing I learned to love – that automation.' Violet's eyes were dry and she clenched her jaw while she looked at me.

I examined her tight face and said, 'But I thought you didn't understand what happened to Mark.'

'I *don't* understand what happened to him. All I know is that he went away one thing and came back another. It took a long, long time to even begin to see that clearly. He had to demonstrate his falseness for years before I could really look behind the mask. Bill refused to see it, but he and I were both part of it. Did we cause it? I don't know. Did we ruin him? I don't know, but I think he must have felt that we were throwing him away. I'll tell you this,

I hate Lucille, too, even though she can't help the way she is – all boarded up and shut down like a condemned house. That's how I think of her. I felt sorry for her in the beginning, after Bill left her, but all that pity is gone. And I hate Bill, too, for dying on me. He never went to the doctor. He smoked and drank and stewed in his own melancholy, and I keep thinking he should have been harder, tougher, meaner, angrier, not so goddamned guilty about everything all the time, that he should have been stronger for me!' She paused for several seconds. Her lashes were shiny black from her tears and I could see the small red veins in her eyes. She swallowed. 'I needed somebody, Leo. I've been so alone with my hate. You've been so kind to me, and I used your kindness.'

I started to smile then. At first, I had no idea why I was amused. It was a little like giggling at a funeral or laughing when someone brings you news of a terrible car accident, but I realized that it was her honesty that made me smile. She was trying so hard to tell me the truth about herself as she knew it, and after the innumerable lies and thefts and the murder we had lived through together, her self-criticism seemed comic. It made me think of a nun in the confessional booth whispering her meager sins to a priest who is guilty of far worse.

When she saw the smile, she said, 'It's not funny, Leo.'

'Yes,' I said, 'it is. People can't help what they feel. It's what they do that counts, and as far as

I can tell, you've done nothing wrong. When you and Bill sent Mark back to Lucille, you thought you were doing what was right. People can't do more than that. Now it's your turn to listen to me. As it turns out, I have no power over my feelings either, but it was a mistake to talk to you about them. I wish I could take back what I said – for my sake as well as yours. I lost my head. It's that simple, but there's nothing I can do about it now.'

Violet's green eyes regarded me steadily as she put her hands on my shoulders and began to stroke my arms. I was caught off guard for a moment by her touch, but I couldn't resist the happiness it brought me, and I felt my muscles relax. It had been a long time since I had felt someone's hands on me like that, and I actually tried to remember the last time. When Erica came for Bill's funeral, I thought.

'I've decided to go away,' Violet said. 'I can't be here anymore. It's not Bill. I like being close to his things. It's Mark. I can't be near him anymore, not even in the same city. I don't want to see him again. A friend of mine in Paris invited me to give a seminar at the American University, and I've decided to do it, even though it's just for a few months. I'm leaving in two weeks. I was going to tell you at dinner but then the phone rang, and . . .' Her face contorted for a second and then she continued, 'I'm lucky that you love me. I'm really lucky.'

I began a reply, but Violet put her finger to my

lips. 'Don't talk. I have to tell you something else. I don't think it could go on, because I'm too confused. I'm broken, you see, not whole.' She moved her hands to my neck and rubbed it softly. 'But we can be together tonight if you want. I do love you very much, maybe not exactly the way you would like me to, but . . .'

She stopped talking because I reached for her hands and pulled them gently away from my neck. I continued to hold them in mine while I looked at her face. I knew that I wanted her badly. I had forgotten what it was not to want her, but I didn't want her sacrifice – that sweet offering she held out to me, because I imagined my greed and lust accepted but not returned, and that picture of my desire made me quail. I shook my head at her while two large tears spilled onto her cheeks. She had been kneeling throughout our talk and she put her head down on one of my thighs for a second before she stood up, led me over to the sofa, sat down beside me, and leaned her head against my shoulder. I put my arm around her and we sat together for a long time without saying anything.

I remembered Bill in Vermont then, walking out the door of Bowery Two just before dinner. I saw him through the kitchen window of the Vermont house, and although it was an uncommonly lucid memory, I felt no emotion or nostalgia. I was merely a voyeur of my own life, a cold spectator who looks on at other people going about their daily routines. Bill lifted his hand to greet Matthew and

Mark from the top of the stairs, and then paused to light a cigarette. I saw him stride across the lawn toward the farmhouse while Matt tugged at his arm, my son looking up at Bill. Mark was grinning as he staggered behind them and feigned a spastic disorder – holding one arm akimbo and waving the other helplessly in front of him. I surveyed the large kitchen in my mind and saw Erica and Violet pitting olives at the table. I heard the screen door slam, and at the sound, the two women looked up at Bill. Smoke rose up from the butt between his fingers, which were stained with blue and green paint, and as he sucked on the cigarette, I could see that his thoughts were still in the studio, that he wasn't ready to talk to anyone yet. Behind him, the boys had crouched down to look for the garter snake who lived under the front step. No one spoke, and in the quiet, I could hear the ticking of the clock that hung to the right of the door – a big-faced old school clock with clear black numbers – and I found myself struggling to understand how time can be measured on a disc, a circle with hands that return to the same positions over and over again. That logical revolution looked like a mistake. Time isn't circular, I thought. That's wrong. But the memory didn't let go of me. It continued – vehement, acute, inescapable. Violet glanced at the clock and pointed at Bill. 'You're a stinky mess, my love. Go wash. You've got exactly twenty minutes.'

★　　★　　★

Violet left New York on December ninth in the late afternoon. The low sky was beginning to darken, and a few tiny flakes of snow had started to fall. I carried her heavy suitcase down the stairs and left it on the sidewalk while I hailed a cab for her. She was wearing her long navy blue coat, which tied around her waist, and a white fur hat that I had always liked. The driver popped the trunk, and we lifted the suitcase into it together. While we said good-bye, I clutched at what was there – Violet's face coming toward mine, the smell of her in the cold air, the hug, and then the quick kiss on my mouth, not my cheek, the sound of the car door opening, then slamming, her hand at the window and her eyes with a tender, sorry look in them under the fringe of her hat. I followed the yellow taxi up Greene Street as Violet craned her neck and waved again. At the end of block, I watched the cab turn onto Grand Street. I didn't leave until it had travelled some distance from me – a shrunken yellow thing lost in the jumble of traffic. When I felt that it was just about the size of the taxi in my painting, I walked back up the block to my door.

My eyes started to go on me the following year. I thought that the haze in my vision was caused by strain from my work or maybe cataracts. When the ophthalmologist told me there was nothing to be done, because the form of macular degeneration I had was of the wet rather than the dry sort, I nodded, thanked him, and stood up to leave. He must have found my response perverse, because he frowned at me. I told him I had been lucky with my health so far, and I wasn't surprised by illnesses that had no cure. He said that was un-American, and I agreed. Over the years the haze turned into fog, and then into the thick clouds that block my vision now. I've always been able to see the periphery of things, which allows me to walk without a cane, and I can still negotiate my way on the subway. The daily effort of shaving became too hard, however, and I grew a beard. I have it trimmed every month by a man in the Village who insists on calling me Leon. I don't bother to correct him anymore.

Erica remains a half presence in my life. We talk more often on the telephone and write fewer letters, and every July we spend two weeks together in Vermont. This July was our third year, and I'm sure we will continue the tradition. Fourteen days out of 365 seems to be enough for us. We don't stay in the old farmhouse, but we aren't far away, and last year we drove up the hill, parked the car, walked around the lawn, and peeked through the windows of the empty house. Erica isn't strong. Headaches continue to interrupt her life, rendering her a semi-invalid for days, sometimes weeks, but she still teaches with fervor and writes a lot. In April 1998, Erica published *Nanda's Tears: Repression and Release in the Work of Henry James*. At home in Berkeley, she often spends the weekends with Daisy, now a pudgy eight-year-old girl enamoured of rap music.

Next spring, I will finally retire. My world will shrink then, and I'll miss my students and Avery Library and my office and Jack. Because my colleagues and students know what I've lost – Matthew, Erica, and my eyes – they have turned me into a venerable figure. I suppose a near-blind art history professor gives off a whiff of the romantic. But nobody at Columbia knows that I lost Violet, too. As it turns out, she and Erica are about equidistant from me these days, one in Paris, one in Berkeley, and I, who never moved, occupy the middle ground in New York. Violet lives in a small apartment in the Marais not far from the Bastille. Every December, she returns to New York for a few days before she flies home to Minnesota for Christmas. She always spends a day with Dan in New Jersey, who, she says, is doing a little better. He still paces, chain-smokes, makes the O sign with his fingers, and speaks several decibels louder than most people, and he has yet to master the ordinary business of living day to day. It's all hard – cleaning, shopping, preparing meals – and yet Violet feels that everything about Dan is a little less Dan than before, as if his whole being has subsided a notch or turned one shade lighter. He is still writing poems and occasionally a scene for a play but is less prolific than he once was, and the scraps of paper and manuscript pages that lie scattered about his one-room apartment are covered with verse or bits of dialogue followed by ellipses. Age and thirty years of potent drugs have dulled Dan a bit, but that muting seems to have made his life a bit easier.

Four years ago, Violet's sister, Alice, married Edward. A year later, at the age of forty, she gave birth to a daughter named Rose. Violet is crazy about Rose, and every year she arrives in New York with a suitcase stuffed with Parisian dolls and dresses to bring to the angel in Minneapolis. I hear from Violet every two or three months. She sends me an audiotape in lieu of a letter, and I listen to her news and her rambling thoughts about her work. Her book *The Automatons of Late Capitalism* includes chapters entitled 'Manic Shopping,' 'Advertising and the Artificial Body,' 'Lies and the Internet,' and 'The Parasitic Pyschopath as Ideal Consumer.' Her research has taken her from the eighteenth century into the present, from the French physician Pinel to a living psychiatrist named Kernberg. The terms and etiologies of the illness she is studying have changed with time, but Violet has tracked it in all its shifting incarnations: *folie lucide*, moral insanity, moral idiocy, sociopathy, psychopathy, and antisocial personality – ASP for short. These days psychiatrists use checklists for the disorder, which they revise and update by committee, but among the features most often included are glibness and charm, pathological lying, lack of empathy and remorse, impulsivity, cunning and manipulativeness, early behavior problems, and a failure to learn from mistakes or respond to punishment. Every broad idea in the book will be illustrated by individual cases – the countless stories Violet has been collecting from people over the years.

Neither Violet nor I ever mention the night I told her I loved her, but my confession still lies between us like a shared bruise. It has created a new delicacy and inhibition in us that I regret, but no real discomfort. She always spends an evening with me when she comes for her yearly visit, and while I'm making her dinner, I notice that I try to suppress the most obvious signs of my joy, but after an hour or so I lose that self-consciousness, and we lapse into a familiar intimacy that is almost, but not quite, what it was before. Erica tells me that there is a man called Yves in Violet's life and that they have an 'arrangement' – a circumscribed liason that involves hotels – but Violet doesn't speak to me of him. We talk about the people we have in common: Erica, Lazlo, Pinky, Bernie, Bill, Matthew, and Mark.

Mark turns up every once in a while, and then he vanishes again. With money Bill had set aside for him, he enrolled in the School of Visual Arts and impressed his mother and even Violet (who followed his school career from Paris) with his first-semester grades, which arrived in the mail – all A's and B's. But when Lucille called the registrar's office for some information during Mark's second semester, she discovered that Mark wasn't a student. The grades were clever forgeries done on a computer. After a week and a half of school in the

536

fall, he had collected his tuition money, which was refunded directly to him, and had run off with a girl named Mickey. In the spring, he had enrolled again, taken the money again, and disappeared. He calls his mother from time to time, saying that he's in New Orleans or California or Michigan, but nobody knows for sure. Teenie Gold, who is now twenty-two and a student at the Fashion Institute of Technology, sends me a Christmas card every year. Two years ago, she wrote that a friend of hers thought he had spotted Mark in New York leaving a music store with a pile of CDs, but he wasn't a hundred percent sure.

I don't want to see Mark again or speak to him again, but that doesn't mean that I'm free of him. At night, when every sound is amplified by the relative quiet of the building, my nerves race, and I feel blind in the darkness. I hear him in the hallway outside my door or on the fire escape. I hear him in Matt's room, even though I know he isn't there. I see him, too, in visions that are half memory, half invention. I see him in Bill's arms, his small head nestled against his father's shoulder. I see Violet throwing a towel around him after his bath and kissing his neck. I see him with Matt outside the house in Vermont, walking toward the woods with their arms over each other's shoulders. I see him wrapping a cigar box in masking tape. I see him as Harpo Marx honking madly on his horn, and I see him outside the hotel room in Nashville, looking on while Teddy Giles slams my head into the wall.

Lazlo tells me that Teddy Giles is a model prisoner. In the beginning there were those who speculated that Giles might be killed in prison for a crime unpopular even among criminals, but it seems that he is well liked by everyone, especially the guards. Not long after his arrest, the *New Yorker* carried an article on Giles. The journalist had done his homework, and some mysteries were solved. I discovered that Giles's mother had never been a prostitute or a waitress. She wasn't dead, but alive in Tucson, Arizona, refusing to speak to the press. Teddy Giles (who was christened Allan Johnson) grew up in a middle-class suburb outside Cleveland. His father, who worked as an accountant, left his wife when Teddy was one and a half and moved to Florida, but he continued to support his wife and son. According to one of Giles's aunts, Mrs Johnson suffered a severe depression and was hospitalized a month after her husband's departure. Giles was farmed out to a grandmother and spent most of his early years between his mother and various other family members. At fourteen, he was expelled from school and began to travel. After that, the journalist lost Allan Johnson's trail and didn't pick it up again until he surfaced in New York as Teddy Giles. The writer made the usual comments about violence, pornography, and American culture. He pondered the ugly content of Giles's work, its brief, sensational rise in the art world, the dangers of censorship, and the bleakness of it all. The man wrote well and soberly, but as I

538

read the article I was overcome by a feeling that he was saying what he knew his readers expected him to say, that the article, with its smooth language and received ideas, would unsettle nobody. On one of the pages there was a photograph of Allan Johnson when he was seven – one of those badly taken grade-school portraits with a fake sky as the backdrop. He had once been a cute kid with blond hair and protruding ears.

Lazlo works for me in the afternoons. He sees well what I see poorly, and together we make an efficient team. I pay him a good salary, and I think he mostly enjoys the work. Three evenings a week, he comes and reads to me purely for pleasure. When Pinky can get the baby-sitter to stay late, she comes along, too, but often falls asleep on the sofa before the reading is over. Will, also known as Willy, Wee Willy, Winky, and the Winker was two and a half last month. The Finkelman offspring is a devil for running, hopping, and climbing. When his parents bring him over for a visit, he leaps on me as if I were his personal jungle gym and leaves no part of my aging body untrampled. I'm fond of the redheaded little dervish, however, and sometimes when he crawls over me and puts his fingers on my face or touches my head, I feel a small vibration in his hands that makes me wonder if the Winker hasn't inherited his father's unusual sensitivities.

Will, however, isn't ready for an evening of *The Man Without Qualities*, which his father has been reading to me for the past two months. For such a laconic person, Lazlo reads pretty well. He is careful about punctuation and rarely stumbles over words. From time to time, he pauses after a passage and makes a sound – a kind of snort that moves from his throat and up through his nose. I look forward to the snorts, which I've dubbed 'Finkelmanian laughter,' because by matching snort to sentence, I've finally gained access to the comic depths in Lazlo I always suspected were there. His is a dry, restrained, often black humor, well suited to Musil. At thirty-five, Laz isn't young anymore. I have no impression that he's aged physically at all, but that may be because he's never modified his hair, glasses, or neon trousers, and my eyes are fuzzy. Lazlo has a dealer now, but he sells too little to make the dealer happy. Nevertheless, he plows on with his kinetic Tinkertoys, which now hold small objects and flags with quotations on them. I know he reads Musil with an eye for a sharp quote. Like his mentor, Bill, Lazlo is attracted to purity. He has an ascetic streak. But Laz belongs to another generation, and his observant eyes have been fixed too long on the vanities, corruptions, cruelties, foibles, fortunes, and falls of New York's art world to have remained untouched by it. A tone of cynicism sometimes creeps into his voice when he talks about shows.

Last spring, he and I started listening to Mets games on the radio. It's late August now and there's excited talk about a possible Subway Series. Neither Laz nor I has ever been a rabid fan.

We listen for two fans who died, and we take their pleasure in soaring home runs, hard-hit doubles, beautiful slides into third and a scuffle on first about whether the guy was really out. I enjoy the language of baseball – sliders, fastballs, knuckleballs, a can of corn – and I like listening to the games on the radio and to Bob Murphy inviting us to stay tuned for 'the happy recap.' The play-by-play has started to excite me more than I would have expected. Last week, I actually popped up from my chair and cheered.

Lazlo likes to take out the portfolios of Matt's drawings and look at them. When my eyes tire, he sometimes describes the scenes to me. I lie back in my chair and listen to him tell about the tiny people in Matthew's New York. Last week, he described a picture of Dave: 'Dave's chilling out in his chair. He's looking kind of beat, but his eyes are open. I like the way Matt did the old guy's beard with those little squiggly lines and the white craypas over them. Good old Dave,' Lazlo said. 'He's dreaming about some old girlfriend probably. He's going over the whole sad mess in his mind. I can tell, because Matt stuck a little wrinkle between his eyebrows.'

Lazlo's been my right-hand man when it comes to the book on Bill. For several years it's been growing and shrinking and then growing again. I want it to be finished before Bill's retrospective in 2002 at the Whitney. Early in the summer, I stopped the revisions I was dictating to Lazlo in

541

order to write these pages. I told him I had a personal project that I had to take care of before we could continue. He suspects the truth. He knows that I dusted off my old manual typewriter for the occasion and have been typing in a trance every day for hours. I chose my old Olympia because my fingers don't lose their position on the keys as easily as on a computer. 'You're straining your eyes, Leo,' he tells me. 'You should let me help you with whatever it is.' But he can't help me with this story.

Before she left for Paris, Violet told me that she had left a box of Bill's books on the Bowery for me. She had saved volumes she knew I would like and that might help me with my work. 'They're all marked,' she said, 'and some of them have long notes in the margins.' I didn't pick up those books for over two months. When I finally went to get them, Mr Bob trailed after me, sweeping while he delivered his harangue. I was robbing Bill's ghost, violating the sacred ground of the dead, cheating Beauty of her inheritance. When I pointed to my name written in Violet's hand on a cardboard box, Bob was tongue-tied for a moment but rebounded immediately with a long discourse on a possessed breakfront he had tracked down in Flushing twenty years earlier. When I walked out the front door carrying the small box in my arms, he punished me with a rather perfunctory blessing.

Violet hasn't given up the Bowery studio. She

still pays the rent for herself and Mr Bob. Eventually, Mr Aiello or his heirs will want to do something with the building, but for now it's a sagging, forgotten structure inhabited by a mad but highly articulate old man. Bob gets most of his nourishment in soup kitchens these days. About once a month, I go and check on him or send Lazlo to do it when I feel I'm not up to the old man's monologues. Whenever I make the trip, I bring along a bag of groceries and am forced to endure Bob's whining about my choices. Once he accused me of having 'no palate.' Nevertheless, I've sensed a slight softening in his attitude toward me. His hostility is a little less vituperative, and his benedictions have become longer and more florid. It isn't altruism that prompts my visits to Mr Bob but my eagerness to listen to his ornate farewells, to hear him invoke the radiance of the Godhead, the seraphim, the Holy Dove, and the Bloody Lamb. I look forward to his creative perversions of the psalms. His favorite is Psalm 38, which he alters freely for his purposes, calling on God to keep my loins free of loathsome disease and to maintain the soundness of my flesh. 'O Lord, let him not be bowed down greatly,' Bob bellowed after me the last time I was on the Bowery. 'Let him not go mourning all the day long.'

I didn't find Violet's letters until May. I had opened some of the other books, but never the volume of da Vinci drawings. I was saving it for when I began to research *Icarus*. I felt sure that

Bill's unfinished work had been influenced by the drawings, not in any direct way but because the artist had made drawings for a flying bird-machine. I had been avoiding *Icarus*. It seemed impossible to write about it without mentioning Mark. As soon as I opened the volume, the five letters spilled out. After only seconds, I understood what I had found and started reading. I read and rested, read and rested, nearly panting from the strain but hungry for the next word. It's good that no one saw me deciphering those love letters. Heaving, dizzy, blinking, and straining, I finally managed to get through all five during the course of a couple of hours, and then I closed my eyes and kept them shut for a long time.

'Do you remember when you told me I had beautiful knees? I never liked my knees. In fact, I thought they were ugly. But your eyes have rehabilitated them. Whether I see you again or not, I'm going to live out my life with these two beautiful knees.' The letters were full of little thoughts like that one, but she also wrote: 'It's important now to tell you that I love you. I held back, because I was a coward. But I'm yelling it now. And even if I lose you, I'll always say to myself, 'I had that. I had him, and it was delirious and sacred and sweet.' If you let me, I'll always dote on your whole odd, savage, painting self.'

Before I mailed the letters to Violet in Paris, I xeroxed them and put the copies in my drawer. I wish I had been nobler. To resist reading them was probably beyond me, but if my eyes had been better, I might not have made those copies. I don't keep them to study their contents. That's too difficult. I keep the letters as objects, charmed by their various metonymies. When I take out my things now, I rarely separate Violet's letters to Bill from the little photo of the two of them, but I keep the bit of cardboard and Matthew's knife far away from the other things. The doughnuts eaten in secret and the stolen gift are heavy with Mark and with my fear. The fear pre-dates the murder of Rafael Hernandez, and when I play my game of mobile objects, I'm often tempted to move the photographs of my aunt, uncle, grandparents, and the twins near the knife and the fragment of the box. Then the game flirts with terror. It moves me so close to the edge that I have a sensation of falling, as if I had hurled myself off the edge of a building. I plummet downward, and in the speed of the fall I lose myself in something formless but deafening. It's like entering a scream – being a scream.

And then I withdraw, backing away from the edge like a phobic. I make a different arrangement. Talismans, icons, incantations – these fragments are my frail shields of meaning. The game's moves must be rational. I force myself to make a coherent argument for every grouping, but at bottom the game is magic. I'm its necromancer calling on the spirits of the dead, the missing, and the imaginary. Like O painting a slab of beef because he's hungry, I invoke ghosts that can't satisfy me. But the invocation has a power all its own. The objects become muses of memory.

Every story we tell about ourselves can only be told in the past tense. It winds backward from where we now stand, no longer the actors in the story but its spectators who have chosen to speak. The trail behind us is sometimes marked by stones like the ones Hansel first left behind him. Other times, the path is gone, because the birds flew down and ate up all the crumbs at sunrise. The story flies over the blanks, filling them in with the hypotaxis of an 'and' or an 'and then.' I've done it in these pages to stay on a path I know is interrupted by shallow pits and several deep holes. Writing is a way to trace my hunger, and hunger is nothing if not a void.

In one version of the story, the burnt piece of doughnut box might stand for hunger. I think Mark was always starved for something. But what? He wanted me to believe him, admire him. He wanted it badly for at least as long as he looked into my eyes. Maybe that need was the one thing that was whole and true in him, and it made him radiant. It didn't matter that he felt little or nothing for me or that he had to pretend to get my admiration. What mattered was that he felt my belief. But the pleasure he took in pleasing others never lasted. Insatiable, he gorged on crackers and doughnuts, on stolen things and money, on pharmaceuticals and on the chase itself.

I have no object for Lucille in my drawer. It

would have been easy to save some scrap of her, but I never did. Bill pursued her for a long time, a creature in his mind whom he could never locate. Maybe Mark was looking for her, too. I don't know. Even I followed her for a while, until I came to a dead end. The idea of Lucille was strong, but I don't know what that idea was except maybe evasion itself, which is best expressed by nothing. Bill turned what eluded him into real things that would carry the weight of his needs and doubts and wishes – paintings, boxes, doors, and all those children on videotape. Father of thousands. Dirt and paint and wine and cigarettes and hope. Bill. Father of Mark. I can still see him rocking his little boy in the blue boat bed he built for him on the Bowery, and I can hear him singing in a voice that was low and hoarse, 'Take a walk on the wild side.' Bill loved his changeling child, his blank son, his Ghosty Boy. He loved the boy-man who is still roaming from city to city and is still reaching into his travelling bag to find a face to wear and a voice to use.

Violet is still looking for the sickness that moves in the air, the Zeitgeist that mumbles to its victims: scream, starve, eat, kill. She's looking for the idea-winds that gust through people's minds and then become scars on the landscape. But how the contagions move from outside to inside isn't clear. They move in language, pictures, feelings, and in something else I can't name, something between and among us. There are days when

547

I find myself walking through the rooms of an apartment in Berlin – Mommsenstrasse 11. The furniture is a little blurry and all the people are gone, but I can feel the sweep of the empty rooms and the light that comes through the windows. A bitter nowhere. I turn away from the place as my father did, and I think about the day he stopped looking for their names on the lists, about the day he knew. It's hard to live with nonsense – gruesome, unspeakable nonsense. He couldn't do it. Before she died, my mother shrank. She looked very small in the hospital bed, and her freckled arm over the sheet was like a stick with pale loose skin. It was all Berlin and flight and Hampstead and German and confusion by then. Forty years had vanished from her head, and she called out for my father. Mutti in the dark.

Violet packed up Bill's work clothes and took them along to Paris. I imagine that she still puts them on from time to time, for comfort. When I think of Violet in Bill's ragged shirt and paint-smeared jeans, I give her a Camel to smoke, and I call the image in my mind *Self-Portrait*. I never imagine her at the piano anymore. The lesson finally ended with a real kiss that sent her far away from me. It's odd the way life works, the way it mutates and wanders, the way one thing becomes another. Matthew drew an old man many times, and he called him Dave. Years go by, and it turns out that he was drawing his own father. I am Dave now, Dave with patches on his eyes.

Another family has moved in upstairs. Two years ago, Violet sold the loft for a lot of money to the Wakefields. Every evening I hear their two children, Jacob and Chloe. They shake the light fixtures on my ceiling with their ritual war dances before they go to bed. Jacob is five and Chloe is three, and noise is their business. I suppose if they thumped for hours on end, I would be annoyed, but I've grown accustomed to their routine explosions around seven o'clock. Jacob sleeps in Mark's old room, and Chloe sleeps in what used to be Violet's study. In the living room, there's a plastic slide where the red sofa used to be. Every true story has several possible endings. This is mine: the children upstairs must be asleep, because the rooms above me are quiet. It's eight-thirty in the evening on August 30; 2000. I've had my supper, and I've put away the dishes. I'm going to stop typing now, move to my chair, and rest my eyes. In half an hour, Lazlo is coming to read to me.

ACKNOWLEDGMENTS

Although this book is a work of fiction and its story and characters are imaginary, the numerous references to hysteria, eating disorders, and psychopathy are taken from a wide range of sources. Among them are Georges Didi-Huberman's *Invention de l'hysterie* (Macula); *A History of Private Life: From the Fires of Revolution to the Great War*, volume 4, general editors Philippe Ariès and Georges Duby, volume editor Michelle Perrot (Harvard University Press), in which I found the barking women of Josselin; Hilde Bruch's *Eating Disorders: Obesity, Anorexia Nervosa and the Person Within* (Basic Books), which includes the story of the fat little boy who thinks his insides are made of jelly; and Rudolph M. Bell's *Holy Anorexia* (University of Chicago Press), in which Bell gives an analysis of Catherine Benincasa's extreme fasting. The evolving terminology, checklists, general descriptions, and possible etiologies of what is now called psychopathy or antisocial personality were culled from several works: *The Roots of Crime* by Edward Glover, M.D. (International Universities Press);

the third and fourth editions of the American Psychiatric Association's *Diagnostic and Statistical Manual* (DSM-III and DSM-IV); *Abnormalities of the Personality: Within and Beyond the Realm of Treatment* by Michael H. Stone, M.D. (W. W. Norton and Co.); *Impulsivity: Theory, Assessment, and Treatment,* edited by Christopher D. Webster and Margaret A Jackson *(Guilford Press); Severe Personality Disorders: Psychotherapeutic Strategies* (Yale University Press) and *Aggression in Personality Disorders and Perversions* (Yale University Press), both by Otto F. Kernberg; the three volumes of John Bowlby's *Attachment and Loss* (Basic Books); Hervey Cleckley's *The Mask of Sanity,* fifth edition (Emily S. Cleckley); and the following books by D. W. Winnicott: *Deprivation and Delinquency* (Routledge), *The Maturational Process and the Facilitating Environment* (Maresfield Library), *The Family and Individual Development* (Routledge), *Holding and Interpretation* (Grove Press), and *Playing and Reality* (Routledge).

I want to thank Ricky Jay for *Jay's Journal of Anomalies,* from which I borrowed the hunger artist Sacco, who starved for crowds in London, and the apocryphal story of Descartes's automaton. He was also kind enough to let me peek into several rare volumes in his private library that contained medical reports on the status of people who purported to subsist on nothing but air and odors.

I am also indebted to Dr Finn Skårderud, both for his books and for his conversations with me

551

about contemporary culture and eating disorders. The references in the novel to J. M. Barrie and Lord Byron, as well as the story of the bulimic patient who vomited into plastic bags and left them hidden in her mother's house, come from him. His books include: *Sultekunsternere* (Hunger Artists), *Sterk Svak: Håndboken om spise forstyrrelser* (Strong Weak: A Handbook on Eating Disorders), and *Uro: En reise i det moderne selvet* (Unrest: A Journey in the Modern Self).

Last, I am deeply grateful to my sister, Asti Hustvedt, for her original research and thoughts on hysteria. The ideas in Violet's dissertation closely resemble those in Asti's unpublished Ph.D. thesis, 'Science Fictions: Villiers de L'Isle-Adam's *L'eve future* and Late-Nineteenth-Century Medical Constructions of Femininity' (New York University, 1996). I benefited too from the research she has done in the Salpêtrière Hospital archives for her forthcoming book, *Living Dolls*, to be published by Norton. I also want to thank her for her close reading of the novel and its references to hysteria and for her ongoing conversations with me about the mysteries of culture, medicine, and illness.